A BLACKBIRD IN TWILIGHT

'It's obvious to me what caused the revolt,' said the thin Councillor.

'Yes?'

'Melkavesh. The rumours of her rallying Vardrav against Gorethria incited them.' Xaedrek agreed but he said nothing. He knew what was coming next.

'Sire,' said Amnek, leaning forward in his chair, 'why don't you find her, have her assassinated?' His face in shadow was almost black, but his eyes were luminous, making him look more than ever like a bird of prey.

'I know where she is,' Xaedrek replied evenly. 'She's in Charhn, by a sensible guess. But even if we sent an assassin to find her, with her power they would never get near her.'

'You mean, because she can far-see . . . and you cannot . . .'

About the Author

Freda Warrington was born in Leicester in 1956
and studied graphic design at Loughborough
College of Art and Design. She has worked as an
in-house designer for a local building company in
Hitchin. She is now a freelance designer and lives
near Leicester. Her other books in this series, A
BLACKBIRD IN SILVER, A BLACKBIRD IN
DARKNESS and A BLACKBIRD IN AMBER,
have all been published with great success.

'Enjoyably readable fantasy . . . many cuts above
the average'

Anne McCaffrey

A Blackbird in Twilight

FREDA WARRINGTON

NEW ENGLISH LIBRARY
Hodder and Stoughton

First published in Great Britain in
1988 by New English Library
Paperbacks

An NEL Paperback Original

Printed and bound in Great
Britain for Hodder and Stoughton
Paperbacks, a division of Hodder
and Stoughton Limited, Mill
Road, Dunton Green, Sevenoaks,
Kent TN13 2YA (Editorial Office:
47 Bedford Square, London
WC1B 3DP) by Richard Clay
Limited, Bungay, Suffolk.
Photoset by Rowland
Phototypesetting Limited,
Bury St Edmunds, Suffolk.

British Library C.I.P.

Warrington, Freda
  A blackbird in twilight.
  I. Title
  823'.914[F]

  ISBN 0-450-48908-6

Dedicated with love to Mic, Tim and Stella,
Sue (Charlotte), and my heroine, Suzanne . . .
for the priceless gift of friendship.

Contents

Prelude   1
1 The Essence of Far-sight   5
2 Daughter of the Moons   22
3 Beyond the Circle   43
4 In a Red Crystal Sky   66
5 The Aludrian Sea   87
6 Heldavrain   112
7 Fliya's Path   133
8 White Shadows of Evil   158
9 'Xaedrek will destroy you'   186
10 On the Storm-wind   206
11 Reparation   227
12 A Messenger from Charhn   246
13 Children of Dark and Light   261
14 'My name was Ahag-Ga'   284
15 Ashes of Ice   306
16 Moonrise   325
17 The Circles of the World   352

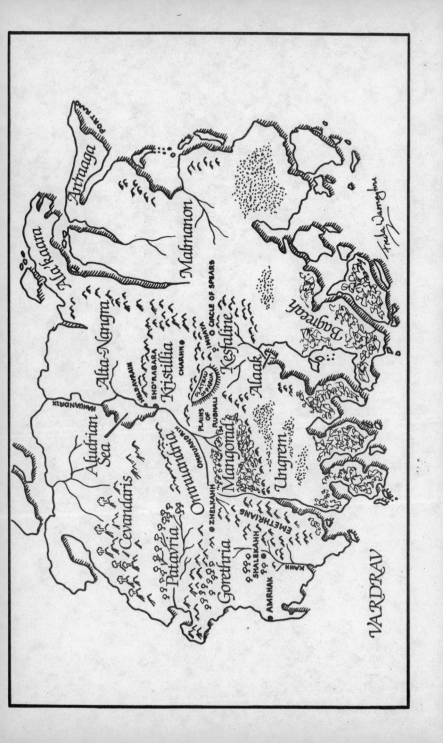

Prelude

IN A pearl-grey nothingness that lay between the Planes, two beings met in conflict. One was the Lady of H'tebhmella, in anger a terrible figure of diamond and blue fire; the other, hardly visible, was a Guardian, shrouded from head to foot in the same neutral grey as his surroundings.

'Stand aside,' he said, 'and let me pass.'

'No, Ferdanice. Now I've found you, I command you to listen to me,' said the Lady. 'This Earth is not like any other. The three planes with which it intersects may be in separate dimensions, but they are symbiotic, as essential to the world as it is to them. If you go on with this, you will destroy the balance between them.'

No human could have faced the cold purity of her rage, but the Grey One was unmoved. 'We can't have everything, my Lady. There is a greater balance at issue. Why must the H'tebhmellians always obstruct the Guardians? We should be working together.'

'The Guardians are always concerned only with the movement of mindless powers, never the welfare of Earth. Even those of the White Plane Hrannekh Ol and the Black Plane Hrunnesh care more for mankind than do the Grey Ones. I am not human, yet I have a thousand times more humanity than you.'

Ferdanice laughed. 'I know things are difficult on Earth. You expected perfection the moment the Serpent died? You said yourself that new evils would appear in its place. I am trying to help the world evolve in a way that will eradicate certain of those evils – in the first instance, by helping Melkavesh to defeat Xaedrek.'

1

'That war will be an appalling thing, I agree. But the consequences of your "help" will be worse.'

'I tire of this, my Lady. Why don't you admit the true reason for your objection? The Blue Plane H'tebhmella is a static dimension. You are simply terrified of any sort of change. But I cannot let you interfere.'

'You are wrong, Ferdanice,' the Lady replied. 'You know what the result will be and you don't care. Melkavesh must be warned.'

'You'll do nothing of the sort! Now, if you've finished, I must return to Earth and see that Falmeryn completes his errand for me.'

'Grey One, I cannot let you.' She raised her hands, palms outwards. Ribbons of light began to curl around the Guardian, interweaving and hardening until he appeared to be imprisoned in a cage of brilliant blue glass.

'No – no – you can't do this!' he cried. 'I demand that you release me. How long do you think you can hold me here?'

'For as long as I must.'

'Long enough for Xaedrek to win the war? No.' The Grey One seemed to swell within the cage. The pale mist around them quivered, contracted into a cloud and swathed itself round the Lady. She wavered, but held the blue cage intact. 'And now we are prisoners of each other, and we shall fight until one of us breaks free. Don't be a fool, my Lady. You know I'm stronger than you.'

There was no witness to the conflict that sent them spiralling between the threads of the Universe; only a blackbird, who tumbled past them in her own headlong flight towards Earth. They did not see her.

It was after the death of the Serpent that Miril had flown into the dawn sky, chirruping her joy at the world's rebirth and her own. The flight had carried her between the stars, through other times, but she had flown foo far and now something was calling her urgently, insistently back to Earth. Some part of the Serpent was not quite dead. She was the world's Hope and she was needed.

Yet the world eluded her. Time after time she reached it,

flew over its oceans like a burnished leaf until she found those who needed her. She could watch them moving and talking, but it was as if they were very far away behind a pane of glass. She could not make them see or hear her. Then, like any trapped bird, she would fling herself again and again at the glass, singing stridently for just one soul to notice her and call her name, until at last the Earth slid away into another part of space and she must start her search anew.

1

The Essence of Far-sight

EMPEROR XAEDREK of Gorethria rode out into the streets of Shalekahh to survey the damage for himself. As always he took a minimal guard, just four men and the young Duke Valamek. He refused to let anyone think that a slaves' revolt, however violent, had been anything to unnerve him.

The city, he noted with satisfaction, was almost back to normal. It was astonishing what effect an impending inspection by the Emperor could have on the speed of repairs. The burned houses had been restored, the blood scrubbed from the white marble streets. It had been part of the slaves' punishment to complete the work under maximum duress.

Riding into the city's main square, Xaedrek looked round appreciatively at the graceful houses, towers and spires. Fountains glittered between rows of stately beeches, their metallic purple foliage rustling against a storm-washed sky. The sun was hot, the buildings all ice and crystal. There was no city on Earth to compare with Shalekahh.

But in the centre of the square, three bodies turned slowly on a gibbet.

The crowd lining the square had been cheering wildly as Xaedrek approached, but something in his manner caused a sudden hush to fall on them. He had been smiling; now his face took on a dangerously neutral expression. Looking neither to left nor right he led his retinue towards the gibbet, while the normally self-possessed Gorethrians watched him with growing anxiety. Fear rose like heat from the few Vardravian slaves in the crowd.

The Emperor halted his horse in front of the platform. An officer came forward to meet him, hurriedly removing his winged black helmet and giving the formal bow and salute.

'Your Majesty, I am honoured to meet you. I am Captain Reshek, of the Fortress of Execution.' His smile was very white against his dark skin.

Xaedrek studied the bodies and said nothing. One was Cevandarish, a thickset man with bushy black hair and beard. Next to him hung an Alta-Nangran, his sallow skin now purple and his slanted eyes bulging. The third was a Kristillian.

'As Your Majesty doubtless knows, these were the leaders of the revolt,' Reshek went on proudly. 'We think they will prove an effective deterrent to any further trouble.'

Xaedrek said, 'Take them down.'

'Your Majesty?'

'Take the bodies down. Their purpose has been served and they are an eyesore.' He leaned forward in the saddle and said in a confidential tone, 'Do you not know that Kristillians are exempt from execution?'

The Captain's smile vanished. 'Of course, Sire, but this case was so heinous that an example had to be –'

'No exceptions. Kristillians are too valuable in my research to be wasted. Why make this one a martyr? It would have been better to show that he's no different from any other slave.'

Reshek swallowed, and sweat broke out on his forehead. Xaedrek's tone was pleasant, and he was taking care not to humiliate the officer by being overheard, but that meant nothing. He was well known for suddenly ordering punishments and executions in that same friendly voice.

'Did you authorise the hanging yourself, Captain?'

'Yes, Your Majesty. I take full responsibility.'

'I see.' Xaedrek straightened up and looked thoughtfully at the Kristillian, leaving the officer in a limbo of dread. This quality of menace that the Emperor possessed was indefinable yet only too real, particularly to those who had displeased him. It was not physical power, for Xaedrek was no warrior. He was slim and graceful, his face aristocratic

6

with arched eyebrows and a well-shaped mouth. His brown skin had the merest sheen of purple to it, and although he was only thirty-five, his long black hair was turning white at the front. He lacked the grim look of most Gorethrians, but his eyes made up for that; they shone like jewels, the irises a disconcertingly vivid ruby-red.

His necromantic power (which he preferred to be thought of as 'scientific') was known and feared, and it was no secret that he could defend himself better than any bodyguard. Just before the revolt, a Cevandarish would-be assassin had broken through his guards, with a poisoned knife. There had been many witnesses to the bronze fire that Xaedrek had summoned from nowhere and unleashed at his attacker, rendering him a mass of charcoal and bubbling grease.

That was cause enough for the Emperor to be treated with a healthy respect, but his true source of power was simply his personality. He had a quality of stillness, an aura of self-containment so intense that it seemed electric. It magnetised as much as it repelled.

'So, Captain,' Xaedrek said at last, 'you took it on yourself to make an exception to my rules. Knowing better than the Emperor is not a crime, but it is a dangerous thing in practice.'

'I am sorry, Sire.' Reshek held himself straight, but his face had gone slate-grey. 'I acted as I thought best.'

'I know. And to take full responsibility as you have is a very commendable thing. Don't look so worried! I am not about to have you hung on the gallows in their place. It would be a waste to execute a soldier of your obvious ability.'

The officer almost fainted with relief. 'Thank you, Your Majesty,' he whispered, bowing. A weak smile reappeared on his lips.

'On the contrary, I'm sure much better use can be made of your military skills. An extended tour of Alta-Nangra as a foot soldier will be an ideal opportunity for you to reflect on the importance of obedience.'

It was a disgrace as bad as death. Reshek gasped in dismay, and began to plead before he could stop himself, but one cold look from the Emperor cut him off. The matter was closed, and Xaedrek's thoughts were already elsewhere.

Turning to the tall young man at his side, he said quietly, 'Duke Valamek, you can arrange his transfer. Now let's return to the palace.'

He turned his horse. The crowd did not know what had passed between him and the officer, but he was smiling again. Almost feverishly, their tension vapourised into an atonal roar of adulation.

When Xaedrek arrived at the palace, he went straight to his chambers, intending to change out of the elaborate silk riding gear. Lord Amnek, however, had anticipated him and was already waiting in the anteroom. Xaedrek masked his irritation.

'Sire, I will of course wait while you change, but we must talk.'

'No, it's all right, Amnek,' Xaedrek sighed, pushing open the door to his bedchamber. 'Come in.'

For some reason the curtains were closed. He went across to open them, and light spilled blue and silver across the jewelled furniture, a filigree screen, the silks and velvets of the hangings. He indicated for Amnek to sit at a small jade table, and went to fetch another chair from beside the bed.

'I trust you found the city more settled, Sire,' said the Councillor, arranging the folds of his grey robe.

'The revolt is over, with twelve fatalities – including the six Gorethrians poisoned by their own servants,' Xaedrek replied, leaning on the back of the chair. His crimson jacket and breeches were like a blood-splash in the soft light. 'Of course, there are several hundred Vardravians dead – mostly Cevandarish, Alta-Nangrans and Alaakians. The survivors are being detained for use in the amulin process, and those who did not take part are under strict curfew.'

'They should all be punished.'

'No, Amnek. I believe in rewarding good behaviour. Still, I can't imagine what possessed them to try it. They must have known what the result would be. Perhaps they thought it worth committing suicide to inconvenience us.'

'It's obvious to me what caused it,' said the thin Councillor.

'Yes?'

8

'Melkavesh. The rumours of her rallying Vardrav against Gorethria incited them.'

Xaedrek agreed, but he said nothing. He knew what was coming next.

'Sire,' said Amnek, leaning forward in his chair, 'why don't you find her, have her assassinated?' His face in shadow was almost black, but his eyes were luminous, making him look more than ever like a bird of prey.

'I know where she is,' Xaedrek replied evenly. 'She's in Charhn, by a sensible guess. But even if we sent an assassin to find her, with her power they would never get near her.'

'You mean, because she can far-see.' Amnek looked pointedly at a small phial in the centre of the table. It contained pearly liquid shot through with pinkish veins, which every now and then twitched as if alive. 'She can far-see, and you cannot.'

'We've had this argument before. I would put up with it from no one but you, but my patience has a limit.' Xaedrek spoke more in sorrow than annoyance. Lord Amnek had been his mentor when, as a boy, Xaedrek's parents had been killed in battle. Amnek had encouraged his passionate love of Gorethria, instilled in him his own scientific ruthlessness. He and his wife Shavarish had been Xaedrek's closest colleagues, and he had appointed them to the Inner Council on becoming Emperor ten years ago. There had been great respect and friendship between them – but no longer. Since Shavarish died, Amnek clung to the mourning grey, and had lost his scientific coldness.

'I'll pursue the argument until I get a satisfactory answer,' Amnek said fiercely. 'You must find Melkavesh. She killed Shavarish!'

Xaedrek remained calm, but his eyes would have terrified anyone except Lord Amnek. 'Not technically. Melkavesh gave Irem Ol Thangiol the amulin, only intending him to escape. It was his decision to sabotage the amulin machine. He did not set out to kill Shavarish. Don't demean her death; she died in the bravest Gorethrian way, trying to stop him.'

'You demean her death by defending Melkavesh and that damned Kristillian!'

9

'I am not defending them. I am pointing out the truth of the case. I am concerned at the way the lines of logic have blurred in your mind.' Xaedrek knew that what he said was not getting through. He had thought of retiring Amnek, but he was so short of scientists that he could not consider it until after the war with Kristillia was won. Why could they not all be like Lady Lirurmish, still diamond-sharp in her one hundred and seventeenth year?

'You question my logic, Sire? What has happened to your own? You *could* have far-sight – it is there in that phial – and yet you refuse to take advantage of it. That, to my mind, verges on criminal lunacy!'

A menacing smile touched Xaedrek's lips. 'I am not only a criminal lunatic but a singularly poor communicator, if I have to explain my reasons yet again.'

'*Please spare us that,*' a new voice broke in, making Xaedrek jump so violently that his heart almost stopped.

'Ah'garith!' he said angrily. The voice had come from behind the screen. He pulled it aside and found the woman-demon sitting on a couch, her legs tucked primly under her, wearing a green satin robe that she appeared to have taken from his wardrobe. He should have seen her through the filigree-work; more importantly, he should have *sensed* her presence the moment he stepped into the antechamber. 'How long have you been there? Amnek, did you let her in?'

'No. I did not know she was here either.'

'Well, Ah'garith, I would like to know what you mean by intruding on my private rooms and eavesdropping.' Xaedrek spoke coldly, but he was trembling. He willed himself to calm down.

'You should lock your doors. I apologise, *Sire*.' She uncurled herself and began to walk towards him. In form she was a stately old woman, fair-skinned and white-haired, but the body was stolen and what lurked inside was not human. She reminded Xaedrek of the swollen white insects that insinuated themselves into cracks in the palace garden. 'What I have overheard has made me sick. You could have equal power to Melkavesh. You demanded far-sight. I worked tirelessly to achieve it, yet now you shun it!'

'I though you'd got over this, Ah'garith. Surely you're not still sulking?'

This remark increased the demon's rage. 'Lord Amnek is right. You take amulin freely, yet you will not touch the ichor. What's the difference? You were so disgusted by the experiment that created the ichor that you made me dismantle it and kill the subjects. Yet you still keep phials of the stuff. You are like an archer saying, "What shall I shoot with?" while the bow lies at your elbow!'

Xaedrek was used to the reptilian slither of her voice, but it still nauseated him. He said, 'There is a difference. The power that Melkavesh possesses naturally is as bright and pure as lightning. I am not a natural Sorcerer, I can only command the power by taking amulin, but even amulin – despite the way it is made – is clean by comparison to the ichor. It is a corrupt and corrupting substance, Ah'garith. But you don't know what I mean, do you?'

'Don't insult my intelligence, Sire. You mean the ichor is evil – like me, like the Serpent. Well, I'll tell you something. The power, whatever its source, is all the same power! Where do you think it came from? It is the Serpent M'gulfn's power, dispersed around the Earth when that noble being was murdered. Whoever wields it has a little of the Serpent in them. So why be so fussy about its origin?'

'She has a point,' said Amnek.

Xaedrek looked from one to the other, and decided he was wasting his breath arguing with them. 'Please go to the mansion, Ah'garith. There are plenty of slaves to be working on, and we need all the amulin we can produce for the army. I will think about what you've said.' Apparently not appeased by his diplomacy, she gave him a poisonous look and stormed out, slamming the door. Xaedrek sat down opposite Amnek and let out a sigh.

'Her petulance is becoming intolerable. I sometimes wish I had never summoned her. If only I didn't need her power . . .'

'She is naturally resentful about the destruction of her experiment, Sire. If you take the ichor, I'm sure she will calm down.'

11

'Oh, I'm sure she will.' Xaedrek picked up the phial and rolled it between his finger and thumb.

'Sire, you are not afraid of her, are you?' His fingers drummed like spider's legs on the table. 'I pursue this not just because of Shavarish, but for Gorethria's sake. You never used to be so cautious. What became of the questing scientist?'

'If you are so enthusiastic, try it yourself,' Xaedrek said, and smiled at Amnek's expression of distaste. 'We'll see. I'm sure it would deliver the power and far-sight she claims, but only at a price . . . The problem is that her goal and mine are totally opposed. I want a strong Gorethria presiding over a healthy Empire; she would like to destroy everyone and everything on Earth, using us as a stepping-stone on her way. It's all right while I can keep her in check, but to allow her free rein with her "experiments" could be disastrous.'

'No wonder she is so resentful, Sire.'

'What do you mean?'

'You do not trust her. You've no proof of her intents; she has served you obediently for ten years, and I think you are being unnecessarily suspicious.'

'Do you?' Xaedrek raised his eyebrows, and gazed thoughtfully at the Councillor. 'It's by not trusting her that I remain in control. Don't you know what the Shana used to do to those who summoned them, when the Serpent was alive and they had the power? They possessed them. They made slaves of them, physically and mentally, and leached everything out of them, reason, strength and sanity. That's what Ah'garith would like to do to me.'

Amnek seemed shocked. His eyes were strange, as if they were not quite looking in the same direction. Xaedrek was concerned for him, but there was no time for sympathy with a war to be won. It would not bring Shavarish back.

'I don't see that you have any choice, Sire,' said Amnek eventually. 'You need far-sight. You must destroy Melka-vesh. I think you will bring yourself to test the ichor . . . otherwise you would have disposed of it without a second thought.'

Xaedrek looked broodingly at him, and the silence came

12

down between them like a sheet of frost. Then he stood up and opened the door. 'I will have to bid you goodnight, my friend. I am tired and hungry, and I need time to think.'

'Of course.' The Councillor rose graciously. Xaedrek was tall, but Amnek was half a head taller, even with the slight stoop that made him seem older than he was. 'Good night, my Emperor.'

He crossed the anteroom, but just as he reached the far door, Xaedrek said, 'Amnek, you will be careful with Ah'garith, won't you?'

Amnek's aquiline nose wrinkled slightly. 'I hardly think she has such designs on me.'

'Maybe not, but I've let you work alone with her a lot . . . perhaps too much. Just be on your guard, that's all.'

Xaedrek bathed, dined alone in his chambers, and worked on senate papers until he felt able to sleep. But every time he drifted into a doze, images of almost physical unpleasantness tormented him awake. Finally his recurring dream of the moons began, and at that he gave up the struggle, climbed out of bed and pulled on a robe of violet satin.

Outside it was dark, but the sky rumbled and throbbed with strange colours. He crossed to the window and looked out at the palace gardens, where trees were being dragged into elongated shapes by the wind. A bank of grimy purple cloud was outlined by bursts of silver-white lightning, while spheres of orange and green fire sped along the eastern horizon, over towards the Emethrian mountains. Xaedrek shook his head grimly. Once the Emethrians had been no more to him than a wild and savage aspect of Gorethria's beauty; now he could not think of them without thinking of Melkavesh, who had miraculously survived crossing the black peaks after she had fled from Shalekahh. He wondered what she was doing now – in Kristillia, with Gorethria's enemies.

No rain was falling. The air seemed to bristle with static, and he could taste the acrid tang of electrical discharges. Statues of past Emperors stood pale as ghosts in the avenues of trees, oblivious to the storm. One day, he thought, my statue will stand there – and how will I be remembered? As Gorethria's greatest Emperor? Unlikely, he thought with a dry smile. There is only one way I wish to be remembered: as a Gorethrian citizen who loved his country with absolute, single-minded passion, whose every action was for her benefit, no matter how great the cost. That's the most to which any Gorethrian, however mighty or humble, can aspire.

The storm intrigued him. It was typical Gorethrian weather, yet it was more than that; it was a manifestation of the weird energies that had been released by the Serpent's death some twenty-five years earlier. Magical, supernatural, hyperphysical – all such terms fitted, and the possibilities it offered were beyond imagination. Melkavesh had claimed that only natural Sorcerers could or should use the power, and she had condemned Xaedrek's methods out of hand.

'Sorcery has its own laws,' she had said. 'It should only be wielded by those with the latent ability to draw the power. To do otherwise is to break the natural law, and the result is corruption of the power and of those who wield it. You're using a demon, a creature which by rights should be dead, and whose aims are purely evil. You have to maim and murder to gain the power, and then what is it used for? Nothing constructive. More killing, warfare, domination over others. Can't you see that it's wrong? I want you to stop.'

'You're asking me to stop,' he had replied, 'and the power will remain the privilege of the lucky few, and Gorethria will sink into oblivion?' She had hardly been able to find an answer to that. Doubtless she was right, but he could not allow moral concerns to interfere with Gorethria's welfare.

He tried not to think about Melkavesh. One problem at a time.

Ah'garith was the only demon to have outlived her creator, the Serpent. All the other Shana had perished. She was trapped in a human body, her power so reduced that she could hardly use it herself, only act as a channel to feed it into the crystalline powder that Xaedrek had named amulin. It gave him the abilities of a pseudo-Sorcerer, and

14

administered in smaller quantities to his soldiers it made the army all but invincible.

Gorethria had been in a state of chaos when, purely out of curiosity, he had first summoned the Shanin. Even without her help he knew he would still have become Emperor, for that was a matter of foresight and strength. But her hyperphysical power had been essential in reconquering the Empire, and he could not do without it.

None of the conquests had been easy, but all had eventually fallen to the dark tide of Xaedrek's troops. Only Kristillia was still free, and had already held out for an impossibly long time. They had no supernatural power, only fanatical determination – but now they also had Melkavesh on their side. He was not complacent about conquering them. Special measures would have to be taken, but he was a patient man and the challenge would only make the victory sweeter.

Xaedrek did not hate the Kristillians. He felt almost nothing for them at all. Apart from the political consideration that a free Kristillia would always be a danger, they were simply the missing piece needed to complete his glorious picture of the Empire.

He had to win, and he needed every advantage. Melkavesh possessed a skill by which she could observe almost any event or place she chose, which meant Gorethria could have no secrets from her. Perhaps she was even watching him now, he thought with a shudder. He needed the same skill, Ah'garith claimed to have delivered it, yet he hesitated . . .

He picked up the phial and studied it, as he had done many times over the past few days. It looked so innocuous, yet he could not forget the hideous experiment that had created it. It lurked in the back of his mind like a blinding headache; three humans deformed and blended into one three-lobed monster, pain sweating from them like terror. The flesh-like surface on which they lay had throbbed with a sickly bloodstained glare, filtering into them all that was negative in the Earth's energy. It was unspeakably repellent. Ah'garith had set it up without consulting him, and had proudly presented it to him as the source of all the power he could dream of. His revulsion had been so intense that he had ordered her to destroy it at once.

He had tried to explain. 'There is a certain dignity in simple suffering. When I see an enemy staring at me from defiant eyes, and I look back, we understand each other. However much pain he is in, we both know that if the positions were reversed, he would deal with me in a similar way, and so we are equal. But this is different; this deformation of mind and body is an utter corruption of everything I have set out to make Gorethria . . .'

Ah'garith had not understood, of course. Neither, to his surprise, had Amnek. He thought his Emperor was being unscientific. He could not see that the power was wrong because it emanated from the heart of the demon's vilest desires.

Xaedrek had anticipated something like this. A Shanin could not change its nature. However helpful, however quiescent Ah'garith seemed to be, behind the façade was a mass of resentment and evil intent. She did not really want to help Gorethria; she wanted to destroy it. She loathed Xaedrek because she could not enslave him, and the only thing that kept her under control was the tenuous bargain, the fact that she needed him as much as he needed her. In fact she clung to him like a parasite, and much as he longed to dispose of her, she appeared to be indestructible. He dreaded her breaking free.

Yet Xaedrek had kept the ichor, which was the transmuted blood drawn from the beings' veins. His indecision was out of character. If he swallowed the liquid – his gorge rose at the thought – it would give him greater power than amulin could provide. But his suspicion that it would also put him at Ah'garith's mercy could not be assuaged by any amount of reassurance on the demon's part. It was too tempting, too obvious.

But he needed far-sight . . . He put the phial down and went to close the curtains, intending to go back to bed. Then he started violently. For a moment there seemed to be a silvery face smudged against the pane, and the room was suddenly full of a metallic whispering.

16

He turned round, convinced Ah'garith was in the room; but that was impossible, the doors were locked and she could not spirit herself from place to place. His heart pounded as he scanned every corner of the chamber. There was nothing there.

Then he realised that the strange whispering was not inside the room but outside, caused by some aberration of the wind. Lightning cast all manner of strange shadows, easily translated into faces or other shapes.

He shut the curtains, exasperated. He was not normally prone to irrational fears, and it only served to prove that he had let the ichor problem get completely out of hand. To sit alone brooding was to stray onto the fringes of insanity, Ah'garith's domain. Perhaps Amnek was right; he should treat it as a scientific matter, one that would benefit by research.

He put on an overmantle of red silk and made his way out into the marble corridors of the palace.

The late Emperor Meshurek's suite of rooms had been sealed for many years until Xaedrek had reopened them and put them to use. Some sensitive folk claimed there was still an aura of evil in the chambers where Meshurek had summoned a demon and gradually gone insane, and the terror which some Vardravians felt at being there was useful in persuading intractable prisoners to co-operate.

Slipping quietly into a side room, Xaedrek seated himself before a pane of glass which appeared from the other side to be a mirror. It gave a clear view of the bedchamber. Honey-coloured lamplight filled the room, casting blurred golden highlights on the great bed with its carved posts and bejewelled cover, the curtains fringed with precious stones, a couch shaped like a golden leopard.

The two prisoners in the room were awake and talking quietly. The woman was sitting upright against the bedhead, while the man lay spreadeagled across the cover, his head cradled in her lap. Their attitude was somehow childlike, putting Xaedrek in mind of a girl comforting her sick brother while both waited, stoical and terrified, for some dreadful punishment.

17

He looked at them, and he looked at the phial of ichor which he had brought with him. What effect would it have? It would give power, undoubtedly, but there could be all manner of unpleasant side effects. He leaned forward, trying to catch what the prisoners were saying.

The man was a Kristillian, Irem Ol Thangiol, on whom Xaedrek had been conducting some interesting experiments with amulin. The woman, Anixa, was a Kesfalian who had been the court dressmaker until Xaedrek had caught her trying to free Irem Ol Thangiol several days ago. Since then he had kept them here in no physical discomfort, but with every reason to believe something terrible was going to happen to them. Each day he observed them drawing closer together, wilting under the strain of continual fear and becoming more and more dependent on each other. This concern for each other had the desired effect, which was to sharpen their anticipation of their fate.

Anixa was stroking the man's brow gently as they talked. She was a small, dark woman, no longer young but retaining an elfin quality. Her colouring was typically Kesfalian; dark bronze skin dappled with lighter patches of sheeny blue-gold, eyes the colour of pale honey, hair curving down either side of her face like two long, black wings. It was obvious that the Kristillian adored her. As for him, he was tall and had once been powerfully built, but weight had been burned off him by amulin-fever, and his muscles were wasted and flabby from under-use. The green silk gown hung on him pitifully.

Xaedrek was observing all this when he distinctly heard the woman mention Melkavesh.

'Anixa, don't talk of her, don't mention her name,' Ol Thangiol said anxiously. 'He watches us – I'm sure he does.'

At this, she seemed to freeze, although her sombre expression did not change. For a second her hand was poised in mid-air, then she resumed her caressing of his tangled reddish hair and beard. 'I've something to confess,' she said in a flat tone. 'I've been trying all night to tell you – I could not.'

'What is it? I won't be angry, whatever it is.'

Xaedrek was astonished at how lucid Ol Thangiol was; a few days earlier he had been out of his mind with fever and madness. Anixa seemed to have worked wonders on him.

'I told Xaedrek about Melkavesh.'

He tried to lift his head. 'Told him – what?'

'Everything I knew. How she came to me, how I let her hide so she could disguise herself and trick Xaedrek, how she fled into the mountains.'

'By the moons, Anixa –'

'I know how shameful it was.' There was an icy light of self-condemnation in her eyes. 'I will carry the shame of it for the rest of my life, and I need no one else, not even you, to tell me how wicked and unforgivable it was.'

'No – no, you misunderstand.' He reached up quickly to clasp her hand. 'My love – what did he do to you to make you tell him?'

'Nothing. It was the threat of what he would do to you if I stayed silent that did it,' she whispered.

'Gods,' murmured Ol Thangiol, squeezing his eyes shut. 'You told him for my sake. I don't think there's anything Xaedrek could do to me that he hasn't done already.'

'Nevertheless, I could not let him –'

'Hush. I would have done the same. All that matters is that you weren't harmed.'

'No. He's done nothing to hurt me yet. But you see, there's no point now in us not talking of Melkavesh. We can say what we like; he already knows.'

At this the man's head tipped back and he began to laugh, long and silently, and his mirth was like the shuddering of total despair. Anixa's face did not change. She only watched quietly until he had subsided.

'All right then,' he said at last. 'Let us talk of her, and let Xaedrek tremble – for she is going to destroy him.'

Xaedrek was unmoved by their pathetic courage, and decided he had heard enough. He went to a side table and poured a strong-flavoured spirit into a goblet, mixing it well with water and honey. On a thought he added a pinch of white powder and stirred it with a glass rod. Finally he drew the stopper from the phial and let the pearlescent liquid drip into the goblet. A few pinkish tendrils drifted to the surface, but he did not think they would be noticed. He sniffed at it, and could discern nothing except the odour of the spirit.

Irem Ol Thangiol had been an excellent subject for experiment and had yielded some useful results, but he was burnt out. Anixa, on the other hand, was strong and healthy. He had known she would prove useful for something.

He went into the anteroom used as an office, where Duke Valamek was seated at the desk. He had not been long in Xaedrek's service, but was proving a gifted scientist. Xaedrek hoped he would one day prove worthy to replace Shavarish on the Inner Council.

'Valamek, the very man,' he said amicably. 'I expect you're tired, if you've been on duty all night.'

'No, I'm quite all right, Sire.' He stood hurriedly and bowed his head.

'There's no need to be so formal – not in private, anyway.' Xaedrek smiled. 'You can go off early, if you'll do one thing for me first. Take this goblet and make sure Madam Anixa drinks it, will you? If she looks like objecting, remind her of what could happen to Ol Thangiol.'

'Of course, Sire.'

'I've put in a powder to prevent it making her sick, but be careful. Come out and lock the door as soon as she's finished it.'

He went back to the mirror and watched as Valamek entered the room. Anixa and Irem Ol Thangiol raised their heads and became as tense as terrified deer. Valamek approached them; words were exchanged. For a long moment Anixa stared at the goblet with that unreadable gaze that Xaedrek found intriguing. Then slowly, reluctantly, she reached out and lifted the vessel to her mouth and drained it. Her expression did not change. She handed the goblet back to Valamek with her eyes fixed on him like cold moonlight shining through flakes of amber. The Gorethrian strode out and relocked the door.

'Thank you, Valamek,' said Xaedrek. 'As you go out, would you tell the guards I am not to be disturbed, please?'

'Yes, Sire, at once. Good morning.'

In the chamber, Anixa showed no immediate reaction. She said something that sounded like, 'I don't know what it was. I don't care,' and she wiped her lips and leaned listlessly back against the bedhead, her eyes closed. Then Xaedrek saw her chest begin to rise and fall with her quickened breathing, and he saw sweat break out on her dark face. She half leaped, half fell off the bed, and stood frantically rubbing at her throat. A pale light glistened around her.

'Beloved, what is it?' cried Ol Thangiol, sitting up in consternation.

'I think Xaedrek has poisoned me,' she gasped. 'I don't know – oh, by the moons, help me!' She staggered against a table, and the lamp on it rocked wildly. The Kristillian – who could barely stand – struggled across to help her.

Xaedrek left the mirror, made his way round to the door and quietly let himself into the chamber. Anixa was thrashing in Ol Thangiol's arms as he tried to help her back to the bed, and it was a moment before they noticed him. Then they both froze.

As he stood ominously before them the Emperor looked – to Anixa's eyes – no less than beautiful. The soft golden lamplight made his dark face seem radiant and sublime as a statue's, and his eyes were hypnotic wells of light. Indeed, he might have been one of the statues of past Emperors come to life, for he had that same idealised aspect of benevolence and tranquillity. But he was not cold marble; he was warm and alive, animated by a compelling presence so strong that the Kesfalian woman felt her own spirit curling in on itself like a dead leaf before a fire. She was not sure that he was evil; she was no longer sure of anything. A slight smile touched his lips.

'Well, Madam Anixa,' he said. 'How do you feel?'

21

2

Daughter of the Moons

'ARE YOU afraid of heights?' asked the priest, Irem Ol Melemen.

'I don't think Lady Melkavesh is frightened of anything,' said Queen Afil An Mora, lifting the hem of her robe clear of the top step.

Melkavesh smiled politely, thinking, *If only you knew.* 'No, I don't mind heights.'

The King, who was preceding them onto the balcony, gave a slight gasp and said, 'It's just as well.'

The tallest spire of the Crystal City seemed to be swimming in blueness, more part of the sky than the ground. The view was dizzying. The towers all around them gleamed like wind-sculpted ice awash with pastel colours, only the twin-domed temple shining pure white. Beyond the wall the plainer buildings of the Outer City were scattered like a mosaic down the sides of the hill. Trees rustled in the winding streets. Part of the second wall could be seen like a meandering rim of pearl, but Charhn spilled out beyond it until it was lost in the arms of the fells.

The fells rolled north, south and east like giant waves frozen in palest green velvet, with outcrops of quartz foaming on their crests. A golden haze sifted over them. To the west lay farmland and the chain of towns and villages that lay along the river winding towards Ehd'rabara.

Kristillia, Melkavesh was thinking, might lack Gorethria's vividness, but was as beautiful in its own way. She leaned over the void without fear, but with an intense, unexpected pang of love.

'It's a long time since I last came up here,' said King Afil Es Thendil breathlessly. 'An unsurpassed view, if you can survive the climb – and the dizziness. We wanted you to see it.' The balcony encircling the spire had an outer wall and a low inner wall which served as a bench. Melkavesh and the King and Queen sat down, but the priest remained with his back to the spire as if he were glued there.

'I have no nerve for this,' he said cheerfully. 'But to come up here every now and then is a compulsion. And perfect for private conversations, of course.'

'Alas, that we have lost the skills with which our ancestors built the City,' said the King.

Melkavesh smiled. 'I hope you'll recapture them. It's wonderful here.'

'Where is your friend Kharan?' the Queen asked in a peculiar tone.

'Oh – she wanted to stay with her baby, I think.' Melkavesh was glad of Irem Ol Melemen's presence, there being a distinct tension between the King and Queen. Both were happily talking to her, but not to each other. 'We're grateful to you for making us so at home in the royal mansion.'

'Nonsense,' said Afil Es Thendil, smiling. 'It can't even begin to repay what you are doing for us – for Kristillia and all Vardrav.'

The King was a thin, slightly stooped man with a pleasant face that often bore a grave expression. His beard and shoulder-length hair were a gingery golden-brown. Almost all Kristillians had reddish hair of various shades, and their skin had a marbled look of gold, ivory and brown swirling together. He and the Queen wore amber robes and cloaks of sage velvet, while Irem Ol Melemen – a clean-shaven, well-built man – wore the indigo chasuble of a priest. The Queen, with her mane of dark hair drawn back from her face, was extraordinarily beautiful, yet there was a coldness about her beauty that made her seem unapproachable.

Melkavesh said, 'Believe me, I'll do everything in my power to help you defeat Xaedrek.'

'You do understand,' said the Queen, 'that Kristillia will

23

never be safe until Gorethria is not only defeated, but destroyed?'

'That is my aim,' said Melkavesh quietly. 'To oust them from the whole of Vardrav.'

'More troops are coming in from other countries every day.' The King leaned forward enthusiastically. The tower seemed to sway, and Ol Melemen closed his eyes. 'Listen to me, we used to call them "refugees", and now they are "troops"! But there *is* a difference. They are coming for a reason; not just to escape the Gorethrians, but to fight back! They're coming from Kesfaline, Malmanon, Alta-Nangra; even as far away as Ala'kaara and Cevandaris.'

'They are very brave men and women,' said the priest. 'Fliya knows how many are being slain by the Gorethrians on their way.'

Es Thendil frowned. 'But they cannot slay them all. They can't stop the flood. Melkavesh has given us a banner to rally to.'

'I knew my strange hair would prove useful for something,' she said with a grin. Her father, Ashurek, had passed on the dark brown-violet skin, aristocratic features and grimly set mouth of a pure Gorethrian. But from her mother, Silvren, she had the startling Athrainian-blonde hair that had been her downfall with Xaedrek and her salvation with the Kristillians; a shining waist-length cascade with all shades of gold in it. Her eyes, the only compromise, were brilliant golden-green.

'Forgive me, Lady Melkavesh, but I know very little about you,' said An Mora. 'Is it true you are Ashurek's daughter? I only know what the King has said – if I can believe that.'

'I forgot I haven't told Your Majesty,' Melkavesh said quickly, before the Queen's remark took on any greater significance. 'I know you must find it hard to trust me, being half Gorethrian. Ashurek was Meshurek's brother, and he would have been Emperor if he'd stayed. But he renounced Gorethria totally, and he brought me up to believe . . .' It was hard for her to say it. 'To believe they are evil. That was why he and Silvren felt they couldn't stay on this Earth, and

24

went to a world named Ikonus, where I was born. Sorcerers abounded there, and I was nothing unusual. But I had to come back to this Earth. I don't know why – it was a compulsion, like being called home.'

'But you went to Gorethria first,' said An Mora.

'I went to see if the Empire still existed. I won my way into Xaedrek's confidence to investigate the supposed sorcerous powers he has. I found out that they were false and corrupt; and that's why I came here, because the only way to destroy the Empire and purge the evil is by war.'

Es Thendil was listening intently. Melkavesh had never felt unimportant, and it did not seem strange to her that a king was hanging on her every word. She went on, 'I don't regret coming back. I love Earth, I'm more at home here than ever I was on Ikonus. But I feel very alone sometimes. There are no other Sorcerers; not yet, anyway. The power of sorcery is a new-born thing, released by the Serpent's death, and when latent wielders of the power are born they will need my help and guidance . . . Your Majesty, you look doubtful.'

'It is only that you have made no mention of the moons, Jaed and Fliya,' the Queen replied. 'They influence everything. I can't believe such a profound change has taken place that doesn't involve them.'

Privately Melkavesh thought that the Kristillians' worship of the moons was no more than a superstition that gave them hope and unity against Gorethria, but she could not say as much without causing grave offence. She said carefully, 'Perhaps the moons are of significance. I don't know much about your religion, so it would be presumptuous of me to speculate.'

'It would take days to explain in full, but I can tell you a little of its history,' said Irem Ol Melemen. His face, rather fleshy, had a friendly expression that seldom betrayed his true thoughts. 'The first priestess was a wise woman – a Kesfalian, in fact – who saved Kristillia from an unspecified menace several thousand years ago. There is no record of what exactly she did, but my own theory is that a demon was wreaking havoc, and she banished it by slaying the

25

summoner. Then she directed people's thoughts away from the Serpent M'gulfn and towards the moons instead.'

'Replacing evil with a reverence for nature,' said Melkavesh.

'Exactly. And the wise woman's name was Fliya. The moons were nameless in those days – or had other names that are forgotten. Then, three thousand years ago, there is said to have been a strange conjunction of the Planes that made them become visible in the sky. This conjunction was supposed to have caused such disruption that a chunk of one of the moons was torn away and fell to Earth.

'Thereupon a Kristillian decided to fashion the fallen rock into a temple to the moons. Fliya was well pleased and took him as her husband, and he built the Crystal City around the temple. The man's name was Jaed, the founder of Charhn. When they died, it was believed that their spirits passed into the moons to watch over Kristillia and Kesfaline.'

'Of course, we do not believe that the temple really is made of rock from the moon itself,' said the King, 'and Jaed and Fliya themselves are mythical figures, but –'

Ol Melemen cut across him sharply. 'There is no proof that they did *not* exist. Whether the legend is true or not is beside the point. The myth is symbolic, and what it symbolises is the basis of our faith. The moons are not invisible gods, they are very real bodies that have great influence over the Earth. They represent all that is good, and in return for our reverence they protect us. The first time Gorethria conquered us a thousand years ago they destroyed much of our knowledge and skill, and the logic behind many of our philosophies was lost. But at least they could not steal our faith.'

At the mention of Gorethria, the King's expression changed. 'It's remarkable what we have held onto, being under Gorethria's domination for centuries,' he said in a low voice. 'We have been free of them less than thirty years. We thought the nightmare was over, but now there's Xaedrek to drag us down again. But this time we are not going to fail!' He spoke fiercely, and for a few moments the Queen's eyes on him contained empathy, not coldness.

'Of course, there is an aspect of our belief that we've never lost,' said Ol Melemen, 'which is that an enchantress would one day come and bring the "power of the moons" into its own. What could that refer to, except sorcery? And you are here – so don't be too swift to dismiss our religion as mere superstition.'

'I don't,' said Melkavesh, chastened. 'No, I don't. There is much in Kristillia that is closed to me, outside my experience. A dormant strength that I cannot touch. It is in all of you, and I think it's the reason why Xaedrek cannot conquer you.'

Even the Queen's eyes were warmer now, and she actually reached out and laid her hand on Melkavesh's. 'And you have truly renounced Gorethria?'

It was a jarring note, but she answered fiercely, 'Of course! Xaedrek's necromancy is so wrong – so alien, so unnatural to me that even now I can hardly bear to think about it. There's more at stake than Kristillia's freedom. If his vile methods spread before true Sorcerers gain a foothold, the whole future of Earth could be sullied by an evil as bad as the Serpent.'

They were staring at her, transfixed by the feeling in her voice, the crusading glow of her eyes. Like Xaedrek, she had a natural gift of charisma and knew how to use it; but it was not calculated, and the effect it had still took her aback.

'I believe passionately in true sorcery and in freedom,' she said, 'and believe me, I'll give my lifeblood to help Kristillia win.'

There was a moment of silence. The city seemed frozen, eternal. A flock of white birds soared overhead and swooped down through the void as if plunging into an invisible ocean.

'You are our inspiration, Melkavesh,' said Es Thendil, his eyes bright. 'And we are all so, so glad you came.'

Melkavesh had enjoyed their company, but she was not sorry when evening came and she could retreat to her room in the royal mansion. She needed solitude, a chance to think.

The chamber was sparse by Gorethrian standards, but

27

mahogany furniture and walls of rose-red stone gave it a warm feel. She poured herself a glass of brown wine and sat on the bed, leaning against the high, carved headboard. It is so easy, she thought moodily, to put on a show of confidence for them. But when I first came here, it was not a show.

Her arrival in Charhn had been a time of pure euphoria, particularly after the arduous 4,000 mile journey from Shale-kahh. The Kristillians had been suspicious of her Gorethrian face at first, but she had won them over, not by a show of sorcery, but by the force of her personality. That and the moon talisman she had been wearing, given to her by Ol Melemen's brother, Irem Ol Thangiol – and of course her bright hair, which seemed to prove that she was not Gorethrian. For the Kristillians it had become the outward mark of her sorcery and their hope of freedom. And now she received adulation wherever she went.

It had been the same with the tribespeople of Mangorad, whom she had also rallied to her cause during the journey. They had been more difficult than the Kristillians, because they were less responsive to reason and she had had to play on their superstitions to win them over. Once swayed, the Mangorians' devotion was slavish and unbreakable. The Kristillians, however, were a far more intellectual people and she knew that the slightest wavering of her confidence might lose them.

She had promised them so much. Sorcery, sorcery. On a transcendent level her inner vision was as strong as ever; a destiny awaited her that was as vast and all-encompassing as space, and she was rushing towards it on a tide of fiery optimism, bearing all of Vardrav with her. That vision was inside her, heart and soul. But on a practical level, could she offer Kristillia anything at all?

There was her power, but it had a limit and could not destroy even a hundredth of Xaedrek's army. Unlike him, she could not distribute the power to all and sundry; and even had she been able to, it was contrary to her strict Sorcerer's Oath to abuse it in such a way.

Then there was far-sight. In theory she could watch every move Xaedrek made, anticipate every step of the invasion until he did not stand a chance. But even that was not as easy as everyone thought.

She sighed, rubbed at her forehead, and set the glass aside.

She was not omniscient. She could not far-see all the time, nor could she see more than one scene at once. It was rare that knowledge leapt at her; normally she must go seeking it, often with no idea of what she was looking for. The process was deeply tiring. Night after night she lay in her bed, not sleeping but sending her mind questing out into Shalekahh for as long as she could bear it. When she ceased, she would be drained to the point of exhaustion.

Once, on Ikonus, far-seeing had been easy. On this Earth everything about sorcery was difficult. There was something wrong with the power, as if it were not flowing freely through the Earth but being blocked in some way. Its birth was incomplete. As hard as she tried to find out why, she could not, but the impediment was real enough and resulted in pain and exhaustion every time she used her power. When she had first set foot on Earth the shock had almost crippled her. Since then her tolerance to the pain had increased, but it never went away and put a severe limit on what she could do.

She should have solved the problem by now. But no answer came, and every failure left her more tightly wound, with frustration and anger pounding inside her skull, eating away at her belief in herself.

It was time to try again. She eased herself down on the bed, tried to relax, closed her eyes. A faint blonde shimmer enveloped her body. She slid slowly into the trance of far-sight, loosening her mind and freeing it like an arrow into the night.

There was a swerving, dizzy sensation, as if she were not quite in control. That worried her, but she steadied herself and rotated gently, like an all-seeing eye. Quite involuntarily she found herself above the spire, with the Inner City a forest of crystal shadows below her. The temple of Jaed and Fliya was shining like translucent white glass, and she was drawn towards it like a moth seeking light. She could almost see through the walls, see the countless diffused circles of candlelight and taste the fragrant smokes. The priests and priestesses were moving in a slow, swaying dance under the twin domes, circling the statues of Jaed and Fliya that had eyes like moons . . . The dance was hypnotising her. Their chanting drifted from the open doors like a soft, unintentional reprimand.

'We give thanks to the moons Jaed and Fliya for bestowing the gift of their daughter. All praise and thanks to the moons for sending our hope, the enchantress.'

This thanksgiving was for *her*! Mortified, Melkavesh reeled away and with a surge of power, thrust herself away and into the night sky. As it was, the last thing she wanted was their gratitude.

She was travelling swift as thought now, spearing towards Shalekahh. The night sky was like blue-black glass, arrayed with a glittering field of stars. The two moons were above the horizon, Jaed in crescent and Fliya half full, giving every tree and rock a faint double shadow. Below her, Kristillia slanted away towards the edges of the world. It was a country completely landlocked apart from a short stretch of coastline along the Aludrian Sea.

It was towards Aludria that she felt herself pulled now, as if by an invisible magnetism. She fought the pull, but it was strong and distorted her path into a curve. She was losing speed. Drawing on the reserves of her distant body she thrust herself onwards, but the further she went the harder it was becoming. In this form she could feel no pain and might not know she had over-exerted herself until it was too late. Sorcerers had killed themselves by being too ambitious . . .

No time for caution now. Suddenly she was past the resistance and plunging into Shalekahh, but all seemed blurred and disjointed. Walls leaned at strange angles, night and day overlaid each other, scenes were obscured by distorting prisms, and voices echoed from the far end of whirling tunnels. She was trying too hard and she would pay for it later, but she could not leave without learning something . . .

There was something about a machine . . . She could not make sense of it, but it sent spirals of dread grinding through her like corkscrews. Perhaps it was to do with the vile experiment that Ah'garith had set up . . . She directed her thoughts to the cell where it had been but, to her astonishment, it was gone.

A source of such gross power, and they had destroyed it? She would have wept with relief if the vacuum of far-seeing had allowed any expression of emotion, but woven with the relief was a deeper suspicion. She must understand – She quested towards Xaedrek, could not find him, could only hear obscure murmurings.

Melkavesh strained desperately for understanding. She would snap like a taut thread if she pushed herself any harder, but she would rather break than return without learning what it meant –

A whiplash of blackness blinded her. She was no longer in Shalekahh but hurtling through the night sky. The thread of her self had not broken but recoiled, and with the momentum she could not resist the pull that was drawing her towards the Aludrian Sea.

Then something strange happened. Although the landscape was still receding beneath her, all at once it seemed she was not moving. She felt she had hung there all her life with the world perpetually growing tinier yet staying the same, while the moons were growing larger and larger, pulling her towards them yet never seeming any closer.

In a moment of sheer terror she knew she had lost consciousness and was touching the threshold between astral projection and a dream. This had never happened to her before. It meant she was still outside her body but no longer in control; and with no idea of what to do, her first instinct was to return to her body.

In an instant, it seemed she was back in bed. She could feel the covers under her hand, a strand of hair pressed into her cheek, see the moonlight shining on the flags – so *real* – but like a sleeper who is convinced he has woken up only to find the nightmare continuing, she knew she was still dreaming. The room fell away and she gasped with sudden vertigo. Now there was a dark mass heaving and swaying beneath her, catching points of light on its surface. A sea . . .

The dream took her prisoner then, and she no longer knew

she was dreaming. It was one she had had many times before, but trapped in it she had no memory of those previous times. The moons were still above her, no longer benign and distant but close enough to touch. They were huge and threatening and heavy, and she could sense the weight of them, a billion tons of rock poised to descend on her. Weight flowed from them in slow, ponderous waves, pressing down on her head and chest, crushing her rib-cage until she struggled and gasped for breath. This was intolerable – she must wake up –

The globes were pushing her down towards the sea, and however desperately she fought, she could not resist them. She felt the awful sensation of falling – the leaping of her stomach, the panic of losing control – and she felt the air rushing past, the water slamming into her back, the waves closing over her head. Her ears were singing, her head bursting. She opened her mouth and swallowed cold sea water as she flailed desperately to reach the surface. But the moons forced her deeper. All was black, but she could sense the waves of gravity pulsing from them like an invisible, heavy light which contained the answer –

A century later, Melkavesh found herself bobbing on the surface of a milky-green sea, looking up into the face of a child with long hair the rich plum-red of Gorethrian maples. She was leaning over the rail of a ship with a small bird on her shoulder. It resembled a blackbird, except that it was the same colour as her hair.

The child was Filmoriel, yet it could not be, Filmoriel was still a baby, and the bird – the bird was flying straight towards her now. Melkavesh raised her arms to fend it off, but just before it reached her, it seemed to slam into a pane of glass. She watched, helpless, as it turned in a flurry of wings to fling itself again and again at the glass with such desperation that she was suddenly weeping, shouting, begging for it to stop –

'What's wrong?' said a voice.

'I'm drowning,' Melkavesh croaked, and woke up.

There was a face bending over her, a kind face full of concern, brown eyes gathering light.

'Kharan. Oh, Kharan, thank the gods you're here.' She

sat up, gasping, dripping with sweat, her ribs spiked with iron. The pain and fear were so intense that she flung herself off the bed as if to escape them, then stood hugging herself, holding herself in place. She thought she must have roused the whole mansion, until she realised that her cries had been voiceless, and that –

That there was no one with her in the room.

'Oh, gods,' she sobbed. 'Gods.' She staggered to a cabinet and tried to light the lamp standing on it with palsied hands. 'It's over. It's all right, you fool, it's over.'

She would recover, but it would take time for the shock and exhaustion to wear off. After that she had to face the consequences of another failure . . .

It had just been wishful thinking, the idea of Kharan being there to comfort her after the nightmare. In reality she was alone, but that was something she was used to.

The next morning, Kharan sat idly in front of a mirror, trimming her dark brown hair. It had grown long and straggly in the journey from Shalekahh, and she thought it suited her better at jaw length. The face looking back at her was light-skinned with a dusky rose sheen, slightly too long and square-jawed to be called pretty. She was at a loss to know what drew men to her, with or without encouragement. It must be my smile, she thought, pulling faces at herself. Filmoriel watched from the crib beside her with wide grey-violet eyes.

Kharan put the scissors down and turned to her. 'Well, what do you think? Not much? At least there's some colour in my face again. More than in yours, miss. You're as fair-skinned as Falmeryn. Oh, I wish he could have seen you. We could have had a bet on what colour that excuse for hair is going to turn. I think red –'

A soft knock at the door cut short this diverting one-way conversation. 'Come in, Melkavesh,' she called, forgetting that the Sorceress usually rapped briskly and walked straight in. There was no response. Puzzled, she went to open the door and found King Afil Es Thendil standing there.

'Oh, it's you,' she said. 'Come in.'

'Kharan, my dear, forgive me for disturbing you. If it's inconvenient –'

'No, of course not.' She smiled. 'You know I said you could talk to me whenever you needed to.' He kissed her, but she turned her cheek to his lips. He did not seem to notice the gesture.

'How is Filmoriel?' he asked, bending over the crib.

'Very well. And how is the Queen?'

'Must you always mention her?' He sat down at the little mahogany table in the centre of the room and straightened his amber robe. Over it he wore a blue tabard with a bronze belt, and a bronze circlet on his hair. 'She is barely speaking to me.'

'Has it occurred to you that if she finds out she will probably kill me?'

'She will not find out, and no one will harm you, my dear.'

'She has eyes to see the way you look at me!' Kharan sat opposite him. 'Es Thendil, are you sure this isn't a mistake?'

He looked away from her, shaking his head. 'Oh, Kharan, what can I say? It was a marriage of political necessity. We are cousins, we grew up together, and I – and I never liked her. I respect her, but there is something about her that I can't love.'

'That's not your fault. But does she love you?'

'I – I don't know whether it is love, or possessiveness. She can be so cold! But the moment I saw you I sensed a warmth about you, something in your character, your eyes –' he shrugged helplessly. 'Something magical. This has never happened to me before, I have never loved anyone as I love you.'

Kharan avoided his doe-like eyes, and looked down at her fingers, white against the table top. 'You call her cold, but I haven't exactly encouraged you.'

'But you are yourself with me. That means everything.'

'And An Mora isn't?'

He sighed and folded his hands. 'She expects me to be always perfect, always a king. We must be stoical and never express our doubts. An admirable philosophy, I'm sure, but I cannot live up to it. Sometimes I thought I'd go mad for want of someone to talk to. You are a sympathetic listener, Kharan, and much more . . .' His hands folded over hers, and she made herself meet his eyes.

'Es Thendil, I am very fond of you. You're one of the nicest people I have ever met, and I suppose either you or the Queen will be unhappy whatever I do. But I haven't been quite honest with you. I owe you the truth, because after I've told you, you may not want to see me again.'

'My dear, I'm sure you can't have done anything that terrible,' he said gently. 'What is it?'

She held his gaze and stated quietly, 'I used to be the Emperor Xaedrek's mistress.'

His shock was even worse than she had anticipated. His fingers skittered backwards across the table and he pressed himself into the chair back as if she had announced that she was a plague carrier. For a long moment he stared at her, his eyes wide with undisguised horror – and then he leaned hesitantly forward again, shaking his head. 'By the moons. You poor child. How did this come to be?'

'Well, I was in Shalekahh as a slave, of course,' she said as lightly as she could. 'I grew up in An'raaga, an orphan with about thirty others. When we were old enough, the adults who had looked after us sold us to Bagreean slave-traders. Eventually I was taken to Shalekahh where I found myself working as a kitchen maid for a nobleman, one Duke Xaedrek. By the time he became Emperor, I was established as his mistress. I was seventeen years old then.'

'It must have been a terrible ordeal,' he breathed. She smiled thinly. 'How long did it go on?'

'I lived in the palace with him for nine years.' She watched his mouth soundlessly frame the word *nine* and then she continued. 'It was not easy; the Gorethrian courtiers hated me, and so did the Vardravian servants. I had not one single friend, but I didn't care, because in an odd way I was happy. I had what I wanted, you see – status, riches, an easy life.'

Afil Es Thendil's gingery brows almost met with perplexity. 'Wait – forgive me, Kharan, I assumed you meant he had forced you. Are you saying that you lived with him of your own accord?'

'Yes. I suppose I could have let you think he forced me, but I want to tell you the truth.'

'But how could you?' he cried. 'That monstrous man –'

'Ah, but in person he is not monstrous. He is perfectly amicable and charming. In all the time I knew him he never said an unkind word to me or gave me any cause to fear him. He used to say that what had first attracted him to me was that I did not fear him; most other people did, you see.' There was a catch in her voice and she swallowed hard before continuing, 'As to why, it was my way of getting even with the Gorethrians. They enslaved us, despised us and took everything we had. I thought that by becoming Xaedrek's mistress, I had made myself their equal. I believed it for a long time. Pure self-delusion.'

She fell silent. The King asked, 'Are you all right? You've gone a dreadful colour.'

'I'm fine.' She drew a deep breath. 'I closed my eyes to Xaedrek's evil. I mean, I knew he did terrible things, but I simply pretended it had nothing to do with me. Then one day I chanced to go into the mansion where his "scientific" work took place, and I found it full of his victims – Vardravians, some of them An'raagans, horribly burned and in terrible physical and mental pain. He had been experimenting on them, using them to produce his necromantic power. After that I couldn't close my eyes any longer. It was such a shock – not just to see the reality of the vile things he was doing – but to confront my own wickedness. Do you understand? As long as I stayed with him I was condoning it. I hated myself. I wanted to run away from him, but I couldn't even do that. I was too much of a coward.'

The King stood up and went over to the window, as if – she thought – he could not bear to look at her. He mumbled indistinctly, 'Go on. I'm listening.'

'So I began avoiding him, even hiding in the stables to delay going back to the palace. And there I met one of the grooms, a man called Falmeryn. He was from Forluin – he'd been captured by slave-traders while on a voyage to Vardrav, and put to work in the Imperial mews. He was so different from Xaedrek, who was all surface charm and ice. He was

36

gentle and good and warm-hearted, and he was the first real friend I'd ever had. Until I met him, I hadn't believed there was any such thing as love; he proved me wrong. I loved Falmeryn to the point of madness and, the Lady help him, he loved me. So we tried to escape. We knew it was insane and bound to end in disaster, but we tried anyway. I think we got all of half a mile from the palace gates before Xaedrek's guards caught us.

'That was the last time I ever saw Falmeryn.' A sob escaped her and she tried to turn it into a cough, hoping Es Thendil had not noticed. But he was looking at her, shaken by the unselfconscious misery betrayed in every line of her drooping shoulders and neck. 'And I think it was the first time I really saw Xaedrek as other Vardravians did. I can't explain what it is about him that's so terrifying; he was perfectly civilised yet so cold – and he confused me. I couldn't believe he'd ever felt much for me, yet he gave the impression he was really hurt that I'd preferred Falmeryn to him. To this day I don't know whether he was acting or not. But he had no compunction about putting the two of us to death – even though I'd been his companion for so many years.'

'Death?' the King cried. 'And he'd never said an unkind word?'

She gave a humourless smile. 'It was the first time I'd crossed him, you see. Xaedrek has certain values. He is as kind and chivalrous as you could wish to those he finds agreeable; but displease him once and the punishment is swift and final. And completely without malice – that's the most disturbing thing of all. He's a perfectionist . . . and I was no longer perfect.'

'But you survived. How was that?'

'Melkavesh saved me. I was being taken to the Fortress of Execution to be beheaded. Suddenly this woman was there – Gorethrian, but with bright golden hair – just one woman against four guards, yet she was scattering them across the street like a whirlwind. I hardly remember anything about it; Xaedrek had offered me a drug to stop me being afraid – very considerate of him – and, being a coward, I had taken it.'

'Did she also rescue Falmeryn?' Es Thendril asked innocently.

Kharan did not answer for a long time. When she did, her voice was hoarse and unsteady. 'No. He's dead. Xaedrek refused to tell me what would happen to him because – because he did not want the knowledge to torment me. He couldn't guess how my imagination would torment me instead, the endless images of Falmeryn being executed by every Gorethrian method there was . . . or perhaps he could. No, I don't know what happened to him, I just know he's dead.'

It was a long time since she had wept for Falmeryn, but speaking of him brought it all back, and she could not restrain the spasm of crying that shook her. The King did not touch her; he only offered her a square of cotton on which she gratefully wiped her nose.

'You must have loved him very much.'

'Oh, I did. You can't imagine – I'd never met anyone like him, and never will again. For a time I wished I'd never met Melkavesh, that my execution had gone ahead. But I was pregnant, and I decided I had to live for the sake of Falmeryn's child. I nearly lost her as well, because of that terrible journey through the Emethrians. I remember it so vividly – we were in cave sheltering from the weather. I couldn't sleep for the pain I was in, and the storm and the night seemed to go on forever. I really thought the mountains themselves were revenging themselves on me by tearing my child away. Eventually Melkavesh made me sleep and when I woke, I was convinced I'd lost the baby, that my last link to Falmeryn was severed. I would not wish it even on Xaedrek himself to want to die that badly.' She closed her eyes, stunned by the vividness of her memories. 'I was wrapped up in a cloak, so numb I couldn't even feel the rock under me. I remember the storm had stopped, and there was a square of sunlight on the cave wall. And then Melkavesh showed me the tiny baby – alive. She had saved her life by sorcery.' Kharan looked up at the King with an expression of solemn awe that almost made him weep with her. 'Filmoriel is a miracle. She's Falmeryn's daughter and she's all I've got – more than that, she's all I want. I live only for her.'

'And you are still mourning Falmeryn,' Es Thendil said sadly.

'Yes, I am, but I can't help that. Perhaps it's dangerous to have something so perfect, because when you lose it, it destroys your whole life.'

'You could try to rebuild it. You ought to.'

'What for?' she exclaimed. 'You already have a wife, and I – I don't think I can love anyone. What would be the point? I'm sorry, Es Thendil. I suppose I ought not to speak like that to a king. Still less to a friend.'

'It's all right. You can say what you like to me.' He put his arms round her and she leaned against him, suddenly grateful for his kindness. 'It doesn't matter about the past.'

'I'm trying to tell you that after Falmeryn, anything else is meaningless. I live my whole life for Filmoriel, and I have nothing left to give you. I'm sorry.'

Es Thendil went back to his seat and folded his bony hands on the edge of the table. 'If you really wish me to go away and not come back, I will.'

'Perhaps it would be best . . . But I just haven't the heart.' She smiled weakly.

'I wish I had the strength, Kharan, believe me. I feel it's you I've known all my life, and the Queen who is a stranger to me. Who else could I say this to? I don't feel like a king; I feel like a man faced with an enormously tall and forbidding mountain which owes absolutely nothing to me, least of all its existence. The prospect of holding Kristillia against Gorethria is like forever scrambling up its frozen sides, and never reaching the peak.'

She reached across and touched his hand. 'No one thinks you will let them down. You are a good king and everyone loves you.'

'I find no joy in responsibility,' he said. 'I was not really brought up to be a king; Gorethria still ruled us when I was a child, and the Royal Family had to live in hiding with peasants in the northern mountains. That was the only life I knew for my first ten years. When the Empire fell apart after Meshurek's reign and it seemed Gorethria itself would be destroyed, I was brought out of the mountains and crowned.

We thought our centuries of slavery were over – then Xaedrek came, and it's as if time has run in a circle back to a thousand years ago, when all of Vardrav had fallen except Kristillia, and for us it was only a matter of time. And here I am, charged with the responsibility of breaking the circle, feeling totally inadequate to the task.'

Kharan said nothing, but her heart went out to him. In his way he was as alone as Xaedrek, but unlike Xaedrek he hated his position. An unhappy marriage only made the burden greater.

Without bitterness, he went on, 'I'm sure An Mora does not still dream of rain blowing across the red mountains, or yearn for the drudgery and simplicity of our childhood. The past is gone behind a veil of rain, and dreaming of it only makes my task harder. You must understand, my dear, I am not trying to shirk my responsibility. I regard it as a very grave and serious duty. I will transfer the burden to no one else, not An Mora, not Melkavesh; and whether I succeed or fail, no one shall say that I did not love and serve Kristillia as I should.'

The sun was sinking in a lake of ruby light, turning the royal mansion from rose to fiery crimson. From the parapets, Melkavesh and Kharan could see the roofs and treetops of Charhn, hear the faint sounds of marching feet, hoofbeats and birdsong. They walked slowly, their arms linked, listening as the sounds dwindled to the chirping of a solitary bird.

'I still can't believe we're here,' Kharan said. 'Do you remember the nights we spent in the mouth of some freezing cave, or soaked to the skin in that damned jungle? Sometimes I think I'll wake up there and find this was all a dream!'

'I'm glad you like it here,' said Melkavesh.

'Oh, I do. Shalekahh was so cold, all marble and metal. Kristillia feels almost like home. Filmoriel is thriving here too.'

'She's a survivor, like her mother.'

'If I survive the Queen's jealousy.'

'There's no reason for her to be upset, if you're discreet.

Listen, if you and Es Thendil can find some happiness after all that's happened to you, I can't see any harm in it.'

'Can't you?' said Kharan softly. 'I'm fond of him, but it means nothing. I didn't mean to cause the Queen such pain. He says she is cold, but I think she is an intensely shy woman who can't express her love.'

'Then refuse to see him!'

'I can't, Mel. He needs me.' Kharan gave a bleak smile. 'And I can't even care enough about the Queen to refuse him. It just doesn't seem to matter either way.'

'You've lost someone, and it's very hard to get over,' Melkavesh said, putting an arm round her shoulders.

'All this sympathy, there must be something wrong with you!' It was meant light-heartedly, but then Kharan looked more closely at her companion and said concernedly, 'There is something wrong, isn't there? What is it?'

'The same as always, but worse,' was the short reply. 'I tried to spy on Xaedrek, but it was harder than ever this time.'

'Mel, you were still tired from the previous time. You'll make yourself ill.'

'I know. Don't lecture me.'

'Well, I'm worried about you. Look, you are Kristillia's shining light, and I don't doubt your leadership qualities, but how are you actually going to help them?'

'To be honest, I don't know yet. But I'm going to find a way. Kharan, it's essential that I appear supremely confident! What use would it be to admit my doubts? No one can solve my problems except me.'

'Problems? This is a war we are talking about.'

'I know,' said Melkavesh tightly, disengaging her arm and turning away. 'Everyone is afraid, Kharan. It's going to happen anyway, whether I help the King or not.'

'Yes, but the thing is, if the Kristillians had been left to their own devices, although they'd have fought bravely, it would probably have been over quickly. But with you leading them they'll think they're invincible. But they're not. The war will drag on and it will end in the most horrific massacre.'

Melkavesh swung round, her eyes luminous with anger

41

under the fiercely slanting brows. 'What do you imagine I
think of every waking moment? Why do I nearly kill myself
trying to far-see?'

They faced each other for a long moment, but Kharan
held her gaze squarely, with no intention of apologising.
Eventually Melkavesh turned away to lean on the parapet,
and stared into a sunset that was streaked with fire and blood.

She had a tendency to act first and think later, and for
once it seemed her over-confidence had led her to a disastrous
misjudgement. She could inspire Kristillia; she could unite
all the oppressed nations of Vardrav; she could lead them
like one vast multi-coloured arrowhead against Xaedrek's
legions. But unless she found the key to the theurgic power
and unlocked it for Kristillia's use, all would be as Kharan
said. Defeat, genocide, disaster.

3

Beyond the Circle

THE CITY of Shalekahh seemed as delicate as eggshell, quivering as if it might shatter at any moment. Falmeryn wished it would. He willed the perfect spires to craze, the slabs to be torn up and blown away like a membrane, leaving only grass under them, hills and freedom –

But Shalekahh remained. His horse's sides heaved under his legs, foam flew from its lips. Kharan rode desperately at his side. Her mouth was open and her face white with terror as she urged her horse on, but its hooves were sliding about as if the marble had turned to ice. They were galloping on the spot. The street before them stretched out longer and longer until it became a white filament attenuated to infinity, while behind them their pursuers came on like a line of flame.

Then, with a scrabbling of hooves, Kharan's horse went down. Falmeryn was suddenly on his feet, running back to her, his own mount vanished. It took him forever to reach her. They seemed to be completely alone in the street, yet the moment he touched her the Imperial guards appeared from everywhere, fire and black metal, to tear her out of his arms and carry her away.

'Falmeryn, Falmeryn,' she cried. 'They're going to kill me!'

Kharan, he mouthed, unable to make a sound, *Kharan*. Her head was twisted back towards him, her face a paper mask over bone.

She was already dead.

*   *   *

Someone was shaking him. He hauled himself out of the nightmare, gasping, trembling, sweating, to find an anxious Kesfalian face bending over him.

'My poor boy, I couldn't wake you up, I thought you were ill,' said the man.

'No – I'm all right, Cristanice. It was just a bad dream.' Falmeryn swung his legs over the side of the wooden pallet and sat up stiffly. Sunlight was filtering through the small window of the cubicle, warming the stone walls to golden-brown and pooling on the umber tiles of the floor. 'What time is it?'

'Second hour after sunrise. You've overslept. You may be a guest here, but you still have to work like the rest of us. An astronomer and they set me to picking apricots, I don't know how I stand the degradation.'

Falmeryn smiled. 'I'm sorry, Cristanice. I'll come and help you.'

'Good. Breakfast first, if they've left you anything.' The Kesfalian was a short, plump man, wearing the brown robe and braided black hair of a sage. His face was round and small-featured, his tawny eyes pale against the dappled bronze skin. 'And don't keep calling me Cristanice, it's so cumbersome.'

'Cristan. I'll try to remember.' Falmeryn dressed quickly in a loose white shirt, linen breeches and sandals, and went to the main hall where a few men and women were still seated at the refectory table. The walls were lined with sleeping pallets. Sun streamed through the windows, and Falmeryn saw that most of the Kesfalians were already at work in the gardens. He breakfasted hurriedly on bread and fruit, put on a straw hat, and went out to join Cristan.

Half the valley was still in shadow, the sun having only just crested the cliffs. But it was already warm, and the cloistered building glowed like honey in its rays. From the building, with its red-tiled roof and a tower at one end, the gardens spread out in a patchwork of green and russet, enclosed in an almost perfect circle by a ring of cliffs. Falmeryn paused on the edge of the orchard to look up at

44

them rising sheer and jagged against the sky, and hardly noticed Cristan placing a basket in his hands.

'If you're awake yet, perhaps you'd like to start work,' the astonomer said grumpily. 'Are you sure you're well?'

'Yes.' He began to pull fruit from the lowest branches of a tree. 'I can't seem to shake off the nightmare, that's all.'

The valley was called the Circle of Spears, and to the sages of Kesfaline it was a safe and peaceful refuge from the Gorethrian conquerors. But to Falmeryn it was beginning to feel like a prison.

In different circumstances he might have been happy here. The Circle had an atmosphere of peace that reminded him of his own land, Forluin, and the Kesfalians were a gentle people for whom he had come to feel great affection. But he could not forget the strange events that had brought him here, nor that there was a world beyond the Circle where Emperor Xaedrek's legions enslaved almost the whole of Vardrav.

A voice broke his reverie, and he became aware that time had passed and that Cristan had been addressing him without success for several seconds.

'What did you say?'

'Nothing of consequence. I merely asked what your nightmare was about.' He put down a full basket and picked up an empty one. 'I might as well have been talking to the tree.'

'I'm sorry. I was miles away.' He drew a breath. He had been trying to forget the dream, and Cristan had reminded him again. Then it occurred to him that he had told no one anything about himself since he arrived, and that it might help to talk. 'It was about . . . something that happened to me.'

'Something terrible, by your voice,' Cristan said gently. 'If you'd rather not –'

'No. I'd like to tell you.'

'In that case, let's rest for a while. It's too hot to work, anyway.'

'It's easier if I tell you from the beginning.' Falmeryn sat down against a tree-trunk and stretched out his long legs on the grass. By contrast to the Kesfalians he was tall and fair-skinned, with dark grey eyes and chestnut hair falling to his shoulders. There was no hint of his traumatic experiences in his face, which still retained the clear, haunting beauty that all the Forluinish possessed; only a shadow of introspection in his eyes. He went on, 'I left Forluin to go on a trading voyage to An'raaga. I never dreamed I wouldn't be going back. I left the ship on my own in Port Raag, and I was seized by men who take slaves for the Gorethrians. They took me to Shalekahh, where I was eventually set to work in the Emperor's stables.'

'Dear me, that must have been dreadful,' Cristan muttered.

'No, it wasn't, not really. I wasn't badly treated. The worst thing was missing my family.' He paused. His memories of Forluin were still painful, even though he had not seen his country for five or more years. His ship was certain to have returned without him, and his loved ones must long ago have given him up for dead. It tore at him to think of them – their loss, and his grief, and no prospect of ever going home. He could still see his mother, Arlena, with her silver-blonde hair and sweet face, her arm around her brother Estarinel's waist as she watched *The Silver Staff* slide out of the harbour . . . 'You can't know what a hold Forluin has on its children. It is like this valley, only ten times more beautiful.'

'I don't know much about it, but I've heard people say there's an enchantment on the place.'

'I don't know about that. It's true we have the protection of the Blue Plane, H'tebhmella. Or maybe we're just arrogant to think we're different.'

'You, Falmeryn, are the least arrogant person I've ever met!'

'But, you see, because Forluin is so isolated we tend to think that the rest of the world doesn't affect us. Even after I'd arrived in Vardrav, it took me a long, long time to think otherwise. I witnessed Gorethria's evil every day, and still I felt it had nothing to do with me. But no more . . .'

'What happened to change your mind?'

'There was a girl I loved in Shalekahh. Her name was Kharan. The Gorethrians killed her,' he said shortly. He did not add that Kharan had been the Emperor Xaedrek's mistress, and that if she and Falmeryn had not fallen in love, she would still have been alive. 'We tried to escape the city, but Xaedrek's guards caught us. That's what my dream was about. They took her away and I never saw her again, but I was told – I was told she would be executed.'

'Take your time,' Cristan said kindly.

'I was condemned to death as well. I was savaged by a pack of hounds and left for dead. I only survived because Ferdanice healed me and sent Raphon to bring me here.'

'I wondered why you were so restless here, so keen to join in a war which I thought had nothing to do with you. But you've certainly been given good cause to hate the Gorethrians.'

'But it's not revenge I want. There was so much more. While I was travelling with Raphon, I saw them slaying and capturing Ungremish tribespeople who were virtually unarmed. And in Kesfaline itself it's as bad. Haven't you ever been outside? The Gorethrians are using the farmers as slaves, taking all the riches out of the land. They are so powerful, and so arrogant!'

'I know. I have been outside. We are isolated here, but not ignorant.'

'I'm sorry,' Falmeryn said. 'I just feel I must do something to stop them. I couldn't go back to Forluin, even if I had the chance, while Xaedrek's evil goes unchecked. I want to go to Kristillia and join the fight. I'll probably die in the attempt, but it's the least I can do – for Kharan's sake, and for those poor Ungremish who died because they had helped me.'

'My poor friend,' said Cristan, patting his arm. 'This is a terrible burden to carry.'

'As I said, it was Ferdanice who had me brought here. He saved my life not out of kindness but because he needs someone to run an errand, and apparently I was in the right place at the right time. But I've been here for weeks, and Ferdanice seems to have vanished. I can't stay forever. Where is he?'

'I don't know. He often spends long periods outside the

Circle. But you're not Ferdanice's prisoner. You don't have to stay, surely?'

Falmeryn sighed. 'I promised I'd wait until he came back. This thing he wants me to do – he said it was something that will help Kristillia win the war. But he never said he'd be so long.'

'What is this – hm – errand?'

'He told me not to speak of it.'

Cristan frowned. 'Why would Ferdanice keep anything secret from the rest of us? I think you ought to tell me.'

Falmeryn hesitated. There was no love lost between him and Ferdanice, whose callousness had caused needless suffering to Raphon, himself and others. He said, 'You don't know who Ferdanice is, do you?'

'Eh? He's just a Kesfalian, like myself. A scholar, trying to protect our philosophies from the Gorethrians.'

'Cristan, do you know what the Guardians are?'

The astonomer folded his hands over his round abdomen. 'They are said to be supernatural beings who bring balance to the powers of the universe, so that neither positive nor negative becomes too dominant. If they exist.'

'So would you say that they are good or evil?'

'Oh – well, neither, I suppose. Neutral.'

'And if they exist, might they not be able to take on a human form and pass unnoticed on Earth, if they had a reason to?'

'What a very peculiar train of thought. I think you have a touch of the sun.'

'Not at all. Think about it. How could Ferdanice have saved me when I was thousands of miles from here, how could he have contact with Raphon, who was from the Black Plane, how –'

'Enough!' Cristan sat up straight, so stunned that the blue-gold dappling on his skin had bleached to ivory. 'Falmeryn, I don't think you could tell a lie if you tried. I don't want to believe it. I can't, but –'

'It's true. Ferdanice is really a Grey One.'

The astronomer subsided against the tree and said gravely, 'I think you'd better tell me the rest, my boy.'

'When Raphon led me through the cave maze to get here, Ferdanice met us and took us to a cavern where he showed me a bright patch of rock at the bottom of a chasm. He said it was a stone from one of the moons, Fliya. He wants me to take it to an enchantress called Melkavesh in Charhn. Apparently it will help her against Xaedrek. But I can't go until the stone has been retrieved.'

Cristan's frown deepened. 'This goes against all our beliefs. We revere the moons and I totally condemn any violation of them! I knew the moon stone was there – at least, I'd heard rumours of it – and it should never have been brought to Earth. There could be great danger in moving it. Oh, gods.' He leaned forward and pulled at Falmeryn's arm. 'I study the moons every day. They are central to our philosophy, they guide us. This may sound foolish, but it's no worse than you saying Ferdanice is a Guardian; the moons have long predicted that an enchantress will come who will deliver us to some kind of disaster.'

Falmeryn felt something darkening, tightening behind his eyes. 'You mean Ferdanice is trying to make me the instrument of it?'

'You're miles ahead of me. I don't know what I mean. I hate to say it, but I've never liked Ferdanice. Don't do it, my friend.'

Falmeryn closed his eyes, and saw the red-gold glow implode into a flood of memories that would not be stemmed. Torchlight flashing on wet cave walls; Raphon's shining black limbs moving in a feeble struggle for life; a child with hair like rubies, insubstantial as a reflection yet compellingly real as she stretched out her hands in a plea for Falmeryn not to go to the Circle of Spears, not to trust Ferdanice. He did not know who or what she was. But the most persistent image was of Cristan's orrery. He had often stood in the observatory while the astronomer turned the handle and the rings slid into life, carrying the Earth with its dancing moons around the copper orb that represented the sun. But in his vision it seemed the orrery was working without human aid against the glassy void of space. The motion was never-ending, hypnotic. And as he watched, it seemed that he was looking

49

not at a model but at the Earth itself, and seeing it change in a way he did not understand . . .

He opened his eyes, sat up with a jolt. He looked up at the glass-domed tower that housed the orrery, and just for a moment he thought he could see Ferdanice's face pressed against the inside of the glass. A spasm that was not quite fear went through him.

'I gave my word, Cristan,' he said unsteadily. 'Whether it's right or wrong, I gave my word to help him.'

'Perhaps that was rather ill considered, as you have such strong doubts.'

'I had no choice. Raphon was dying on Earth and desperately needed to return to the Black Plane. Ferdanice made me promise to take the moon stone in exchange for his life!'

Cristan began to exclaim in disgust, but Falmeryn was no longer listening. Something else had possessed him, and he was climbing to his feet as he went on, 'Perhaps something's wrong. Perhaps Ferdanice has been delayed somewhere, and I should just take the moon stone and go.' He was already walking away through the trees; walking, then running towards the building.

In the base of the tower was a staircase spiralling down into the caves that lay under the valley. Falmeryn was not fully rational, but he thought to collect a lamp, a mallet and a chisel before descending into the darkness. A thrill of cold went through him, sharpening his sense of urgency into determination. He had to find the moon stone, had to escape the Circle.

It was more by luck than sense that he found his way to the tortuous path along which Ferdanice had once led him. The lip of the chasm took him by surprise and he almost overbalanced, hardly believing he had found it. He held the lamp out over the edge and saw the slick grey expanse of rock many feet below. And there, reflecting the lamplight, was the small patch of brightness that he remembered.

Ferdanice had said, 'We have to wait for the pull of the moons to draw it to the surface before we can recover it.'

It seemed brighter, Falmeryn thought. He lowered himself over the lip and began the long climb into the chasm. It was not hard, but the rocks were slippery and he was trembling by the time he reached the bottom. The surface that stretched before him resembled a lake of fossilised ice, and he hesitated before cautiously trusting his weight to it.

It was not ice, but solid rock. He walked over to the bright patch and saw, as he had suspected, that it was not on the surface but under it, trapped as if beneath a thick slab of crystal. He knelt down and ran his hands over it, finding it cold and glassy to the touch. To have protected the moon stone by sealing it in rock was something only the Guardians could have done, and there seemed only one way to remove it.

He put the chisel to the rock and brought the mallet down. The shock jarred his arm, the chisel skidded. He struck again and again until the darkness rang with echoes, but the rock would not yield so much as a chip. The air chilled his hot skin and the ache in his arms began to transmute itself into fear of the caves themselves.

Then a light swam above him. He looked up, shielding his eyes, and saw Cristan leaning over the edge of the chasm.

'It's no good, Falmeryn,' he called. 'Even if you could dig it out, you know the only way out of the Circle is through the cave maze, and you'd never find your way through. I'm not even sure of it myself. I'm not taking sides in this. You'll just have to wait for Ferdanice, however long it takes.'

'Yes. All right,' Falmeryn said hoarsely. The strange fever had burned itself out and he felt both desolate and foolish.

'Come on then. Come back to the surface and help me finish in that wretched orchard.'

'I wish you would kill me. Death would be better than this,' Anixa said in a low voice.

'Don't talk nonsense,' Xaedrek replied. 'This is not a torture or a punishment. Merely . . . a trial. Something medical.' He was holding her up by the arms, and she trembled like a bird in his grasp. 'Do you feel ill? Answer carefully now. Do you really feel ill, or have any pain?'

'I feel faint.'

'That's nothing. A symptom of panic. Try to calm down, and it will pass.' He settled her down on the leopard couch and sat beside her, while Ol Thangiol watched fearfully from the bed.

Anixa took a few deep breaths and rubbed at her forehead. 'I'm calm now,' she said, an acid note in her voice. 'What was that stuff?'

'Just answer the question.'

'No, I do not feel ill and no, I have no pain.'

'Good. You see, I have not poisoned you at all. So, what made you think I had?'

'I don't know. Something inside me – like a ball of light in my stomach, suddenly spreading out into my veins. It felt strange – not hot or cold, but smooth – like silk. I'm sure this is making no sense.'

'No, you're doing very well,' said Xaedrek. His kind tone made her shudder. 'Do you still feel this now?'

'A little. It's not unpleasant.'

'And how strong do you feel?'

'Not strong at all.'

'Are you sure? Look.' He plucked her left hand out of her lap and held it in front of her face. A pale radiance gleamed from it, faint but clearly visible and with a curiously oily look to it. She gasped. 'Can't you feel this light inside yourself? You could do anything you want with it. For example, move the lamp on that table without touching it. Try for me.'

For a moment she tried to defy him, but there was something about Xaedrek that crumbled the strongest resistance without him saying a word. She began to think about moving the lamp, and as she did so sweat burst from her pores like tears and she found herself trembling and sobbing. Lightning was searing her limbs, lightning crackling all over her body, while a terrible vision thrummed in her head – something to do with a pale monster from which a ghastly, bloodstained power emanated. The table went over with a crash, the lamp fell and went out – but the chamber was not dark. A hideous light flickered round it, and it was coming from Anixa.

She cried out in terror, beating her hands against the black material of her dress as if to put out a fire. Irem Ol Thangiol

52

was on his feet and coming towards them, crying out in concern. Xaedrek quickly stood up and intercepted him.

'Go back to the bed and stay there,' he said calmly. The Kristillian obeyed, too afraid and weak to do otherwise. Xaedrek went to the window and drew back the heavy curtains, letting a grim, bluish twilight fill the room. The storm had subsided, but the atmosphere still had a tense, electric quality that echoed the power pouring from Anixa.

'It's dawn,' he said, sitting beside her again. The glow was fading now, but she was wide-eyed and shuddering, still rubbing her hands compulsively on her thighs. Xaedrek actually put his arm round her, which filled her with renewed revulsion. But when he moved his other hand to restrain her frantic movements, he did so with such calm gentleness that she felt almost hypnotised. 'Nothing to be afraid of,' he murmured, clasping both her hands in his own. She nodded. Her shuddering stilled.

'You see, you are not as weak as you think. With this power you could do anything you wish. Perhaps you could even kill me. Break down the door. Escape the palace with the guards falling before you like dolls. What do you think? Would you like to try?'

Anixa swallowed hard, and forced her dry tongue and throat to work. 'You're mocking me.'

'Not at all.'

'It's a trick. You know I can't.'

Xaedrek smiled, and brushed a line of sweat from her neck with a gentle hand. 'Yes, Anixa, I know you can't. But not because you haven't the power, do you understand? Only because you are afraid of me. I give you the power, and still you dare not use it.'

Her eyes jerked up to meet his, cold as frozen topaz in her sullen face. 'I hope it makes you happy, knowing that.'

'Not really.' He withdrew his hands. 'It makes me rather sad. I only respect those who can overcome fear. Never mind, Anixa, this is not a trial of your courage, only of the substance I gave you. Now tell me, how do you feel in your mind? Set emotions aside, and look beyond them.'

'I feel strange. Disorientated.'

'Close your eyes. I want to know if you can see anything beyond this room.'

She obeyed. After a moment her eyes flew open, and she gasped, 'I can still see Irem Ol Thangiol on the bed – with my eyes shut!'

'Good. Don't be alarmed. Try to see beyond this chamber – into the corridor, for example.'

Her lids closed again, and after a minute she grasped his arm, forgetting herself. 'Guards! They're changing the watch!' she cried breathlessly.

'And beyond that?'

Something went wrong then. Anixa sent her mind questing beyond the palace, out into the graceful white streets of Shalekahh, luminous in the dawn. She saw hawks circling against the sky. And then all the visions came at once; different places, different times, one sky sliding into another and each filled with birds, all flapping, calling on a thousand different notes. Her head was filled with birds. And there were people, countless people whispering and talking and shouting all at once, drifting through her mind in a blur of different clothes, landscapes, languages. Image after image slanted across her brain, each at a different disorientating angle so that it seemed she was being tossed on giant waves, or turning over and over in mid-air. Confusion and panic possessed her, but she could not make the images stop, *could not close her eyes* –

It had gone on for years, it seemed. Years in a snowstorm of visions, when suddenly she felt a pain in the side of her face, and her eyes flew open. The chamber whirled slowly to a halt, and she stared in disbelief at the bed, Ol Thangiol, Xaedrek. It was all so still and quiet, and she could not even think where she was.

'I apologise for hitting you, but you were screaming,' Xaedrek said matter-of-factly. 'Are you all right?'

'I think so.'

'What did you see?' He was frowning. Perhaps the ichor was useless after all, and did nothing except induce madness. It took Anixa a long time to answer, but he waited patiently, holding her hands.

Eventually she said, 'Everything.'

'Everything? Explain.'

Anixa did her best to describe the visions, although it was scarcely possible to put the experience into words. Her throat ached with loathing. She wanted to die. But even as she sank deeper into misery, Xaedrek's hopes were soaring. He listened intently, and when she had finished he rose and paced slowly round the room.

Far-sight. The ichor really did give far-sight.

No one could handle the power with skill the first time they used it; it was not surprising Anixa had been overwhelmed. It would take practice to sift through those visions, focusing only on the ones that were wanted. At least he had some idea of what to expect, and as yet the ichor seemed to have no drastic ill effects.

Elation gripped him, and he had to force himself to recall that the ichor had one final trial to undergo.

'You've done very well, Anixa,' he said with a genuine warmth that seemed to shock her. He suddenly felt very well disposed towards her; after all, she had done nothing terribly wrong. Unlike the Kristillian, who had murdered Shavarish, her crimes had been very minor. 'You will excuse me while I go and send for someone.'

He went to speak to a guard, and as he returned he heard Ol Thangiol ask in a hoarse tone, 'Could you do it? Could you kill him?' Anixa did not reply. He smiled to himself, and went back into the room.

A few minutes later there was a knock on the door and Ah'garith came in. Irem Ol Thangiol scrambled off the bed, flew across to the window and clawed at it in a frantic attempt to escape. Anixa was at his side in an instant, clinging to him and trying to calm him. To her obvious relief, Xaedrek made the Shanin stay by the door.

'Ah'garith, do you sense anything strange about this woman?' he asked.

'No, Sire, but if I could go closer –'

'You don't need to do that. Just use your supernatural powers of perception.' She did not hear the sarcasm in his voice. After a moment she said, 'She has taken the ichor!'

'Well done, Ah'garith, most impressive.'

'Dangerous, Sire –'

'Why? Does it make her stronger than you?'

He knew this was a difficult question for the demon to answer. If she said no, it would imply that she could dominate anyone who had taken the ichor; but if she said yes, she would be admitting that they would be stronger than her – and that she had created something that would be very dangerous in the wrong hands.

'Dangerous – because you've made her powerful,' she said.

'Strong enough to overpower you?'

The Shanin scowled. 'No, Sire.'

'I see. Come here, Anixa. Come – I won't let Ah'garith near you, I promise.' Unable to disobey, Anixa walked woodenly over to Xaedrek and did not resist as he put his hands on her shoulders and held her before him. He was watching her, expecting some reaction, but her face showed nothing.

'Does Ah'garith frighten you, Anixa?'

'A little. I hate her, if you must know. She's like the drink you gave me, and the power. Horrible.'

'All right. But do you feel any awe of her? How can I put it – any loss of will, as if you want to obey her?'

Anixa shivered violently. 'No. Just disgust. You are all disgusting.'

'I don't know what you are trying to prove, Sire,' said Ah'garith testily.

'Don't you, really? Thank you, Ah'garith, you may leave us now.' He held the door open as she glided out, muttering, and closed it behind her. Anixa was weeping with a curious self-containment; she stood upright, her arms clasped across her stomach, her expression as cold and enigmatic as ever. Yet tears flowed from her eyes as if she were trying to wash her soul clean.

Xaedrek stood a moment in thought. He would have to give Anixa a drug to sedate her for a few days, just in case she suddenly found her courage and did something drastic. It seemed possible. He also wanted to observe how quickly the effects of the ichor wore off. But so far, all had gone very well indeed.

'Madame Anixa, listen to me,' he said gently. 'Of necessity I have to be harsh with wrongdoers. No doubt I have caused you a great deal of fear and discomfort, for which I apologise. You have served me so well here this morning that I am prepared to pardon your misdemeanours and let you return to your duties as a dressmaker. All I require is your co-operation for a few more days, and an assurance that you will perform no further acts of disloyalty.'

She stared at him, stunned. The power still skittered over her arms and shoulders. 'You'd let me go?'

'Yes. As soon as the ichor wears off.'

'Perhaps it never will,' she murmured.

'I'm sure it will, in no more than a day, probably. Then you'll be free.'

'Free him,' she said sharply, pointing at the Kristillian. 'Let us both go. Leave him alone.'

'You know I can't. He murdered a Gorethrian noble-woman.'

'In that case, I don't want to be set free,' she said, tilting her chin defiantly. 'I want to stay with him. I'd rather die with him than sew another robe for a Gorethrian courtier.'

'You're being very foolish. Very well, if you insist. The offer remains open if you change your mind.' Another challenge to her courage.

'I won't,' she said. 'And you needn't fear I'll use your filthy power against you. I won't – not because I'm afraid of you, but because it *is* filthy. It and you. By the moons I pray that Melkavesh may destroy you.'

'Thank you for those few words of encouragement,' Xaedrek remarked, and smiling at her, he left the room. He felt too elated to let her stubbornness affect him.

As he went over the events in his mind, however, his natural caution reasserted itself. Everything had gone *too* well. There had been no sign at all that the ichor had put Anixa in Ah'garith's power, but that proved nothing. Ah'garith must have known what he was trying to do, and it would have been easy for her to play the innocent and pretend she could not possess the woman.

His earlier disquiet returned, and with it the taint of Ah'garith's vile experiment. The truth was that he still had no answer, and would have none until he tried the ichor for himself.

The meeting of the Inner Council took place in the Oval Audience Chamber, where slender black columns alternated with ones of marble, and every surface was delicately figured with opal, platinum and jet. The only colour in the room was in the silken gowns of the Councillors, which glowed as richly as flowers from the palace garden.

The Inner Council had been selected by Xaedrek from the 300-strong Senate. They were men and women whom he valued both for their scientific and military skills, and for their absolute loyalty. Yet they were all people who did not fear him, who were able to argue with him as equals. He had implicit trust in no one except himself, but these were the nearest he had to true friends.

Only eleven out of the twelve members were present. Amnek sat protectively by Shavarish's empty chair as if defying Xaedrek to replace her. Next to him at the oval table sat Lady Lirurmish, primarily a scientist but able to turn her hand to anything. Although she was tiny and stick thin, with only a wisp of white hair left on her dark scalp, she was still full of the fierce joy in life that, to Xaedrek, personified everything that was great about Gorethria.

High Commander Baramek, sitting opposite, made Lirurmish seem as small as a doll. In stark contrast to the silks around him, his dress uniform was predominantly black and made his massive frame even more formidable. Xaedrek clapped him on the shoulder as he walked past to take his place at the head of the table.

'I have called this meeting, as you've no doubt guessed, to discuss war plans,' the Emperor said. 'You are aware – without any disrespect to our High Commander – that conventional forays against Kristillia have so far failed. Undoubtedly, with a new strategy and a greater number of troops, we would eventually defeat them, but given their unprecedented strength it could well be a hard and long drawn-out campaign, with heavy losses. Is it not so, Commander?'

Baramek nodded grimly. 'Nevertheless, the army is ready to do whatever is required of us, Sire.'

'No one could be more proud of the army and of you, Commander, than I am. I know that every last soldier is willing to die for Gorethria. However, I don't want to inflict unnecessary hardship on the troops. For this invasion I have something very different in mind.'

No one spoke, but Xaedrek noticed Baramek and Amnek staring at each other in an unfriendly manner.

'Three people in this room already know of the new plans, namely, the High Commander, Lady Lirurmish and Lord Amnek. I am telling the rest of you in the strictest confidence, and there are certain reasons why I cannot go into any detail. Not even the Senate are to be told, and knowledge is to be limited to those directly involved. I trust this is clear.'

There was a murmuring of assent. He continued; 'I am talking about battle machines, weapons so terrible that they will crush the Kristillians like flies.' He looked round at their various expressions: surprise, excitement, cynicism. 'No doubt this sounds improbable, but Lirurmish, Amnek and I have already begun the designs and carried out some tests. They will work.'

'When will they be ready?' asked Galdrek, a dour-faced man who was Xaedrek's main adviser on Vardravian affairs.

'Such a project cannot be hurried. The invasion will have to be delayed another two years or so.'

'That is two years in which the Kristillians could grow even stronger.'

'But it doesn't matter if they do. The point of the machines is that nothing can stand against them, nothing at all. Two years are negligible in the history of the Empire.'

'Where are they going to be built, Sire?'

'In Cevandaris, where they have the skills and the materials; massive furnaces in the sides of volcanoes, unique metals, and unsurpassed craftsmanship. The Cevandarish slaves will have to be put to work under very strict surveillance to prevent spying, naturally, but that is no problem. Lady Lirurmish will be leading the team.'

'With all due respect, my lady,' said Galdrek, 'are you sure it's wise to be undertaking such an arduous journey at your advanced age?'

'Are you a physician, Galdrek?' she snapped.

'Well, yes, I am, in fact,' he said with a half-smile.

'In that case, I shall ask your advice when I am sick. Until then, you can keep your opinions to yourself!'

Everyone laughed at this and Xaedrek relaxed back in his chair, knowing that the meeting was going well. Then Amnek said, 'What about Melkavesh?'

'What about her?' A cold look came into Xaedrek's eyes.

'Who knows what manner of help she will give the Kristillians, if she finds out about these machines in advance?'

'Three points, Lord Amnek. Firstly, simply knowing about the machines may lose us the element of surprise, but it won't reduce their effectiveness. Secondly, Melkavesh's power is a wholly personal one which, unlike amulin, she cannot bestow on others. Thirdly, she will be found and destroyed long before then.'

Amnek fell quiet, but his long thin hands were bunched up like talons. More questions followed, and Xaedrek handled them all with his usual diplomatic skill until the meeting ended with most of the Councillors happy. He wished them good day and went to his private office.

A few moments later there was a knock on the door and he found Baramek outside. 'I'm sorry to disturb you, Sire,' he said. His heavy features seemed carved from obsidian and lacked the aquiline beauty of most Gorethrians. His hair was brushed back from his brow, and his eyes were a hot ochre yellow. Many feared him as much as they feared Xaedrek – and loved him equally.

'Not at all, my friend. Come in. Is anything wrong?'

'I think you know what it is. These machines disturb me. How will they work?'

'They will be powered by amulin. Hyperphysics.'

'Sorcery?'

60

'If you like.'

Baramek's lips narrowed. 'I don't like the sound of it. I've never approved of the men being given amulin before going into battle. It's wrong and unnatural.'

'Unsporting?' Xaedrek smiled, and went to pour two cups of wine. 'Come now, Baramek. I know you are a traditonalist and regard anything out of the ordinary with deep suspicion. There's nothing wrong in that. But the world itself is changing. We have to stay ahead. Supernatural or scientific, every source of strength is only a tool for Gorethria to use in her advancement. Our values stay the same.'

'Sire, my loyalty to you is absolute, and I will do whatever you require of me. But I have seen what one demon can do, and I can't help having my doubts about anything even remotely similar.'

Xaedrek's face did not change, but inwardly he felt a qualm. His predecessor Meshurek II had summoned a demon which had destroyed him and almost wrecked the Empire. Xaedrek's whole strategy in taking the throne had hinged on discrediting Meshurek. No one except Amnek knew that Ah'garith herself was a disguised demon; most believed she was just an old Tearnian woman with an extraordinary skill. If anyone, particularly Baramek, discovered the truth, the result for Xaedrek could be disastrous.

In a mansion not far from the palace, Amnek descended a flight of steps and pushed open the door to a subterranean room. He was just in time to see a charred body being dragged across the floor by two guards, watched by Valamek and Ah'garith. He stood aside until the guards had removed the corpse from the room, then turned to the young man.

'Duke Valamek, I will take over from you for an hour,' he said.

'Are you sure, Lord Amnek? You must be very busy –'

'Go and have a rest,' Amnek said firmly, holding the door open. As Valamek passed, he added accusingly, 'You don't look well.'

'No, I am quite all right,' Valamek said, swallowing. 'But I have not been supervising the amulin process for long.'

61

'You will get used to it. The Emperor and I are very impressed at how hard you've been working, but you must not overdo it.'

'I wish someone would be as solicitous about my welfare,' Ah'garith muttered sourly as Amnek closed the double doors behind the Duke. She came forward, rubbing her hands, her eyes fish pale. 'You wanted to see me, my lord?'

Amnek walked across to the delicate structure of rods that dominated the room. Some were made of gold, others of glass with streams of light rippling continuously along them. Tracing a finger along one of them, he said, 'It's about the experiment you dismantled. Could you set up another?'

Ah'garith's mouth stretched in a grimace. 'I would if I could. But Xaedrek has forbidden it, and I must obey my summoner.'

'You set it up without his permission in the first place.'

'But I had taken amulin, which increased my power for a time. Now he's forbidden that as well. What are you getting at?'

'I am concerned for Xaedrek,' Amnek replied. 'When he saw the experiment, it was the first time I'd seen him quail. Until then I'd thought he'd learned what I taught him only too well, that nothing could move him. So much for the scientist! I blame Melkavesh for affecting him in this way – and I am only saying this for his own good.'

'My sentiments exactly. But Xaedrek has tested the ichor . . . on a prisoner. He was impressed. He'll soon try it for himself, and once he has a taste of the stuff, his scruples will vanish.'

'But it won't harm him, will it? Be honest with me.'

'Harm him? Of course not! How could you think it? He will see sense, and give us full rein to experiment as we will.'

Amnek turned round and put a dark hand on her shoulder. He towered over her, his vulturine face threatening. 'Why do you want it so badly, demon? What will you gain? Your own power?'

'The Shana were made to serve mankind,' she replied primly. 'I am chained to Xaedrek and Gorethria.'

'But you'd like to be free.'

Suddenly Ah'garith became agitated, as if the feelings she usually suppressed had burst to the surface. 'You don't know what hell this is, being imprisoned in this lumpen shape! To be powerless! To spend all day, every day, with that force flowing into me from the ground and out again – never able to hold on to it or use it. Do you know how powerful I used to be?' Her eyes glinted like colourless venom. 'When I looked at people, they fell down in fear and begged to be allowed to serve me. I could have stretched out my hand and rent this mansion with a thought. I could bring chaos and terror at whim, and I was surrounded by siblings who were the same. Now I am alone, and I have nothing. All I get is insults and abuse. I am scratching in the Earth to find even a fraction of the strength I once possessed, while this accursed new "sorcery" whirls all around me and through me and I cannot seize hold of it any more than a human can the wind! Have you any idea how much I hate my existence? Have you any idea how much I hate natural Sorcerers? *Melkavesh, that damnable witch Melkavesh!*'

'You're shouting, Ah'garith. Calm yourself.' The Shanin subsided abruptly. Amnek went on in a tone like the soft hiss of a razor cut, 'Do you know, I feel rather sorry for you. My own emotions are similar.'

'You're mocking me, Lord Amnek. You've had nothing taken from you. You couldn't know.'

'Ah, but I have. My wife Shavarish was taken from me. While she was alive, I took her as much for granted as my own heart. Now she is gone, I feel as you do. Trapped, powerless and futile. Nothing matters . . . except making Melkavesh pay.'

'Now I understand you.' Her manner changed in an instant to being sympathetic and conspiratorial. 'I have been mistaken about you. *You* are the one with finer feelings – not Xaedrek. We must help each other, my lord.'

As she finished speaking, someone rapped on the door and Amnek found the guards outside, holding a Patavrian slave. 'Are you ready for the next subject, my lord?' asked one.

Amnek scratched his temple, then waved them into the

room irritably. He watched without feeling as they forced the little black-skinned man into a gap in the structure, and locked the rods that would hold him in place. He struggled and whimpered feebly, completely unhinged by terror. Once he was secure in the gold and glass cage, the guards left and Amnek shut the doors.

'Our conversation has gone far enough, demon. Let us get on with the work in hand.'

'Very well.' Ah'garith went to the end of the mechanism and stood on a triangular area that throbbed like living muscle set into the floor. It was a kind of lens that helped to focus hyperphysical energy through her body. She grasped two rods, set her forehead to the end of a third, and began to summon the power.

The rods began to glow, the structure became an ethereal, sinister net of light. The Patavrian convulsed against the rods, but he could not escape the energy that now began to flow into him and accumulate until he blazed like a miniature sun.

The human element was essential. It was the catalyst that gave amulin its potency.

The moment the energy reached its critical point, it began to pour out of the victim's body in a river of static, crackling fiercely along the rods until it spiralled into a glass sphere filled with powdered crystals. The whole room was ablaze with white fire, the air vibrating with the humming of the mechanism and the hoarse screams of the Patavrian.

Amnek watched the procedure carefully, judging the moment at which to terminate it. As soon as the cries grew weaker and the light began to fluctuate, he called Ah'garith to stop. As she stepped off the lens, the dazzling whiteness faded and the room swam back into focus. Then Amnek went to the sphere and noted with satisfaction that the crystals had turned the pale gold of perfect amulin. This substance had already won back the Empire, he mused; now it would be the very lifeblood of the machines that would finish Kristillia once and for all . . .

'Shall I call the guards?' said Ah'garith.

Amnek started. 'Oh, yes, yes, have that thing taken away

and the next one brought,' he said, not even glancing up.

As pure and clean as lightning was this power, so Xaedrek said; but like lightning it was lethal to whatever it touched. The slave's tormented cries had ceased. Now he hung sense-less in the cage, his body blackened and swollen as if it had boiled from within, plasma running down his face like tears.

4

In a Red Crystal Sky

XAEDREK HAD honeyed the ichor for Anixa, but did not do so for himself. He eyed the phial for a moment, then – before nausea weakened his resolve – he raised it to his lips and drained it in one quick, convulsive swallow.

It was not as bad as he had expected. Almost tasteless, really, with a slight bitterness and gelatinous quality to it, like raw egg white. He sat back and waited for it to take effect.

He had taken precautions against Ah'garith overpowering him while he was vulnerable to the ichor by removing himself to an isolated villa on the edge of the Emethrians. Ah'garith remained in Shalekahh under Amnek's supervision. For once Xaedrek had brought a heavy guard with him, because he did not want to affect the trial by taking amulin and ichor together – and without amulin, he had no hyperphysical power.

He had told no one his reason for going to the villa. The guards did their job unquestioningly and even Duke Valamek, his assistant, was not allowed to witness the experiment.

For a few moments, he felt nothing. Then, just as Anixa had described, there was a warm implosion in his stomach, a feeling like silk ribbons uncurling along his veins. It was not painful, but decidedly strange, and very different from the dark fire of amulin. This was more like an intoxicating lightness swimming into his limbs, and looking at his hands he saw radiance sweating from them like pearl beads.

Now his awareness began to change, as if it was becoming greater, shifting into a new perspective. Everything seemed paler. He stood up slowly, looked round the room, and fixed his attention on a heavy chest. Dare he try to use the power? He had barely thought it when ropes of light snaked from his hands and the chest suddenly soared upwards as if weightless. In a split second he mastered his shock, controlled the chest before it smashed into the ceiling, and lowered it soundlessly back to the floor.

Xaedrek was breathing fast, verging on laughter. Ah'garith had promised power greater than amulin, and she had not lied. This felt immeasurably stronger, and there was also a seductive pleasure in using it, as if a satin light were gliding over and through him. But he was aware that the ichor was affecting his mind in another, subtler way, like a drug. He still had reason and judgement, yet it was as if some part of his personality were changing, becoming hysterical and rabid – like Ah'garith.

At that, his laughter died. There was no cause for exhilaration. The electricity exuding from him looked as pure as day, but he could see blood in the light, white shadows of evil.

He sat down again. Those shadows were layers overlying his sight, and it seemed that everything he desired to know was set before him and would be discovered by gradually peeling the layers away. Apprehensively, he gripped the chair arms, closed his eyes, and waited for the onslaught of far-visions.

Nothing Anixa had said could have prepared him for the reality of the experience. It began gently, with a hissing like the distant sliding of snow, but the hiss became a roar and then the images came down like an avalanche, suffocating, almost bearing his mind away with them. Xaedrek hung on. A small part of his mind remained aloof from all emotion, simply observing, and he clung to that detachment as if to a rock.

He knew the avalanche would not stop unless he opened his eyes, but he could not. He pushed down his terror. A thousand landscapes, a thousand skies slanted through his

67

brain, and the sound was the roar of a million voices. If he could only focus on one scene and make sense of it . . .

A line of troops, moving towards Zhelkahh. The effort of concentration sent pains shooting through his skull, but he fixed his attention on them and kept it there until the other images became no more distracting than rain. And if he could travel with those soldiers, surely he could send his mind ahead of them, questing along the Vardrav Way and ultimately into Kristillia . . .

He opened his eyes and let out a breath of relief as the room shimmered into focus. The visions were still clamouring round the edge of his brain, but he needed a moment to steady himself before plunging into them again. He *could* control them. It was a matter of practice. His suspicion of Ah'garith was forgotten as his eyelids fell and the storm began again.

When the ichor wore off, several hours later, he felt not relief but frustration. Just as he had been getting somewhere . . . He had learned how to sift through the scenes without being overwhelmed, how to select the ones he wanted and attune himself to the relevant information. He had moved unseen through the marble halls of Shalekahh, flown across the Emethrians. He had also learned that the further he pushed his mind, the harder it became.

'But that is also a matter of practice,' he said to himself, and smiled. Soon Melkavesh would not be able to keep a single secret from him. Perhaps the power of the ichor would be enough to kill her, from a distance, without the inconvenience of dispatching an assassin.

He moved around the room, stretching his stiff limbs, and refreshing himself with water and fruit. How soon, he wondered, would it be safe to take another dose of the ichor? There seemed to be no ill effects, apart from a faint buzzing in the ears and a slight sense of oppression. He did not even think of Ah'garith.

Far-sight, far-sight at last. He went to the window and looked at the dark bulk of the Emethrians against the sky. Once he understood the power, it could be extended to others and a network set up across the Empire that would secure Gorethria's power for ever. Messages could be sent instantaneously, troops monitored and moved on a thought. Nothing would be hidden. With such power, even conquering Tearn became a possibility . . .

'Oh, Melkavesh, you are a fool,' he said. 'You could have shared this with me, and instead you threw it away for ridiculous ideals that even a child would laugh at.'

Melkavesh had come to him out of nowhere, apparently offering the promise of supernatural power that would enable him to dispose of Ah'garith. With her hair dyed black and a false identity he had believed her a pure Gorethrian, an innocent whose unique power he could mould to his own design. But she had swiftly shown her true colours, spouting idealistic nonsense about dismantling the Empire, ceasing to make war on other nations – effectively reducing Gorethria to nothing.

With parents such as Ashurek and Silvren, he thought disdainfully, such misguided notions were only to be expected. Yet there was something about her he did not understand. She had sworn that she loved Gorethria as much as he did, and he still believed she had meant it, and remained a true Gorethrian, heart and soul. How then could she so easily turn her back on her own country and side with its enemies? They had been lovers. He had asked her to marry him, offering her a share of the throne and all the power she could have desired, if only she would become his ally and use her unique power for Gorethria's benefit.

She had agreed at first, then demanded ridiculous conditions; that he renounce his own hyperphysical power and – quite unbelievable – withdraw his troops from the Empire. He had tried to make her see reason, but this had only led to an argument which ended with them trying to kill each other. She had fled, and his attempts to catch her had failed.

In a way he regretted having been so harsh with her. If only he had been less dogmatic he might have talked her round or even tricked her into acquiescence. He had need of her now, but she was gone.

It was not that he loved her, for Xaedrek would never put

a single human being above Gorethria. Together they could have been the most powerful Emperor and Empress ever, which would have been all to the nation's good. And if she had stayed, the dilemma of the ichor and the need to build battle-machines would never have arisen. 'You have much to answer for, my lady,' he murmured, moving away from the window.

At the thought of the ichor, his curiosity transformed into a positive desire to take another dose. He opened a gold and ruby travelling case and took out two more phials of the milky fluid. It might be dangerous to take so much. He should have experimented further with Anixa. Still, it was not caution that had won back the Empire. He swallowed the contents of the phials quickly, one after the other, before he had time to feel them gelling in his throat. Then he lay down flat on a rug, trying to relax as he waited for the images to flood in.

The power was overwhelming this time, wild as lightning yet smooth as silk. He felt no fear, only exhilarating confidence, and he thought, *Why waste any more time? Why not go straight to Melkavesh? There is nowhere she can hide from me now, nothing she can do to defend herself.*

Almost without effort he slid between the infinite layers of knowledge, peeling them away until he saw Charhn open up beneath him like a flower.

The Mangorian leader, N'golem, came up the hill as fast as his reptilian mount could carry him, shouting angrily at Melkavesh.

'We were winning. They tricked us!' He shook his spear at the battle raging in the valley. The Kristillians, held to siege inside their camp, had been on the point of falling to the Mangorian and Malmanish troops. Then a reserve division of Kristillians had ambushed the attackers from behind, and were now winning a swift victory.

Melkavesh urged her horse away from the royal party to meet N'golem, shocked to see that he was genuinely angry.

'Kristillian deceivers!' he snarled. His teeth were bared, and with his slate-blue skin and hairless, domed skull he looked fearsome. Like his fellow tribesmen he went naked except for pectorals and loin coverings of beads, and metal serpents twined round his arms.

'N'golem, it's only an exercise!' She caught the U'adruil's bridle before the beast charged in front of the King, and had trouble halting it. She wished the Mangorians would overcome their hatred of horses and dispense with the cumbersome lizards. 'Be reasonable. How do you think we'll defeat the Gorethrians, without tricks?'

N'golem subsided, but his eyes were still fierce in his narrow face. 'I apologise, my lady. But *you* are our leader – not the Kristillians. We will not be humiliated by them.'

'No one's trying to humiliate you! You must learn to co-operate with them. We're all on the same side. Now go down and make sure no tribesmen are injured.'

N'golem obeyed, and Melkavesh turned her horse back to the hill peak from which the King and Queen, Irem Ol Melemen, Kharan and a number of officers were watching the battle.

'Problems?' Irem Ol Melemen asked.

'It's just the Mangorians taking the exercise rather too seriously.'

'It's difficult to take any aspect of this war too seriously,' said the King. 'Still, all our other Vardravian allies are firm friends. I don't know why Mangorad has to be different. It won't do.'

'I know,' said Melkavesh. 'Don't worry about them, they'll obey me. They are a strange people. They were too long isolated in the jungle, and they used to worship the Serpent – until I explained it was dead.'

'And now they worship you,' said the Queen.

Melkavesh did not reply.

The battle was over now; the 'injured' were picking themselves up out of the mud, the Kristillians and the lithe, silver-skinned Malmanish embracing each other, laughing. The hundred or so Mangorians sorted themselves out into a sullen group, separate from the rest.

'I think I'll go down and speak to them,' she said. 'Not just N'golem's people, I mean all of them.'

'They'll appreciate that,' said Afil Es Thendil, nodding. 'I'll come with you.'

They were in the fells outside Charhn, with the city gleaming chalk pale to the west. The soft green valleys were dotted with army camps, countless hide tents with smoke curling up between them. Refugees had come from Malmanon, Kesfaline, Alaak and Ungrem to be formed into armies under Kristillian leadership.

Veils of moisture were sheeting down from the fells' rugged heights, more mist than rain. Oblique sunlight turned the haze to bronze, brushed everything with powdered copper, made the outcrops of quartz gleam like milk-curds. As Melkavesh rode down the fellside, the soldiers quickly fell into ranks and began to cheer effusively.

'Mellorn! *Mellorn!*'

They all knew her as Mellorn now. It was the name given to her by her parents; she had adopted the name Melkavesh on her arrival in Gorethria. But it had unfortunate connotations for the Kristillians, who had first been conquered by an Empress Melkavesh, so, in public at least, she found it expedient to call herself Mellorn.

Their enthusiasm for her was almost embarrassing. They loved Es Thendil, yet their regard for Melkavesh was as great, and she felt a deep stirring of love for them in return. The toughness of the Kristillians' makeshift, mud-spattered uniforms could not obscure the fierce pride that shone from them. Men and women alike carried themselves like dancers. They were totally lacking in self-pity, toughened by centuries of defying Gorethria, yet still full of joy in life and friendship.

She raised a hand for silence and began to speak the words of praise and encouragement which they were obviously longing to hear.

Kharan, watching from the hill-top, took care to stay clear of the Queen and found herself next to a Kristillian woman wearing the battle-dress of a senior officer. She was riding a large brown mare.

'Mellorn can afford to be free and easy with her praise,'

said the woman. 'It's me who's got to make herself unpopular by pointing out everything they did wrong.'

'But you won!' Kharan looked at her, surprised.

'We won, but it was a close thing – too damned close. What did you think?'

'I thought the Kristillians were superb – but I'm no expert,' she replied diffidently.

'It's good to meet someone who's not ashamed to admit it. You must be Kharan – Mellorn's companion?'

'Yes, that's right.'

The woman extended a hand. 'I am Haeth Im Nerek.'

Kharan gasped involuntarily. 'Oh, *you* are the Battle Marshal!'

'Yes. Why, who did you think it was?'

She pointed at a huge, bearded officer next to An Mora. 'Melkavesh has mentioned you, but I assumed – being Baramek's counterpart – you'd be equally . . . well, I thought he –'

'Oh, no, that's General En Scanon.' The woman grinned. 'Don't let the outside fool you. I am as tough as Baramek – I need to be.'

Battle Marshal Haeth Im Nerek was a small, slim yet sturdily built woman who seemed impossibly young for the duties that were hers. Her uncompromising face was framed by shaggy, gingery-brown hair, and she had startling light blue eyes that suggested Alaakian blood. From what Melkavesh had said, she had a powerful ego that was more than matched by a keen, military mind.

'It's just that you don't seem –'

'Experienced enough? My parents were soldiers; I was virtually born with a sword in my hand.' She shrugged dismissively. 'Soldiering's the only thing I can do. I just happen to do it a damn sight better than anyone else. What about you, though? How on Earth did you come to be with a woman like Mellorn?'

From Im Nerek's tone, Kharan gathered that she was one of the few Kristillians less than enamoured with the enchantress. 'It's a long story,' she said, watching Melkavesh turn and start to ride up the hill.

And she saw Es Thendil hold back his horse for Melkavesh to go first, just as if *she* were the monarch – not he. She looked the part. She was a tall, powerful figure in officer's garb of leather breeches, high boots and a breastplate burnished to the gloss of a ripe chestnut. With her bitter-brown skin and the umber horse beneath her, she seemed carved from earth – except for a deep green cloak clasped with bronze, and her sun-brilliant hair loose on her shoulders. This must be how the Vardravians saw her; an awesome and untouchable vessel for the strange fires of the Earth, separate from the rest of humanity but self-contained, needing no one. There was only Melkavesh, dark and bright; only her, the earth and the mist and a wild, sweeping sky.

The moment was lost. Melkavesh was approaching them, smiling and saluting. While Es Thendil went to speak to General En Scanon, Melkavesh joined Kharan and the Battle Marshal.

'Have you two been introduced?' she asked.

'We did the job ourselves,' said Im Nerek, 'and it's refreshing to meet someone who does not pretend to be a military expert.'

'Are you suggesting that I do?' Melkavesh raised her eyebrows. She had already had a number of fiery arguments with the Battle Marshal, and had no wish for another.

'You know a lot, Lady Mellorn, but it's all from books and training exercises. It's no substitute for the real thing.'

'I'll grant you that. But you must admit that the army is bound to be jaded after years of holding Gorethria off, and can only benefit by a fresh approach.'

'You have ideas and the energy to put them into action, I'm sure,' said Im Nerek sarcastically, 'and when I need your advice, I'll let you know.'

Melkavesh bit back a retort. She was in an awkward position. Es Thendil had appointed her joint adviser to himself and the Battle Marshal, but from the start Im Nerek had treated her with deep resentment and suspicion. She was determined that no one – enchantress or otherwise – was going to undermine her command. Melkavesh could understand how she felt, but she also knew it was essential for changes to be made.

'They're excellent fighters, Im Nerek, but I have to say this whether you like it or not. They look scruffy, like brigands.'

The Battle Marshal gave a scornful laugh. 'They're bound to. They're fighting men and women, and they have just come through a battle.'

'I'm not talking about a bit of mud. I want to see them all helmeted and equipped to the standard of the King's own guard. Leather breeches and proper boots, tunics held in with belts and not just any bit of thonging they can lay their hands on, and everyone wearing a breastplate with a shirt underneath.'

'Is that all?' Im Nerek fixed her with a dissecting blue stare.

'For a start,' Melkavesh said icily.

'I take it that's an order, then.'

'I –' Melkavesh bit her lip, stopped trying to stare her down. 'No, of course not. Look, I do try to curb my habit of ordering people about. You know how it is . . .'

'Yes, but I make sure I restrict my orders to those over whom I actually do have command.'

'It's advice, Im Nerek,' she sighed. 'I know you think it doesn't matter, but it does. When the Gorethrians march onto the battle field, they look as splendid as eagles, and that doesn't just happen –'

'No, it takes a great deal of wealth, most of it stolen from Vardrav.'

'More than that, it takes a lot of hard work, but the result is that they march into battle feeling invincible – because they know they look it.'

'Don't lecture me on dress, Mellorn, and still less on morale. You have not seen the Kristillians go into battle yet, but I promise you'll have no cause to be ashamed of us!'

'I'm sure I won't.' However angry Im Nerek sounded, she was not one to ignore a sound suggestion, and there would probably be an improvement in the army's turnout within a week. Melkavesh only wished she could lessen

75

the antagonism between them. 'I'm not criticising their fighting skills. They must be good to have held Gorethria back for so long. When they tried to invade before, how did you defeat them?'

Im Nerek pulled a face. 'It wasn't exactly a defeat. Baramek was over-confident and didn't bring enough men. They had to make what you could call a strategic withdrawal. Since then we've had a so-called truce – more a stalemate, really. There's been a fair amount of fighting along the borders.'

'But what about amulin?'

'What about it?'

'Well, it gives Xaedrek's soldiers pseudo-sorcerous powers in battle; their arrows and spears always meet their mark, they can even kill their opponents without touching them. Even outnumbering them, how did you stand against that?'

'By sheer bloody-mindedness,' said Im Nerek.

'Come on, there's more to it than you want to admit.'

'I'm telling you, Lady Mellorn, we are damned good fighters and whatever warped magic Xaedrek calls down on our heads, it's no match for the simple will to survive.'

Her tone made it clear that the Sorceress had overstepped the mark, but Melkavesh could not let the matter drop. 'You accused the Gorethrians of over-confidence. Let's hope it won't be our downfall as well.'

'If we are over-confident, it is down to one person, and that is not myself,' the Battle Marshal retorted. Melkavesh dropped her gaze. 'No, Lady Mellorn, I know just how hard a fight it is going to be. I am a realist, but I also have beliefs. To be honest, I don't know how we have withstood Xaedrek's necromancy. We believe that the moons protect us, and as far as I'm concerned, it is true.'

'It may well be. I'd like to make Kristillia even stronger, by sorcery.'

Haeth Im Nerek was not appeased by this. She replied flatly, 'That's between you and the King. As for myself, I do not need the aid of "sorcery", good, bad or otherwise. My unadorned fighting skills have served Kristillia well enough so far, and that's the way it will stay.'

Melkavesh said no more. Something told her that she

would never win the Battle Marshal's confidence, and she would only make things worse by trying.

The exercise completed, the royal group turned away and began the ride back to the city. Amber sunlight shone through the mist, gilding Charhn's roofs and drawing exquisite colours from the spires of the Inner City. As they approached the gate, Melkavesh found Afil Es Thendil at her side, saying something that she could not hear over the shouting of the crowd.

'*Mellorn! Mellorn!*' The people lining the streets were dressed in simple cotton robes and cloaks, and they were mostly children and old people. All the able-bodied were in the army. But they had the same grace and pride, the same darkly burning eyes as the warriors. Her heart went out to them.

'Lady Mellorn,' the King said in a louder voice. Their horses walked in step with necks arched and black-brown manes flowing.

'I'm sorry, Your Majesty, what did you say?'

'That they make me feel very humble, and quite inadequate to my task.'

'And me,' said Melkavesh, without meaning to. The King looked around as if to make sure no one could overhear them.

'Mellorn, forgive me if I speak out of place, but is anything troubling you? You seem – rather distracted. And Kharan is worried that you're exhausting yourself.'

'Oh, is she?' Melkavesh said sharply, then softened her voice. She could not go on deceiving Es Thendil by pretending nothing was wrong. 'The truth is, I *am* worried. I had hoped to find a way of helping you by sorcery that would guarantee Gorethria's defeat. So far I've found nothing. Whatever is blocking my power is getting worse, and I'm even finding it hard to far-see now. It's as if something's deflecting the power . . . you know, as lodestones push each other apart?'

'I see,' said the King, frowning. 'You mean you don't know what Xaedrek's doing?'

'Oh, I will find out, don't fear,' she said quickly. 'How can

I explain what's wrong? On Ikonus, the power of sorcery was protected by a Sphere which hovered above the School of Sorcery like a giant blob of mercury. It acted as a kind of lens which let through only the positive aspects of the power and filtered out the bad. My mother, Silvren, always said that this Earth should be protected by something similar. I disagreed; the Sphere made everything perfect on Ikonus to the point of sterility. This world is different, wilder and more savage, and I believed something like the Sphere would do it no good. Now I'm not sure . . .'

'I don't think I quite follow, but go on.'

'It's the demon, Ah'garith. She should have died with the Serpent. It may simply be her presence that's blocking the true potential of the power. Either something she's created, or she herself, is acting as a lens that has the opposite function to the Sphere; it lets through only evil.'

Es Thendil's marbled skin had gone quite pale. 'This sounds terrible. Is there nothing you can do?'

She saw then the folly of speaking the truth. She had to restore his confidence before the despair permeated any deeper. 'I am trying all the time, and it's only a matter of time before I find the answer,' she said brightly. 'Don't let it worry you. It's my battle, and there's nothing anyone . . .'

She trailed off, suddenly distracted by a hideous sensation like fingernails scratching down the inside of her skull. The King's face seemed frozen in an expression of horror, and she could no longer feel her horse moving under her. 'Help me,' she heard herself say. Time hung suspended; then there was a flash of activity, horses milling round her, voices asking if she was all right; then silence again.

She managed to raise her head, but everything was in slow motion. She could see the royal mansion gleaming red through the trees. It was at a strange angle, as if she were no longer on her horse – then there was another burst of noise, Kharan bending over her and saying, 'Mel, what's wrong? Please speak to me!'

'Help – stand up,' she croaked. The city swung dizzily, and she found herself upright, supported between Kharan and Ol Melemen. 'Someone –'

She could not explain. All she knew was that someone was trying to far-see, to spy on her. Another Sorcerer –

Xaedrek.

'Take me to my room,' she said with an effort that made everything turn white.

'Yes, I'll stay with you,' said Kharan.

'No! Must – be alone. Promise . . .'

She did not hear the reply. The city looked unreal, painted on chalk, the chalk crumbling to dust and blowing away, leaving only the vision of her inner eye; a lifeless grey surface like slush, a vile, intimate probing like a scalpel stabbing repeatedly into her brain, and a voice whispering, 'Melkavesh. *Melkavesh.*'

She knew she was lying on a bed, but she could not feel it under her. If she opened her eyes, she could see no more than with them closed. She was paralysed. She had nowhere to go except inwards, down into the trance of far-sight, convulsively drawing energy as if it were air to keep her alive.

Light, at last light and shapes that began to make sense. She was questing through a slaty-blue infinity where stars as numberless as snowflakes glittered in a mist of zodiacal radiance. She sought Shalekahh, yet it seemed she was being pulled another way, not to Aludria this time but to the source of the call . . .

She gave in to it, and the pain went away.

A jewelled thread led her mind to the Emethrian mountains, an elegant Gorethrian villa she had never seen before. She found herself in a room with a marble floor and silk hangings. Far-sight lent everything a strange miniaturised quality, like the distortion of a lens, but dazzling in its clarity. There was some simple furniture, a gold and ruby travelling case, and a silk rug on which Xaedrek lay as quiet as death.

Her journey was not over yet. She was drifting down towards his forehead, no longer on the defensive but ready to attack whatever lay within his mind.

And as she sought him, so Xaedrek sought her.

Not yet adept but learning fast, he floated enmeshed in

the silken visions that the ichor had bestowed. The large dose he had taken made his mind seem splintered, as vast as space itself, filled with an infinity of images like sheets of milky crystal on which scenes were sketched in translucent colours. Everything was edged with white fire. It was difficult to control the visions, but once he had fixed his mind on Charhn, he found Melkavesh with ease. As he clawed his way through the confusion to find her at the centre, he saw her collapse . . .

A kind of stillness enfolded him. The jostling images fell away until there was only one; the Sorceress lying in a darkened room, the cover rising and falling softly with her breathing.

He paused. This was the first time he had seen her since she had fled.

But he was still on the outside, and he did not know if there was a way to see into her thoughts. Hardly able to believe this was happening, he drew back a little, revelling in the implications. From now on she could have no secrets from him. The Kristillians could not move a single platoon, not a single man, without him knowing and pre-empting them. Perhaps Melkavesh could do the same, but if so, her advantage was gone for ever. How harmless she looked, asleep . . .

No, not asleep. Far-seeing. Trying to enter his mind as he was trying to enter hers.

They were falling towards each other now; caught in each other's gravity. Xaedrek felt her power as a lightning shock of silver and gold; but the power she felt from him was acidic, bloodstained, like Ah'garith's hand wielding the scalpel that stabbed and stabbed into the core of her brain.

The next instant, a cold unseen wall slammed into her and she was suddenly nowhere, turning over and over in a blank sky. With an intense shock of recognition she suddenly saw Xaedrek – and he, catapulted into the void by the same impact, saw her.

They were disembodied, yet they were face to face. Fragmented faces – huge transparent eyes, skin seen so close that every tiny hair was magnified and delineated with a gossamer light. There was disbelief and pure horror on both sides. They were fighting ineffectually to separate themselves, but to no avail; as helpless as feathers they were swept together and merged into one as they tumbled through a night sky frosted with unknown constellations.

In far-seeing there was no room for emotion, but shock destroyed even that barrier. They were clinging as they fell, all their thoughts shared, all differences between them vanishing. They were enmeshed, identical. The same fires burned in them, the same ideals and loves . . . and it seemed the firmament was coalescing around them into a sphere that was almost physical, evoking the essence of a place and time rather than its substance. Hints of shapes; a sweep of silken drapery, the gleam of jewelled furniture and satin sheets, all bathed in silver-blue twilight. There was rain beating at the window, light shining through the rain. No conflict, no evil. Only two souls lost in each other, everything forgotten except their passion.

We had this, they told each other. *We should not have destroyed it. We are two halves of a whole . . . twin beings, like Jaed and Fliya.*

There was something terrible in the ecstasy, the unexpectedness of it, the sense of helpless surrender. However blissful it was, it could not last. The intensity of the memory faded and lost its hold on them, and the obdurate element in each of them began to rebel. Like a cell dividing into two, they slid out of each other's grasp.

And like the moons, we must be for ever separate.

Everything had become very still. The sensation of falling had passed. They were facing each other, very close, filling each other's vision. To Melkavesh, Xaedrek's pupil could have been a black sun from which gleaming ruby spokes radiated across a red crystal sky. To him, her iris seemed a sunlit green sea fringed by dark ferns.

Communication between them was swift and painful. They felt each other's shock and anger; they experienced the nuances of a thousand subtler emotions, questions, recriminations. They touched each other with the poignant regret of lost love. But at last they found themselves at the centre

81

of the deadlock that had originally forced them apart. Immovable principles; Xaedrek's belief in Gorethria's superiority; Melkavesh's devotion to the laws of natural sorcery and humanity.

How have you stolen the skill of far-sight? she asked. *It's Ah'garith's doing, isn't it? The power is vile. Xaedrek, give it up before it destroys us all.*

He replied, *Melkavesh, I know you love Gorethria. Please stop fighting me. Come back.*

Never. It's far too late. I cannot allow you to have an equal advantage, nor to abuse a gift which is the right of natural sorcerers alone.

She felt him laugh. *How will you stop me?*

It was not a conscious decision on Melkavesh's part. Pure instinct took over as she began to gather her power and mesh the strands into a veil, which she then began to draw down between them.

He realised at once what she was trying to do. He could not stop her. Just before they lost sight of one another, there was a moment heavy with mutual reluctance and regret. Then, with sinister and mechanical determination, Xaedrek began to add his power to hers. Strings of thick, blood-tainted ichor began to weave themselves into the veil.

Melkavesh recoiled and almost lost control. She had not expected this. Recovering herself, she renewed her efforts and poured streams of energy into the screen. It thickened, spreading out to infinity until it was a vast impenetrable barrier between them. The veil had become a Wall and she was alone, stunned and bereft in a wasteland of shadows.

She drew back from the Wall, horrified at what he had forced her to do. There could be no more contact between them. He could not destroy the Wall, but neither could she, and she feared she had lost more than she had gained.

Put it to the test.

She slid away into another dimension and sent her mind swooping towards Gorethria. If she could not spy on Xaedrek, there were many other things she needed to see. Even as she did so, Xaedrek was arrowing towards Kristillia –

Only to find themselves hurtling towards a surface as

82

featureless as the inside of a shell. There was the shock of falling, total disorientation – and suddenly Xaedrek was back in a mountain villa, Melkavesh in a chamber of red stone.

In creating the Wall they had blocked out everything, destroyed each other's far-sight totally.

Again and again they returned to the trance and tried to push past the barrier, but each time they found only the Wall, the sense of plummeting into nothingness.

The final time, Xaedrek fell and kept on falling. With horror he realised that the ichor had worn off and he had no power to extricate himself. *Melkavesh had won and he would fall for ever . . .*

He came out of the trance with a shout that brought Valamek and the guards running. He saw them in the doorway, he saw the room reassemble itself around him, but he was so shaken that he could hardly move.

'Get out!' he yelled. Astonished, they obeyed hastily. It was almost unknown for Xaedrek to raise his voice, which made it all the more alarming.

Alone, he staggered to a table and leaned on it with his head in his hands. He felt sick, so bitterly angry that he could have wept. 'All the risks – all the trouble and care I took with the ichor – wasted! No sooner do I discover the gift than it is lost!'

He could not know how much worse it was for Melkavesh.

She came round not angry, but aching with grief. The skill she had lost was not newly acquired, but something she had taken for granted for years and years. It was like losing her eyesight or hearing. Worse, every time she had tried to find a way through the Wall she had found herself immersed in the necromancy that had helped to build it.

She could stand no more. She felt contaminated. Surely nothing would ever scrub the slime from her skin or rid her mouth of the metallic taste of blood. It was not Xaedrek; it was Ah'garith, the damnable Shanin. Shivering in the tousled bed, she knew she had touched on the horror that Silvren and Ashurek had known in the Dark Regions, and she wondered if she would ever feel clean – or quite sane – again.

Exhaustion weighed her down, but with an effort she dragged herself off the bed. It was dark, and she was afraid. Until this night she had not understood just how insidious and evil the demon truly was. The knowledge was intolerable, like a scar ripped open to reveal a stinging red wound in her mind; and with it came a profound blackness of spirit that drained all her courage.

For the first time in her life, she was terrified. She could not face anything, anything at all.

Kharan had respected Melkavesh's wish to be left alone, but she had not slept. All evening and all night Melkavesh had remained locked in her room, and although Kharan had knocked once or twice there had been no response. She had spent the intervening time alternately sitting by Filmoriel's crib and pacing around the room.

Finally she lay on the bed and fell into a restless doze, only to be woken up by the door scraping open.

Kharan sprang off the bed, astonished to see Melkavesh shambling into the room like a ghost. She could hardly believe her eyes. The Sorceress's face was all shadows as if the substance had been sucked out of it, leaving only skin stretched over bone. Her eyes were enormous and haunted, her hair a pale tangle. Not speaking, she sat on the end of Kharan's bed and pulled her cloak around herself as if she were freezing.

'Mel, what is it?' Kharan gasped. 'You look awful. For pity's sake, tell me what's wrong.' She sat next to her and took Melkavesh's long dark hand in her own. She could feel her shaking through the velvet of the cloak. For a long, long time she did not speak, only sat there pressed against Kharan, trembling.

'Please say something, Mel. You're frightening me. Is it something to do with Xaedrek?' It was terrible to see her like this when normally she was so buoyant and unquenchable.

'I've lost –' she choked.

'Lost what?' Kharan put an arm round her shoulders. Melkavesh leaned on her and began to weep with the abandonment of a child.

'The ability to far-see,' she sobbed hoarsely. 'It's lost. Gone.'

'How?'

Melkavesh could not reply, but Kharan saw from her grief that it had hit her not merely as a misfortune but as a bereavement. She wept with her, tears rolling from her eyes onto the Sorceress's head.

Eventually Melkavesh straightened up and uttered a deep, shuddering sigh. 'It's disastrous, Kharan. I can't pretend otherwise. I can't watch Xaedrek any more, and I've no way of finding out whether he can still watch us. Without far-sight, what help can I give the Kristillians?'

She pulled away and stood rigid in the centre of the room. Kharan ached for her, but something in Melkavesh's stance made her feel excluded, as if – despite everything they had been through together – the enchantress still felt she had no one to turn to. Kharan remembered the times when she had yearned for some of Melkavesh's strength, the impression she gave of being in control of her own destiny. But such freedom had its price. Now Kharan could admire her, sympathise with her – but envy her, never.

'Have something to drink,' she suggested. 'Stay in here and rest. Things won't seem so bad in the morning, they never do.'

But when Melkavesh turned towards her, the look in her eyes made Kharan flinch. It was obvious she had found no relief or comfort in weeping, and the sheen of tears had been replaced by viridian madness.

'I won't be here in the morning,' she said flatly, striding to the door.

'Where are you going?' Suddenly dizzy with foreboding, Kharan jumped up and seized her arm. 'Melkavesh, tell me where you're going? If you do something stupid –'

The Sorceress did not reply or pause. The door was open, she was through it, but Kharan was thrust back into the room with such force that she ended up sprawled across the bed. Filmoriel woke up and wailed. Winded, sick with alarm, Kharan found her feet and stumbled out into the corridor.

'Melkavesh!'

The corridor was empty. Kharan stood shaking between the stone walls, rubbing the backs of her arms. A moment later she heard the shouts and footsteps of guards turning out in quick response to her scream, but she made no move to run and meet them. It was pointless. Melkavesh was gone and there was nothing Kharan could do, never anything she could do.

5

The Aludrian Sea

MELKAVESH RODE swiftly and she rode alone, her face set savagely against the wind.

Her mount was no earthly horse, but a spectral one conjured by sorcery. It was formed of yellow light through which a skeleton could be seen in faint silhouette, with eyes like wells of flame in the skull. The mane and tail were plumes of aureate fire.

She had lost her far-sight, but at least her other skills had not left her. The effort of sustaining the horse drained her, but she relished the pain like a penance, pushing the horse higher and faster until her bones ached and her spine felt like a column of lead. The wind whipped tears from her eyes and iced the sweat on her brow. There was no other way to purge her despair.

No one had seen her leave Charhn, for she had cloaked herself against being seen. This did not make her invisible, but it meant those she passed would retain no memory of having seen her – nor a horse that galloped on air and trailed fire from its hooves.

The city was far behind her now. She was heading northwest, with no aim in mind but to find a wilderness as bleak as her soul. Time ceased to mean anything as the fells rolled beneath her; the sky went from black to blue to colourless several times over, but she hardly noticed. When she stopped to rest it was only because exhaustion forced her to, and then she fell into such heavy sleep that she remembered nothing of it. The flight seemed continuous, endless. She ate nothing.

Sorcery nourished her but, if she went on, sorcery would kill her.

There was a forest ahead. She could not quite raise the horse clear of the tree-tops, so for a time it galloped hock deep in the foliage. The breeze blowing up at her was damp, earth-scented. In the distance she could see the line of red mountains that divided Kristillia from Alta-Nangra. She had swift-travelled hundreds of miles from Charhn, and beyond those peaks lay a true wilderness in which she could lose herself, never go back –

What am I trying to escape? Whatever it is, I can never be free of it, because it's inside me . . .

Whether it was despair or sheer exhaustion that brought her down, she did not know; but the horse evaporated and she was suddenly crashing through the trees to land painfully on the forest floor.

Oblivion claimed her almost at once. When she awoke she was so stiff and cold that she could barely move. Melkavesh had the impression that she had blacked out for at least a day. It was dawn. She looked up at the canopy and went dizzy at the height of the trunks dwindling into a bright silver haze.

Groaning, her joints feeling like rusted iron, Melkavesh pulled herself to sit against a tree-trunk. One more try. She closed her eyes and loosed her mind, but all she saw was the blank malevolent grey of the Wall. She came out of the trance with a scream. It was hopeless, the Wall was there for ever. She hugged her stomach and retched, emptiness into emptiness.

When she found the strength to stand up, all her efforts to reconjure the horse failed. This had happened to her before – *never on Ikonus, blessed Ikonus, where the power flowed so easily* – and the only cure was to wait until her energy returned. It could be hours or days. Numb, stranded on a shore far beyond misery or rage, she began to walk aimlessly through the forest.

She told herself she had no direction, yet something was pulling her. There was no other reason for her to have headed west rather than directly north. Her skill for sensing the geography of an area from a distance and finding her way through it unerringly without a compass or map was not strictly sorcerous, and that at least had not left her. She tried to block out the knowledge, but the shadow-shapes persisted and it was no surprise at all when the trees ended and she walked out into jagged hills. She had never seen them before yet their outlines were familiar, as were the mountains massed like red clouds on the horizon, and the great solitary trees on the hilltops.

Melkavesh walked on. Perhaps she fell down and slept at some stage; she did not remember or care. She made no attempt to fight the pull but went with it resignedly, feeling that whatever wanted her there so badly might as well have her.

Everything else that had happened to her on Earth had been a challenge to be met joyfully. But the Wall was terrifying because it could not be challenged; it simply *was*, and it was as impassive and indestructible as the sky. And she had helped to create it.

Mother, Mother, would you have done what I have, littered your path with broken Oaths? Would you have given up at the first true difficulty? It was the only coherent thought she had had in a long while. No answer came.

It was late afternoon – of the next day, or perhaps the one after – when she climbed a final hill and looked down at the view she had known would be there. The low sun dazzled her, outlining every grass blade with white gold, glittering on a line of water along the horizon. It was the inland Sea, Aludria.

She had been drawn here perpetually while trying to far-see; now she had been drawn here bodily. Too heartsick even to feel curious, she walked woodenly towards the shore. The grass ended at a line of tumbled rocks, red-gold in colour like the narrow beach that lay below them. Melkavesh scrambled down them and was at the water's edge in a few strides, staring out across the sea, her hands on her hips as if she were issuing a bitter challenge.

'Well, here I am,' she muttered. 'What do you want of me?'

Behind her, the landscape lay wild and desolate; before her, the sea filled the horizon, reflecting the sun's globe in an ever-moving pathway of platinum and glass. The air was sweet and mild. A few seabirds wheeled high above her but there was no other sign of life, nothing left in the world to offer her any comfort or hope.

I have never needed them, she told herself fiercely. What she felt was not self-pity but brutal self-condemnation. Failure was hard enough to accept when it only affected herself; when it meant disaster for others, it was impossible. It was her first taste of fallibility, and she did not know how to cope with it. *I am dying*, she thought. *If I do not eat, if I push myself on like this, I shall die. Is it the best thing – not for me, but for the Kristillians?*

The water looked gentle, tempting. She took off her cloak and boots, left them rolled up on the sand and went barefoot into the waves. She relished the sensation of sand sliding under her feet, water swirling round her ankles. The criss-cross patterns it made were hypnotic.

No one asked me to come to this Earth, not Silvren, not the Guardians, not even the Lady of H'tebhmella herself. I came here for myself. I thought I was special, that I could do anything – pure egotism, so I can hardly complain when it rebounds on me . . . The water is not cold. It would be swift . . .

She looked up, and only then did she see Jaed and Fliya hanging like discs of lacy bone in the sky. At the sight of them something seemed to break within her.

'You wanted me here, so I came!' she cried. 'At least tell me what you want of me, you tricksters! Tell me!'

In her fury she lost her balance. The sand slid away under her left heel and she stumbled, trying to find firmer ground. But the sand was sinking swiftly beneath her, and no matter what she did, she could not right herself. She flailed wildly and fell headlong in the foam. Horribly, her toes were enveloped not in sliding sand but in a hole rimmed by a hard, sharp edge like a row of teeth. The water was gurgling wildly around her and her nose and ears were full of it. Coughing, she struggled to drag herself forward, but the surface turned to liquid under her hands, there was nothing she could grip. The hard edges clamped onto her ankles like a man-trap, sending a thrill of pain through her – and she found herself being dragged backwards and downwards through the waves.

For a few seconds the foam rushed loudly through her ears, the sea closed over her head and the sound became thick and muffled. Her eyes were open, but she could make out nothing; all was vitreous green, full of bubbles and lozenges of light. Her chest tightened with the desperate need for breath.

That was when she realised that the last thing she wanted to do was die.

She had not tried to use sorcery for two days, but it rose now in an instinctive flood that pre-empted thought. Even as she flailed helplessly, she saw the aura gathering round her hands and felt a ball of power crackle down to destroy her attacker.

There was a faint impact, shock waves thrumming through the water. The thing holding her legs paused, but it did not let go. If anything it was dragging her down faster than before.

The pressure in her head increased; the tightness in her lungs filled her with black dizziness. Consciousness was slipping away, but her desire to survive was so overpowering that she forced herself to cling to it. With the water rushing past her and the steel pain in her legs, concentration was almost impossible and it was a fight to drag power into her body and hold it there. *Don't panic, don't try to breathe*, she told herself frantically. The water was numbingly cold. But just as she thought she was certain to drown, she sensed the vermeil radiance of her power beginning to fill her lungs and pump life-saving energy through her blood.

The pressure eased. The black stars faded and her vision cleared. She no longer felt the need to breathe air; sorcery kept her alive, as if the water had become her natural element. But that brought its own pain, and she did not know how long it could last.

Green shadows loomed beneath her, and suddenly she was being dragged at wild speed between rock walls. She flung out her hands to protect herself, seeing the last of daylight as a rippling greenish ribbon far above her. They were in a crevasse. It was too dark to perceive her captor as anything more than a rounded shell, silhouetted against a blue-green glow that came from beneath them . . . *You're not going to drown. Stay calm.* Then the crevasse widened, and they were plunging through a vast cave towards a sandy floor.

The creature decelerated and set itself down gently, sending sand pluming up through the water. She had intended to wait and see what happened, but her fear overrode sense and she flung out a great detonation of power. Its reaction was unexpected. Any normal beast would have been flung away, probably killed, but the sea-creature only shuddered, convulsed – and tightened its iron grip on her legs.

She opened her mouth wide in agony. The next moment the being seemed to spit her out, and she drifted down to the sea-bed, watching a cloud of some dull brown substance billowing out around her ankles. It took her several seconds to realise that it was her own blood, pouring from her legs, and that her right calf was broken just above the ankle.

The pain was unspeakable. For a long time she lay immobile on the sand in shock, the slow pulse of power barely keeping her alive. It was so cold. She could not see the thing that had seized her; all she could see was sand, shells and a few waving fronds of seaweed, blurred by the rippling water. The sourceless glow illuminated everything but made nothing clear.

Very soon I will be dead, and oh, I do not want to die, I can't die with so much unfinished . . .

Why did the creature not attack her again? She presumed it had meant to eat her, and as her power had so little effect on it there was nothing to stop it. She could not move, could not find enough strength even to edge out of its reach.

Calm, I must keep calm. There were ways to detach herself from pain, she had learned them at the School of Sorcery. *So hard to concentrate . . .* Somehow she managed to half sit up, only for her leg to flare into jagged red agony. She tried to cry out, swallowed water, and for several seconds battled between the instinct to breathe and the necessity not to.

Theurgy was keeping her alive but if she sucked in water she would begin to drown. She was on the point of passing out when, unexpectedly, the pain stopped. Her viewpoint changed. She was upright and floating, and looking down she saw her own body lying on the sea-bed.

She realised what had happened; it was an involuntary astral projection, something any Sorcerer might experience under great stress. It did not bode well for her body, which was even more vulnerable with her mind outside it. *I must go back, I must,* she thought frantically, sinking down again, dreading the pain she would feel. But just before she reached her body she froze with an intense feeling that something was watching her.

She let her astral form drift upwards, turning slowly. It took her a while to take in what she was seeing, and when she did she could barely comprehend it. The cave she was in was a vast natural amphitheatre, filled with what seemed at first glance to be rows and rows of boulders. The smallest were some ten feet in diameter, the largest at least seventy. But a few seconds' observation convinced her that these were living creatures. Their shells were all roughly spherical in shape, with eight ribs running from crown to base, but the variations on that form seemed infinite. Their colours were startling in the gloom; there were luminous blues, metallic greens shading to turquoise, vivid hues of mandarin, crimson and magenta. No two were alike. Their ribs varied from simple ridges to rows of spines or scalloped crests on which tendrils swayed like anemones. Some of the shells had a lattice-work structure through which their insides could be seen, transparent and pulsing with an aquamarine light of their own.

These creatures were themselves the source of the glow she had seen, and she felt an inexplicable sense of familiarity, of something waiting to be recognised.

Near her body she saw the creature that had captured her. It was no more than twelve feet across and a silky pinkish-grey with white nodes running down its surface. Through the round orifice on top she could see hard ridges champing together, and a blue glow from within whenever they opened.

The radial symmetry allowed for no features, certainly not eyes – so why did she feel they were watching her?

The creature began to move, as if she had stunned it and it was just recovering. If it seized her body there was nothing she could do. But it did not go near her; it simply rose up, and as it did so she saw trailing from beneath it a mass of tentacles, clear as glass and shining with the same cyan light. It was moving to join its fellows. Unable to stop herself she followed it, and as she floated above them they all began to rise up around her, as if to acknowledge her presence.

At that she forgot her predicament, forgot everything except her profound awe.

They were vast spheres rising on columns that would dwarf those of the greatest palace, and those columns were like ropes and rippling veils of light. She marvelled at the colours of their shells, the tendrils and fans undulating along their ridges, the delicate fretworks of silica. They were impossibly frail, impossibly beautiful. Could they be aware of her? Of her body perhaps, as a fragment of food – but to sense her astral presence seemed impossible. Yet she felt herself being drawn towards one, and suddenly she was inside it as if enfolded in the luminescent heart of a jellyfish. The underwater glow surrounded her and filled her, so familiar that it seemed part of her.

This creature is conscious, she thought incredulously. She reached out to touch it with her mind. It was alien. It had no clear thoughts, and what intelligence it possessed was slow and unfathomable. Yet there was something –

Recognition. It knows I am here. And it recognises me!

In a moment of shock and excitement, she realised why the glow seemed so familiar to her. It was the same extramundane energy as her own. Somehow they absorbed it from the Earth and stored it within their bodies. They did not wield it, it was simply part of them; and where her power was golden-white and vigorous, theirs was blue-green, slow and viscid. And yet it was the same, pure and untainted, the opposite of the vile energy that Ah'garith drew.

Perhaps that was why they had captured her. *To greet me, to tell me something?* She flung out wordless questions to the

94

creature, but all that came back was a blunt pulsation that expressed no more than, *We exist.*

And that was all there was to know. All she could give in return was acknowledgement, a mental gesture of reverence. Then, with reluctance, she eased her mind out of the shell and began to drift back to her body.

The thought of returning appalled her, but if she did not she would die, her astral self would wink out of existence. The instant she returned, discomfort flooded her; her broken leg felt like a dead thing twice its normal size. Her head throbbed, the water pressure hurt her ears. Somehow she must find the power to heal herself and return to the surface, but however hard she tried she could not move. Shadows moved over her. Looking up, she saw three of the sea-creatures directly above her and descending.

Alarm twisted in her stomach. Not understanding her danger they might kill her without meaning to, and she was totally vulnerable. She shut her eyes and shivered as she felt their tentacles drape across her. What if they contained stinging cells? Bracing herself for the pain she thought, *At least that would be faster than lying here until my power fails altogether and I drown . . .*

There were no stings. What she felt instead was like cool blue sunlight washing through her, just as if another Sorcerer had laid his hands on her and was filling her with his strength. She felt her own energy swell in response, merging with the new power and turning to the silver-blue of healing. They were helping her! In amazement and hope she directed her thoughts to her injured leg and began the mending process.

Healing others was arduous; self-healing could be so un-pleasant that even the most adept of Sorcerers avoided it. It was as if the fragments of bone and burst veins were laid out like a landscape over which she must toil until each cell had been guided back into its proper place. Without the Aludrians it would have been impossible; even with them, her leg felt like a spike of fire and she laboured in misery, wondering if it would not have been easier to drown after all. But after a time it became easier. There was a last burst of agony like a spear of light impaling the tibia, then the energy became a gentler tide, lapping over her legs to soothe the ache and ease her cramped muscles.

It was over. The Aludrians seemed to know, for almost at once they withdrew their tentacles and began to rise again as if on towers of azure crystal. Melkavesh stared at them, so lost in wonder that she would have wept if she could. Then she bent forward to feel her leg.

It ached, but it was whole again. As pain subsided, terror rose in proportion and she dreaded being unable to find a way back to the surface. Helped by the creatures' residual energy, she found the strength to stand up. Then she launched herself off the sea-bed and began to swim slowly upwards.

She dared not look back at the ranks of Aludrians. If she had she might have been transfixed by their beauty and lingered until it was too late. But she still felt the touch of their minds, and tried to send back her own awe, friendship and gratitude.

The crevasse was above her, a glass-green tape of light. The swim seemed to take an age. She was so tired that her body felt weighted, reluctant to float, and every stroke was like hauling herself up a mountain. Just when it seemed her power would fail and her lungs burst, she saw that she was ascending through the upper waters towards a shimmering jade membrane.

The air came as a shock when her head broke the surface. She had almost forgotten what it was to breathe. Her first effort seared her lungs like the raw edge of winter and made her cough so convulsively that she feared she would drown after all. With difficulty she splashed to the shore and managed to crawl clear of the water before collapsing. She lay on the sand, gasping like a landed fish.

I'm still alive, she thought, laughing and crying. *I'm still alive.*

The first thing she noticed was that the light had changed. The sun had gone down, and the sky had turned the clear violet that precedes darkness. She was exhausted and had nowhere to go, but if she stayed on the beach she was unlikely to survive the night. Groaning, she turned on her back. As she moved, she noticed that the shoreline had changed as well. She must have come several miles south. To the right as she faced the sea was a great plug of rock on which stood a castle.

She sat up in surprise and gazed up at its towering bulk. A soft purplish twilight suffused the walls and rimmed the battlements with silver. It was connected to the mainland by a strand of rock fused into a low cliff that had rocks strewn along its base. It would be hard to climb but not impossible. The castle looked ancient and unassailable, but to her eyes there was nothing hostile about it. It was beautiful. It was her salvation.

She lay back, thinking, *I must move. I must climb up to the bridge. I can do it . . .* But instead she closed her eyes, and saw again the other-world of the Aludrians and touched their minds . . .

And only knew she had fallen asleep when she found two faces bending over her.

'She's a Gorethrian,' said the first woman.

'No she's not, Mother,' said the second. 'Not with hair that colour.' They were Kristillians, tall and slender with chestnut hair plaited and coiled round their heads. Both were dressed in wine-red dresses and shawls held with bronze pins.

'I'm Mellorn,' she said weakly, trying to sit up. They stared at her blankly. 'Mellorn. Surely you've heard of me?'

The two women shook their heads and looked at each other. 'She's half drowned. Better take her inside, anyway,' said the younger one.

'As long as she's not Gorethrian.'

'I'm not, I swear.' They helped her to her feet and she hung between them, smearing their shawls with sand and water. Their manner was businesslike, though not unfriendly, yet she felt a sudden touch of wariness about being taken into the castle.

'Wait – who lives there?'

'We do,' said the older woman. 'I am Thaufa En Mianna, and this is my daughter, Thaufa En Faliol. Now save your breath for the climb.'

'Yes, but it is a Kristillian castle, isn't it? Who else lives in it?'

Thaufa En Mianna scowled at her. 'There is no one else at Heldavrain now. I wish there were. En Faliol and I live here alone.'

Melkavesh said no more. She did not have the strength. She let herself be half carried up the cliff path, glad that they did not know who she was. She felt numb, no longer racked by the despair that had almost driven her to suicide, but devoid of all prospects and hopes. She did not even delude herself that the Aludrians could provide any solution to her troubles. All her ambitions were reduced to their simplest essence, food and sleep, and she could see nothing beyond that.

'Poor woman,' said En Faliol as they led her across the bridge towards the courtyard. 'What happened to you? We'll soon have you feeling better.'

When Melkavesh entered Heldavrain Castle, any last trace of wariness vanished. Her only emotion was an overpowering sense of arriving home.

By the time Xaedrek returned to Shalekahh he was in a more collected frame of mind. His fury at Melkavesh still writhed beneath the surface but it was hidden and controlled. He even managed to smile as he opened the door to his office where Amnek and Ah'garith were waiting for him.

'Good day to you, Sire,' said Amnek. 'I trust you had a pleasant – er – journey?'

'Not particularly,' he replied. The sight of them depressed him. They seemed elongated, ghoulish figures, one light grey and one dark grey, looming over him in a room too small to contain them. He brushed past them and went to close the velvet curtains. 'What I have to say will not take long.'

'Sire?' said Ah'garith, twisting her hands together.

'It's about this.' Xaedrek turned towards them with the same cool smile on his lips and a phial of ichor in his hand. He held it out to the Shanin. Perplexed, she reached out to take it, but just before her fingers touched his he deliberately drew back and let it fall to the floor. It smashed on the marble tiles, spewing a pool of pearly liquid that lay pulsing by the hem of her robe. Then he went to sit on the edge of his desk, regarding them gravely. Both looked bewildered.

'I don't understand,' said the demon.

'Useless, Ah'garith. The ichor is absolutely useless. I have destroyed the rest. That was the last of it. There will be no more experiments.'

He thought she would burst with fury, and allowed himself an inward laugh at her dismay. She must have been confident that he would give her permission to reinstate her vile 're-search' – and judging by Amnek's equally unhappy expression, so had he.

'Useless?' she raged. 'That's impossible, Sire. Impossible! Did you not go away expressly to try it?'

'What a very clever guess, demon. Yes, I tried it, and I found Melkavesh almost at once. You never warned me that she might have her own defence against my far-sight. As soon as she realised, she created a Wall against me through which I cannot penetrate – not to spy on her, not to see anything.'

'You should have used the ichor's power to stop her!'

'I could not. Our power was equal. In fact, I helped her.'

'You did what?' Amnek cried.

'I had to. It was the only way I could prevent her from continuing to spy on me. Now, if there's any justice, I trust she has also completely lost her far-sight.'

'This is disastrous!' Amnek looked as if he might attempt murder, but Xaedrek silenced him with a glacial look.

'In a way, I'm glad,' he said quietly. 'There's no need for the ichor now, and no point in wasting any more time on it. In view of that, and of its unpleasant nature, Ah'garith, I expressly forbid you to set up any more experiments.'

'Your Majesty!'

'That is enough.' Xaedrek suddenly felt he hated them both, thrusting their hope and dismay at him like a voracious thirst that only he could slake. What was wrong with them? He had expected no better from the Shanin, but *Amnek* –

The room oppressed him, as if the air were full of invisible, whispering figures. He had to escape. He stood up slowly, saying, 'I gave the ichor a fair trial. I've no more to say on the subject. From now on all our energies will be devoted to producing amulin and perfecting the battle machines. Is this understood?'

'Yes, Sire,' they replied sullenly.

'Good. Now I am going to pay a visit to Anixa and Irem Ol Thangiol, and I do not wish to be disturbed.'

When the Emperor had gone, Amnek turned on the demon, furious. 'Destroyed it all? How could he? You led me to believe that once he'd taken the ichor he would forget his reservations, let us set up networks of lenses and take as many victims as necessary. We'd give Gorethria all the power she needs, and finish Melkavesh once and for all. So what went wrong, demon?' He bent over her, gripping her shoulder with a claw-like hand. 'Damn you for a fool. You think you know everything – but how little you know him.'

'Don't touch me, Lord Amnek,' she hissed. 'I told you what I believed to be true.'

'If so, you underestimated him in one very serious respect. He has great self-discipline. He is not a man to become addicted to anything. If he can resist even such a temptation as the ichor, for you to think you could manipulate him was a gross misjudgement.'

'Ah, so it was my fault. I should have realised. Whatever would you and Xaedrek do without me to blame for everything that goes wrong?' Her metallic voice grated on Amnek's ears and he found himself looking around the room for a weapon. There was an ornamental knife on the desk . . . 'Well, just listen to this. The ichor he has already taken is enough.'

'What do you mean?'

'I mean, my lord, that it is too late for Xaedrek. He had some inkling of the ichor's hidden purpose, and that's why he was so cautious with it, travelled miles to try it, and has finally destroyed what was left. But it has availed him nothing. Even one dose gives me some advantage and several doses will make him decidedly . . . pliable.'

'You're talking of possession,' Amnek whispered, aghast.

'No, no –'

'Destroying his mind, enslaving him – that was never what I intended! Gorethria's benefit was all I –'

'Lord Amnek, I am talking of making him less obstinate. As he only took a small amount of ichor it will be a gradual process, and he'll never know what's happening. But the change is in motion and there's nothing, nothing he can do to stop it.'

'Gods.' Amnek closed his eyes and saw a vivid, horrific image; Xaedrek, the greatest man he had ever known, reduced to the wretched slave of the demon, his brilliant mind destroyed.

'I've been blind. He warned me about you, but all I could think of was avenging Shavarish . . .'

'I like single-minded people. They're the easiest,' said the Shanin, starting to giggle. The next thing Amnek knew, the knife was in his hand and he had thrust the demon to the floor and was driving the blade repeatedly into her chest. The sound she made was horrible. *She was still laughing.*

The breath turned thick in his throat and he began to tremble. His blows became more frantic, but Ah'garith suddenly seized his wrist in a bone-hard grip that he could not break. He wrestled against her. The face grinning into his was that of a mild old woman, but the eyes were like lakes of mercury, mad and unhuman. Suddenly his frenzy turned to terror, and all his strength left him. He rolled away from her, the knife fell from his hand, and he curled up like a child shuddering in a nightmare.

'Oh, my lord, see what a mess you've made of my robe.' The satin was torn, but she had shed not one drop of blood. She leaned over and put her face very close to his, and he seemed to see another face superimposed on it; that of a silver, asexual being with a leering red mouth. Her smell made him heave. 'You can't kill me. Nothing can, except Miril, and she, the Serpent curse her, is dead.'

'Leave me alone.' Amnek felt his bones softening to cartilage, his capacity for judgement dissolving in a colourless lake where there was only mockery and malevolence and evil for its own sake. He was already in her power. Perhaps he had been all along.

'Too late, my lord. What made you think I can only possess Xaedrek? I'll have you all in time.'

'Fiend.'

She stood up and kicked him. 'Don't call me that. I am your master now. Oh, get up – there is great pleasure in tormenting you, but I need your help. You will tell Xaedrek nothing of this conversation, do you understand?'

'Yes,' Amnek said helplessly.

'Good, because we are going to go on playing Xaedrek's stupid game until his stupid war is over. That's an entertainment I don't want to miss, and I can be patient for a year or two. Unless, of course, he provokes me beyond endurance before then.'

Amnek climbed to his feet and leaned heavily on the desk, unable to stop himself bowing to the demon. He was shivering with misery. Shavarish's sapphire eyes haunted him and all he could think of was the way he had betrayed Xaedrek without ever meaning to. *Betrayed him. He was my Emperor, and the nearest we had to a son.* He said hoarsely, 'What happens afterwards?'

'After I possess him his orders will cease to bind me. I shall amuse myself with this world just as I please, and everyone, every single human being, is going to pay for the murder of the Serpent M'gulfn a thousand times over.'

Still trying to shake off the feeling of oppression, Xaedrek went to Meshurek's suite to see Anixa and Irem Old Thangiol. He sat watching them through the mirror for a long time, thinking about a plan he had formed but never put into action.

Amulin, he had discovered, gave Irem Ol Thangiol's blood very interesting properties. It was something peculiar to Kristillians, but not to all of them; of the others he had experimented on, only two had yielded similar results before dying in agony. Now there was only Ol Thangiol left. Until Kristillia was conquered and an unlimited supply of subjects available, the man was indispensable and Xaedrek was glad he had given him a chance to recover his health.

Anixa had worked a miracle. They were devoted to each

other, and their love, as he had once told Amnek, was the lever by which they could be persuaded to do anything.

Yes, it would work. If it had worked with an eagle, how much more effective it would be with a human. Smiling to himself, he walked round and let himself into the chamber.

Their faces fell at the sight of him. The Kristillian closed his eyes, but Anixa kept her sullen amber gaze fixed on the Emperor. He said pleasantly, 'There's no need to look so alarmed. I trust you are both well, and that you don't regret staying here, Anixa. If you remember, I did give you the option of leaving, and it was your own choice to remain a prisoner. Now I need your help.'

'I will do nothing to help Gorethria.'

'I appreciate your noble sentiments,' he said softly. 'But your conscience may be easy in the knowledge that you were forced into it. Do you remember your friend Melkavesh?'

Anixa did not reply.

'Well, how would you like to pay her a visit in Kristillia?'

King Afil Es Thendil had called the Council of War long before Melkavesh had vanished, and even without her it still had to go ahead. Leaders and representatives of his Vardravian allies had travelled thousands of miles in great danger to take part. Their strategy for defeating Xaedrek hinged on this meeting.

His throne room was modest compared to Xaedrek's glacial hall, but it had a grandeur of its own. The rose-red stone of the walls glowed warmly in the light of an immense stained glass window that soared up behind the throne dais, casting pools of coloured light onto the floor. The throne faced an ornate double door, and on either side of the room were rows of tiered seats carved from mahogany where a hundred Vardravians sat. Another two hundred or so were crammed into the space in front of the throne.

There were Kesfalians, white-skinned folk from Alaak and Ala'kaara, Malmanish soldiers, even a handful of tribes-people from the deserts of Ungrem, with bronze skin and creamy robes. On either side of the dais, there was a line of tall chairs. Irem Ol Melemen sat on one side with his senior priests, clad in vestments of deep orange and indigo; on the other side were Haeth Im Nerek, several Kristillian generals, and Prince Rar An Tolis of Ehd'rabara.

The Prince, a distant cousin of Es Thendil, was an elderly man with long silver hair and white brows bristling over eyes that always seemed half closed. He carried himself proudly, and concealed his bony frame beneath robes of the Ehd'rabaran colours, dark blue, peacock and silver.

With him had come the representatives of the races who would help to defend Ehd'rabara; huge Cevandarish warriors, and sallow-faced men from Alta-Nangra. N'golem and the priestess U'garet of Mangorad sat uneasily alongside them.

Kharan was sitting next to Haeth Im Nerek, feeling uncomfortably conspicuous amid the officers. But the Battle Marshal had taken the trouble to save her a seat, and however out of place she felt at the meeting she had to hear what was going to be said. She twisted a fold of her skirt between her fingers, unable to stop brooding about Melkavesh.

Im Nerek leaned over and whispered, 'Don't worry, my sister. She'll be back. I couldn't be so lucky as to have lost her for good.'

'I can't help it. It's so unlike her . . .' Kharan glanced up at the King and Queen enthroned on the dais. They looked regal in state robes of green and amber velvet trimmed with gold, but their expressions were tense and solemn. She looked away before she caught Es Thendil's eye.

'My beloved friends and allies, I am deeply grateful for your attendance here today,' the King began. 'I know the terrible risks you have taken to leave your own countries, the losses you have suffered on your way. Gorethria forces us to this, but it is to end Gorethria's tyranny once and for all that this Council of War has been called.'

A huge cheer greeted his words. Kharan found it ironic that he must address them in Gorethrian, the only language they all understood. Es Thendil held up his hand for silence and went on, 'However, I have some grave news to impart. You know it is the enchantress Mellorn who has rallied us to this new effort. Many of you have been eager to see her for the first time. Unfortunately –' His hands opened and closed on the arms of the throne. 'Unfortunately, she is not here. She vanished fourteen days ago after falling ill. She has not been seen since.'

There was an uproar of dismay at this, and Kharan felt sorry for Es Thendil. The Queen's face was like iron.

'Please, my friends,' he said when the noise died down. 'I saw no point in trying to hide the fact from you.'

'Well, where's she gone?' shouted a black-bearded Cevandarish man.

'No one knows, Baron Gartha. As I said, she was unwell. I fear something has happened to her.'

'Or she's deserted us?' suggested a Kesfalian. There were angry shouts at this, particularly from N'golem and U'garet.

'No – no, I am sure she never meant to desert us,' said Es Thendil. 'We've searched for her to no avail. I don't know what more we can do.'

The Kesfalian, a slim man uniformed in green and violet leather, said, 'Perhaps it is just as well she has gone.'

'What are you talking about?' demanded Irem Ol Melemen, standing up.

'I am talking about the foreknowledge divined from Jaed and Fliya that an enchantress would come to save us, only to lead us into a greater disaster.'

'Kristillian prophecies speak of no disaster,' said the priest.

'Then your prophecies are incomplete. Without disrespect, there is a saying that the Kristillians only look outwards; it is the Kesfalians who see inward. I say again, we are better off without her.'

Irem Ol Melemen's pleasant face did not change, and he said in a measured tone, 'I am only Kristillia's chief priest. It is not for me to dispute Kesfaline's greater wisdom. But in this I have to say you are wrong.'

'Unless the disaster is that she's left us,' someone muttered.

The Kesfalian began to speak again, but the King rose to his feet and said sharply, 'Enough! With or without Lady Mellorn there is still a war to be won! This argument is getting us nowhere, and we must go on with the business in hand.' They fell quiet. 'I call upon Battle Marshal Haeth Im

Nerek, the commander-in-chief of the Kristillian army, to give us her view of the situation.'

The Battle Marshal stood up with her feet planted apart and her arms folded. 'The situation is that we have Gorethrian troops patrolling along all our borders, particularly in Kesfaline and along the river Omnuandrix. This has been so since we repelled their last invasion. At present they do not attack us unless we provoke them, although there have been isolated battles and a few occasions when small groups of Gorethrians have infiltrated Kristillia itself. They did not get far.' She gave a grim half-smile. 'They show no signs of preparing for an imminent invasion. My guess is that Xaedrek is biding his time until he can amass extra troops in Omnuandria and Kesfaline.

'The attack, when it comes, will be two-pronged. There is little point in him coming in from Alta-Nangra, when he can reach Charhn so much more easily from Kesfaline. So there will be an attack on Charhn almost certainly from the south. However, the worst of the invasion will be at Ehd'rabara.

'Now, Ehd'rabara guards the mouth of the Omnuandrix where it joins the Aludrian Sea. It is a heavily fortressed town which Xaedrek will try to hold to siege. We need to engage and destroy the army before they reach the walls –'

'If I may interrupt, Battle Marshal,' said Prince Rar An Tolis. He spoke ponderously, as if half asleep, but his narrow eyes were shrewd. 'The Gorethrians have always used the Omnuandrix as a main trade and military route into the Aludrian Sea. We have had great success in blocking their access by obstructing the river . . . harassing their ships in the estuary . . . and so forth. In effect, Ehd'rabara is the gateway to the Empire. It would be Xaedrek's most strategic conquest. Take Ehd'rabara and Kristillia . . . Kristillia would fall automatically.'

'I hope you are not suggesting that there's no point in defending Charhn, cousin,' said the Queen.

'Of course not. But I am saying that Ehd'rabara's importance must not be underestimated. Xaedrek will concentrate his attack upon us and it is, hm . . . imperative that we have sufficient troops to defend us. I think the Battle Marshal understands this.'

'I appreciate it too, cousin,' said Es Thendil quietly. 'I would not withhold men from you simply to save my own skin in Charhn. Ehd'rabara shall have whatever is needed.'

Haeth Im Nerek cleared her throat. 'I'm glad you agree, Your Majesty. In fact, I feel the defence of Ehd'rabara is of such importance that I am asking your permission to conduct the campaign there.'

The King looked stunned. 'But – but – who will take your place at Charhn?'

'General En Scanon, of course. He's every bit as competent as me. Well, almost.'

Es Thendil bowed his head in thought, and Kharan followed his eyes to the colours pooled on the floor and dappling the assembled Vardravians like a shattered rainbow. She tried to lose herself in their warmth, tried not to think of war, of Gorethrians pouring through the streets of Charhn, slaying and burning. Where would Filmoriel be safe?

'Very well,' said the King. 'I shall hate to lose you, Battle Marshal, but I must not be selfish. When you have done all you can here, you may go with Rar An Tolis to Ehd'rabara.'

'Thank you, Your Majesty.' She bowed. 'If it is of any consolation to you, I think we can win this war quite comfortably without the Lady Mellorn.'

'I hope so. I truly hope so.' The King looked round at the other Vardravian leaders, his equals yet all willing to defer to his leadership if it meant the end of Gorethria. 'Protecting Kristillia is only the first stage. We must drive them back and destroy them on their own soil. From every country they now occupy they must be driven back and destroyed.' But over the shouts of concurrence Kharan heard him murmur, 'And in that I believe only Mellorn's power could have helped us. Damn it, Melkavesh, where are you?'

As he spoke, there was a commotion at the back of the throne room. The double doors were pushed open, and three of his guards rushed in excitedly. They were all shouting at once, and no one could hear what they were saying, but a few seconds later another figure strode in, and everyone turned to stare at her.

It was Melkavesh. She might almost have been waiting outside to time her entrance.

Forgetting herself, Kharan stood on her chair and then bent to grip Haeth Im Nerek's shoulders. 'She's back! Oh, thank the Lady, I knew she'd come back!'

'Who could doubt it?' said Im Nerek through clenched teeth.

The crowd parted and Melkavesh strode through them, her eyes fixed on the King and Queen. She looked like herself again, Kharan thought; the gauntness had left her face and there was confidence in her bearing. Light from the window slid over her hair in soft patches of colour. Where she stopped in front of the dais, a yellow pane turned it to such an extraordinary blazing gold that there were gasps of astonishment.

For a time it seemed everyone was holding their breath. The King's lips were working, but no sound came out. Then Melkavesh said, 'Forgive me, Your Majesty. It was wrong of me to go away without saying anything. I had my reasons, and I would like to explain them to you.'

She did seem different, Kharan thought. The arrogance had left her. The King rose and extended a hand, and she climbed the four steps to stand on the dais and address the Vardravians. 'I swift-travelled here in the hopes of being in time for this Council; I apologise for arriving late. I have been to the Aludrian Sea.'

'There and back, in fourteen days? It's a thousand miles away!' Im Nerek whispered.

'As to the reason I left, it was because – because Xaedrek attacked me. He found a way to far-see, and in stopping him I inadvertently destroyed my own Sight.' Above the murmurs of dismay, she went on, 'I am telling you what happened, and what it will mean, so that you can judge for yourselves . . . whether you still want my help.' No one responded. Their eyes were fastened on her. 'The loss of far-sight to a Sorcerer is like being crippled. I left because I needed time to think. At Aludria I discovered –' Kharan wondered why

108

she hesitated. 'I discovered what it was to be in such despair that death seemed preferable to letting you down. I almost did die – and that taught me that I couldn't give up so easily, that I can never give up while there's still a breath of life in my body. I must be honest with you. Xaedrek has the help of a demon, and its presence on Earth is severely limiting my powers. I'd hoped to have found an answer by now. I still mean to keep trying . . . but I can promise no miracle.'

'Can you not return to Shalekahh and kill this demon?' the Queen asked quietly.

'It's indestructible. There would be no point. If there is an answer, I feel it lies at Aludria – but I don't know why. I can offer you no supernatural power, I cannot even far-see for you; the only help I can give is in honing the army to its most efficient, leading them and inspiring them. Anything I *can* do with my own sorcery, I shall do.' Her voice was stronger now, her golden-green eyes shining. 'The Gorethrians have amulin. I can give you nothing similar. But you have already held off the Gorethrians for ten years, because there is a strength in Kristillia that Xaedrek cannot crush. Whatever it is – whether it is bestowed by the moons or simply the passionate desire for freedom – it is more than equal to amulin. My task is to feed that strength, and with all my heart I want to go on helping you. But only – only if you still want me.'

The throne room erupted into a deafening cheer that left no doubt of their feelings. Melkavesh had worked her magic again. She looked sideways at Kharan, with a smile that was almost embarrassed, as if to say, *I did not expect this.* Kharan ran onto the dais and embraced her.

Then everyone was surging forward to greet her, kiss her hand, or kneel to her; even the Kesfalians, who had doubts, even the arrogant Cevandarish. Kharan hung onto her arm through it, and Es Thendil stayed at her other side, trying to speak to her over the noise.

'My lady, I can't tell you how glad I am to see you.' There were tears in his eyes. 'We were all so worried. I couldn't believe you'd deliberately deserted us.'

109

'I would never do that. I love Kristillia, I couldn't leave you. Es Thendil, I don't deserve this.'

'But you do. Your honesty won them. You can't realise how vital it is to have something to inspire us, and they've chosen you, Mellorn.'

'I'll try not to let you down,' she said huskily. 'There's something else I should explain to you. I once made some amulin for Xaedrek, in the hope of stopping him from using humans. I fed my energy directly into the powder, and it worked; but it almost bled me dry. I can't tell you how much I regret helping him, even though it was only false help. I want you to understand that even if I could create something like amulin freely I would not, because it's against my Sorcerer's Oath to misuse the power.'

The King was shaking his head, his face aghast. 'No, no, Mellorn, we would never want you to corrupt your power for our sake. We will survive without amulin or anything like it; the strength of the moons will suffice, as you said. But what did you mean about the "answer" being at the Aludrian Sea?'

'I'm not sure.' She had decided to tell no one about the creatures under the sea, resolved that they would not be used or harmed. 'It's just a feeling. Es Thendil, I have a favour to ask.'

'Anything, my dear.'

'There is a castle there called Heldavrain. There's no one living there except two housekeepers, who told me the Duke and his family left to fight the Gorethrians and never returned.'

'It's true,' the King said sadly. 'I knew the Duke of Heldavrain. A brave man. He and his wife and retainers were slain during one of Xaedrek's previous attempts at invasion.'

'I'm sorry. But is the castle yours?'

'Well, yes – it reverted to the Crown when the Duke died without heirs. Why?'

'Because I would like to go and live there.' Ignoring his startled expression, she continued quickly. 'It would make a perfect School of Sorcery. And it is near to Ehd'rabara. I think I should be there for the invasion.'

'There? Not with us in Charhn?'

'Even I can't be in two places at once.' She smiled, and put her hand on his shoulder. 'Listen, I've been in Charhn for nearly a year. They won't need me here, when they've got you! Xaedrek's bound to concentrate his attack on Ehd'rabara, so I ought to be there.'

'Oh, wonderful,' said Im Nerek, standing next to Kharan.

'Do you have some objection, Battle Marshal?' asked the King.

'Of course not. I said it was wonderful.'

'Oh, Mellorn,' Es Thendil sighed. 'I can't let you go.' She stared at him, dismayed. 'I can't let you go . . . without sending someone with you. Take a hundred of my best soldiers, and whoever else you need to staff Heldavrain. Take them with my blessing.'

Before she could respond, he had turned away to call an end to the Council, requesting them to meet again the following day. It was several minutes before everyone began to file out of the room. As Kharan made to follow Melkavesh off the dais, someone touched her arm and she turned to find the King beside her.

'Kharan, my dear, you are not going to Heldavrain, are you?'

His eyes were so sad that she could hardly bear to reply. 'If Melkavesh goes, I shall go with her. I think Filmoriel will be safer there.'

'What am I going to do without you?'

Kharan glanced over his shoulder and, with a shock, saw the Queen regarding her with a cockatrice glare that seemed to burn into her very soul. It was not An Mora's hatred that distressed her, but the anguish that lay behind it, anguish she had never meant to cause anyone.

Very gently, she extricated her arm from the King's grasp. 'I'm sorry, Es Thendil. It's for the best.'

6

Heldavrain

WHILE LADY LIRURMISH oversaw the construction of
Xaedrek's battle machines, and Falmeryn waited restlessly
in the Circle of Spears, Melkavesh was establishing her
headquarters at Heldavrain.

And in the shadowy intersection between the Planes, Ferdanice and the Lady of H'tebhmella still held each other captive, aware that time on Earth was passing, but with no way of
learning what was happening there. Each grew more desperate, more determined not to let the other go. But the strands
of the sapphire mesh were weakening, breaking one by one,
and Ferdanice was slowly beginning to work his way loose.

No one on Earth knew of their conflict, still less its purpose;
even with far-sight, it was not something that Melkavesh
could have divined. Yet the shock waves of it touched Earth.
In Forluin, an island blessed by its close links with
H'tebhmella, pale blue lightning crazed the deeper blue of
the sky, infusing the inhabitants with a tension that they
could not define. It was not foreboding so much as a vague
sense that something was changing.

In the heart of Forluin, a man and woman walked through
a wood flooded with golden light. They were Falmeryn's
parents, Falin and Arlena. Familiarity with their island's
loveliness never blunted the edge of it, and every day the
Forluinish could view the sweetness of the hills and meadows,
in all their ever-changing moods, as if for the first time. They
loved their land and they loved each other; that made life
simple, and brought them peace.

The Forluinish themselves were a beautiful folk, tall and slim with fair skin and long, shining hair. Foreigners who met them never forgot their radiant faces, the crystal light of their eyes, the aura of gentleness and grace that made them seem almost unearthly. They were long lived and hardly seemed to age, except that their hair turned white when they neared a hundred. Falin, barely half that, was still brown-haired, Arlena silver-blonde.

The Forluinish had everything they could desire, but they were very far from taking their good fortune for granted. It had almost been torn from them once, and since then they had vowed that nothing would be allowed to threaten Forluin again. They worked endlessly to sustain her perfection. And the love they felt for each other was so extreme that the loss of it could almost tear them apart.

'Are you still thinking of Falmeryn?' Falin asked gently.

'I can't help it,' Arlena replied. 'It's over four years since he left, a year since the *Silver Staff* came back without him, but as long as I live I shall never stop – thinking about him, wondering –'

'I know,' he said. 'I know.'

'Oh, why doesn't he come home?' she burst out. Falin pulled her against him, stroked her hair.

'Arlena, he would if he could. You know that.'

She shuddered, fighting tears. 'I can't bear to think that he's dead. I just can't bear it. Falin, I had a very selfish thought – that Estarinel has three grown children, so why couldn't he have lost Farinel, instead of us losing our only child? Unforgivable of me. If we had had ten children, I would have missed Falmeryn as much, and I wouldn't wish this pain on anyone, least of all my brother.'

'Beloved, you're tormenting yourself. There's no need.'

'The worst thing is not knowing. Not knowing what happened to him, if he suffered, and not being able to do anything –'

'Arlena, please stop,' Falin said hoarsely.

A silence poised itself between them, and was shattered by birdsong. She took a ragged breath, and said, 'I'm so sorry, my love. The pain never goes away for either of us.

Most days I can bear it; it's just that today, of all days –'

'It's all right.' He took her arm. 'Come on. Estarinel's waiting for us.'

In another part of the wood, Estarinel and his wife Lilithea stood looking through the shining green canopy at the sky.

'Is something happening, do you think?' she asked.

'I don't know, Lili. I've never seen the sky like this. How does it seem to you?'

'Not frightening . . . but as if something's not quite right . . .'

'. . . with H'tebhmella,' he added thoughtfully.

'If you know something, E'rinel, I wish you'd tell me. There are times when I think you're not here at all, but still half on the Blue Plane. Do you want to go back there?'

He turned to her, and buried his fingers in her luxuriant bronze-brown hair. 'No, Lili. H'tebhmella is exquisite beyond description, but that's the paradox of it. It's too beautiful, and it never changes. I couldn't have stayed there, no one can for long. I belong here with you . . .'

She kissed him, wishing that she did not still need these reassurances from him after all this time. When Estarinel had come home after the Quest of the Serpent, he had been grief-stricken and alienated for a long time. Even now he sometimes seemed distant, as if he were remembering those times, and it still caused her sorrow.

'I did have a dream,' he said after a while.

'Yes, what was it?'

'Something about the Guardians, and that the Lady of H'tebhmella was not on the Blue Plane but in danger. And that Miril could make no one see or hear her.'

Lilithea looked into his gentle dark eyes, worried. 'You've had so many prescient dreams in the past, I shouldn't dismiss it out of hand. What do you think it meant?'

'I've thought about it a lot, but I can't make anything of it. It might just have been . . . memories.' He shook his head, and smiled. 'The prescient dreams I had in the past never made any sense and never helped me at all. It was only

114

afterwards I could say, "Oh, *that* was what it meant"! It's all right. I'm sure there's no danger.'

She slid her arm round his waist. 'Look, there are Falin and Arlena. Shall we go into the grove?'

They entered a circle of young trees, named Sinmiel's Grove, where a number of men and women had already gathered. Among them were Estarinel's son Farinel, his daughters Arviel and Filmorwyn, and his mother Filmorwen. He saw his younger sister, Lothwyn, run across to hug Arlena. His friends Edrien and Luatha were also there, and many others who remembered the coming of the Serpent.

Estarinel and Lilithea went round the circle, kissing and embracing them all. Then, one by one, everyone went to place flowers on a small black obelisk in the centre of the grove, and when that was done they stood in silent vigil around it.

It was twenty-seven years since the accursed day when the Serpent M'gulfn attacked them and laid Forluin to waste, twenty-six years since Medrian, Ashurek and Estarinel had slain it. Then the waters of H'tebhmella itself had flowed across Forluin and helped to heal the stricken land, washing away the last traces of the Worm's poison.

It had been a time of darkness and the most racking despair, yet it had ended and Forluin, as if by a miracle, had survived to become even lovelier than before. There were even some, slain by the Serpent, who had returned to life – Arlena, Lothwyn and their mother among them. But others had not returned. Estarinel had lost his father, Falin his whole family, and other loved ones had also perished. It was to mourn them that they held this yearly vigil; to mourn, and to remind themselves that Forluin's peace was dearly bought and infinitely precious.

With warm sunlight shining through the leaves and the chirruping of the birds, the grove seemed sublimely tranquil. It was hard to believe that Falin's house had once stood here, and that the Serpent itself had crushed it and lain malignly on the ruins before continuing its ghastly flight. All trace of defilement had been removed and the trees planted in its stead, but the obelisk stood there as a grim memorial.

Eventually Estarinel spoke. 'We can never forget that the Serpent came. We must remember it not to cause ourselves sorrow, but to celebrate our present joy and safeguard Forluin for all time.'

Then he saw that Arlena was weeping, and went across to her. He hugged her, meeting Falin's helpless gaze over her head.

'I was thinking of our father,' she said. 'He was so like you, E'rinel, and there was so much of him in Falmeryn as well. It's just . . . It's bad enough to think of those who died when the Serpent came. But to lose Falmeryn now, years later, when we thought nothing more could go wrong – it's so hard to bear. Oh, I am a fool. I should be strong, so why am I frightened?'

'You mustn't be. The Serpent is dead, and nothing can ever be that bad again. We're all here with you, Arlena, and there's nothing to fear.' Estarinel spoke sincerely, but when he looked up at the sky, the weird electricity awoke a sense of unease, the image of the Lady of H'tebhmella in danger. If anything should happen to the Blue Plane, what would become of Forluin?

Kharan had dreaded the journey to Heldavrain, but it proved to be nowhere near as arduous as she had feared. The horrible journey she and Melkavesh had made from Shalekahh to Charn was fresh in her mind as they set off; but with a great convoy of horses, soldiers and pack animals, plenty of food and a proper camp each night, they travelled in tolerable comfort.

The Kristillian horses were heavy animals who compensated for their ugliness with a proud carriage and sweet temperament. In colour they ranged from pale gold to black through every shade of brown, and a herd of them running wild across the fells was a glorious sight. Kharan's own mount was a brown gelding named Sabil, Melkavesh's a mare named Faara. For her second journey to Aludria, she had decided to ride a non-spectral mount at conventional speed.

The Malmanish, a slender folk with dark silver skin, had their own lightly built greys which they rode without bit or saddle. The Mangorians were mounted on their reptilian U'adruils, with the rest of the tribe marching barefoot as they had from Mangorad. They still refused to mix with the other Vardravians. As the King had promised, he had provided one hundred of the best Kristillian cavalry, and the rest of the column was made up of foot-soldiers, mainly Kristillian but with representatives of most of the other races. There were roughly equal numbers of men and women, around five hundred people in all.

An atmosphere of excitement pervaded the convoy, infecting even the sour Mangorians after a time. Melkavesh had lost none of her inspirational glamour for them and there was a feeling of being special, the enchantress's own chosen ones.

Kharan rode at Melkavesh's side with Filmoriel in a sling across her chest, Sabil's rhythmic gait lulling her into daydreams. Thoughts of war seemed a thousand miles away. She had not really wanted to uproot herself from Charhn, but now they were on their way – and Melkavesh happy again – the anxieties that had oppressed her began to lift. She could even remember her last meeting with Afil Es Thendil with sadness rather than agony.

Alone, he had clung to her like a child, yet he had not tried to prolong the moment when they must part for the last time. He had done his best to hide his unhappiness, spare her feelings.

'Do you know what I'll remember most about you?' he had said. 'The way you were always saying, "you're a nice man", or "you're a sweet man". Never "I love you." But you said it with such tenderness that it almost didn't matter.'

'The Queen loves you, Es Thendil,' she replied. 'Please try to forget about me, for her sake. She does know about us and I rather think she'll kill me if I stay any longer.'

'She would never do that. She keeps everything inside. She said something strange to me, you know . . .' He rubbed at his beard. 'It's the only time she's ever mentioned you directly. She asked if you were leaving with Mellorn, and when I said yes, she said, "I wish she were truly leaving. But

117

if she were on the other side of the world she would still be here, like a ghost between us."'

Kharan winced at the memory of the Queen's eyes, the brutally suppressed misery in her bearing. 'Oh, Es Thendil, don't do that to her.'

'I'll try not to,' he said sadly. 'I do know what it's like to compete with a ghost, my dear.'

At that she looked away, stared at her twined fingers. 'I know. I'm sorry. You say you can't talk to her, but I don't think you even try. If you did, you might grow to love her.'

He smiled regretfully. 'I am not a monster to her, Kharan. But I will try. For your sake, I will try.'

Not for mine. For hers, she wanted to say, but could not. Anyway, it was over now. She would always think of him with affection, but he had not even touched the emptiness left in her soul when she had lost Falmeryn.

At Heldavrain, there would be a new beginning.

Melkavesh had already described the castle to her in detail; it was roughly oval in shape with a central courtyard and two watch-towers, one above the gate and one overlooking the sea. There was stabling for forty horses, and ample room for 300 people inside. The Mangorians would prefer to make their own camp on the shore, as would the Malmanish, so that removed the problem of overcrowding. Where the rock bridge joined the cliff, there were several acres of gardens and orchards, sheltered partly by the distant hills and partly by walls. They had been allowed to run wild, but Melkavesh was full of plans for recultivating them, for making Heldavrain independent of Charhn . . . Kharan listened in a dream, not really taking any of it in.

And nothing Melkavesh said could have prepared her for her first sight of it.

The castle came into view as they approached along the shoreline from the south, with the Aludrian Sea rippling like a sheet of golden glass on their left. A massed cheer went up at the sight of it rising sheer from the brilliant water, the watch-towers silhouetted against the sky. As they drew closer, they saw that it was built of no ordinary rock, but one that had the quality of reflecting and intensifying whatever

118

colours were around it, so that on the shore side it glowed emerald green, blending into sunset hues where it faced the sea. The battlements were edged with violet fire. It was immense and ineffably beautiful, with light-patterns playing constantly on the gilded walls.

They paused to gaze at it for a long time.

Later, as they filed along the bridge and under the deep gateway to the courtyard, Thaufa En Mianna and her daughter En Faliol came out to meet them. Melkavesh had told them she would return. They greeted her with a cool friendliness, but when they saw Filmoriel they smiled for the first time and welcomed Kharan like a long-long sister.

Breathless, Kharan turned to Melkavesh and said, 'I don't know how to explain this, but I feel as if I have come home.'

The Sorceress smiled. 'That's just how I felt, the first time I came here. It is home now, Kharan.'

Time fled by at disconcerting speed, leaving no time to brood on the future. The two Kristillian women had only been able to keep a small part of the castle habitable, so there was much work to be done. Everyone in Melkavesh's small army was allotted a task, as carpenter, cook, groom or craftsman, under the supervision of Kharan and En Mianna. The Mangorians hunted for food in the hills while the Kesfalians began to tend the gardens. Until the castle became self-sufficient, Melkavesh had also arranged with Prince Rar An Tolis for supplies to be sent from Ehd'rabara. Heldavrain had come to life, and was barely recognisable as the deserted husk it had been.

Melkavesh commandeered two large rooms overlooking the sea for her own use, one as a bedchamber and one as an office. Kharan took an adjoining room, with En Mianna and her daughter – the only people she trusted to help her take care of Filmoriel – next door. The rooms were large and draughty with uneven floors, the furniture sparse and of a red-brown wood so heavy that it could hardly be moved. The hangings were faded, the beds and couches threadbare. The plumbing also was primitive by Shalekahh's fastidious standards, but at least each chamber had a side room with a water-pump, a stone bath and a fire to heat the water. With repair, they would be reasonably comfortable.

Each room had two long windows through which light and sea reflections streamed in, to be soaked up and given back as a richer glow by the walls. The whole castle was built of this strange stone, that seemed to have no colour except that which fell upon it. So, through the course of a day the chambers would blend from silver to violet, blue to flame, and back to silver as twilight fell; and in darkness they would take on the blush of fire and candlelight.

When she had been Xaedrek's mistress, Kharan had spent her days virtually idle and had had no friends. *However could I have thought I was happy?* Now she had countless friends and was endlessly busy . . . yet there was still a sense of something missing. In the evenings she would gaze out of the window, with Filmoriel sitting on the deep sill, and try to imagine living at Heldavrain for ever.

She could not. The war stood between her and the future like Melkavesh's terrifying Wall.

'Well, you seem happy enough, my love,' she said to her daughter. 'You're lucky you're too young to know what's happening. I wish we could have gone to Forluin. We'd all have been safe there. You'd have liked it there. I suppose you are Forluinish, in a way . . .' The baby looked at her with Falmeryn's eyes, and smiled.

Filmoriel was growing fast. Born prematurely and sustained by sorcery until she was large enough to survive, she was still small for her age. But she seemed to thrive at Heldavrain, and within six months she was walking and uttering her first words.

One day Melkavesh took Kharan and Filmoriel onto the beach, a strange quietness about her as if she wanted to tell them something and could not. When Kharan made to put her daughter on the sand, she said quickly, 'Don't let her go near the water's edge. I've warned everyone against it.'

'Why?'

'There are . . . creatures in the water. The first time I came here, one seized me and I almost drowned.'

'Gods,' Kharan exclaimed, snatching Filmoriel up again. 'What sort of creatures?'

'I think . . . I think they meant no harm. They took me because they were curious. But if it happened to anyone else I'd never forgive myself.'

'What on Earth are you talking about?'

Melkavesh paused. 'I've told no one else this, Kharan. They have a kind of supernatural energy, like mine. They were as primitive as shellfish in a way, yet there was contact between us. I can't far-see, and yet I can still touch the minds of those beings – if you could call them minds. It's a kind of limited far-sight, in a way.'

Kharan looked at her, worried. 'You're not making much sense.'

'It doesn't matter.' She smiled ruefully, and pointed up at the castle. 'Look at that, a School of Sorcery without any students. If only there were already some latent Sorcerers on Earth, I might have had an army of them by now, and Xaedrek wouldn't have stood a chance. But there's only me – and a baby. Whatever is limiting my power is also damping the power in others.'

Kharan did not answer. Filmoriel was twisting round in her arms, staring at something she could not see. Kharan tried to restrain her, saying, 'What is it, darling? What can you see?'

Quite clearly, the child replied, 'Miril.'

'What did she say?' Melkavesh exclaimed.

'Miril,' Kharan said with a shrug. 'Now stop it. There's nothing there.'

'Gone now,' said Filmoriel, and promptly fell asleep.

'Where on Earth did she hear that name?' said Melkavesh. 'Miril was a bird – or at least, she had the form of a bird, but she was a mystical being said to be the opposite of the Serpent. Even the Guardians didn't understand exactly what she was. She died with the Serpent. My father said she was the most beautiful creature he'd ever seen.'

'I know who Miril is. Falmeryn told me.' Kharan looked at Melkavesh and added, 'He also said that Estarinel saw her in Forluin after the Serpent's death – alive.'

121

'That's impossible. Ashurek saw her die, just like a mortal bird.'

'So Estarinel was wrong?'

'He must have been. I don't know.' She picked up a stone and hurled it across the water. 'Oh, Kharan, I thought I knew everything when I came to this Earth. The longer I'm here, the less I understand. I have dreams about the moons that seem to be telling me everything yet tell me nothing; and they always end with a little girl and a bird. And all I know is that the child is Filmoriel and the bird is Miril.'

'I don't know how you can assume it's Filmoriel,' Kharan said angrily.

'Oh, come on.' She reached out to touch the child's rapidly growing mop of hair, a rich deep red that was almost plum. 'Where else have you ever seen hair of such a colour? And I've been dreaming of her since long before she was born. She's the first and only latent Sorceress I've found, but I think there's more to her even than that. Perhaps she really can see Miril when no one else can.'

Kharan turned away, speechless with anger. She hated it when Melkavesh spoke like this, as if Filmoriel were some extraordinary being to be used as a piece in a cosmic puzzle. But she was not. She was her daughter, all she had left of Falmeryn, and Melkavesh had no right to assume anything.

Autumn came, heavy with fruit and warm rains, followed by a dry, mild winter. Almost before they knew it, it was spring again, and they had been at Heldavrain close on a year.

Messengers came and went between the castle, Ehd'rabara and Charn, reporting that there was still no sign of imminent invasion. Each day that passed without news increased their tension like the slow winding of a spring, and through it they had to sustain normal life. Haeth Im Nerek was already at Ehd'rabara with Prince Rar An Tolis. More refugees were arriving in Kristillia every day, eager to join the fight. Melkavesh, wearing her mask of vibrant optimism, swift-travelled to and from Ehd'rabara to liaise with the Battle Marshal and learn as much as she could from the Kristillian scouts who had ventured into Omnuandria to spy.

They were brave people. Of those who went out, few returned.

Melkavesh went herself a few times, under her cloak of invisibility, but learned very little. There were only the usual Gorethrian troops on the far side of the Omnuandrix, nothing that foreshadowed invasion. If anything they were unnaturally quiet, and had even stopped trying to breach the blockades between Ehd'rabara and the Aludrian Sea.

After all this time, her far-sight still had not returned. And now she felt a more sinister change; her power was slowly becoming harder to summon, more of a drain on her strength each time she used it. She began to have nightmares that Ah'garith was sucking the blood from her; and her blood had turned to a ghastly white ichor.

The feeling of helpless terror was returning. Most of the time she could control it, but when she was tired it would bubble to the surface and almost swamp her. It was terrible to know that even her last resort, swift-travelling back to Shalekahh to spy on Xaedrek in person, was lost now. From her short forays, she knew that she simply would not make it.

And even if I could, there is still Ah'garith. She would sense my presence. The way I feel, she might even destroy me.

Twice she dived down to look on the eerie splendour of the Aludrians, but learned no more of them than she had the first time. They offered her no secrets, no power, only themselves. To have tried to take more from them would have been a violation. On the second dive she almost drowned again, and she did not risk a third.

If the deterioration continued, she guessed that by the time the battle came she would have no power left at all. Despair crushed her in its leaden fingers, but each time she would fight back against it, thinking, *I am Ashurek's daughter. If I cannot go into battle as a Socreress, then let it be as a warrior.*

It was summer again when Xaedrek's scheme bore fruit.

The heat, Kharan thought, was never as oppressive as in Gorethria, nor punctuated by such violent storms, but it made everything seem as slow-moving as honey. She stood in her room, her elbows on the window-sill and her chin in her hands, staring out at the blazing white-gold plain that was the sea. En Mianna and En Faliol were with her, talking idly, while Filmoriel played happily on a rug at her feet. All was so peaceful that the idea of war seemed impossible, Gorethria just a fevered dream.

Then she saw the black dot on the water. It was hard to see against the dazzle, and for a moment she thought it was just her imagination. Then En Faliol exclaimed, 'Look, a boat!'

'Are you sure?' Kharan said. 'Melkavesh – Mellorn will be furious if anyone's gone out on the sea.'

'No one has, I'm sure,' said En Mianna. 'That boat is coming in to land – Fliya knows from where.'

'By the Lady, you're right! En Faliol, would you stay with Filmoriel? And En Mianna, find Mellorn quickly, and tell her. I'm going down to the beach.'

By the time Kharan had raced down the endless staircases, across the courtyard and bridge, and picked her way down the cliff, a crowd had already gathered. Two Kristillians were wading through the tide to pull the vessel onto the sand. It was hardly more than a coracle. In it sat a small dark-skinned woman, dressed in a black tunic and trousers.

Kharan shouldered her way through the crowd to get a better view. The Kristillians were helping the woman out of the boat now, and she almost collapsed as she stood up. Her hair hung over her shoulders like seaweed, and now Kharan could see how weak and thin she was, and how familiar, how very familiar –

She stared dumbstruck as the warriors half carried the woman up the beach. She was like a little burnt stick between them. Kharan's heart was pounding, her breath suspended as she came closer and took in every impossible detail of the woman's dappled-bronze skin, the pale amber eyes unfocused with exhaustion.

The Kristillians halted in front of her and the woman looked at her without expression. Just looked, as she had done so often in the past.

'Anixa,' Kharan whispered. 'Is it? Gods, how did you get here?'

There were footsteps on the beach behind them. Anixa's eyes drifted past Kharan and then an expression did appear on her face; one of pure anguish. Everyone turned to see Melkavesh hurrying towards them, her hair like a liquid flame.

'What's going on?' she called.

Kharan seized her arm. 'Mel, it's Anixa.'

Melkavesh stopped dead, even more shocked than Kharan. 'By the Serpent, it really is. What are you doing here? Oh, never mind – just bring her inside, she looks dreadful.'

'No,' said Anixa. 'Lady Melkavesh, I – please would you – help me – inside.'

The Sorceress looked at her, puzzled. 'Yes, of course.' She waved the two men aside, and went to lift Anixa's slight frame in her arms. A second later, something strange happened. Kharan saw her mouth open as if in shock, and then she dropped – *dropped* – Anixa on the sand. For a moment she bent over her, tugging at something on the Kesfalian's hand, and Kharan had the impression of some horrible, unspoken communication between them.

'He made me –' Anixa choked.

Melkavesh lurched away from her then, her eyes blank as if her sanity had evaporated. 'Bastard,' she said. And then she turned and fled back to the castle as if a demon was pursuing her.

'Why the hell did you run away from her like that?' Kharan demanded angrily, standing in the doorway of the office. Anixa was now tucked up in bed in the small room next to En Mianna's, but the Sorceress had not been near her. She sat stiffly behind her desk, giving Kharan a baleful glare that anyone who had known Ashurek would have recognised and fled from.

'I don't wish to discuss it,' she said shortly.

'What on Earth is the matter with you? That's Anixa lying half dead in that room – Anixa, who looked after us and

125

protected us and in effect saved our wretched lives! Don't you understand, she has travelled all the way from Shalekahh on her own to find us? Can't you see how desperate to escape she must have been? I can't get her to tell me anything, but the only reason can be that Xaedrek found out she sheltered us. She's in terrible distress, and all you can do is throw her about and then shun her as if she was carrying a plague!'

'Kharan, will you get out of here.' Melkavesh stood up, her face as impassive and deadly as a cobra's. 'The last thing I need is a speech from you. If I had any sense, I'd have thrown Anixa back in the sea.'

Kharan stared at her, so stunned by this that she could not think, let alone reply. She stalked out, slamming the door with a bang that reverberated along the corridor.

Back in Anixa's room, she went to the bed and anxiously watched the shallow heaving of the Kesfalian's chest as she lay with one hand curled limply on the pillow in a tangle of hair. Once she had been so self-contained and enigmatic that Kharan had been almost afraid of her. Now, for all she was older than Kharan, she seemed like a child.

Thaufa En Mianna was seated by the bed, watching over her. Twilight glimmered ashen-mauve through the windows, and a candle flame gleamed on a bowl of soup lying untouched on a dresser.

'I can get her to take nothing, not even water,' said En Mianna unhappily.

'Perhaps she just needs to rest.' Kharan bit her lip and felt an upsurge of rage. 'En Mianna, would you go and fetch Mellorn? I couldn't make her come, but she might listen to you. I don't know what's wrong with Anixa, but I'm sure only Mellorn can heal her.'

En Mianna returned shortly, saying that the enchantress was now nowhere to be found. Kharan sat at Anixa's side with the anger congealing to a cold, sick fear. Anixa was dying. Melkavesh could have saved her, but Melkavesh was behaving like – like a Gorethrian.

'Lady Kharan?' The Kesfalian's eyes fluttered open, her voice was reed-thin. Kharan shivered at the deferential address, which brought back memories of the Gorethrian court, when Anixa had been her dressmaker – her servant in effect.

'Yes, I'm here,' she said gently, taking her hand. 'You're safe now. It's all right.'

'No. It's not.' Her fingers tightened on Kharan's, as thin and tough as a bird's claws. 'Would that I'd never found you. Fliya, have mercy.'

'Hush.' She stroked Anixa's forehead. 'I remember when I was ill and you looked after me. Now we're the other way round, I shall be just as much a bully in making you rest and eat.'

'I can't. Not while he can see –' An awful shuddering racked her, and her eyes bulged like yellow moons. Kharan was struck by a dreadful revelation. Anixa was not merely suffering the aftermath of a horrific experience; the experience was still going on.

The spasm ended. Anixa's eyes fell shut. Her breathing was no more than a tiny intermittent sigh, and Kharan saw in her the overwhelming malaise that only death could relieve. She recognised it, because she had felt it herself.

'Anixa, please tell me what's wrong. Let us help you.' There was no reply. *Don't die, I beg of you don't die*, she thought. There was a hot mesh of misery tightening in her stomach – and at the centre of it was the knowledge that only one person could be at the root of such torment. Xaedrek.

'Damn you, Xaedrek,' she muttered between rigid jaws. 'And damn you, Melkavesh.'

Thaufa En Mianna crossed the room, graceful as a dancer, to pull a curtain and light a lamp. As she turned, Kharan saw her pause and stare at the doorway, and she looked round to see Melkavesh standing there.

It took all Kharan's self-control to restrain an explosion of rage. 'What the hell do you think you're playing at?' She compressed the passion of a shout into a rough whisper. 'Where've you been? Waiting for her to die? Hoping?'

Melkavesh did not reply. Her arms folded, her face an inscrutable mask, she went woodenly to the bed and looked

127

down at Anixa. At once the Kesfalian's eyes peeled open and stared back with an unsettling larval glow.

After a minute or so, Melkavesh said, 'Well, he must know you've failed by now.'

'Mel, what is this?' Kharan said, seizing her arm. 'You're behaving as if you've lost your mind. For the moons' sake, heal her! You must!'

'Calm down. You don't understand. En Mianna, would you leave us, please?'

The Kristillian gave her a disapproving glance, but obeyed without argument. As she left, Kharan said, '*You* don't understand, if you don't do something to help Anixa *now*, I am going to –'

'Just listen to me.' The words, though quiet, seemed to hit Kharan like an electric shock. It was like arguing with a statue. Melkavesh's will was stronger and, as always, she was forced to defer to it. 'I have not lost my mind. What do you think this is?'

She showed Kharan a silver ring which she was holding carefully in a piece of leather. When she pressed a small stone with her fingernail, a minute needle clicked out on its upper surface.

'It looks like a Gorethrian device.'

'I took it off Anixa's hand. There's poison on it, daelammion by the smell – you know, the stuff that kills with a single drop? Another split second and I would have been dead.'

Kharan had gone dizzy. 'How did you know?'

'Evidently my prescience has not completely deserted me. The moment I touched her I knew what she meant to do, and I knew that Xaedrek had sent her . . . and that he could see me through her eyes.' She ignored Kharan's gasp. 'That's why I ran away and wouldn't come near her. Then I thought, what does it matter? He knows where I am, the damage is done. Isn't it so, Anixa?'

The Kesfalian turned her head from side to side, her face contorted with shame and misery.

'Well, Anixa, haven't you anything to say?'

'Stop it!' Kharan cried. 'You're tormenting her.'

128

'I don't mean to do that. I just want to know . . .' Melkavesh leaned over and held Anixa's chin, forcing her to keep still. 'How could you do this? I know what the Kesfalians are always saying, that I will cause some kind of disaster, but was that vague prophecy enough for you to sell yourself to Xaedrek and betray me?'

'Melkavesh!'

'How could you, Anixa? How could you?'

'*No!*' The word emerged as a scream as she pushed herself up off the pillow. 'I would not have betrayed you for anything – Fliya help me – I had no choice. It was Irem Ol Thaniol . . .'

'Who?' said Melkavesh in astonishment. 'How do you know of him?'

Anixa curled up on her side and began to convulse with painful sobs as if the last remnants of her spirit were being coughed out of her. Kharan had never seen her weep before. She felt like murdering Melkavesh herself.

'Look,' she said, shaking the Sorceress's arm, 'if you heal her, maybe she'll be able to talk to you.'

For the first time, her words got through. 'Yes.' The Sorceress sat down on the edge of the bed. 'You're right, Kharan.' She bent low over the thin form, one hand pressed to Anixa's forehead and the other to her heart, and the silver-blue flames of healing began to flow over them both. Kharan watched anxiously. Presently Anixa turned onto her back, her face peaceful, and Melkavesh drew away with a sigh of exhaustion. 'Would you bring some water?'

Kharan did so, and Melkavesh propped up the Kesfalian and got her to take a drink.

'Will she be all right?'

'I think so,' Melkavesh said grimly. 'She was exhausted and half starved from the journey. But as for the harm Xaedrek's done her, I don't know . . . I've calmed her as much as I can.' She settled her back onto the pillow and said gently, 'I'm sorry, Anixa. I shouldn't have been so harsh with you. But will you please try to tell me what happened to bring you to this?'

She nodded, quiet now but unhappy. 'It was my own fault, Lady Melkavesh.' Haltingly, she explained how she had been

129

fitting Xaedrek for a robe, passed out with fear at the sight of Ah'garith, and been taken to the room where Irem Ol Thangiol was lying ill. 'I had to try to rescue him, for the sake of the fellowship between Kesfaline and Kristillia. It was foolish. Xaedrek was bound to catch us. He imprisoned me with Ol Thangiol and left us together, terrified, until we could not bear to be separated.' As she went on to describe the experiment with the ichor, Melkavesh's expression became very sombre.

'Xaedrek's damnable far-sight,' she muttered. 'What happened after?'

'It wore off, but it left me feeling . . . filthy. And Xaedrek was so pleased . . .' She shuddered. 'He said I could go free. I refused. I wanted to stay with Ol Thangiol . . . When I was in Kesfaline the Gorethrians slew my husband and son, but instead of fighting I went meekly as a slave to Shalekahh and won status by sewing their cursed robes . . .'

'You had to survive.' Melkavesh took her hand gently.

'I'm trying to explain that I had loved no one since losing my family, until I met Ol Thangiol. Xaedrek knew. I thought I was defying him by staying, but when he thought of a new use for me all he had to say was, "Do this, or Ol Thangiol will suffer."'

'Then he gave Ol Thangiol a huge dose of amulin, and drew blood from his veins, and made me drink it. I didn't understand why at first. Then he explained that it made a kind of mind link, so that whatever I saw, Ol Thangiol would see it too, and report it to Xaedrek.'

'He did the same thing once with an eagle,' said Melkavesh. 'Do you remember, Kharan? It tracked us across the Emethrians and tried to kill us.'

'How could I ever forget?' Kharan muttered.

'The blood did something horrible to me,' Anixa went on. 'Whenever I closed my eyes I could see a golden blur that I knew was you, Lady Melkavesh. Xaedrek told me to focus on it and follow it until it led me to you. Every day of the journey I had to drink more of the blood so the effect did not wear off. When I found you, I was to kill you. And if I failed, he said Irem Ol Thangiol would pay.'

130

'The bastard,' Kharan whispered, her face stricken. 'The vile bastard.'

'I knew, Anixa, the moment I touched you. Xaedrek couldn't fool me that easily. Now listen, you're safe here. Everything is going to be all right.'

'But it isn't. I've failed.' Anguish shone in her eyes. 'Ah'garith is tormenting Ol Thangiol. I am mind linked to him, and I feel everything he suffers –'

'Gods.' Melkavesh now looked as sick as Kharan felt. She gripped the woman's hand tighter. 'Look, the far-sight effect will wear off soon. Then you'll be free of it.'

'No – I must take more, or Xaedrek –'

'You will not. I shall destroy any of the blood you've brought with you, and any more daelammion as well.'

'But Ol Thangiol –'

'Anixa, be sensible; what is the point of Xaedrek's torturing him if you are no longer aware of it?'

Anixa turned her head away, squeezing her eyes shut. Her desolation broke Kharan's heart. 'And when the link is broken, I can send him back no comfort, either. He'll have no one, nothing.'

'It will be all right, Anixa.' Melkavesh's voice barely held steady. 'Xaedrek is not vindictive. He blames himself when he fails, not others.'

'But that doesn't stop them suffering.'

'I'd help Ol Thangiol if I could. When the war's over and Xaedrek dead, I'll do all I can to find him.' She looked into the Kesfalian's amber eyes as if trying to see along the mind link, see Xaedrek himself through Irem Ol Thangiol's eyes – just as she had once done with the eagle. It was another way to far-see, but she did not have the energy to pursue it, nor the stomach for another taste of the Wall. She only said, 'If Xaedrek can hear me, he had better know that this futile attempt on my life has only made it more certain that I will destroy him.'

Anixa broke the gaze, and said with strangely forlorn self-possession, 'Forgive me, my lady. I would rather have died than betrayed you in this way. Perhaps it is better that I die, than live with this burden of shame.'

'No, Anixa. None of it is your fault. If anyone's, it's mine.' Melkavesh stroked her forehead. 'I can't let you go back to Shalekahh, but you'll be safe here. Now, will you try to get some sleep? Kharan will sit with you. Gods, you poor thing.'

She and Kharan met each other's eyes. There was peace between them now, and a grim understanding that needed no words. Anixa's arrival seemed to presage a dark future, making them only too aware of the invisible chain of days that was winding them relentlessly towards war.

7

Fliya's Path

'How LONG have I been here now, Cristan?' Falmeryn asked, squinting against the platinum blaze of the sun.

'I don't know, but it seems an eternity when you ask me that question every day,' the astronomer replied gloomily.

'Not every day, surely?' Falmeryn said with a rueful smile. They moved into the shade of the orchard and sat down against a tree. The valley, lying in a swirl of green and blue and russet, as ever belied the savagery of the world outside. 'It's more than two and a half years, and there's still no sign of Ferdanice.'

'Someone who'd been outside came back this morning, and when the sages heard what he had to say, they put a ban on anyone else entering or leaving the Circle. Did you see him?'

'Yes. Apparently there are now so many Imperial troops massing in the Imhayan Hills that the invasion of Kristillia must be imminent. If I don't go soon, it'll be too late for the enchantress to do anything with the moon stone.'

'Well, Falmeryn, you have a choice. Either defy the ban and join the fight – if you can find your way out – or stay here in safety until it's over. I recommend the latter. But resign yourself to the fact that that treacherous brute Ferdanice is not coming back.' The Kesfalian pulled his hat over his eyes and made to sleep. 'The more I think of him, the more indignant I feel. A Guardian, pretending to be one of us!'

Falmeryn closed his eyes, trying to decide what to do. There seemed no answer. A shadow fell across his lids and he looked up to find a figure, backlit by leafy sunlight, standing in front of him as if it had appeared from nowhere. It was Ferdanice. He sat up, startled, and shook the astronomer's arm.

'Well, Cristan and Falmeryn,' said Ferdanice. 'I am so glad you've found time to stop work and have such an interesting talk.'

He was wearing the brown robe of a sage, and had the same dappled skin and braided black hair. But he was tall and angular, with a heavy-boned face and hollow cheeks. His eyes were like discs of citrine ice.

'Ah, Ferdanice.' Cristan was flustered. 'We were just discussing –'

'I heard. Falmeryn, there are certain matters that I asked you not to discuss with anyone,' he said shortly.

The Forluinishman stood up and faced him. 'Where have you been? You never led me to believe I'd be here close on three years. A few weeks, you said!'

'Nevertheless, that was no reason to break the confidence.' There was a tense, challenging silence between them, and Falmeryn sensed that Ferdanice was in a very unpleasant mood.

'Cristan is the only one I've told. I had to talk to someone. You seemed to have forgotten all about me.'

'I was unavoidably detained. I've had trouble enough coming back here at all, without further trouble from you.' Then his expression became less harsh, and he placed a paternal hand on Falmeryn's shoulder. 'Never mind. The damage is done. You're quite right in saying that if you don't leave now, you will be too late.'

'You mean you want me to leave immediately?' Falmeryn gasped. The idea of escaping the Circle had become so abstract that the reality of it floored him.

'Yes. Go and find yourself some very warm travelling clothes and as much food as you can carry –'

'One moment,' said Cristan sharply. He had scrambled to his feet and was brushing grass and leaves off his robe. 'I have been told some extraordinary things about you, that you are not really human but a Guardian, and that you mean to interfere with our moons. I'd like a straight answer, Ferdanice. Is it true?'

The sage looked exasperated. 'Yes, Cristan, it's true that I am a Grey One, as some like to call us. Please don't look at me as if I were a demon. I haven't planted myself here for the express purpose of harming anyone.'

'Then why deceive us?'

'I chose this as a suitable place to hide the moon stone and watch over it until it was needed. Before you condemn me, ask yourself how the Circle of Spears has remained undetected by the Gorethrians all these centuries?'

Cristan foundered. 'Well, the cliffs – the cave maze –'

'They'd have found a way in eventually. No, Cristan, the Circle is safe because it is under my protection. Are you ready, Falmeryn?'

The astronomer was gaping at him, speechless. Ferdanice began to walk towards the building, then turned back and said, 'As you know everything, you may as well come and help us. We can talk as we go.'

The caves beneath the Circle of Spears were vast and black as night. Cristan's torch seemed to magnify the darkness, sending huge shadows swooping round them with the slightest movement. Although Falmeryn had been here twice before, his previous visits had only sensitised him to the eerie atmosphere, and he felt his anxiety becoming irrational.

As Ferdanice had advised, he had put on leggings, coat and boots of fleece-lined leather. He was uncomfortably warm in them, but shivered at the coldness of the air on his face. There was a pack of food on his back, and a knife at his belt. As soon as they had retrieved the moon stone, Ferdanice would guide him through the short labyrinth and out into the Imhayan hills. At present he felt he would rather face the entire Gorethrian army than another hour in the caves.

'I'm afraid I still don't understand,' said Cristan. He and Ferdanice were leading the way along the tortuous path and Falmeryn followed, listening in silence to their conversation. 'What exactly do you intend to do with the moon stone?'

'I will try to explain, but I must be brief. We haven't much time,' Ferdanice said with measured patience. 'The Guardians are not gods. We don't create the powers of the universe and we don't make the laws which govern them. We are there merely to enforce the laws – or indeed to break them at times. Strictly speaking I should not be interfering as directly as this, but I was alone among the Guardians in anticipating the need for the moon stone. I took advantage of a peculiar conjunction of the Planes some three thousand years ago to pass through to Fliya and bring the Stone to Earth. It has lain dormant ever since, ready for the time when the Serpent M'gulfn would die and a new power awaken within it. Now the moon stone is essential in shaping the Earth's future. Do you understand so far?'

'I'm not sure. Are you saying that you should not really be doing this?'

Ferdanice shrugged. 'Sometimes it is necessary to give mankind a push in the right direction. But there is a limit to how much I can do, which is why I need Falmeryn to take it to where it's needed.'

'Needed – for what?' said Cristan. 'What do you mean about the Serpent, and shaping the future?'

'The great Serpent that once held sway over this Earth was a creature of vast negative energy. It had to be slain before it destroyed the balance and dragged Earth into stagnation. However, its death was only the beginning of the change; the birth pangs are not yet over, as it were. Its destruction released a wild power, the potential for "sorcery", as some call it, but the power is . . . how can I put it . . . out of alignment, obscured. The result is that there are too few real Sorcerers, while others are abusing the energy in a very dangerous way. Although I doubt that she realises it as yet, the enchantress Melkavesh needs the moon stone in order to free the power and bring it to its true potential. To keep the balance.'

'I don't know,' the astronomer muttered. 'I don't know what to think. It sounds as if the result could be cataclysmic. I hope you're going to give her some guidance.'

'We cannot.' Ferdanice sounded almost embarrassed. 'She

136

is part of the power, but the Guardians are outside it. It is up to her to discover what must be done.'

'You mean you don't know? You're setting in motion some huge disruption of the cosmos and you don't know what the result will be?'

'Not as such, but it's for the Earth's good. There is a degree of risk in any change, and overall it will be beneficial.'

'Risk?' They had reached the edge of the chasm, and Ferdanice made much of helping Cristan to climb down the rock face, obviously – Falmeryn thought – hoping to end the conversation. But Cristan was not to be so easily diverted. 'I'm sure the Guardians are wiser than me,' he went on breathlessly, 'but are you sure you really understand what you're doing? You're aware of the moons' prediction that this enchantress may cause some kind of catastrophe, and all I can see is that you're helping her in it. It goes against all our beliefs! We revere the moons – we do not violate them – and to have torn part of Fliya away is a very dangerous sacrilege. I thought you believed it too! But, of course, why should you? You are not one of us.'

'Don't be angry, Cristan,' Ferdanice said, gently persuasive. 'Try to understand. The transition must take place. It's absolutely essential if the Earth is to have a future, and it must not be prevented. Your anxieties are groundless. The moon stone will give the enchantress the power to defeat Xaedrek, if she uses it well. Would you deprive Kesfaline and Kristillia of that, for the sake of an obscure prophecy?'

Falmeryn listened to this with a taut, sick feeling in his stomach. He had already been given the same explanation. Ferdanice sounded so plausible, yet there was always the hardness behind his eyes, his alienness and lack of conscience.

'I don't know,' Cristan said unhappily. 'I won't try to stop you, but I don't like it at all.'

They reached the bottom of the chasm, and torchlight danced on the weird lake of crystal. Ferdanice had given Falmeryn a bronze circlet with a cabochon that lay flat against his forehead and gave out a silver-blue light of its own. It resembled a large opal, but the Guardian had said the light was produced by thousands of tiny, luminescent insects. The beam shone faintly on the grey-white surface, except for one patch of white brilliance.

'The stone of Fliya,' said Ferdanice. His sandals slapped on the rock as he hurried over to it and knelt down. 'Cristan, hold the torch steady. It still isn't quite at the surface.'

'I tried to dig it out, over a year ago,' said Falmeryn. 'I could make no impression on it.'

'No, you wouldn't. But it was a brave effort.' From a bag slung over his shoulder, the sage took a black gemstone and began to score a circle, about a foot in diameter, in the crust. The moon stone gleamed beneath it as if through a pane of ice. When the circle was complete he bore down on one side, but it would not budge. He cursed and scored round it several times more. The gem slowly carved deeper as if the impervious rock had turned to wax.

As he worked, Falmeryn's tension increased. There seemed to be an icy static in the darkness, a sensation like tiny spiders running across his skin. Blue sparks danced in the edge of his vision. At first he thought it was his imagination, but when his hair began to crackle and stand on end, he knew otherwise. Ferdanice glanced up and adopted an air of grave urgency.

'I protected it too well,' he muttered. 'Falmeryn, help me, quickly.' With all their strength they pushed down on the round section, while Cristan hovered anxiously over them. Suddenly it gave with a loud crack and Ferdanice lifted it out, a disc an inch thick. The hollow beneath was filled with a fine, bright dust.

'Oh, no,' said Ferdanice, staring at it. 'It was a solid piece of stone when I first embedded it; the pressure of the rock crystal seems to have crushed it to nothing. Never mind.' He took a square of vellum and a pouch out of his bag and snapped, 'What are you waiting for?'

Hurriedly, Falmeryn began to scoop up the powder and heap it onto the vellum. When they had retrieved as much as they could, the sage tied it into a firm package and slid it into the leather pouch, which he then handed to Falmeryn.

The pouch was not large. It fitted in his cupped hands, but

138

was far heavier than it had any right to be. He weighed it for a moment, then stood up and strapped it securely to his belt.

'Good,' said Ferdanice with relief. 'That's done. Now, a small change of plan about your journey –'

As he spoke, a hiss of blue stars in the darkness made them all jump, and Cristan looked round in alarm. 'What was that?'

'Damn her,' the sage muttered. Then, briskly, 'It's nothing. Cristan, there's no point in you coming any further with us – can you find your way back alone?'

'Yes, of course, but what about the torch?'

'Take it, we don't need it. Please go now.'

The small astronomer hesitated. 'I'm not at all happy about this. I don't blame you, Falmeryn, I just hope the Guardians know what they're doing. Well, goodbye, at last.'

Falmeryn suddenly realised he would not see Cristan again, nor the Circle that had been home for so long. By the time he found something to say, Cristan was already beginning to climb the chasm wall. The unsaid words closed his throat, and the sense of something being unfinished seemed to exacerbate his anxiety.

'Come on, Falmeryn,' said the Guardian. 'Hurry.'

His hand closed like a bone vice on Falmeryn's arm, forcing him to turn reluctantly away from Cristan. The torch flame had left a chain of purple blossoms hanging across his eyes, and soon the only light was the beam from the jewel on his brow.

He said, 'This isn't the way we came. It's not the way to the cave maze, either . . .' He was alarmed by Ferdanice's air of preoccupation, and his unease was fast deepening.

'There is more than one way out of the caves, and this is a better one. It's just somewhat longer.'

'Longer?'

'You can't walk through all those Gorethrian troops. This way you will avoid the worst of it, and have a much better chance. I'd do more for you if I could, but I have – ah – problems to attend to.'

'What do you mean?'

Ferdanice ignored the question. 'Listen, there's less time

than I thought. You will find the enchantress Melkavesh in Charhn. I think they call her Mellorn. You cannot get lost, because there is some stone from the other moon Jaed in the city. The moon stones attract each other. You will find yourself being pulled in a certain direction, and thus drawn to Charhn as if by a thread. Do you understand?'

'In a way, but –'

'Trust me. Now, there's something further you must know. The rock from Jaed fell to Earth some three thousand years ago. That was why I had to bring the substance of Fliya here – to keep the balance, you see? Tell the enchantress she will need stone from both moons. Can you remember that?'

'Yes.'

'Good.' Ferdanice was walking faster now, almost running across the quartz lake. All around them the air seemed to be hissing and singing without sound. The sage swore under his breath.

'What's wrong?' Falmeryn exclaimed. Now there was a sense of the air whirling – or the cave turning while the air remained still. He felt his hair drifting into a cloud, and saw sapphire sparks dancing on the sage's head. Suddenly the whole cavern was alive with light motes; they were even crackling between the fine hairs on his hands.

And now the sparks were converging into streams, spiralling faster and faster as they coalesced into a glittering sphere. The lake was bathed in azure light, such an exquisite contrast to the darkness that Falmeryn was transfixed by it. He was vaguely aware of Ferdanice tugging at his arm, trying to take him in another direction, but whichever way they turned the sphere was still in front of them. They came to a halt, and out of it stepped the Lady of H'tebhmella.

She was tall, unearthly and beautiful as morning, but there was nothing gentle about her. She seemed all fierce anger, with her hair blowing out on an unseen wind, her eyes as pure as diamonds, and her hands enveloped in ice-blue fire.

'Guardian!' she said. Her voice was low, yet it filled the cave like the clear, stern note of a bell.

'Run,' Ferdanice barked at Falmeryn. 'I'll deal with her. Run, I command you!' But Falmeryn had no intention of

140

obeying. He tried to shake the sage off and for a moment they grappled and skidded on the waxy surface. Then the Lady's arm came down between them and Falmeryn found himself lifted as if by a wave of light and cast down a few feet away. He was on his back, with the Lady's awesome form looming above him.

'Ferdanice, you cannot go on evading me,' she was saying. 'You must listen. You have given insufficient thought to what you are doing. The moon stone should never have been brought to Earth.'

'I have heard enough of this argument. I've heard years of it,' Ferdanice replied. 'How dare the H'tebhmellians presume to interfere with our essential business? Go back to the Blue Plane!'

'Do not speak to me of interference. The Grey Ones know full well that they are not meant to intervene physically on Earth. Such meddling has brought disaster in the past. Can you never learn? We of H'tebhmella care for the Earth herself. You care only for the balance of mindless powers. In this case you *must* let things alone, even if it means leaving them less than perfect. I believe that many of your fellows agree with me.'

'Enough.' The Guardian's gaunt frame was vibrant with anger, and Falmeryn had a sudden intuition that the Lady was in danger. He did not think. He simply leapt up and flung himself at Ferdanice.

The sage crumpled beneath him, and there was a dull thud as his skull struck the rock. A moment of terrible stillness followed. Falmeryn levered himself up on his hands, gasping for breath – and saw the hollow-cheeked face beneath him slack and expressionless, the eyes lifeless crescents.

He had killed Ferdanice.

His brain whirling, he stood up shakily to find that the Lady of H'tebhmella was no longer there. The sphere was still spinning before him, and very distant within it he saw figures in pale silhouette, and heard the faint echo of two voices raised in argument. It was impossible to hear what they were saying. The light was fading now, carrying them away to another Plane.

A terrible misery and yearning overwhelmed him. The Blue Plane H'tebhmella was a legendary dimension of tranquillity, sacred to the Forluinish, and he knew the light was an Entrance Point. He had to speak to the Lady. With a last, desperate effort he sprang into the centre of it as if into a bottomless lake.

Solid stone jarred his legs. He fell to his knees, gagging with the pain. He was still in the cave, but he was alone. The Entrance Point had gone, taking the Lady with it.

The shock of what had happened recoiled on him like a snapped bow string, and for a few seconds he could not move under the weight of his despair. When he recovered enough to sit back on his heels, the light on his brow illuminated the body of Ferdanice.

'Gods,' Falmeryn muttered, shuddering. He leapt to his feet, yelling, 'Cristan! Cristan, are you still there?' There was no answer. He bowed his head. 'Gods, Ferdanice, I only meant to stop you. Not to kill you . . .'

'You did not,' a thin voice cut in. His heart lurched in terror and he turned, shaking, to see who – or what – had spoken.

The voice had not emanated from the corpse. It had come from a gauzy figure standing a few feet away. It was small and slight and shone with a faint ashen light of its own, and he felt sure that if he tore the gauze away there would be no human flesh underneath.

'Ferdanice?' he gasped.

'Yes, it's me,' the figure replied. 'I'm sorry if my appearance alarms you. This is my true form – or one of them, at least.'

'I thought I'd killed you.'

'Nothing of the sort. I chose that moment to vacate the human body so that I could fight the Lady on equal terms.'

Falmeryn took this in, and his shock was swept away by a mixture of relief and fury. 'The Lady!' he cried. 'What have you done to her? If you've harmed her, so help me, I *will* find a way to kill you!'

'Please, please.' The Grey One raised his gauzy hands. 'I meant fight as in debate. I only required her to return to her own Plane, which she has done. She is perfectly safe, and I am far too lenient, considering it was her who delayed me all this time. I will have to ensure she does not trouble us further.'

'Trouble us?' Falmeryn gasped. 'I've a mind to fling this accursed moon stone into the nearest abyss. I was prepared to give you the benefit of the doubt against Cristan – but if the Lady herself says this is wrong, it's her I believe – not you.'

'You cannot refuse me. You gave your word to go if I spared Raphon,' the Guardian said softly.

'Oh, yes, you sent Raphon back to Hrunnesh – after he was so weak he could hardly have completed your errand anyway. I was manipulated into agreeing, and you know it.' There was an ominous silence. He added, 'Now I suppose there will be another bargain. Either I take the Stone, or you'll leave me here to perish.'

'I could say something like that.' In a more conciliatory tone, he said, 'Listen, my friend, we've had this argument before. The Lady only objects, like the Kesfalians, because she is over-cautious and does not fully understand. As a timeless being from a timeless domain, she fears any kind of change, even when it is for the best.'

'But you said even the Grey Ones can't predict what the result of the change will be. Perhaps she knows and has been trying to tell you! Perhaps you already know,' he added accusingly, 'and are hiding the truth. You've pointed out yourself that the Guardians' view of good and evil is so grey that they can barely tell them apart. What is not bad to you may be disastrous to us.'

'That's not exactly what I said.' The Guardian's tone became menacing, not quite human. 'And I have had enough of this conversation. I would strike you down here and take the stone myself if I could, but I've already overstepped my limits, and I have business in another domain. So you are going to Charn for me, and that is an end of it.'

Suddenly the sense of being utterly alone in an alien presence came strongly to Falmeryn, and the diaphanous figure of the Grey One enlarged to fill his whole field of vision. The atmosphere reverberated with cobweb whispers. 'Must I force you? Or will you be sensible and keep your word?'

Falmeryn withstood the aura for as long as he could, but it overcame him. It was not a sense of evil that defeated him, but an overwhelming blank indifference that seemed to suck all the joy from his spirit. Never again, having glimpsed that infinite grey ocean, would he say that neutrality had no power.

'Very well. I'll keep my word.'

At once the Guardian resumed more normal proportions, but the whispering went on and the cavern thronged with half-seen pale figures.

'Good. Make sure you do, because my time on Earth is over and I am relying on you. Don't be pessimistic, my friend, think of it as a way to defeat Xaedrek. Now my brethren summon me and I must go.'

'Wait!' cried Falmeryn, alarmed. 'You must guide me out of the caves, at least!'

'I told you, follow the pull of the moon stone. Let it be your guide and it will lead you to safety.' His voice was fading to a whisper, indistinguishable from the rest. He raised an arm to point, and the other figures lifted their arms in perfect synchronisation as if they were a myriad reflections of one being. '*Hurry*,' they sighed. '*There is so little time.*' They froze in that attitude like figures sketched on a scrim, and then they all fell to ashes and blew away into the depths of the caves.

Falmeryn was alone. Beyond the pool of light cast by the opal, the blackness seemed immense and heavy with the billions of tons of rock that enclosed it. Fear surged inside him, and only the knowledge that panic would achieve nothing enabled him to fight it down. Trembling, only just in control, he began to walk slowly across the smooth expanse of crystal.

Let the moon stone guide you . . .

At once he became aware that a strange magnetic drag was taking him in a precise direction. The sensation was so disconcerting that he almost lost his footing, and he soon found that if he tried to resist the pull, the pouch became impossibly heavy. So, the Guardian had told him the truth about one thing, at least.

He was relieved to reach the edge of the fossilised lake, but as he climbed up to the rim he knew he faced an even more hostile region. The light flickered on stalagmite columns that soared up to the distant vault of the roof. Warm browns and reds, purples and soft greens gleamed on their surfaces, locked within the glassy sheen that covered everything. The cavern's beauty was awesome, but to Falmeryn it seemed unutterably sinister.

He set off briskly, but the floor was a tangle of boulders and nodules, and there was no clear path. He found himself constantly scrambling around stalagmite bosses or jumping from one rock to the next, and whenever he had to deviate from the moon stone's path, its sudden weight almost pulled him over. He was soon gasping with exertion, but his dread of being trapped in the caves forced him on relentlessly. He could only be grateful that the pull was so definite – but he dared not let himself wonder what would happen if the way was barred by solid rock.

'He said I would not get lost,' he reminded himself. But Ferdanice had been known to make mistakes.

As he toiled on he thought of the Circle of Spears, which no longer seemed a prison but a heavenly refuge – lost, like Forluin, for ever. The memory of the Kesfalians haunted him. They were a reserved people compared to the Forluinish, yet he had come to feel a strong affection for them. They deserved better than to be ravaged by Xaedrek, he thought, or used by such as Ferdanice . . .

The roof was angling downwards, and he saw the glint of calcite straws hanging from it. Alarm welled up in his throat. He dreaded the cave becoming confined. He tried to climb faster, hardly noticing the pain as he slipped and bruised himself. A draught slapped like ice against his hot skin, and he surmounted a boulder and found himself looking into a tunnel of polished limestone.

He almost cried out with relief. It was high enough to walk upright, and the magnetic line was drawing him directly through it. Water splashed underfoot as he ran to see what lay beyond.

The tunnel was long, but presently it opened out into a cavern festooned with stalactite curtains. They were white and reflected a spectral glow like moonlight from the jewel. When he reached the far side he found that the floor fell away into a chasm, but it did not seem deep and there was a ledge of flowstone leading round it on the right. He set foot on it cautiously, finding it slippery but broad enough to traverse safely.

He had been in the caves for several hours by now, and the combined fear and exertion had drained his strength. He was unaware of how exhausted he was, until half-way along the ledge it suddenly overcame him and he all but collapsed.

His shoulders were stinging, and his whole body throbbed with tension. He leaned back against a nodule of flowstone for a few minutes, breathing deeply until the ache eased off. Then he sat up and took off his pack with unsteady hands.

Below the ledge, pale curtains of calcite flowed down into shadow, and above him, half-seen rocks took on alarming shapes. His mind was over-sensitised, and he could do nothing to prevent ghastly images taking over from logical thought. The last time he had felt so afraid and fatigued had been while trying to outrun the Gorethrian hound pack . . . Trying to put the hideous memories from his mind, he drank deeply from his water flask and forced himself to eat.

It would have been good to sleep, but he could not relax. He was beginning to shiver, and longed to be out of the eerie cavern. The mournful drip of water echoing from every surface seemed to be growing louder, and through it he thought he could hear other sounds; the scratch of claws on rock, the soft, thick breathing of an animal –

He looked round, his heart thudding. It was not his imagination. On the ledge some twenty feet ahead of him, there stood a wild cat the size of a leopard. She was watching him, motionless apart from the sinuous flick of her tail.

Falmeryn's first thought was that if such a creature could enter the caves, then the way out could not be far. But this fleeting hope was obliterated by the look in her eyes. She was a beautiful creature, with pale rust-red fur, a slender face, eyes like golden agates. Once he might have felt empathy with her and have been able to win her confidence, but no more. Xaedrek's hunt had torn something from his soul. The same look had been fixed on him by the Gorethrian hounds just before they sprang, and in that moment, reason deserted him and he was swept back in time to the same blinding red terror, the knowledge that having faced this once he could not face it again . . .

The leopard smelled his terror and growled. An electric shock of dread went through him, and with it another unpleasant sensation, like the heat of amulin in his veins; the desire to kill.

Everything took on a horrible dreamlike clarity as he slid the knife from his belt and rose into a crouch. The coldness of the hilt made his hand ache. The instant he moved, the leopard bared her teeth and sprang.

He lunged forward to meet her, but she flung her whole weight at him and the momentum carried him backwards off the ledge. There was a moment of breathless suspension. Then rock slammed into his shoulder and they were tumbling and sliding, tangled together, down a limestone flow as smooth as ice.

Twenty feet down they collided with a boulder and came to rest, Falmeryn on his back and the cat crouched on top. Pain throbbed through him, but he was aware only of the weight of her paws on his shoulders, the liquid eyes, the wet incisors curving near his face. Her snarl rumbled in his ears and the carnivorous blast of her breath made him gag. He thrust his elbow into her throat and struggled frantically to force her head away.

His right arm seemed paralysed. He could hardly feel the knife. But a mindless instinct had taken him over and somehow he jerked his hand upwards and felt the blade slice through the soft belly fur and into the creature's guts.

A warm sticky flood burst over his legs. Her snarl rose to a caterwaul of pain. He cut deeper, pierced her lung, and suddenly her weight lost all its elastic poise and slumped on him like a sack of rocks.

He was being smothered. With the last of his strength he managed to half roll over and drag himself from under the corpse. He struggled to his hands and knees and remained there for a moment, staring at the crimson lake spreading out under the slender, furry form; then faintness overcame him and he crawled away and collapsed into a lurching vortex.

For a long time, there was only dizziness and pain. He had struck his head in the fall, and his back and limbs throbbed to the bone. His lungs were raw, every breath an effort. He lay very still and prayed silently for the cave to cease spinning and falling beneath him.

When at last he recovered enough to sit up, he had no idea how much time had passed. He was still shuddering with pain and shock, and at the sight of the leopard's corpse the shudders became dry sobs. Something about her filled him with grief, as if she had been more than an animal and he had not slain but murdered her . . .

In normal circumstances, he would not have harmed the cat for anything – any more than he would have killed a human being, even a Gorethrian. *Life is precious, it is not our right to destroy it*, he thought wretchedly. That was what they believed in Forluin, but in the outside world that philosophy could be corrupted with the swiftness of mockery. He *had* killed a man. A Gorethrian officer had forced him to take amulin and face him in a sword fight. Falmeryn had won, but in victory there had only been guilt and heartsickness, the horrible memory of amulin burning in his veins, destroying compassion and replacing it with ruthless blood lust. When facing the leopard he had felt the same sliding away of conscience, and the knowledge brought him to despair. Could it be that, taken even once, amulin corrupted for ever?

'Or perhaps it is me,' he whispered. His throat was sore. 'I want to blame Xaedrek, but perhaps it's my own weakness that has made me capable of killing. First a man and now this . . .'

Somehow the leopard's death seemed worse.

He swayed dizzily to his feet and limped towards the slope of flowstone down which he had fallen. It was only twenty feet to the top, and it had plenty of apparent foot-holds. But the moment he started to climb, he knew he would never gain the top. The rock slid under his hands like soap, and he was so weak that he could barely co-ordinate his limbs. Because he was trying to move against the moon stone's line of attraction, the pouch had become like a boulder at his hip and he could not summon the strength to resist it. Eventually exhaustion overwhelmed him and he gave up. He could not climb with the moon stone. Neither could he leave it behind; besides breaking his word to Ferdanice, he needed it to guide him.

Desperation swirled in him, but he forced himself to be positive. He could not regain the ledge, but he could still follow the moon stone's path. Surely it would lead him out eventually. With that thought, he stumbled away from the ledge, found the unseen thread and let it draw him down into the chasm.

His pack was still on top of the ledge, he realised in dismay. But at least he had not lost the circlet, and he had never been more grateful for its thin watery beam dissolving the darkness.

The chasm led down into a warren of small, dark caves, overgrown with stalactites. It grew much colder. Subterranean draughts moved sluggishly past him, and the air seemed tense with the echoes of dripping water and creaking rock. His fatigue was persistent, worsened by the frequent necessity of resisting the pull as he skirted rocks and crevices. It was a relief when each obstacle was past and he could fall like a sleepwalker into the invisible current.

But all the time it felt wrong. He knew he should have stayed on the ledge. The Stone of Fliya offered no guidance except the shortest distance between itself and Charhn, regardless of what obstacles lay in the way. He was hopelessly lost, and the feeling that he was being drawn into a dead end crept over him. The further he went, the less possible it was to turn back. Yet there was always the wretched, persistent belief that if he only went a little further, he would find a way out; and so he drove himself on, ignoring tiredness and hunger.

Hours passed. He felt despair pressing on him in the blackness, insanity piled up like the masses of rock above him, and he knew that if he did not escape soon he would begin to go mad. He missed Raphon desperately. The Hrunneshian had been a strange companion, unhuman and disquieting, yet during their journey to Kesfaline Falmeryn had grown used to the neman's gentle presence. Now Raphon was safe on the Black Plane Hrunnesh, and Falmeryn would not have wished it otherwise, but at this moment, desperately alone, he would have done anything to have the neman with him again.

He stopped to drink from a pool, and must have fallen asleep, for he suddenly found himself in a dream of Forluin. It was poignant and tormenting, for although he knew he was dreaming, it was as vivid as life. He was with his mother, Arlena, and his father, Falin; he walked and spoke with them in the meadows, and it was all so real that he could pluck leaves and see every tiny vein, smell the scent of flowers, hear bees droning in the pollen-gold light. He thought, How could I have left? It had only been a trading voyage, no one was compelled to go, and how foolish to imagine that An'raaga was as safe as Forluin . . . The capture by slave-traders and the hellish journey to Shalekahh seemed a life-time ago, a thick grey curtain drawn between him and his family. Yet here he was with them again, and they were telling him how the ship had come home without him, and how much he was missed by his loved ones. Their eyes were so sad. And although he explained again and again what had happened and that he was still alive, they never seemed to hear him . . .

'I know you'd come home if you could,' said Arlena.

He woke violently, disorientated. He had been convinced that he was at home, and reality descended on him with unspeakable horror. He jumped up and went blindly onwards in a haze of dread.

The cavern became lower and narrower until it attenuated to a passage through which he had to walk bent almost

150

double. His heart beat thickly and he tried to turn back once or twice, but the pouch's weight would not permit it. He began to think, *What a terrible way to die. So slow, and so lonely. I would rather the Gorethrian hounds had finished me . . .*

'Lady of H'tebhmella, help me,' he muttered. He recalled bitterly the way she had appeared, only to be banished by Ferdanice. Longing for her to return was just another hopeless dream. He knew that she had once come to save Estarinel, imprisoned in a nightmarish castle, and that he must now be experiencing at least a taste of what Estarinel had suffered. The H'tebhmellians had always watched over the Forluinish . . .

'Beloved Lady, if you can hear me, help me,' he whispered. Then he shouted, '*Please!*'

The sound set up an echo that seemed to go on and on until he wished he had stayed silent. But there was no response. He had expected none.

He went on more slowly now, with his hands pressed to the rough stone on either side as if he were unconsciously trying to prevent the walls from closing in. His fingers were numb with cold. Presently, the tunnel widened out and he found himself on the brink of a subterranean lake.

He paused, stricken by the sensation that he was trespassing in an underground domain where humans had no place. Small stalagmites stood around the edges, doubled in length by their reflections in the looking-glass surface; white and delicate and never before seen by human eyes. He felt like weeping, not for himself but for something he could not define.

'I'll have to cross the lake, or go back,' he said quietly. There was no way round it. At least the roof rose just enough for him to walk upright. He stepped into the freezing water and began to wade slowly towards the other side.

At first ankle deep, it soon came over his knees and he felt icy trickles running down inside his boots. He hoped it would go no deeper. If he had to swim, he was sure the cold would be the end of him.

Half-way across, he trod on something soft.

151

He snatched his foot away and froze, hardly daring to look down. The surface was like black glass, and under it he caught a glimpse of something white writhing round his ankles. He caught his breath, made to run – but then the water erupted into a maelstrom of foam.

The creature he had disturbed was thrashing madly round his legs, and as he tried to extricate himself he became aware that the chaos was spreading outwards until the whole lake was heaving like a storm-blown sea. Water splashed over him. A paralysing disgust tightened round his throat, and he obeyed his instinct to flee towards the far side. His feet came free of the coils, but he took only two or three steps before they entangled him again. He went headlong, and the water slapped into him like a sheet of ice.

The shock almost stopped his heart. Water filled his ears and nose, and he could see nothing except bubbles swirling in ink. It seemed impossible to drown in such shallow water, yet he could not surface. He thrashed as wildly as the things around him, twisted onto his back, and finally thrust his face into the air. As he did so, a pale head rose up beside him.

He got a brief impression of a vermiform body, a moustache of white tendrils above a small mouth, and round sightless eyes. He tried to draw a breath, swallowed water, and began to choke. Through the blur of discomfort and panic, he saw the thing loom over him and lunge forward in an arc that took it across his chest.

He lurched sideways in the water, managing to roll over and find the lake bottom with his knees. The creature was curled round his waist now, soft and boneless. Coughing violently, he knelt up and with infinite revulsion, plucked the thing from him. It was very long, and as he struggled to rid himself of it it clung round his wrists like an obscene maggot-pale scarf. He staggered to his feet and managed to fling it away, but there were others surging round his legs. Sobbing for breath, he ploughed frantically towards the far edge of the lake.

Twice more he fell before he gained it, but at last he dragged himself onto bare rock and lay convulsed in a horrible fight for air. Behind him, the lake became still apart from the occasional ripple arrowing across it.

He coughed the water away and found his breath, but he could do nothing to fight the terrible wintry cold that had enveloped him. His clothes were sodden. His skull ached with the cold. There seemed to be knives thrust through his ears, but the rest of his body felt numb, heavy as granite.

They said it was painless to die of cold. You just fall asleep . . .

But disgust forced him to move away from the water, and once he had found his feet, it seemed easier to keep walking than to stop.

Beyond the lake, the passageway narrowed again to become even more claustrophobic than before. Drained of everything except physical misery, he continued mechanically, even when he had to crawl on his hands and knees. This was still the moon stone's path, and he still had the light on his forehead. But as the tunnel began to angle downwards, the pouch started to drag on him. It could not even be called a tunnel now; it was just a rudimentary fissure leading down into the Earth.

The cold deepened. The walls were beaded with ice, and his clothes stiffened as the water and leopard's blood froze on them. His progress was painfully slow, and the blackness of exhaustion kept bursting across his eyes. Crawling blindly, one arm went elbow deep through an ice crust into freezing water, and the shock brought him to a halt.

He sank back against the rock wall, blinking dazedly. He was in a tiny, oval chamber with a roof just high enough for him to sit upright. But it was a dead end. The floor vanished under a dark pool, and the roof came down to meet the water. There was no way onwards.

With that realisation, all his suppressed terror came flooding through him. He was far from rational and very near collapse. *I must turn back,* he thought. *I gave my word. Turn back –*

And then he remembered the lake. He could not face the lake again. And he did not have the strength.

That was when the last veil of self-delusion was torn away,

and he found himself staring at the inevitability of death. There was no way on, no way back, and he was certain to die of cold and starvation. Strange that it seemed so impossible to bear, after he had faced it so many times before in different ways; but for some reason it grew harder, not easier.

He thought he should feel stoical and resigned, but he did not. He felt only bitterness. There was still something he had to do, he could not die with it unfinished . . .

'I don't exist,' he said to himself, resting his head back and staring wide-eyed into nothingness. 'Everyone in Forluin believes I am already dead. So do the Gorethrians. There was only Ferdanice who knew otherwise, and he's vanished into another domain for ever. I do not exist . . .'

The loneliness of it was what made it so hard. If there was anyone to mourn him, they had already done so long ago. And he thought, was this how Kharan had felt? At that the last layer of memory peeled away, leaving only the raw centre of his misery.

Kharan. Her warmth, her expressive eyes. Gone.

'You make Forluin sound so beautiful,' she had said once, as they lay enfolded in each other's arms in a hayloft, their refuge. 'You'd take me back with you?'

'Of course,' he had replied. 'I'm not going back without you.'

Pain seized his throat. His eyes burned. It had seemed impossible that they would not escape together, somehow find a ship and sail back to Forluin. Time and time again he had visualised their arrival, the cliffs gleaming under a blue sky as he led her onto the shore, his family greeting her with joy and love . . . And he had made Kharan believe the dream as well.

She had understood the danger they were in; he had not. She had tried to warn him, but he had not listened; he had deluded her with false hope of escape. Only when Xaedrek's guards caught them outside the palace gates did he truly understand why she had been so cautious, so afraid . . . and then it was too late.

That was the worst memory of all. Kharan in his arms one moment, begging him to flee without her – the next torn

154

from him by Gorethrian guards and marched away. That was the last time he had seen her, but Xaedrek had taken great pains to explain exactly what would happen to her. She was to be beheaded.

Beheaded. It was unimaginable. He shuddered, closed his eyes in denial. The dream was one of love, survival, safety in Forluin – it could not end in the absoluteness of death. But it had, and Falmeryn blamed himself. If only he had perceived the danger, if only he had had the strength, he would have sent her back to the palace and told her they must not see each other again. She would not have been happy, but at least she would have been *alive*.

Long-suppressed grief overcame him and he could think of nothing, nothing but her. Even being trapped in the caves no longer mattered. It was so unfair that he had been rescued by Ferdanice for his own nefarious reasons, while she had died . . .

But his eyes remained dry. He could not weep. The grief was simply a raw, cold torment which held no hope of meeting her again, even in death. There was no relief in it, but, Falmeryn thought, I deserve none. I am as much to blame as Xaedrek himself.

If he had expected death to come easily, he was wrong. Despite his utter weariness, he felt wide awake, his mind thronging with unbearable thoughts. He crawled forward to the edge of the pool and scooped up a handful of water to soothe his raw throat. He did not even notice the chill of it. Leaning over the water, he was startled to see his reflection staring back at him – his face as white as a blind worm from the lake, his eyes and cheekbones carved out of shadow. His hair was a long uncombed tangle, held out of his eyes by the circlet, and the jewel in its centre flashed on the water like a star.

'Kharan, if this is my punishment for failing you,' he said brokenly, 'then I can bear it. But I wish you were with me at the end.'

Softly, a few inches from his ear, a small voice replied, 'I am here.'

Now I know I have gone mad, he thought. He sat back on

155

his heels, his frozen clothes crackling as he moved. And he looked up and saw facing him, with her knees almost touching his, a child of no more than three.

He knew she was not real. Yet he knew that he was not hallucinating, that she was actually there, because he had seen her before. He had dreamed about her, and when Raphon had been leading him towards the Circle of Spears, she had appeared several times as if warning him not to go there. She had seemed much older then, sometimes almost a woman, but it was unquestionably the same girl. She was unmistakable; the sweet face that reminded him of Kharan's, the wide violet eyes, and above all the rich, deep red of her hair. On her shoulder there nestled a bird of the exact same colour.

He stared at her, speechless. His first reaction, quite illogical, was that she must be frozen in her thin white gown. He wanted to reach out to her, but she was bathed in the light of another time and place, and he knew his hands would pass through her. All his other thoughts were swept away; there was only the child. As always, he had the disturbing feeling that he should recognise her, and understand her connection with him – but it was like struggling to recall a dream that has slid beyond the edge of memory.

'Can you hear me?' he asked, terrified that she would vanish.

'Of course I can,' she said. 'You needed me, so I'm here.'

'Who are you?'

She frowned as if she could not understand why he had asked such a pointless question. 'It's me!' she exclaimed. 'You mustn't go to sleep here. You must go on.'

'I can't. There's no way through.'

'But you must!' Her lower lip twitched, her eyes became luminous with tears. Suddenly his fear was all for her, not himself. 'Miril said you must.'

'Miril?' he gasped.

'This is Miril,' she said, raising a hand to stroke the bird's silky throat. 'Now do you understand?'

Gods, he thought, closing his eyes. *It is an hallucination after all.* But when he opened them again, she was still there.

'You have to go under the water and swim.' She pointed at the pool. 'It will be cold, but it won't be for long.'

'I can't,' he said hoarsely. 'I've no strength left.'

'Please!' she cried. Tears ran down her cheeks. 'We've come here to show you the way out. It will be all right. Miril and I will go first.'

'No . . .' Her vulnerability cut through him like a knife, and his head was spinning. But her eyes were compelling, more compelling even than his horror of crawling into the underwater passage. He loved her; he could not refuse her.

'You must follow me. Do you promise?'

'Yes.'

With that she leaned forward and seemed to dissolve as she slid head first into the pool. He was alone again. Shaking, he stared at the dark water and wondered if he had imagined her after all. If so, there could be no way out, only death; but as death was certain anyway, better a swift than a slow one.

With stiff limbs he shrugged himself out of the thick jacket, took a deep breath, and began to wriggle forwards into the water. The passage was narrow and rough, and the roof rock scraped the circlet from his head. Darkness swallowed him, his lungs strained with fear; but he felt the chill of the water not at all.

8

White Shadows of Evil

ZHELKAHH, THE Black City, was Shalekahh's sibling in negative. It had the same harmonious architecture, the same elegant towers, but the resemblance ended there. Set into an inky mountainside, it dominated the pass between the Emethrians like a fortress at the gates of hell. There was no touch of colour to relieve its sable walls. When the clouds came billowing down from the heights, its highest towers were lost to view and it seemed to rear up into the sky for ever, as forbidding as the mountains themselves.

'I never feel at ease here,' said Xaedrek. 'I don't know how you can prefer it to Shalekahh.'

'Zhelkahh is my home, Sire, far more than Shalekahh can ever be,' Baramek replied.

'The gateway to the Empire . . .'

Baramek nodded. 'The Gorethrians here are of a different character, less cerebral, perhaps, but closer to the realities of war. It's a true warrior's city.'

Rank upon rank of soldiers stood ready to greet the Emperor and his retinue as they rode under the massive arch. Their uniforms, cloaks and helmets shone, like the city itself, with the lustre of jet; but the citizens lining the streets wore bright robes as if in defiance of their surroundings. A roar went up from them as the Imperial party approached.

Zhelkahh, by long tradition, was the gathering place for the Gorethrian troops before they began their long march through Omnuandria to Kristillia. More divisions were arriving all the time. Every day brought the invasion of

158

Kristillia closer, and the arrival of Xaedrek and the High Commander transformed the atmosphere to one of pure electricity.

The scene was one to bring pride to any Gorethrian, terror to their enemies. Even the grim-faced Baramek was moved to shake his head in wonder and exchange a smile with his Emperor.

Xaedrek, however, could not share fully in the crowd's exuberance. Something held him back, a pressure that seemed to be at once inside him and outside, as if the air was crackling with dark fire. He was used to storms, but the one that threatened seemed more ominous than usual; the clouds felt heavy, as taut as a skin on which some massive creature was blundering about, seeking a way through. Surely if the pressure burst, the sky itself would be torn apart and the Earth swallowed into another dimension . . .

'Sire, are you all right?' said a voice at his side, very quietly.

Xaedrek looked round, startled out of his reverie. 'Yes, Valamek, quite all right.'

'It's been a very tiring journey,' said the young Duke.

'Indeed, but it's over now.' Ahead of them loomed the Imperial residence, a black palace set high in the mountainside, with spires that pierced the clouds. The sight of it increased his tension. 'And we shall not see Shalekahh again until the war is won . . .'

The retinue came to a halt before a sweep of steps, where the residence staff, guards and Omnuandrian slaves were standing ready to welcome the Emperor. They came forward briskly with salutes and formal greetings, while grooms held the horses and helped the nobles to dismount.

'Sire, my wife is here. I have not seen her for almost a year,' said Baramek. Xaedrek saw the tall woman dressed in blue silk, waiting higher up on the steps. With her were two girls, one of about thirteen and the other a couple of years younger, both very dignified.

'I hardly recognise your daughters. They are young ladies now,' said Xaedrek. 'How old is Surukish, eleven?'

'Not quite ten, Sire.'

'Is that all?' Xaedrek smiled. 'Go on, Baramek. Go and greet them. Official duty can wait.'

'Thank you, Sire.' The High Commander gave a rare smile and climbed the steps to receive the loving embraces of his family. Xaedrek watched for a moment, then turned to see Amnek and Ah'garith standing by the litter on which the amulin machine, dismantled and carefully loaded, had been brought from Shalekahh.

'Valamek, would you help Lord Amnek ensure that the machine is properly reassembled without damage?'

'Of course, Sire.'

Xaedrek pointed at a second, smaller litter. 'And before you do that, have Irem Ol Thangiol comfortably ensconced in a suitable room. I want to see if he's got anything to tell me.'

Within, the Imperial residence was considerably less grim than the exterior suggested. The rooms were lined with coloured marbles, hung with bright tapestries and lit by lamps. Yet Xaedrek felt no more at ease inside; he was still acutely aware of the electricity building in the sky. Gorethria had a fierce climate that responded like a harp string to the touch of any unseen force. The first time he had noticed a worsening of the weather, it had presaged Ah'garith's arrival and their discovery of a way to tap the new powers raging through the Earth. Now he was aware of a further change, but this time it was not wild and challenging. It was slow, sinister, oppressive, and each time he tried to pin down the reason, it would slide away into fog.

Xaedrek walked over to the ruby-studded black couch where Irem Ol Thangiol lay writhing against his bonds. Lamps gleamed on walls of polished stone that was veined with rust-red and silver; the effect was one of opulent gloom. He put a hand on Ol Thangiol's thin shoulder and stood looking down at him thoughtfully.

Xaedrek had always been clear-minded, one step ahead of Ah'garith, but now there were times when his thoughts seemed clouded and everything around him receded into a grey haze. Grey – like the terrible Wall that stood between

160

him and Melkavesh. The dreams he used to have, of the moons and a child with red hair, had vanished. They had never been pleasant, but what replaced them was worse. Sometimes he woke feeling he had not slept at all, but had spent the night trapped in the limbo of the Wall.

There was no time to brood on it. Preparations for the invasion were proceeding smoothly under Baramek's eye, and they were only waiting now for word from Lirurmish that the battle machines were ready. Then they could be brought from Cevandaris, and the long trek to Kristillia begun. Xaedrek intended to lead the invasion, and he could not afford to let vague feelings and foolish nightmares interfere with progress.

It had not helped, of course, that Anixa had failed to slay Melkavesh.

It had happened just before they left Shalekahh. Seeing all that was happening as if through Anixa's eyes, Irem Ol Thangiol had described her arrival at the castle . . . the crowd on the beach . . . Melkavesh, solicitous and suspecting nothing.

'Urge her to do it now,' Xaedrek had said.

The Kristillian had cried out, sobbed, then said, 'No – too late – Melkavesh knows –'

Xaedrek, coldly furious, had then done exactly what he had promised in the event of Anixa's failure. He had allowed Ah'garith to torment Irem Ol Thangiol. The Kristillian dreaded her so greatly that she only had to touch him to make him scream with fear.

'Let me dismember him, Sire,' she had said, 'a little at a time. A hand, for a start, with the threat of more. That will bring the Kesfalian shrew to her senses.'

'No. He's more use to me in one piece, and I am not allowing it just to gratify your desires.' The demon's request had sickened him. As soon as he realised that no amount of torture was going to make Anixa kill Melkavesh, he banished Ah'garith and concentrated instead on Ol Thangiol's indistinct parroting of their conversation.

He should have known that Melkavesh was not so easily to be disposed of. She had guessed most of it, Anixa had

161

told her the rest, and now his spying advantage was lost. The amulin-enhanced blood that created the link would wear off soon. But just for a second, it seemed the Kristillian's eyes had turned green-gold, and he could hear Melkavesh's voice saying, '. . . *this futile attempt on my life has only made it more certain that I will destroy him.*'

Then the contact was gone. He had broken the news to Amnek as gently as possible, expecting rage; instead the Councillor had been over-controlled, asking question after question while his eyes seemed both glazed and demented. Xaedrek knew that another attack on Melkavesh was pointless; he had accepted that he could not slay her before the battle, but he could not make Amnek see it. Eventually he had stopped trying.

In a way, Xaedrek was glad Anixa had failed. It would make the final confrontation with Melkavesh that much sweeter.

He made an effort to return his thoughts to the present, concerned that it was such an effort. Perhaps it was simply tiredness. He bent over the Kristillian, trying to put Zhelkahh's atmosphere from his mind.

'Now, Irem Ol Thangiol, I trust you are rested after the journey?' he said. 'I want you to tell me what you can see in Kesfaline.'

'Anixa . . . Anixa . . .'

'Forget her, Ol Thangiol. She's gone. Concentrate on Kesfaline.'

'General Kadurik . . . moving troops . . . through Imhaya . . .'

Xaedrek was now using the mind link to more useful effect. He had given Ol Thangiol's blood to an officer serving General Kadurik, who was masterminding the attack on Charhn from Kesfaline. Thus he could monitor the movements of Imperial troops from several thousand miles away.

Unfortunately, it could not last. He could not give Ol Thangiol more amulin or take more blood without killing him, and there was no one to take his place. There had been few enough Kristillians to experiment on; of those, only two

162

had yielded similar results, and they, less resilient than Ol Thangiol, had died.

No matter. After the war, Kristillia would be his, and all things might become possible . . .

He suddenly became aware that his mind was wandering. He could not concentrate on what Ol Thangiol was saying. A thundercrack that sounded like the palace being rent from top to bottom, made him start violently, and at that he went to look out of the window, perturbed.

Outside, the clouds were boiling low in the streets, and a saw-edged wind began to hurl wave after wave of rain across Zhelkahh. People were scattering, already drenched to the skin and frantic to avoid the spears of lightning. Even by Gorethrian standards it was a storm of unprecedented savagery, and as it went on Xaedrek felt as if it were slowly draining his strength away . . .

He became angry. There was a reason for all of this – the weather, his state of mind – and he was determined to get to the root of it. He went to summon Ah'garith and Amnek. By the time they arrived, he felt so weak that he had to lean on the back of the couch to keep himself upright.

'I do hope you are not ill, Sire,' said the Shanin. 'You don't look yourself.'

'The journey was arduous. You haven't rested properly,' said Amnek.

Xaedrek looked at them, trying to clear his thoughts. Ah'garith had been absurdly obedient since the incident with the ichor, almost as if she were mocking him. Amnek went about his various duties lifelessly, and only the mention of Melkavesh or Shavarish could stir any reaction in him. There was something very wrong, and had been for a long time, yet he could not seem to perceive what it was . . .

'Ah'garith, this storm is not natural.' He managed to produce his usual, cool tone.

'What of it, Sire?'

'You don't seem surprised. I would like to know if it's any of your doing. And if so, how did you acquire the power?'

'If I *could* produce such weather, Sire, would it not be a delightful way to put fear into the hearts of your enemies?'

'I suppose it would.' On the couch, Ol Thangiol moaned in fear of the Shanin. They ignored him. 'But answer my question.'

'I don't understand why you asked it, Sire.'

'Don't you? Then I'll explain. Instinct tells me, Ah'garith, that you created this storm – and the power to create it is being drawn out of me.'

Ah'garith grinned vaguely and shrugged. 'What an odd thing to say, Sire.'

'Is it? It's nothing to do with the ichor, of course. You would not dream of creating a substance that would give me power, only to link me inextricably to you.'

'Of course not!' the demon cried indignantly.

Amnek came forward to put a hand on his arm. 'Sire, we are concerned. There is something wrong with you.'

Xaedrek shook him off. 'Not with me, Amnek. With you. I am sick of the game you've been playing, Ah'garith, and I want an end to it before it puts our invasion plans in jeopardy. Do you understand me?'

'Game?' Her mouth stretched into an ugly oblong.

Xaedrek could normally control his temper, but now it seemed to be slipping away from him. 'You think you are indispensable and indestructible. I hope you are confident enough to put it to the test, because I promise you, demon, that I am going to dispose of you, whatever the cost.'

Ah'garith did not answer. She looked at Amnek, and whatever the Councillor saw in her face made him cry, 'No!'

'I did say, my lord, "Unless he provokes me beyond endurance".'

'*Don't,*' Amnek said faintly.

'Be silent! Remember our agreement to help each other . . .' She turned slowly towards Xaedrek. He made to say something but could not; suddenly the room was lurching like a ship and their voices seemed to be coming at him from a great distance, at once too loud and too soft. He could not find his balance. All was confusion. They were leaning over him in a nebula of ochre lights, hideously enlarged, Amnek tall and arachnoid, Ah'garith with her kindly old woman's face, stretching out her hands to him –

164

He was not aware of stumbling away from the couch, only that he was suddenly pressed against a wall with a tapestry prickling his back through the thin satin of his robe. True fear was an emotion alien to him, yet he could only interpret the tightness in his stomach as that. It began there and spilled coldly through his body, and its source was the malevolence emanating from Ah'garith.

There were other tapestries about the room, and the figures in them seemed to be alive, jostling and whispering and grinning at him . . . each of their expressions a tiny echo of the Shanin's grin as she advanced on him.

He saw her now not as an old woman, but as she had once been in the Serpent's time: an argent figure, naked and asexual and gleaming with a beauty that was at once evil and fascinating. Her eyes were mercury orbs, her mouth wet and red as blood. He had occasionally glimpsed this image faintly overlaid on her human form – but now it was the silvery form that seemed like solid flesh, the human one illusory. And as she approached, he was suffused by a depraved and irresistible desire to fall to his knees in worship.

He knew what was happening, yet he could do nothing to stop it. The Shanin was possessing him. Was this how Meshurek had felt? The loss of will; judgement and reason sliding away; insanity bunching in the folds of his brain? It was the very thing he had sworn, *sworn* he would never allow to happen, and yet how suddenly it had come, completely without warning –

No. There had been warnings, and he had not noticed them. Silently, hopelessly, he cursed himself. The grey dreams, the times when everything had seemed cloudy and distant and Valamek had asked concernedly if he was not working too hard. He remembered now, but too late. And there was the one thing it went back to: a discoloured ribbon of thought leading to the ichor. His instinct that it would enable Ah'garith to possess him had been right, but he had never guessed that so few doses were all she needed to work on. But why had she chosen this moment – when the war was still in the balance?

165

'Why?' he gasped. Sweat broke from his forehead and his knees buckled, but he would not kneel to anyone, least of all the vile demon. He gripped the tapestry behind him and hung on to it, feeling the fabric turning damp under his palms.

'Why what, Sire?' Ah'garith's voice hurt his ears like the scream of metal on metal. The ghastly silver face swam in front of him, too close, and on a level as if she had increased in height. Her aura made him retch; sickly sweet as blood, choking as dust-heavy cobwebs.

'Amnek, help me,' he coughed, but the gaunt figure did not move. He could see the hawkish nose in silhouette and one eye glinting palely. The look in it told Xaedrek everything.

'Don't ask me to help you,' Amnek said, his voice thin and strained. 'You failed to kill Melkavesh again. I think you do not want to kill her. I think you are as guilty as she of Shavarish's death.'

'Amnek, for heaven's sake!' Xaedrek cried hoarsely. 'There is no logic in what you are saying. The demon has deluded you . . . gods . . .' He broke off, sick and weak with despair and shaking so convulsively that he could not form his thoughts into words.

He had suspected – he had even warned Amnek not to work too closely with the Shanin. But the realisation descended on him that Amnek had been in Ah'garith's power by then. Xaedrek knew it was his own fault. He had underestimated the dangers, he had thought Amnek as strong as himself – and by the time he had issued the warning, it had already been too late.

He could have wept at Amnek's betrayal of him. This man, in place of the father he had lost, had infused him with the scientific approach and the passionate devotion to Gorethria that were the very motivating forces of his life. Amnek had always been there, strong and single-minded. But his wife's death had unhinged him, making him easy fodder for the demon. Now he stood there like a skeletal parody of his former self, eaten up with vengefulness – a pitiful reflection of Ah'garith herself.

'Amnek,' he whispered. His head fell forward. His elbows bent so that he began to slide down towards the floor. His ears reverberated with the Shanin's giggling.

'You wanted to know why, Sire,' she said. 'By M'gulfn's breath, do you need to ask? I answered your summons in good faith, but from the very first moment we met you have treated me with the utmost contempt. You have consistently used me, insulted me, abused my trust – the Kristillian on that couch has received better treatment at your hands than have I!'

'That may be so, but it was still infinitely better than you deserved.' Xaedrek raised his head. 'I meant, why now? Why not wait until the war is over? Destroy my mind and you reduce Gorethria's chances of winning.'

'What do I care about your wretched war?' the demon shrieked. 'I hope you lose! I hope you and the witch kill each other! No, my Emperor.' Her voice became thick with mockery and malice. 'Gorethria means nothing to me. I only want to destroy it as Meheg-Ba destroyed it. You have often pointed this out to me yourself, so it must be true, mustn't it?'

'Amnek, listen to her,' Xaedrek said desperately. 'For Gorethria's sake, if not mine, stop her.'

'What can I do, Sire?' was the thin response. 'You summoned her. You knew the risks, you said, and you could control her. But I am hers now, and this is where your cleverness has brought us.'

'Yes, you knew the risks,' the Shanin said primly. 'As to why I chose this moment, it's as good as any. I want you to understand that from the moment you first swallowed the ichor I could have possessed you at any time I chose. I was playing with you. I set the trap and you walked into it. Far-sight!' Xaedrek closed his eyes, but he could still see her, and her voice seemed to go on and on like the scrabbling of insect claws on stone. 'But it's your fault. You goaded me. You failed to slay the witch Melkavesh, and that distressed Amnek, who is my friend – more a friend to me than ever you were. And you expressed your hatred of me once too often! Well, I don't care now. You'll never have the chance to dispose of me because I have you now and I will never let you go. I have waited years for this, my beloved, mindless puppet-Emperor. Think of Meshurek and weep!'

History was repeating itself. How, he wondered in the turmoil of the nightmare, could this be happening after all the care he had taken to avoid it?

Foreknowledge was not prevention.

He was still on his feet with his arms locked rigid and his hands clenched on the tapestry, but now a great weight was bearing down on his skull. There was a membrane stretched across his field of vision, dull orange shot through with red veins which pulsated in time to a heavy, painful heartbeat. The rhythm seemed full of ghastly implications, half-memories . . . blackness draining like ink from a bed-chamber, lightning glinting on the white hair and malevolent eyes of an old woman, three deformed creatures lying on a throbbing lens, the stench of metal and burning flesh. The pressure was unbearable. He could not breathe. And he felt that if only the membrane would burst, there would be relief – the demon would let the pain stop, soothe him, nurture him . . .

There was a sudden agony as if a split had opened his spine and was working up through the bones of his skull, forcing them apart. The membrane exploded in redness, and then it seemed he was in another place, divorced from his physical self.

A dark swamp stretched to infinity all around him, oozing with brownish-blue discolourations. The atmosphere was dense, quivering with all that might bring any human to despair: envy and hatred, pain and loss, spite and sadism. Misery sweated from the ground. Xaedrek cried out inwardly and struggled, but there was no escape from this hell, and the worst thing of all was the soul-destroying pettiness of it. Evil for its own sake was as hollow, meaningless and terrifying as the delusions of madness.

'The Dark Regions,' said the Shanin at his side. It was fully in its true form now, like a lime-white ghoul.

'The Dark Regions no longer exist,' Xaedrek gasped.

'They still exist in my mind. I shall re-create them on

168

Earth. From now on, my Emperor, you shall be my slave and help me to achieve my goal. The witch Melkavesh will never keep her hands on the power she so fatuously calls sorcery. I shall have it all, drawn through my lenses and my human victims to be wielded by a chosen few. Will you help me?'

'No.'

The demon smiled. 'Oh, Xaedrek, I never thought to meet one who could match Ashurek for spirit.'

'Don't compare me with that Empire-wrecker.'

'Why not? In the circumstances, the comparison is more than apt. Resist me all you like. It amuses me, as does wondering how long it will take you to realise that you are already in my power, and nothing you say, or do, or think, can change that.'

Xaedrek knew the demon was right. His mind felt as glutinous as the swamp itself, his intellect liquefied in the centrifuge of horror. He could utter words of weak defiance, but his only real desire was to serve the Shanin. It was the source of everything: pain, pleasure, life itself. Worshipping it no longer seemed wrong. Gorethria no longer seemed important.

And yet through this morass of delusion, one small part of his mind remained detached, like an eye observing everything that happened with purely scientific interest. He had always had this capacity, even in dreams or the most terrible of situations, simply to watch. And what he saw was very interesting.

Thought processes turned awry by a flood of negative energy; a purely physical process really, with terror and other emotions as a subjective by-product. He wondered if it could be reversed. The possession had occurred against his will, but will itself was only an abstraction. Logically it could not be taken away, even by such a creature as the Shanin.

'We both know you are mine,' Ah'garith muttered into his ear, 'but I want to hear you say it. Go on. Admit that you are my slave and will bow obediently to me for as long as I see fit.' There was a tremor of excitement in her voice and he knew she was relishing the prospect of torturing him into slow acquiescence. The realisation nauseated him, but now the cold part of his psyche took over.

'All right,' he said.

'What?'

'I will say whatever you want to hear, on one small condition. Let us go back to the chamber.'

'Ha, can you not withstand this place, which is only a pale echo of the true Dark Regions?'

'We can come back here presently, if you like, but I would like to return to the physical world so that I may have a drink of water.'

'Ah.' The demon seemed surprised, then amused. 'Very well! This is your own tactic, is it not, my Emperor? To be momentarily kind to your victims, in order to make the subsequent torture that much more effective? What an excellent idea! Be assured, every insult, every humiliation you have heaped on me shall be paid back a hundredfold.'

With that, Xaedrek suddenly found himself in the room again. He straightened up slowly, feeling cold, weak and fever-drained. The terrible pressure in his head had eased, but he felt dazed, with little more understanding of the situation than a dog that fawns upon the master who has whipped it. Ah'garith's broad, silver face leered at him, and out of the corner of his eye he could see Amnek standing near the couch, staring at him. Yet his scientific eye remained separate, watching – and experimenting.

'What are you doing?' Amnek asked.

'He wants water,' said the Shanin mockingly. 'Fetch some, so that he may moisten his throat in preparation for the pretty speech he is going to make me.'

Xaedrek watched as Amnek went to a side table and filled a goblet from a jug. He leaned back against the tapestry, letting his left hand move to a little hidden pouch in the side of his belt. His nails met glass and were bent back painfully as he struggled to release a small stopper without it falling to the floor. At last it came loose, and he gripped the glass phial between his fingers and waited for Amnek to bring him the water. Ah'garith had noticed nothing.

Amnek placed the goblet in his right hand and stepped

back, glowering at him. Ah'garith continued to grin. Xaedrek paused a moment, then, before either of them realised what he was doing, he brought his left hand forward to tip a stream of pale gold powder into the water. He drained it and flung both the goblet and the phial onto the floor before the demon had time to react.

She gave a hiss of anger, and seized his throat, her fingers excruciating him like bone rods. But a second later, she began to shake with mirth.

'Amulin!' she cried. 'You idiot! What use do you think that is against me? Perhaps it gave you equal strength once, when I was all but powerless, but it will not avail you now. It was I who made it!'

Xaedrek looked back at her through half-closed lids. The detached eye slid into the centre of his mind like a cool glass orb and took him over. All his terror, disgust and humiliation slid away, and he suddenly discovered that he had lost his fear of her. She no longer seemed horrifying, only faintly ridiculous. He smiled.

'No, Ah'garith, you did not make this particular amulin. When Melkavesh was with me, I had her make a batch or two. There was no human subject. She simply passed her powers directly into the crystals. Her power is in me now, pure and uncorrupt.'

The Shanin stared at him, at a loss for words. In the silence, Xaedrek felt the golden fire of the amulin racing through his veins, a tide of positive power that drove the demonic corruption from his brain. Comprehension began to return, his strength came back and his sight cleared. And following that came a flood of anger, passionate conviction. Life took on its true meaning again.

There were ghosts thronging in the room, Gorethrians with dark, ascetic faces and fierce eyes, filling him with the fervour that had driven Gorethria to prove her supremacy over the world. They were the faces from the Hall of Portraits, the past rulers of Gorethria, and their strength was filling him, lifting him on a storm wind. *Gorethria must survive,* they told him. *It is your destiny. You must destroy our enemies . . .*

Xaedrek gathered an incandescent sphere of stars and hurled it at Ah'garith. Sparks skittered all over the walls and floor; a tapestry began to smoulder, and Irem Ol Thangiol gave a moan of fear, not understanding what was happening. The demon stood as if facing a wind, but did not fall. When the force of the blast died she leaned towards him, her face contorted like a gargoyle's.

'You cannot do this,' she muttered. 'I have possessed you. For you to defy me is impossible.' Her aura was overwhelming, god-like, and for a second he almost believed her. Then the fire rose in him, and he answered her with a second burst of power.

Still she remained standing, but her silver body was shredding away before his eyes, leaving only the human form beneath. He thought he had weakened her. Only when she raised her hands and unleashed a great shield of argent flame did he realise that she had been gathering the energy into herself to hurl at him. He summoned an amulin aura and retaliated with all his strength. There was a hissing of gold and silver static, and he saw Ah'garith stagger backwards, her face aghast – but in the same instant he was thrown to the floor with a ball of searing brilliance exploding in his mind. There was a moment of intense pain, mixed with dismay and fury at his defeat. Then, claiming him as the demon could not, unconsciousness pulled him down as relentlessly as gravity.

'Falmeryn.'

The voice must have come from inside his head, he thought. He was under water, his head throbbing with blackness and the deadly cold as he edged his way along the narrow rock passage. Then the muffled water sounds burst into raw clarity, and there was air against his face, air searing his lungs. Still the blackness, and the icy walls of rock around him . . . but room at least to drag himself from the water and stand up.

It was hardly possible to be so numb and still be able to move. He had to keep going for the child's sake. He could see her ahead of him, just a hint of ruby hair or the gleam of a white arm, leading him on down the endless tunnel.

'*Falmeryn.*' The voice again. The darkness was spinning round him and he almost fell. It would be so pleasant just to sleep, but there was something he must do, something so important . . . He could not rest until he had remembered what it was . . .

'Keep him warm,' said the voice. Was it the child speaking to him? No, it was an hallucination. He was drunk with exhaustion. It seemed he had been stumbling along the tunnel for hours, even days, able to keep going only because a whirl of delirium had lifted his mind out of his bodily discomfort.

When grey threads began to penetrate the blackness, he did not recognise it as light. It seemed only a fog to obscure the red-haired girl from his sight . . . Had he fallen asleep on his feet? She was gone, and he was lying on his side on rock, with no idea of how long he had been there. He was being dazzled by lamplight or candle flame – or daylight . . .

He was lying half in and half out of a hole hardly bigger than a warren, overhung with grass and surrounded by bushes. Sunlight backlit foliage, cobwebbed the grass with jewels. He was out of the caves . . . and he felt safe here, reluctant to move. It might almost have been a bed cocooning him, the leaves just an illusion, a memory . . . No. He must move, he had an urgent task to complete.

The air felt lukewarm on his skin as he stood up, and the cold had become an ache so deep that he hardly felt it. His clothes were wet and heavy. He had forgotten about the moon stone, until he felt its weight at his belt and recalled that he was supposed to follow its pull. *Why? Try to remember* . . .

He was in a wood that was thickly overgrown with bushes and bracken. The green fresh scent reminded him of Forluin but he could not be there, he was in . . . Kesfaline, was it? He felt at once eerily calm and mentally dislocated as he forged through the undergrowth.

'He's sleeping now. I'll stay with him.'

Half asleep on his feet again. He shook himself. Something had alerted him and he looked around to see shadows in

173

the trees ahead resolving themselves into black cloaks and winged helms –

Gorethrians. He flung himself flat in the bracken, jolted back to reality by an uprush of fear. They were on horseback and they were riding towards him, and if they had not seen him already they would surely find him. He could hear the thud of hoofbeats, the swish of branches as they approached. A cold sweat sheeted over his body. They passed by so close that they were inches from trampling him, yet they did not stop. He lay there for a long time before he could believe that they had not seen him.

He knew he must be on the border of Kesfaline and Kristillia, an area that swarmed with Gorethrian legions. He was beyond fearing for himself; his terror was that he would be prevented from finishing the task. He went on in a state of alarm, exacerbated by his exhaustion until it seemed he foundered through purgatory, unable to tell reality from hallucination. He needed help. He must reach Kristillia . . .

He found the village by chance. He came to the edge of the trees and saw the white cottages nestled into the side of a hill ahead of him, with a small domed temple in the centre. The sight filled him with relief, then desperation. He must cross open ground to reach it, and what if there were Gorethrians in the area? They would see him at once.

But he had to try. He looked about him to make sure all was quiet, and then broke from the edge of the trees and raced towards the hill.

He was too weak to run; pain zigzagged through his chest and made him stumble. Too far. There was the familiar, hideous dream of running against paralysis and then the culmination of his worst dreads; Gorethrians rising up before him out of nowhere, a line of savage black fire standing between him and his refuge.

Demons of fire and black metal, unassailable, all strength and careless arrogance. Cottages spewing smoke and flame, villagers cut down as they fled . . .

He was falling, screaming. Raphon should have been with him but Raphon was not there. He was alone. He was in the entrance to the cave again, knowing that everything he had

174

just been through he would have to go through again; and it was too much. He needed to sleep. The rock and earth and grass that cocooned him seemed to be resolving itself into a bed, everything fading to a soft, uniform reddish-brown . . .

'Falmeryn?' said the voice again. 'Can you hear me?'

'Raphon?' He struggled to sit up, but gentle hands pushed him back onto the bed. He was shaking and sweating.

'Don't try to move. Just lie quietly, and I'll bring you some water.' The voice belonged to a woman with copper hair drawn back from a babyish, round face, and brown eyes like berries against the soft marbling of her skin. She was small, dressed in a rust-coloured robe with a dark blue overmantle. The throbbing behind his eyes eased at her touch, but it terrified him to discover he had no memory of where he was.

'Who are you?' he said with difficulty.

'The priestess.' She frowned. 'Don't you remember?'

'No,' he said. 'Help me.'

'You came to the village two days ago, and the villagers brought you to me. You're in the temple of Jaed and Fliya.' His vision was becoming clearer now, and he saw that he was in a simple, bare room. Walls, floor and ceiling were all the same soft hue of terracotta, and dust hung across the room in shafts of sunlight. 'You were quite lucid when you arrived; you said you were fleeing the Gorethrians and had to reach Charhn urgently. Then you collapsed. You've been very ill. Your body was so cold I thought you'd die.'

As she spoke, his memory returned. He understood now. Unconscious, he had been reliving over and over again the way he had escaped the caves and found the village; and it had all been true, except for the last part. He had crossed into Kristillia without knowing it. The Gorethrians between him and the village had been conjured out of nightmare. In reality he had reached it safely . . . it came back to him now, pouring out his story to the Kristillians, being taken up the hill to the temple. They must have thought he was deranged.

'I do remember,' he said. 'I'm sorry. I must have put you to a great deal of trouble.'

175

'Not at all. It's why I am here,' she said, stroking his forehead. 'How do you feel now?'

'Much better. It's the first time I've felt warm in days.' He remembered standing at the door of the temple, looking into her astonished eyes as he tried to explain his plight. Whatever he had told her, none of it could have made any sense. 'I'm so grateful for your kindness. You said I've been here two days? Gods, I've already lost too much time.'

'You can't leave until you're strong enough.'

'But I must. What exactly did I tell you? Did I mention the moon stone?'

'You said that you'd been lost in the caves under Imhaya, and that you must find the enchantress in Charhn,' the priestess said sombrely. 'You didn't explain why – not clearly, anyway. Won't you tell me?'

He parted his lips, then found that he could not bring himself to speak of Ferdanice. The priestess was gentle and good-natured and he trusted her, but he suddenly felt locked within himself, unable to confide in anyone. He said, 'I've been entrusted with something that is supposed to help the enchantress to defeat Xaedrek. I have to go to Charhn to find her and if I don't leave soon it will be too late. That's all I can say.'

It took her some time to reply to this. Her eyes were round with surprise and anxiety. In the silence, Falmeryn suddenly had a terrible thought and sat up, looking wildly round the room. 'The moon stone – where is it? There was a pouch – attached to my belt –'

'It's all right,' she said reassuringly. 'All your possessions are safe. But I – I don't know what to say to you. I don't disbelieve you, Falmeryn, far from it, this is a matter too great for me. I think I'd better take you to Charhn.'

'That isn't necessary – if I could just borrow a horse –'

'It's my duty,' she said, but her eyes on him were warm.

'Thank you.' He lay back on the pillow with a sigh. 'We really should go at once.'

'Tomorrow,' she said firmly. 'It's still too soon, but you must have one more day's rest at least. I'll find you some fresh clothes, and arrange for our horses and supplies.' She had barely finished speaking before he drifted back into sleep, and this time found peace.

From the moment they left the village, Falmeryn felt sure there was something following them.

The feeling persisted for days, as they rode north across Kristillia's rich landscape, but failed to resolve into a more material threat. He began to believe that the shadows in the night were only ghosts of his own dreadful memories. He did not alarm the priestess by mentioning it.

It was she who said, on the third day, 'I think we have company.'

'What do you mean?' A chilly spasm of fear went through him.

'Perhaps we'll see them later.' She was smiling, quite unconcerned, but that did nothing to ease his apprehension.

They were travelling now between chasm walls, luxuriantly overgrown and rich with springs and wild fruit trees. Falmeryn knew from the moon stone's pull that they were travelling in the right direction. When they had to deviate from the exact path, his horse bore the sudden weight that in the caves had almost pulled him off his feet. He was weak and his lungs were still painful, but with mild weather, good food and the priestess's care, he was recovering. Ferdanice must have known that the Forluinish were a resilient race, he thought wryly.

Evening was falling as they came in sight of a tower soaring up out of the ravine, for at least two hundred feet. It stood in awesome silhouette against the sky, strangely tapered and with an uneven, ruined look. Falmeryn stared at it for a long time before registering that it was part of a statue. As they rode closer they saw that two giant feet were planted on a base the size of a hillock, and folds of carved drapery rose up to end abruptly at the hips.

'We believe it was a statue of Fliya,' the priestess said with quiet reverence. 'There is one of Jaed further to the west that is just a single leg.'

'How were they destroyed?'

'Who knows? Perhaps they were never finished. Come, we can rest by the base tonight. Let Fliya shelter us.'

They tethered the horses and made camp against the sheer wall of stone, but Falmeryn could not relax with the statue looming over him into the night sky. There was something unspeakably weird about this place, and the undergrowth seemed full of moving, breathing shadows.

'Look,' whispered the priestess, clutching his arm. 'We are privileged.'

They had lit a small fire, and in its glow Falmeryn saw his fears brought to life. There were moon leopards pacing past them, scores of them, flowing like satin that was dappled in all shades from red to silver fawn. They were all grace and cool feline beauty, like – like the one he had killed in the caves.

And they knew. They looked at him and *they knew*.

He must have uttered an involuntary gasp of fear, because the priestess said softly, 'Don't be afraid. They only attack if they are threatened. We never kill them, because they are sacred to us. I knew a hunter once who slew one; the others came and tore him to pieces.'

'Oh, gods,' Falmeryn murmured, his throat constricted. 'You'd better go – get out of here now. It's me they want.'

He heard her catch her breath. 'What have you done?'

'When I was trapped in the caves, I was attacked by one and I killed it.'

She was shaking suddenly, her voice uneven. 'There was blood on your clothes – I wondered –'

'Please go. You must save yourself.'

'No. I'm staying.' She pressed closer to him, and he felt the warmth of fear coming from her. He could not force her to leave him. They clung together, counting each heartbeat as the moon leopards paced back and forth, their tails flicking, their eyes glowing as they judged him. He was defence-less. He had a sword, but he would not use it; he felt he had no right. Their law was everything and he was part of it, bound by it, so weighed with guilt that he was ready to die before he harmed another of them.

Then one of the creatures detached itself from the others and came round the fire towards him. He could not move, not even when it put its face level with his. In terrible detail he saw the elongated pupils, the irises like layer upon layer

178

of golden enamel, a velvety nose with drops of moisture on the hairs. The look was fierce, pitiless, self-contained – and yet he felt a love for the creature that it would never feel for him. He could bear no more. He closed his eyes and waited for the teeth and claws to break his flesh.

The pain did not come. There was a noiseless sighing of the air. When he dared to open his eyes, the moon leopards had gone.

'Falmeryn,' the priestess gasped, 'oh, thank Fliya!'

'I don't understand,' he said faintly.

'They've spared you. They won't come back.'

'Why? Because we were by the statue?'

'I doubt it.' She shuddered, and laughed nervously. 'Perhaps they recognised something in you, that you never meant to kill their sibling – or that you're not theirs to judge. I don't know.'

'You didn't have to stay with me. I don't know what to say. You are incredibly brave.'

'I was terrified! It was only my duty as a priestess – oh, that is a lie. I couldn't bear to lose you, Falmeryn.' He had relaxed his grip on her, but she still clung to him. He was lost for words. All he could do was lift her to her feet and say very gently, 'I think we should move on. The moon leopards may not return, but I'd feel safer if we travelled through the night and found somewhere to rest at dawn.'

It was on the ninth day that they came in sight of Charhn. They rode up through a curve between the fells, and saw the Crystal City before them, shining with diamond-soft colours. Falmeryn sensed the pull of the moon stone growing stronger in response.

'It's so long since I saw Charhn; it only seems to grow more beautiful,' said the priestess.

'It is lovely.' He urged his horse into a canter. 'Do you know where we can find the enchantress?'

'No,' she called as her horse drew level. 'I know very little about her. We'll go to the Temple of Jaed and Fliya. The priests there will know.'

The walls were heavily manned, but within, Charhn

seemed almost deserted. Those too young or too old to fight had been evacuated to outlying villages; the rest were part of the army stationed on the fells. At the gate to the Inner City, they dismounted and went on foot, and now Falmeryn felt the moon stone pulling so strongly that he almost lost his balance.

The priestess made him wait at the door of the Temple while she went in alone. He stood looking at the smooth whiteness of its walls, thinking back on the journey with a knot in his stomach. For all her child-like appearance, she was brave and capable; but she was also sweet-natured, and too guileless to hide her love for him. It pained him that he could not return her feelings. Once, in Forluin, it had been second nature to receive and give affection to everyone around him; that was the Forluinish way, as natural to them as breathing.

No longer, he thought bitterly, recalling the priestess's sad face as night after night he had wrapped himself in his cloak to sleep alone. Perhaps his ability to love had died with Kharan. Should he blame Xaedrek, or Ferdanice – or himself, for not being stronger?

'Greetings, Falmeryn of Forluin.' The voice made him start. There was a priest standing in the doorway, a middle-aged man with a long, sharp face and dark hair. 'Our sister has told me about you. I think you had better come inside.'

Within the Temple, a cool twilight enfolded him and the air was sweet with flowers and perfumed smoke. The Temple had the shape of two overlapping circles, and in the centre of each stood an immense statue, one male and one female. Each bore a globe of rock. Falmeryn gazed at them, fascinated by the frozen folds of their robes, the creamy limbs with every muscle perfectly delineated, the crisply carved hair. Their eyes were like moons, their faces tranquil and benevolent. Glints of candlelight caught on the silver rails that enclosed their bases.

'They represent the moons. The man is Jaed, the woman Fliya,' said the priest, leading Falmeryn to a central dais where the priestess was waiting. 'Now, will you show me this stone that you claim is the substance of Fliya?'

'I was told to take it to the enchantress, Mellorn. No disrespect, but it's her I really need to speak to. Can I see her?'

The priest looked grave, and rubbed at his chin. Eventually he said, 'The enchantress, I'm sorry to have to tell you, is not here. She went to Heldavrain many months ago.'

'Where's that?'

'North of Ehd'rabara. A thousand miles from here.'

'Oh, no.' Falmeryn closed his eyes, stupefied. 'I don't believe it. It's vital that I reach her!'

The priestess slid her hand through his arm, but he did not look at her. He did his best to explain about Ferdanice, but she and the priest both seemed at a loss.

'Unfortunately, our chief priest Irem Ol Melemen is not here either,' the priest said. 'He would know what to do . . . However, as I am empowered to act in his place, I must make a decision.'

'You mean, decide whether you believe me or not?' Falmeryn said. He took the pouch from his belt and carefully opened the square of vellum. The dust within gleamed palely. 'Can you really judge what this is, whether it's good or evil? I don't know whether what I'm doing is right or wrong. I can't think about it any more. The only thing I'm certain of is that the enchantress needs this to defeat Xaedrek!'

'I believe him, brother,' said the priestess.

'I don't disbelieve him . . .' The priest gazed at the dust, perplexed. 'You're right, Falmeryn, I cannot act as a judge in this matter. It is too great for me. I think you must go to Ehd'rabara with all speed. The invasion could be at any time. I'll take full responsibility myself – you shall have good horses, and soldiers to accompany you.'

'Thank you,' said Falmeryn. 'But there's something else. Ferdanice said that Mellorn would also need stone from Jaed, and that it was in Charhn somewhere.'

The priest ran a hand over his hair, seeming almost embarrassed. 'We say that the Temple itself is built of the rock that fell from Jaed – but we are also aware that it is only – hm – a myth.'

'Perhaps it isn't. The dust of Fliya has drawn me here like a lodestone.'

'We must have faith, my brother,' said the priestess. 'Let us chip a piece from the base of Jaed's statue. If anyone has to take the blame for defacing the Temple, let it be me!'

Dubiously, the priest agreed. The rock was not hard, and they managed to lever out a loose fragment that weighed roughly the same as the dust. When replaced in the pouch, the shard and the vellum package clung snugly together like magnets.

'I'm grateful for your help,' Falmeryn said. He turned to the priestess. 'And especially for yours.'

'Don't start saying farewell.' She put a finger to his lips. 'I'm coming to Heldavrain with you.'

'Sire. Sire!'

A voice penetrated the blackness, urgent yet very far away. Xaedrek stirred, but he could make no sense of anything. Someone was shaking him . . .

'Amnek?' he murmured, opening his eyes. He saw a face floating in a grey haze, and a sudden rush of memory made him struggle to sit up.

'Sire! By the gods, I thought you were dead. Don't try to get up – I'll fetch a physician.'

It was Valamek. Finding himself alive, seeing the concerned face of the Duke hovering over him, Xaedrek breathed a huge sigh of relief and slumped back onto the floor. His head was splitting, his body sore and bruised. Valamek began to bundle up a garment to place under his head, but Xaedrek stayed his hand.

'It's all right, Valamek. I don't need the physician.' With an effort, he held onto the young man's arm and rose painfully to his feet.

'But, Sire –' Valamek cried helplessly, knowing it was no use arguing with him. 'Let me help you to a chair, at least.'

'Where are they? Have they been arrested?'

'Who, Sire?' Xaedrek did not reply. He observed that the couch where Irem Ol Thangiol had been lying was empty,

182

and he sank heavily into the chair. 'Sire, what happened to you?'

'You don't know?'

'No – I heard a commotion, but when I came in and found you on the floor, there was no one else here.'

'And you did not see Amnek and Ah'garith leave? It could only have been a minute ago.'

Valamek frowned. 'All the time you were in here with them, I was in my office. The door was open, so they could not have left this chamber without me noticing them. But no one came past.'

'Well, they've gone, all the same.'

'And it was they who – who attacked you?' He went to open a window. Feathers of ash from the blackened tapestry blew across the room.

'Yes,' Xaedrek replied grimly. 'They have both betrayed me. Amnek, of all people . . .'

It was Valamek who was outraged and alarmed, while Xaedrek was collected, even thoughtful.

'I'll have the guards begin an immediate search,' Valamek exclaimed, hurrying to the door. 'Do you wish them taken alive, Sire, or executed on sight?'

'Amnek executed. I doubt that they'll get near Ah'garith, and it could be dangerous to try. But, Valamek – as you are the only one who knows an attempt was made on my life, I want you to ensure it remains our secret.' Valamek understood. People must not suspect any vulnerability in their Emperor.

While the young man was gone, Xaedrek leaned on the edge of a table, and cradled his aching head in his hands. Despite the pain, his mind had cleared swiftly. He went through every detail of the preceding events, until the revelation came to him that he had been possessed by the Shanin, *but he was possessed no longer*. It was a hideous mental slavery which no human had ever escaped, and yet Xaedrek, possibly through sheer obstinacy, had somehow broken the spell.

He was sane, and free.

He laughed. His bodily discomfort began to ease. It was

obvious that Ah'garith and Amnek had fled because they knew they could not defeat him. Let them hide where they would; they could not touch him now, and once the conquest of Kristillia was achieved there would be time enough to track them down and destroy them.

Yet Ah'garith's power must have increased for her to have regained her ability to move between dimensions. And she had freed herself of his hold over her . . .

Valamek returned, out of breath.

'It's done, Sire. They're searching every inch of the residence and the city. They'll find them in no time.'

'I doubt it,' the Emperor murmured.

'Sire?' Valamek came to his side, frowning. 'May I ask why they so suddenly turned against you?'

'Differences of opinion, my friend. It was inevitable, though rather unexpected, I must admit.'

'By the gods, Sire,' said Valamek in sudden dismay. 'Without Ah'garith, there will be no more amulin!'

Xaedrek released a slow breath. 'It's not as disastrous as it seems. We have a great deal in store – I saw to that years ago. There is enough for our needs, at least until the war is over. As to them taking Irem Ol Thangiol, that is inconvenient, but I doubt that he would have lived much longer in any case. And after the war we will find a new source of power.'

'Still using human victims?'

'I fear so. I have had a small taste of Melkavesh's sorcery and I agree that it is a pure, clean power infinitely superior to ours,' Xaedrek said sardonically. 'Unfortunately, as she seems to be the only one privileged to wield the power naturally, the rest of us are left no choice but to use artificial means. Yes, Valamek, there will always be human victims.'

As he spoke, there was the tramping of booted feet in the corridor and two of his personal guard strode in with a Gorethrian messenger between them.

'What is it?' Valamek intercepted them, wanting to spare Xaedrek any further disturbance. 'Have you detained Amnek?'

'No, Your Grace,' one of the guards replied. 'But this man

has ridden by swift relay with an urgent message from the Lady Lirurmish in Cevandaris.'

More bad news, Xaedrek thought drily, and turned to look at the messenger. 'Very well, let us hear it.'

The man, still breathless from his ride, bowed smartly and said, 'The Lady Lirurmish's message is simply this. "I am ready when you are." She said you would know what it meant, Your Majesty.'

'I do.' The Emperor's spirits lifted. He knew he was truly free of Ah'garith when he realised that his sense of oppression had vanished. 'Indeed I do. Guards, see that this man receives the full hospitality of my residence, food, rest, fresh clothes – whatever he wants. He has truly gladdened my heart on a day when I thought it impossible.'

'My thanks, Sire!' The messenger bowed again, trying to conceal his delight. When he and the guards had gone, Xaedrek turned back to Valamek, who was smiling broadly.

'I knew Lady Lirurmish would not let us down. The battle machines are ready. So, Valamek, we'll soon be preparing for the long march to the Omnuandrix, meeting Lirurmish on the way . . . Fetch a quill and paper, would you? Better still, we'll adjourn to your office.'

'Sire, you really ought to rest,' Valamek said anxiously.

'Yes, later. First I wish to draft the message that will be sent to the Kristillians when the time comes. One copy to King Afil Es Thendil, and one to Prince Rar An Tolis in Ehd'rabara.' Valamek caught the chilling look in the Emperor's eyes, and almost felt a kind of pity for the Kristillians. 'A courteous message,' Xaedrek went on, 'giving Melkavesh and her allies the chance to surrender without undue bloodshed.'

9

'Xaedrek will destroy you'

AT FIRST light, a horseman in the blue and silver livery of
Ehd'rabara came clattering over the causeway with an urgent
message for Melkavesh. The Mangorian dawn patrol had
intercepted him and were now running beside him, shouting
at the castle guards to raise the portcullis and take him
directly to the Sorceress.

A few minutes later, he was before her desk, waiting
anxiously as she perused the scroll he had brought. Kharan
leaned on the back of her chair, while N'golem, U'garet,
and several Kristillians crowded round to read it.

'This is the actual letter that the Gorethrian envoy gave to
Prince Rar An Tolis? Not a copy?' Melkavesh asked.

'That's the very letter, my lady,' the messenger answered.
'His Highness barely read it before he bade me dispatch it
to you.'

Melkavesh flattened the bottom portion of the roll and
recognised Xaedrek's seal and his strong, elegant signature.
She shivered. It was so familiar, that writing.

There was something even more chilling in the innocuous
formality of the letter's phrasing. The Emperor required
access to trade routes across Kristillia, it said, in accordance
with a treaty of friendship drawn up between their countries
some eight hundred years ago. The Emperor was certain that
the denial of access was an oversight on King Afil Es Thendil's
part, rather than a deliberate breach of the treaty, in which
case he was sure that the King, in the interests of peace and
friendship between their respective countries, would be only

too glad to remedy the matter immediately . . . and so on.

When she had read it she sat gripping the edges until they began to buckle from her fingers' dampness. 'Has the Prince replied yet?'

'He was composing a reply to the effect that if the Gorethrians set one foot on Kristillian soil, they would have Haeth Im Nerek's army to trade with.'

'And what about the King?'

'There hasn't been time for news to reach us from Charhn,' the Ehd'rabara said, 'but if Afil Es Thendil has received a similar demand for surrender, he will undoubtedly have answered it in the same way.'

'This is it, then. War,' Melkavesh said quietly. No one else spoke, but she could feel all their eyes on her. She had striven for this position of power and leadership, but at this moment she feared that the pressure of it would prove more than she could bear. She let the paper snap back into a roll and stood up. 'I'll come to Ehd'rabara immediately.'

The prospect of invasion had hung over Kristillia like a leaden hammer for so long that it had become a backcloth to the more pressing problems of everyday life. Now the waiting was over, the reality of it washed over Melkavesh like a sheet of ice water.

She stood in front of a mirror in her chamber, settling a green velvet cloak on her shoulders. Her reflection gazed back broodingly, a tall Gorethrian woman caparisoned in the dark brown war gear of a Kristillian officer, with long, strapped boots and bronze circles glinting on breastplate and sheath. It could almost have been Ashurek's face staring at her, the same high cheekbones and brilliant eyes. She looked cool, totally self-possessed – and certainly impressive, she thought with a dry smile. Her hair shone like captive sunlight. But a globe of emotion and terror pulsed in her stomach, threatening to burst through the shell of calmness.

She had always known that this moment would come, and imagined it so often that the reality of it became dreamlike. It seemed a lifetime since she had left Shalekahh, although she remembered it as if it had all happened yesterday; only

Filmoriel's growth anchored her to the reality of time. The child was three years old.

Outside, the clouds were swollen like blood blisters and grumbled with distant thunder. For the past few months, Kristillia's usually mild weather had been changing in a sinister way. It was too much to believe that Xaedrek had anything to do with it, yet it was an ominous coincidence that as the invasion drew closer, the sky became ever darker, and affected everyone with its static tension. Melkavesh's percipience told her only that it boded ill; without far-sight, she could not discover its true nature. The frustration of the impediment ground at her, day after day.

Since Anixa's arrival, Xaedrek had made no further attempt on her life. She was more alarmed than relieved. It was as if he saw nothing to fear in her, or was supremely confident of victory – perhaps with reason. She suppressed a spasm of apprehension.

As she got ready, Kharan appeared in the doorway with Filmoriel in her arms.

'Melkavesh,' she said, 'I want to come with you.'

'You what?' The Sorceress swung round, shocked. 'Have you gone mad? The battle will be right under Ehd'rabara's walls. If it comes to the worst, the town itself will be held to siege!'

'I know,' Kharan whispered. Her face was as pale as linen, and her eyes seemed too large, too brilliant.

'Then why ever do you want to come? I never thought it was your vocation to prove yourself a warrior!'

'It isn't. I'd be terrified, but –'

'Then don't think about it. You're safe here,' Melkavesh snapped, unreasonably irritated. Why did Kharan always have to be difficult?

'Maybe so, but I don't *feel* it. I'd feel safer if I was with you.'

'Oh, would you?' She pushed the cloak back over her shoulders and folded her arms. 'And what about Filmoriel? I can't see you leaving her behind, and how safe do you think *she'd* be in the middle of Ehd'rabara, with the Gorethrians storming the walls?'

'If it gets that far, how safe will this castle be?' Kharan's voice was as brittle as a frosted leaf. For a moment they glared at each other, then Kharan walked up to Melkavesh and set her daughter down on the floor. 'Mel, we've been through everything together. Xaedrek nearly killing us both – the Emethrians – Mangorad – and all that's happened since. And now this last thing is going to happen, you're telling me you don't need me any more.'

'It's because I need you, I don't want you to put yourself in danger.' Melkavesh spoke shortly, trying to hide the tremor in her voice. 'And don't make it sound so final. It's just a battle . . .' She turned away, and busied herself unnecessarily checking the weapons laid out on her bed.

'Don't you think it's a bit late to start wrapping me in cotton wool?' Kharan asked. There was no reply. 'Gods, you can be so cold!' she exclaimed.

And saw that Melkavesh was weeping.

Kharan tugged her arm, made her turn round, and then they embraced, tightly and desperately, like sisters who would never see each other again.

'Kharan, I beg you to listen to me and stay in the castle. I'd worry myself sick if I knew you were in the town, and I'll have enough to think about. If not for your own sake, for Filmoriel's.'

Kharan nodded, and leaned her forehead against the taller woman's shoulder. 'Yes, she is the one who matters.'

'Anixa needs you too. Besides, who is going to run my household in my absence, if not you?'

'I suppose you're right.' Kharan slackened her embrace and stepped back, wiping her eyes. 'I just have a – a bad feeling about staying here. I shall be so worried about you.'

'Well, don't be. There's no need.'

'I can't help it. I know things have not gone as you hoped. I have said some terrible things to you at times – that you were responsible for this war, or making it worse than it need be. Perhaps I was unfair. Someone has to stop Xaedrek, and at least you have the courage to try. It's just that you were so arrogant then – and I didn't understand how hard things were going to be for you.'

189

'Nor I,' Melkavesh said quietly. She longed to say something heartening which would at least make Kharan's waiting more bearable, but the platitudes turned to dust on her tongue and what emerged instead was the truth, in all its bleakness. 'I didn't know what doubt was when I first came to this Earth. Now I look back and I think that perhaps the very first step I made took me onto the wrong road. I keep thinking, *there should have been an answer other than war* – and it's just as if Silvren is at my side, speaking the words.

'I was arrogant, marching across Vardrav, stirring up the Mangorians and the Kristillians and never doubting that I was going to unlock some marvellous secret of sorcery that would free Vardrav and put everything right. But I haven't.

'The truth is, there has been no miracle. Perhaps I should accept that there never will be . . . That the "secret" was a self-delusion and all those tantalising dreams of the moons just mind tricks.'

Melkavesh lowered her eyes as she finished, and involuntarily looked straight into the sombre grey gaze of Filmoriel. A faint sense of shock went through her. The child said nothing, but Melkavesh had the eerie feeling that she understood everything that had been said. Filmoriel was a latent Sorceress – the only one Melkavesh had found so far – but that did not explain why Melkavesh had dreamed of her even before she had been born, nor why the child should sometimes see a bird that simply was not there. Filmoriel grew more like the red-haired girl in her dreams every day, and she found it deeply unnerving.

'I don't understand these metaphysical things,' Kharan said, placing a trembling hand on Melkavesh's shoulder. 'I'm just trying to say that regardless of the differences we've had, I do love you dearly and I pray with all my soul that you win and come home safely.'

'I will.' The possibility that Xaedrek might triumph and that any or all of them might be slain could not be spoken, but it hung between them like a stiff, cold fog. And at that moment Melkavesh knew that she loved Kharan as she had loved no one since Silvren and Ashurek; that the An'raagan was her closest, if not her only, friend. And it suddenly seemed she was fighting the war not for the Kristillians, but for her and Filmoriel alone. *Filmoriel, my little Sorceress . . .* But the words constricted her throat and stung her eyes, and she could not speak. With a last hug for Kharan, a kiss for the child, she gathered up her weapons and strode out, not daring to allow herself a backward glance.

The small group of Kristillians rode urgently, their heads down and their shoulders hunched. Sheets of rain flapped around them, and lightning seared across a sky that was the colour of watered mud.

'We'll make for that rock,' the Commander shouted. 'It'll shelter us from the worst of it until it abates!'

The priestess glanced at Falmeryn with a grimace, and he returned the look, trying to ignore the rain trickling down his neck. The horses were alarmed by the storm and galloped with miserably flattened ears, their manes snapping like wet string. Ahead of them, a knoll jutted from the rain-drenched hillside.

How long can we afford to wait? Falmeryn wondered.

They were still several days' ride from Heldavrain. There was no telling when Xaedrek might attack, but with the troops massing in Kesfaline it was undoubtedly imminent. As the party rode further north and west, the weather worsened as if nature itself were in collaboration with Gorethria, and the dread it induced drove them on at a pitch of feverish urgency. Whatever his doubts had been, nothing mattered more than defeating Xaedrek, and Falmeryn's greatest fear was not reaching the enchantress in time.

The pouch strapped to his belt now contained the dust of Fliya and a piece of stone chipped from the dais in the temple. The two substances seemed to cleave together and there was no longer any pull towards Charhn. It was one more weird event in a chain he had given up trying to understand.

They were within fifty yards of the hill now. Falmeryn and the priestess rode in the centre, flanked by the ten warriors with their Commander in the forefront.

'We're so wet already, there doesn't seem much point in sheltering,' the man on Falmeryn's left said wryly. He was about to agree, when a long flash of lightning bleached the landscape to silver and they saw, in the demon-light, a horde of figures flowing round the side of the hill towards them. The hawk helms in silhouette and the horses like liquid flame were unmistakable.

'Ambush!' the Commander yelled. As one the Kristillians drew their spears and swung the horses uphill to get above the Gorethrians, but as they turned they saw more riding out of a hollow on their left. They were trapped. Falmeryn and the priestess drew their swords as the Commander ordered his men into battle formation, but there were only thirteen of them and the Gorethrians numbered at least thirty.

The moment they were in range, the Kristillians hurled their spears. But a brassy halo of amulin surrounded the Gorethrians, and with almost languid ease they swung their blades to knock the spears out of the air. Only one rider fell as a shaft drove into his chest. The Imperial troops wasted no time in throwing spears but closed in from both sides with their swords at the ready. A heartbeat later, the hillside exploded into the fury of battle.

Hooves pounded the grass into mud, and the air was torn by the screams of horses and men, the crunch of metal cleaving leather, sinew and bone. Spheres of false sorcery hissed through the rain; olive and tan sparks drizzled down onto the earth and vanished amid rivulets of blood and rain. Outnumbered as they were, the Kristillians fought back ferociously.

It was not unknown for Gorethrians to penetrate Kristillia in small groups, though they did not usually get this far, and the Commander had not expected an attack. He fought instinctively, but Falmeryn had never been involved in a battle before, and he was wholly unprepared for the speed and chaos of it.

He barely had time to slide his shield onto his arm before there was a Gorethrian bearing down on him. He froze, his horse shied; then a Kristillian warrior swerved in front of

192

him and took the sword blow that had been meant for Falmeryn.

Horrified, he watched the man fall. He had been talking to him a few minutes earlier. He looked around wildly for the priestess, but she had been separated from him in the confusion and there was nothing he could do to protect her. The Gorethrians were all around them. With his heart lurching and his breath rasping painfully, he fought to control his horse as another black-clad rider came plunging towards him.

Falmeryn was no warrior, and knew he did not stand a chance. But as when he had faced the moon leopard, he felt something like amulin searing through him, a loss of inhibition, and he urged his mount forward to meet the attack. He did not merely want to defend himself. He wanted to kill . . .

He took the first blow on his shield, and gasped as the shock jarred through his shoulder. The golden horse was trained to fight and was dancing around him, biting and striking at his own beast, which squealed and tried to retaliate. It was all Falmeryn could do to keep a grip on his sword. He thrust out with it, but the Gorethrian avoided the blow with graceful ease and then he realised it was a woman's face under the dark helm, a woman's face with a cold, mocking smile on her lips.

He made to strike again, but her horse sank its teeth into his arm and he cried out. As he smacked its head away he saw vividly its scarlet nostrils, the sable fire in its eyes. Another blow came, he met it, and for a few moments he fell into the rhythm of swordplay and fended her off. But it could not last. Every blow drained his strength, and he could find no way through her guard – and then she tricked him with a misleading stroke, and her sword came flashing down towards his neck.

In the same instant, his horse reared. The blade slashed the leather of his boot instead, and he felt a ghastly sinking sensation as the beast lost its balance and toppled over backwards. It crashed heavily to the ground, pinning him underneath.

193

Falmeryn lay winded with mud oozing coldly against his skull and a mosaic of black and red flowers exploding across his eyes. He was losing consciousness; his last sight was of the war-horse's belly as the Gorethrian urged it forward and jumped clean over him and his steed. Somehow he knew that the battle was at an end. There were still Gorethrians milling about, but the fighting had stopped . . .

When he came round, a dense, chilling silence blanketed the hill. His horse had gone; he hoped it had escaped unhurt. Clambering painfully to his knees he stared through the rain, waiting for his head to clear so that he could make sense of what he was seeing. Twenty yards away, beneath the knoll where they had planned to shelter, four brown horses stood in a miserable huddle. The rest must have bolted. The Gorethrians were gone, but all over the hillside there were the dark shapes of corpses.

He stood up unsteadily with his mud-sodden cloak swinging around him, oblivious to his aches and bruises. There were about ten Gorethrians, so they had not escaped unscathed, but there were at least as many Kristillians. He stumbled among them, his eyes burning as he saw the familiar faces, blanched and lifeless, with rain running into their mouths. Their limbs were twisted at awkward angles, water and blood had pooled in the folds of their uniforms. He counted eleven; the ten soldiers and their officer, all dead, all, but he could not find the priestess and his breath sawed convulsively through his throat as he went from one body to the next, searching desperately.

Then he saw her. She was half hidden behind the bulk of a large warrior who must have died trying to save her. She seemed so small, just a heap of inky shadow in the gloom. He knelt down to pick her up, and as he did so she groaned and opened her eyes.

'Oh, Falmeryn,' she gasped. 'Oh, praise Jaed and Fliya, you're alive!'

'Hush. Lie still. I'll catch the horses and we'll find a village.'

'No, don't – it's no use. Stay with me.'

Then he felt the visceral slime congealing on her robes, and he knew that she was dying and there was nothing he

194

could do. He sat down and cradled her against him. She had been shivering, but seemed to relax at his touch, and after a moment she looked up at him and whispered, 'Falmeryn, I never dared tell you how much I love you. I suppose I was afraid of sounding foolish. But I can say it now, for I've nothing to lose. I hoped – I hoped so much that in time you might have come to love me as well. Could you have done?'

Falmeryn could barely speak. He swallowed roughly. 'Yes, I could. I do.'

At this she smiled weakly and reached up to grip his hand. He wrapped his arms round her, and the comfort she received from his embrace was so great that it was almost tangible. Because he was there she felt no pain, only happiness, and the realisation came close to destroying him. He had given her so little.

'Then I am already cradled in the arms of Jaed and Fliya,' she said.

'I'm here with you. It's all right . . .'

He bent to kiss her cheek, and felt her last breath against his lips. In death she looked even more like a child – a sleeping child, free of all pain and fear. He let her down very gently onto the grass, composed her body, and found a discarded cloak with which to cover her.

He was weeping openly now, unselfconsciously, for there was no one to see him. Again he had survived as if by chance; and deep inside him was a pure anger against whatever supernatural force perpetually spared him while others died. Still sobbing, he went mechanically about the task of catching a horse and checking it over in preparation to ride.

The Gorethrians seemed to have stolen nothing; the pouch was still at his belt. It was ominous that they had penetrated so far into Kristillia, and that they had been intent not on taking prisoners but on killing. It could only mean that the invasion had already begun. It was more urgent than ever that he reached Heldavrain.

'Damn you, Ferdanice,' he murmured. He swung up into the saddle and looked across the battlefield. 'So much power, and there was nothing you could do to prevent this? If only you'd returned to the Circle of Spears a month, a week

195

earlier, I might have reached the enchantress in time. Or perhaps you hoped I'd be too late . . .'

With the rain washing the tears from his face, he turned away from the corpses of his friends and rode on towards Heldavrain alone.

Ehd'rabara was more imposing than Charhn in its way, though less ethereal. Towers of oyster-pale stone rose from the water's edge in dignified ranks, and floating from each turret was a banner of midnight blue with the double moon symbol picked out in silver. Melkavesh arrived at the north gate to find Haeth Im Nerek waiting for her, a small and dauntless figure in a uniform of umber leather and a green and gold cape. With her were four guards in Prince Rar An Tolis's livery.

'Oh, you've come,' Im Nerek said unenthusiastically. 'On your own?'

'I swift-travelled most of the way,' Melkavesh said, slightly out of breath. 'My army are following on as fast as possible. They should be here this evening.'

'*Your* army. Good.'

'You know what I mean.' She was in no mood for the Battle Marshal's hostility. The journey had enervated her far more than it should have done, and the dark, oppressive weather seemed to worsen her discomfort.

'It's none of my business, of course,' Im Nerek said as they went through the tall gate, 'but you do not look well.'

'I'm perfectly all right,' Melkavesh snapped. Then she said more gently, 'Look, I don't ask you to like me, but hadn't we better forget our personal feelings until the battle's over?'

'I don't dislike you, Lady Mellorn. I simply don't know why you are here. But as long as the King insists I must work with you, so I will.'

'Well, that's magnanimous of you,' she sighed. 'What's the news?'

The Battle Marshal answered matter of factly, 'Grim. There's a large force of Gorethrians mustering on the far bank of the Omnuandrix, led by Baramek himself.'

Again Melkavesh had to force down a wave of dread. As they walked towards the towering keep where Prince Rar An Tolis and the senior officers had their quarters, the sky turned greenish and a sharp wind sprang up. On it Melkavesh could taste something metallic, sinister. She wondered, *Do I appear as confident as Haeth Im Nerek does? And inside, is she as plagued by doubts as I am?*

At the keep, Prince Rar An Tolis greeted Melkavesh warmly, and she was rather surprised to find Irem Ol Melemen there as well, having just arrived from Charhn. He offered no explanation, but she had a groundless feeling that he had been sent to keep an eye on her. The atmosphere was as tense and black as the weather.

A council of war began almost at once, with an officer describing the positions and approximate numbers of Baramek's troops. It was hard for the Kristillians to keep watch on them, he said, because scouts sent across the river often did not return. Melkavesh bowed her head as she listened to this. Now her loss of far-sight was not her problem alone; it was costing other people's lives.

'Send no more scouts,' she said. 'I will cross the river myself and watch them under a guise of invisibility.'

'Thank you, but there's no point now,' Prince Rar An Tolis said slowly. 'We know enough, which is that tomorrow or the day after, the Gorethrians will try to cross the river. I'd rather you saved your energy for the battle itself. Lady Mellorn, we are all very glad that you are here.'

The meeting went on all day, with a continual coming and going of officers and town elders. The apprehension that hung over them became edged with a certain excitement because Melkavesh was with them. She did not even have to do or say anything; the mere sight of her was enough to bring a fevered shine to their eyes. They were so grateful that she had chosen to be here instead of Charhn, but their reverence embarrassed her. She no longer felt worthy of it. What had she really done for them, apart from giving them some inspiration? Nothing . . .

That evening she was allocated a circular chamber in a high tower, part of the senior officers' quarters. Once her

197

soldiers had arrived from Heldavrain, she retired to bed early, hoping to regain the strength she had lost during the journey. Recently even the briefest use of her sorcery tired her, and in darker moments she wondered if all her power was doomed to be drawn into the void that had claimed her far-sight. She could draw energy from a normal storm, but the weird weather that plagued them now seemed to have the opposite effect. It was as if she were being bled . . .

She tried to put the thoughts from her mind, and sleep. She must have dozed off eventually, because she was awoken from a leaden nightmare of Ah'garith by a lamp shining at the end of her bed. Haeth Im Nerek stood there, her uniform dark with rain, her face very grim.

'What is it?' Melkavesh slurred, sitting up and trying to shake off the heavy dream. 'Something wrong?'

'The Gorethrians have made a bridgehead over the river,' said the Battle Marshal.

'In the middle of the night?'

'We suspected they might try it. We were ready for them – at least, we thought we were.' Melkavesh felt her stomach turn cold as Im Nerek went on, 'A landing party ferried across on a barge. The idea was that a small force of our men would take them by surprise before they could gain a foothold.' She paused as if she did not know how to go on.

'And they failed?'

'I was on the hill some distance away when the Commander gave our men the order. It was hard to see what was happening. Our soldiers rushed into the attack, the Gorethrians fought back for a few minutes – then they just turned and ran, and a second later a ball of fire came arcing over from the far bank and landed right in the centre of our troop. A few escaped. Most of them were burned alive.' Her expression did not change, but her eyes were glassy with shock. She moistened her lips. 'They must have had a massive incendiary catapult on the other side, though Fliya knows how it could be so accurate.'

'Gods,' Melkavesh exclaimed, scrambling from the bed. 'Why didn't you take me with you? I could have done something – protected them, destroyed the weapon –'

198

'I didn't think you'd be needed. I wanted you to conserve your strength for the main battle.'

'Or you wanted to prove who is in command, and that you can manage quite well without me?' Melkavesh retorted acidly. There was a pause.

'That was unfair,' Im Nerek breathed. 'If I had known they had such a weapon, I would have asked your help. The blame is mine.'

'I'm sorry,' Melkavesh said stiffly. 'So, what's the situation now?'

'They've established their position, and they're setting up a bridge of barges to bring their troops and horses across. Ingenious.'

'And is there nothing we can do to dislodge them?'

'Not with that weapon there. But they would have got across one way or another in the end, while we wasted any number of men trying to stop them. In fact, it's best we confront them on this side of the river, so that they'll be below us with their line of retreat cut off. Well, now you know the worst, I am going to have some breakfast and then I am returning to the field. You may as well go back to sleep.'

'I shan't get any more sleep tonight. I'll come with you. What time is it?'

'Sunrise,' said Im Nerek with a hollow laugh.

'Sunrise? But it's still pitch dark . . .'

'You explain it, Enchantress.'

There was no turning back now.

By the time Melkavesh had dressed and eaten, daylight was still no more than a diffuse glimmer along the horizon. Ehd'rabara's towers were washed with a dim luminosity and the river glittered like steel under a swollen, green-black sky. Lukewarm rain fell steadily, and there was not even a breath of wind to make the day seem less turbid.

She was not afraid. No Gorethrian about to go into war would admit to feeling anything but savage excitement, and her father's blood was strong in her. Her pulse was pounding in her ears, but her hands were steady on Faara's reins as she rode away from the towering city wall at Haeth Im Nerek's side. Behind them, the huge gate clanged shut as the citizens prepared for a siege.

What gnawed at her was not fear for herself, but a profound sense of wrongness, incompleteness. Somehow events had slid out of her control. Xaedrek was ready for war, but she was not . . . And yet, without her far-sight, would she ever have been ready? She had already spent too long questing through limbo, as blind as a worm. She could bear no more of that. Let it be over, she thought fiercely.

Let it be over.

The same thought haunted King Afil Es Thendil as he waited on a hill-top near Charhn, his horse crunching impatiently at its bit. Afil An Mora was at his side, and both were clad in regal armour of gold-figured leather. A group of generals, standard-bearers and equerries surrounded them.

Their army was arrayed across the hillside below them, a sea of cavalry and infantry which would daunt any foe. The day was bright but overcast, and the air churned with the clammy promise of a storm.

'Even though Mellorn is not here, I almost feel as if she is with us,' Es Thendil said. His voice was muffled and hollow behind his visor, which was fashioned to represent the face of Jaed. 'The troops sense it too. The inspiration she brought us has not faded.'

'And the will to win is everything,' said An Mora from behind the silver and gold visage of Fliya. The tension between them over Kharan had been submerged by the imminence of war. There was a closeness and comradeship between them now which she could only pray would last after victory was won.

'Sire,' said General En Scanon, a large man with a bushy red beard, 'our scouts report that the Gorethrian army is continuing to advance and will come in sight within a few minutes. A General Kadurik is commanding them.'

'Not High Commander Baramek?'

'No, Sire. I assume he is at Ehd'rabara.'

'Well then, let this Kadurik come,' the King said thinly.

200

'We are ready for him.' He was surprised at how calm he felt, after all the doubts and apprehensions of the past years, yet it was not so strange. When choice was gone and his only responsibility was to lead his people into battle, everything became simple.

'I am proud of you,' the Queen said softly. She was almost ashamed of herself for thinking of him as being weak, for not seeing that his strength was buried deep. 'And I am honoured to fight at your side.'

'You did not have to.' He reached out and clasped her gauntleted hand in his own. 'But I am glad.'

'We live or die together. King and Queen. We are one.'

They were silent, looking out over the beloved landscape that had suffered the march of Gorethrian feet for centuries and must now defend its transient freedom yet again. And as they watched, a black line appeared on the horizon and advanced relentlessly – a violation of the soft green fells.

The King's mouth went dry as he saw the size of Kadurik's force. It was just as if a forest had uprooted itself and was flowing towards them; and the forest bristled with spears, and was borne forward on a tide of golden horses.

'By the moons, Im Nerek was wrong,' he said. 'The main brunt of the attack must be here, not at Ehd'rabara! General, do we advance now, or wait until they are closer?'

'We wait, Sire, but presently we will move into the vanguard and I will judge the moment for you to lead the charge . . .' the General trailed off, distracted. 'That is strange. They seem to have halted their advance.'

The Gorethrian lines had come to a standstill for no apparent reason, and seemed to be waiting for something. Es Thendil felt a trickle of sweat run down behind his visor, and could do nothing to brush it away. The sky was a mass of dark cloud, the atmosphere so thick and heavy that it seemed about to explode with collective tension.

'Why have they stopped?' the Queen demanded, but no one answered her. The Kristillian troops began to shift and murmur uneasily. Strange colours crackled on the horizon and a deep, unpleasant humming reached their ears. Moments

201

dragged by as if time itself had become distorted, and still the Imperial army remained in their neat ranks, waiting.

Two miles south of Ehd'rabara, Baramek looked up at the sky and cursed. The darkness had provided useful cover for the crossing, but now it could only be a hindrance.

The bridgehead had proved very successful, if messy. The highly strung horses had churned up the bank as they disembarked, covering themselves and everyone in the vicinity with mud. Officers had directed the men to sluice off the worst of it. Better to ride uncomfortably wet into battle than looking as disreputable as the Kristillians.

That done, the Gorethrians had moved with swift discipline into their ranks; Baramek and his entourage in the forefront, then lines of mounted crossbowmen, followed by the infantry. Blocks of cavalry jog-trotted on the wings. Circuiting the charred corpses of the Kristillians who had tried to stop them the night before, they marched towards the walls of Ehd'rabara.

The hills were colourless in the rain, and to the left the Omnuandrix lay as dull as an iron sword. Then for an unexpected moment, a blade of sunlight forced its way through the clouds and shone on a great curving mass of warriors waiting on the hillside above them.

Baramek, much as he despised the Kristillians, had to admit a grudging admiration for the improvement in their turnout. Their uniforms gleamed like polished wood, bronze circles shone on their breastplates and shields and on the bridles of their powerful horses. There were smaller blocks of other races; he recognised the green and violet tunics of Kesfaline, white faced Ala'kaarans in black battle gear, groups of barbarous Cevandarish warriors, dour Alta-Nangrans. To his surprise there was even a section of blue-skinned Mangorian tribespeople, some of them mounted on giant reptiles. It seemed all of Vardrav had gathered to welcome Xaedrek's army . . .

On a strategic high point to the river side of the army, Baramek picked out the small figure of Haeth Im Nerek amid her heralds and officers. At her side was the unmistakable figure of Melkavesh. She was unhelmeted, and her golden hair – despite the rain – shone like a beacon that would mark her out anywhere on the battlefield. In the gloom, the Sorceress seemed to radiate a light of her own.

Baramek tightened his grip on the reins. He had known her well, so he had thought, and had believed her to be as much a loyal offspring of Gorethria as his own children. Indeed, he would once have been proud to call her his daughter. Her sudden betrayal of Xaedrek had been incredible. How could she have deceived them all so completely – unless her love of Gorethria had been at least partly genuine?

He gave a signal, and a herald raised a white glass horn to her lips and blew the command to halt.

The Kristillian force was huge. Allowing for hidden reserves and those garrisoning the city, Baramek estimated that half of Kristillia's army was here – the other half unquestionably defending Charhn against Kadurik. His own men were outnumbered, and Im Nerek's troops were evidently much better trained and disciplined than the last time he had faced them.

Nevertheless, Baramek's lips narrowed in a smile. They made a brave show, these rebels, but a show was all it was. They were about to learn an extremely unpleasant lesson concerning the inadvisability of defying Gorethria.

His only regret was the manner of it. He loved Xaedrek, but he hated necromancy, and it dismayed him to think that traditional warfare had been ousted by such unclean arts.

'Why don't they attack?' muttered Haeth Im Nerek for the twentieth time. 'What is Baramek playing at?'

'I don't know,' Melkavesh said softly. She had never felt more uneasy. The sense of wrongness was indefinable but immanent, seeming to swell the very sky into a taut, black skin. Even a degree of percipience, which she had still retained despite losing her far-sight, had failed her on this baneful morning.

She had felt a lurch in her stomach on recognising Baramek, clad in a black cloak and hawk-winged helm, and riding a pale gold stallion. The malachite shimmer of amulin was clearly visible around the Gorethrian troops as they stood patiently behind their High Commander, waiting – for what?

'If he doesn't make a move soon, I am going to,' the Battle Marshal said through gritted teeth.

'No, you must not!'

'Why not? He's calling our bluff, that's all. Again he's made the mistake of not bringing enough men, so he's trying to make us think he's got something terrible in reserve.'

'But he really has, I'm sure of it,' Melkavesh said urgently. She could dominate almost anyone when she chose, but Im Nerek was singularly headstrong and impervious to her will. The thought of her rushing hot-bloodedly into battle at this stage turned Melkavesh's stomach to ice. 'Remember the terrible flames he unleashed at your troop last night?'

'That was just a siege engine,' Im Nerek said dismissively, then paused, frowning. 'But I can see no siege engines now, not one. How can he hope to storm the city without?'

'I don't know, but please trust me, Im Nerek. This is no bluff, and if you attack now it could be disastrous.'

The Marshal's eyes gleamed as cold and hard as steel, and Melkavesh had never seen her so obdurate, as if all her hatred of Gorethria had transformed her into a fire-tempered sword. 'Don't let us forget who is in command here, Adviser,' she said in a dangerous tone. 'When I decide to advance, the decision will be right.'

Suddenly a great deal of activity began in the Gorethrian lines, with heralds coming and going between the bridgehead and Baramek's group. Evidently there was some lively communication between the west and east banks; perhaps Baramek had a vast reserve there. Melkavesh closed her eyes, drove her mind outwards in a desperate attempt to see, but as usual was met by the soul-freezing nothingness of the Wall. She withdrew swiftly, shuddering, her head pounding with the slow crescendo of rage, frustration and numbing dread. Was Xaedrek down there somewhere? Looking at Baramek, she saw his helm turned towards her, and although she was much too far away, it seemed she could see his eyes, emanating hostility like pits of yellow lava.

A shadow folded round her heart. It was so dark, and the

darkness seemed to be inside as well as outside herself. Only in the west, across the river, was there any light, and that was a silver rim along the skyline as ghastly as demon light. And silhouetted against the radiance, so small that she thought at first it must be her imagination, she saw black figures moving.

She reached out to grip Haeth Im Nerek's arm, but her fingers closed on thin air. She turned, alarmed, to see the Battle Marshal in the act of signalling the trumpeters to sound the advance.

'No!' Melkavesh cried, but her voice failed her. The nightmare unfolded before her, but she was paralysed, her limbs turned to wood.

Machines. So this is what it meant! Gods, how could I not have seen this? The full implications of her far-blindness fell on her like the moons crashing to Earth, and she thought, *My failure has destroyed us all.*

10

On the Storm-wind

No MORE than a missed heartbeat could have elapsed before Melkavesh found her voice, and her strength.

'Im Nerek!' she cried. She set her heels to Faara's side and barged in front of the Battle Marshal's mare, almost unseating her. 'Stop!'

'How dare you –' Im Nerek began, but Melkavesh interrupted desperately.

'Just listen to me! Hold the advance. There is something coming.'

She pointed, and Haeth Im Nerek squinted at the silver horizon. 'I see nothing,' she snapped.

'Be patient, use your eyes!'

Within a few seconds, the officers and standard bearers knew something was amiss, and their apprehension spread swiftly through the ranks. Soon everyone was staring out across the Omnuandrix. Silence fell over them like a smothering cloak as they watched incredulously, and when even the least keen-sighted of them could no longer dismiss what they saw as imagination, a murmur of consternation broke out that struck through Melkavesh like a knife.

Marching out of the west, outlined by fluid argent brilliance, came black giants – or statues brought to life. They moved with long, swift strides, their arms hanging stiff at their sides, their domed heads facing rigidly forwards. As they came nearer, Melkavesh counted twenty of them, moving in a rank of five across and four deep.

They were on the far bank of the Omnuandrix now, and

despite its great width, she could clearly see them approaching the water's edge without slackening their pace. Her breath stuck in her throat like a rock. The river must stop them – it *must* – but as they reached it they did not even pause. The first rank plunged into the water and waded deeper and deeper until the surface closed over their heads. The others followed.

For a few moments there was utter stillness, except for sinister ripples criss-crossing the river's surface. Everyone watched with breath suspended, while the air thickened with tension until Melkavesh felt she could have sliced it with a sword.

Even the Gorethrians seemed galvanised. Silence . . . and then the sudden, heartstopping *swoosh* as the first colossus burst through the surface and towered upwards with water cascading over its dark, shiny armour.

Screams of shock shattered the tension, and suddenly the air was full of the sounds of roaring water, terrified cries, officers yelling at their men to stay in rank. The figures began to ascend the bank, unstoppable. *Should we hold our ground, should we retreat?* Melkavesh thought wildly, too stunned to make a sensible decision. Im Nerek was open-mouthed, equally at a loss. And still the machines came on, spreading out until they had formed a staggered line along the bank, four hundred yards short of the Kristillian flank and stretching almost to the walls of Ehd'rabara. And there they stopped.

Melkavesh swiftly took in every detail. They were about thirty feet tall, fashioned in a wondrously grotesque simulation of armoured warriors. They were constructed of overlapping metal plates which she could now see were not black but a very dark blue with rainbow strands of colour playing across the surface. A green and copper halo of amulin crackled round each one, and they emitted a penetrating hum that threatened to induce a sick dizziness. A stench of charged metal wafted from them, making her gag as it brought acute and hideous memories of the amulin process. Cevandarish alloys and workmanship had made them, and there was no question as to the evil genius behind them.

'What in the name of all the gods *are* they?' Im Nerek cried.

'The reason why Baramek doesn't need many men.' Melkavesh's voice almost gave out again. 'Or any, for that matter. There must have been one of those things on the bank last night, protecting the bridgehead. And the bridgehead was just the bait to draw us out here . . .'

'Why didn't you tell me? You're the bloody Sorceress! *Why didn't you warn us?*'

'I didn't know Xaedrek had got anything like this. I swear I did not know,' she whispered, thinking, *but I should have guessed*. Her heart felt like some nerveless white thing inside her.

'How the hell do we fight them?'

There was a squeal of articulated joints and one of the machines began to move, heading for the city wall. Before Melkavesh could react, Im Nerek had wheeled her horse round and was yelling at the nearest cavalry troop to pursue and stop it. With great courage they obeyed, bending forward over their horses' necks as they threw a shoal of spears at its impervious shell. Galloping, they caught it up easily and circled the huge feet, striking at them with swords.

It was to no avail. The figure simply walked on, knocking two horses to the ground, and crushing another. When the huge foot lifted, the poor animal could be seen writhing like a mashed insect before it – and its rider – died.

One of the standard bearers uttered a sob, and passed out.

'Call them back!' Melkavesh cried, but Im Nerek ignored her. The cavalrymen continued to harass the colossus's heels, but it was oblivious to them. Halting some fifty yards from the wall, it raised an arm and unleashed an elongated globe of bronze fire at the stonework.

There was a massive explosion, a cascade of rubble masked by a plume of smoke and dust rising into the air. A shock wave both mental and physical broke over the Kristillians, and they began to surge back and forth. As the debris settled, a vast breach could be seen in the wall, with a fan of singed rocks spread out from it. There was a brief instant of disbelief.

Then the Kristillians rushed towards the machine, their fear swept away by outrage.

Melkavesh shouted until she was hoarse, but she could make no one listen or retreat. One platoon were galloping ahead of the rest towards the nearest of the figures, brandishing their spears and yelling. They came within thirty feet of it before it impassively lifted a hand and pointed at them. There was an ear-splitting screech, a beam of hyperphysical power streaking out to meet them, a flash-fire – and where the platoon had been was a blackened mass welded to the ground, the horses caught in mid-stride like half-melted sculptures. The warriors were charred skeletons with their spears still in their hands like sticks of charcoal.

'No,' Melkavesh gasped, bowing her head, fighting the white aura of faintness. 'For the Lady's sake, Im Nerek, call your troops back!'

Im Nerek did not need telling again, and the warriors were already retreating in a disordered mass. Some would have vanished from the battlefield completely, and there were several moments of confusion as the Marshal and her officers raced up and down, cajoling them back into some kind of discipline as they withdrew. Finally the army halted in an uneasy formation some four hundred yards away from the line of automatons.

Melkavesh, however, stood her ground. Most of her own followers had fled with the rest, but a handful remained, N'golem and U'garet among them.

'This is a mightier sorcery than ever you have wielded!' N'golem exclaimed. 'Why don't you retaliate? Are you unable to?'

She looked up at the machines, standing dark and solid against the lowering sky, and felt her hopes and courage failing. She should have known Xaedrek would have planned something terrible; she *had* known, but robbed of her farsight she had been like a blind, crawling thing with no more intuition than the Kristillians who had put all their faith in her. She had visualised all manner of horrors, but never weapons such as these. At this moment she hated Xaedrek with a desperate passion – and loathed herself equally.

'I might destroy one,' she said as Haeth Im Nerek came galloping breathlessly to join them. 'But if I tried –' she swallowed. Her throat was so sticky she could hardly speak. 'You've seen what they're capable of. Just one of them could destroy our whole army or Ehd'rabara itself, as soon as I made a move.'

'Is this what you have brought my people to?' N'golem said softly. She could not reply, but she felt his black eyes fixed broodingly on her as she turned to face the Battle Marshal.

'If they could destroy us so easily, what are they waiting for?' Im Nerek demanded. Melkavesh could see no fear in her, only rage, under iron control.

'Xaedrek is not a wanton destroyer. He'll do just enough to make us surrender.'

'And he expects us to give up without a fight?'

'Im Nerek, for heaven's sake! You *can't* fight them! How many more men must you lose before you believe it?'

'I believe it,' she said coldly, giving Melkavesh a look that said more than all the bitter recriminations she could have thrown at her. 'I'm headstrong, but not a fool. Ah, and now the Gorethrians are making a move at last.'

Melkavesh looked down the hill and saw a small detachment of horsemen, with Baramek at their centre, riding towards them. Two standards – one a golden hawk on purple, the other a black eagle on Xaedrek's own colours, red and white – were held crossed, indicating that a parley was being requested. Im Nerek yelled for her own standard bearers, and led the party off at a hand gallop to meet them.

The Gorethrians seemed dark and enduring as obsidian, the Kristillians a transient entity of earth and fire, as they moved towards each other and met in the rain-darkened sweep of the hillside. Lightning flickered above them; the atmosphere throbbed with the crackling of static and the sickly clean amulin smell. Melkavesh wondered briefly how the automatons were controlled, and whether Xaedrek himself was directing them from the far bank. Then she found herself barely ten feet from Baramek, looking into his harsh ochre eyes.

'My lady Melkavesh,' he said with a kind of indifferent politeness. 'The last time I saw you, I never expected our next meeting to be on opposing sides of a battlefield. Battle Marshal Haeth Im Nerek –' he nodded stiffly, but she returned the greeting with a look that might have cut him in two. 'I have long looked forward to meeting you in person. I am honoured.'

'The privilege is mine, I'm sure,' she said with a sneer. 'Can we get to business?'

'That's why I'm here. In the name of His Majesty Emperor Xaedrek of Gorethria, King of Shalekahh, Imperial Ruler of all the lands and peoples of Vardrav, I come to issue this statement. You have witnessed a small sample of what the battle machines can and will do if you do not surrender. Lay down your arms and you will be spared, but if you attempt any further aggression against the Imperial forces, your entire army will be wiped out and Ehd'rabara razed to the ground.'

It was only then that the full impact of what was happening seemed to hit Im Nerek. Her shoulders rose and fell; her whole frame seemed animated as if by amulin. Ignoring the two Gorethrian officers who were edging round behind her, she urged her mare the few yards between herself and Baramek.

The High Commander was a forbidding figure of black metal and leather, towering over Im Nerek as she turned her small face up to his. Melkavesh rode closely at her side, thinking, *Isn't she afraid of anything?*

'Do you call this a fair fight, Commander Baramek?' Im Nerek said. 'A traditionalist, I thought you were. Warrior against warrior, and may the strongest win. Now I see your men tainted with demonry, statues made to walk by vile magic, necromancy eating Gorethria's guts out like cancer. Is this what your "glorious past" has come to? Gorethria a walking corpse, only able to defeat a simple country like Kristillia by corrupt sorcery?'

Baramek's hands tightened on the reins and his eyes became murderous. But he did not raise his voice as he replied, 'I like it no more than you do, Battle Marshal. I act at my Emperor's command. Now, go back to your troops and tell them to throw down their standards and surrender. You will then ensure that the gates of Ehd'rabara are opened to admit us without resistance. And if you do not –' he pointed to the colossi – 'you know what will happen.'

'You bastard,' Im Nerek spat. 'You bastard! I'll have your head on a pole for this!'

And she wheeled her horse and raced away, her hair flying out like a storm-tattered pennant. The others galloped after her, but Melkavesh held Faara back and faced Baramek. For a moment they looked at each other, and she thought, *He has not changed. He could almost have been my father* . . . He was so different from Ashurek, and yet the regard she had had for him had been almost as great.

Baramek broke the silence. 'Well, Lady Melkavesh? Have you something to add to your comrade's statement?'

'No. I just want to know, is Xaedrek here?'

The Commander's lips twitched. 'Yes. He's here.'

'Where?'

'That is not for me to say.'

'I want to see him.'

'Well, I know he does not wish to see you. What would be the purpose?' He shook his head, grim and almost sad. 'I wish I understood you, Melkavesh. Such love as you once had for Gorethria could not have been feigned. I fail to see how such love can so easily be put aside and betrayed. If you had stayed with us, it need never have come to this!' He glanced with open distaste at the huge figures ranged along the skyline. 'Now, go back to your friends and make sure they surrender as I instructed. Or do you want to make a bloodier mess of this than you already have? We will give you one hour to make the necessary arrangements.'

She wanted to shout, *I hate what Xaedrek has done as much as you do! I had to leave him because he would not stop!* But she could not find the will to speak, nor the strength to stay under Baramek's harsh, accusing gaze. For a moment the old terror she had had of Ashurek, when as a wilful child she had goaded him to anger, flooded through her, and she pulled Faara's head round and sent her pounding up the hill as if through a slow-motion dream of mud.

The full weight of all her mistakes had descended on her like leaden chains. Her failure to kill Xaedrek when she had had the chance, her underestimation of Ah'garith, the stupid and avoidable loss of far-sight . . . So many misjudgements which should have made her realise she was not infallible. But she had gone on blindly believing in herself, and this was the result, betrayal and failure, doom for the Vardravians who had only wanted their freedom. Sorceress! she thought bitterly, feeling the power sparking beneath her skin, knowing that to use it would bring death upon them all. For the first time she wished with all her soul that she had been born without the power; and for the first time she tasted the heart-sickness that had almost destroyed Ashurek.

And on the hill, inanimate save for the deep vibration of energy, the metallic giants waited.

In Charn, also, five terrible battle machines strode into the centre of the Gorethrian lines and stood there, implacably menacing, while the Kristillians stared at them with uncomprehending dismay and terror.

'What is this?' the King cried. 'I have never seen such things before!'

'They are sorcerous,' said An Mora. She kept putting her hands to her helm, ineffectively trying to defend her ears against the machines' sickening drone.

'But Mellorn never mentioned such weapons to us! How could she – I thought –'

'That she was infallible? Either she did not know – or she has betrayed us,' the Queen said shortly.

'No. It cannot be . . .' But doubts crowded into his heart, and his head spun. False hope. Betrayal. A shower of golden hair, and beneath it the face and soul of a pure Gorethrian . . .

A messenger from General Kadurik came galloping up to them, delivered a scroll, and wheeled away. *Surrender*, the message said, *or the battle machines will destroy your army, Charn, and all her inhabitants. If you doubt that they can, a small demonstration should be sufficient to convince Your Majesty.*

Even as he finished reading it, there was a terrible screech and a crack of light. Horses squealed, reared and bolted, and a great plume of earth and rocks showered down on the disordered ranks. A ball of smoke soared towards the heavens. When it had cleared, Es Thendil, struggling to retain control of his horse, looked down and saw a crater gouged out of the earth only a few yards from the front line of his troops. There were several bodies scattered around the rim.

Afil Es Thendil raised a hand to his visor, sick and shaking. 'Fliya help us,' he groaned. 'Why has Mellorn deserted us? We cannot fight this . . .'

There must be something I can do, Melkavesh thought again and again, until the words became meaningless, like a spike stabbing rhythmically into her skull. There must be, *must be*.

She rode up the rain-lashed hill, past Im Nerek's party and the lines of warriors without looking at them. She could not bear to see the look in their eyes, the devastation mingled with unquenchable bravery. She turned her back on them so that no one should see how close she was to weeping, and she rode alone towards the machines as if going to her death.

Hoofbeats behind her. She looked round and found a young herald following her, curly haired and not old enough even to have sprouted a beard.

'My lady . . .' he began. His face was sheened with fear, as much of her as of the fell machines.

'What do you want?' she snapped, more harshly than she meant to.

'The Battle Marshal requests you to go back and talk to her at once.'

'Tell her –' She made an effort to soften her voice. 'Tell her I can't yet. But Baramek's given us an hour to surrender. Now leave me alone.'

He saluted and began to back his horse away, his eyes wide and his hands trembling.

'Go!' she said. 'Get out, quickly!'

She watched him gallop away, but he looked distorted, as if seen through water. She blinked and rubbed her eyes. She could not even see properly, let alone do anything effective with her power. It had not deserted her, but of late it was more capricious than ever. Yet even if it had been at full strength, she doubted that she could have done anything to stop the monstrous army. *Was I never meant to win?* she thought. *How would Silvren have faced this?*

She jumped down from her mare. She removed her sword and buckler and strapped them to the saddle, then sent Faara cantering away towards her fellows. Unarmed, she went on towards the automatons, staring up at them with a mixture of awe, dread and a black, cold anger. Threads of lightning occasionally cracked on the domed heads, but that seemed to add to their power, not damage them. The vibration and the endless rumble of the storm blended into a cacophony that made the very air seem as jagged as a saw edge. The sickly wrongness of the amulin permeated through her nostrils to her very bones.

Part of her was screaming to turn and run. But the obstinate part of her, the stone-cold Gorethrian core of her soul forced her on until she was almost at the foot of one of the machines.

She knew she shone in the gloom like an aurora; she could see the light sparkling round her hands, blue stars blending with the gold. It was a purely involuntary protection, and she could only pray that they did not think she was about to attack them.

They . . . Surely the machines could not have minds of their own? Even Xaedrek was not that clever.

She looked up at the figure, reluctantly fascinated by the way each metal plate fitted over the next. Such superb craftsmanship, powered by what must have been a huge quantity of amulin. She did not know what she hoped to achieve by this confrontation, nor why she was so rashly tempting death.

Because it would be easier to die than face the consequences of my failure.

Her eyesight was worsening. She was seeing a strange double vision, the physical world around her overlaid by glass-green curtains of water and the dim shapes of the Aludrians. She cursed, thinking, *Not now, not now.* It had happened to her before, this involuntary communication with the sea creatures, and it was the only rudiment of far-sight she still had. But it was always they who initiated it, they who ended it. It was of no help to her, and at this moment it was a positive hindrance. Blinking to clear her vision, she stared as if through a watery veil at the machine and saw, in its chest, panes of smoky crystal behind which human shapes moved.

The machines were manned. She saw the outlines of two Gorethrians, watching her. One of them – it could not be – she held her breath, straining her eyes to pick out every detail until she was no longer in doubt.

It was Xaedrek.

At that she forgot everything except her rage, and she leapt backwards to get a clearer view and yelled at the top of her lungs, 'Xaedrek!'

She was not sure he had heard her. He seemed to be saying something to his companion, but then the other man leaned forward and slid the panel open. And now she could see him clearly, and although it was more than three years since she had seen him in the flesh, he looked just the same. A tiny electric shock went through her. So familiar.

'Melkavesh,' he called. 'I was wondering how long it would take you to notice me. Your powers of perception are definitely not what they were.'

'That's true, and you are to blame!'

'There's no need to tax your lungs. I can hear you quite distinctly.' A coppery glow played on his face, giving him a serene, unreadable look that was almost a smile. 'If you lost your far-sight, I also lost mine. And yet without it I have still created the means to win, while it seems you have done nothing. So who has the greater power, O Natural Sorceress?'

'And you're proud of this evil, are you?' Her own sorcery was crackling painfully over her skin as she fought to restrain herself from attacking him. 'Did you spare a moment's thought for the consequences of making such weapons, or of how you're playing into Ah'garith's hands? Damn you, climb down from that thing and face me!'

'No. I am quite comfortable where I am. You speak of

evil, yet you were quite willing to lead the Kristillians into a war in which they might have been massacred. But this way, further bloodshed will be avoided and the conquest made as painless for Kristillia as possible.'

'Oh yes! If I can persuade them to surrender!'

'That is their choice,' Xaedrek answered indifferently. 'If they prefer death, it's all the same to me.'

'Knowing them, they probably do! For the Lady's sake, Xaedrek – *please* take these machines away before it's too late. Can't you see how wrong this is?'

He leaned forward and said in a voice that was quiet yet perfectly clear, 'If not for you, the machines would not have been necessary. I don't know how many more times I have to explain this. If you had stayed with me, we could have destroyed Ah'garith and used your power alone. You know this, so if you are intent on hurling blame, observe how much of it attaches to yourself.'

Sick at heart, Melkavesh knew he was partly right. Was she any better than Xaedrek? Her Oath was in tatters, her dreams turned to ash. What had she brought them to? If not for her, Xaedrek would never have seen the need to create such weapons which now threatened to destroy Kristillia – and all she had given Kristillia in return was false hope.

What would Silvren do? she thought again. *But I am not Silvren. I am not Ashurek. I am Mellorn – Melkavesh.*

'Xaedrek, wait,' she said desperately. 'If you are so sure of your power, prove it. Meet me in a one-to-one battle.'

'A duel?' He raised his eyebrows.

'No machines, no armies. Just the two of us – the victor to decide Gorethria's or Kristillia's fate.'

'You never give up, do you?' Xaedrek said, seeming astonished. 'You don't seem to understand. You have already lost, therefore any further confrontation between us would be utterly pointless.'

She cursed, knowing that the nebula twisting in her head was the shock of despair claiming her. She was Gorethrian. She could not accept defeat any more than Xaedrek could, and being forced to accept it was like drowning.

'And if I'm the loser, why don't you kill me as you kill everything that is no longer pefect?' she cried.

Xaedrek did not answer at once. For a moment he seemed troubled, but then he said icily, 'All in good time. Now go back and persuade your allies to surrender. Valamek, close the panel.'

She heard the dull *clunk* of the pane sliding into place, and Xaedrek became a dim outline again. She stepped back, her head swimming, her mouth sour. Xaedrek was a man of his word, and she knew he would not attack her or the Kristillians before the hour was up. She began to walk away slowly, as if tempting him to kill her, her back prickling with sweat under her war gear. She must return to Im Nerek, insist that she surrender . . . but her feet seemed weighted with lead, and still she could not clear the underwater veil from her eyes. With despair and other emotions wrapped so tightly within her that she felt numb, she turned and began to climb up towards the breach in the city wall.

The rubble was still smoking, and the battlements intact on either side were deserted, although she could hear occasional shouts from within the city. Climbing up on a huge block of stone, hot even through her boots, she saw the corpses of three soldiers sprawled on the debris. So many civilians and children inside the city. *Oh, Kharan, Filmoriel . . .*

She tipped her head back and let the rain fall on her face, losing herself in the skimming black clouds. Even the light on the horizon was gone now, but she could see another light, the turquoise glow of the Aludrians resting on the sea-bed, and she could feel the blunt, deep touching of their minds against hers. Her heart and soul flowed out towards them in silent invocation along the tenuous link. She did not know she was calling to them, not consciously at least. She could not take their power, did not want to. *We are here*, was all they ever told her. And yet she felt a response, as if they knew she was in distress, just as they had known when she was injured, and helped to heal her leg.

Cool power, flowing into her like sunlight . . .

'No,' she gasped, feeling an unpleasant premonition that

218

compounded all her other emotions. 'No, I never meant to involve you . . .'

But they could not understand her words. They could only respond to her need. In her mind's eye she saw them detaching themselves from the sea-bed and drifting upwards like huge bubbles, a few at first, then in shoals. Her vision went with them, between shelves of rock and up towards the wrinkled green surface. And they broke the surface and continued to rise.

Understanding came slowly to her, and it was not a conscious revelation but a gradual wordless shaping of knowledge. Ten minutes went by, then twenty, but for Melkavesh time seemed to have stopped and she was oblivious to the folk gathering nervously on the battlements above and staring down at her, Xaedrek watching her from his machine's chest, Im Nerek riding towards her then halting, baffled.

'I've been calling to her, but she doesn't reply, ma'am,' said the young herald anxiously. 'It's as if she's in a trance.'

'How very convenient for her,' Haeth Im Nerek said caustically. 'I don't know why the Gorethrians are taking their time to kill her, because if they don't, I will –'

She broke off, staring at the northern horizon.

Ballooning up over the skyline came row upon row of immense, shadowy globes, tentacles trailing beneath them like curtains of molten glass. Cyan light spilled from them. They rode the air currents with majestic ease as if the sky, not the sea, was their natural environment. Soundless, other-worldly, the Aludrians bore down on Ehd'rabara like weightless leviathans.

Panic reigned within the city walls. The people did not wait to see if this was another vile sending of Xaedrek's, but fled inside buildings to watch anxiously from the windows. Haeth Im Nerek brusquely sent messengers to order a further withdrawal of the army. Down the hill, the Gorethrians stirred uneasily, staring with a mixture of alarm and fascination at the apparitions.

Only Melkavesh knew what they were, but she was no less awed by their appearance. She had not meant to call them, but now she understood what they could do, a dark hope thrummed within her and she slid deep into a trance of communion. *Impossible, this is impossible* . . . Yet it was happening. They were flying, borne up by preternatural energy. And unless she could control them, they would destroy Ehd'rabara as mindlessly as one of Xaedrek's machines.

Without words she spoke to them, whispered, cajoled. Guiding them was like trying to turn a ship in full sail and she began to ache with the strain. But the deeper she slid into the trance the more their power enmeshed her until she seemed to be at once watching them from the ground and flying with them. Their communication was perfect. They were hers to command.

The battle machines were turning and reforming as the first of the creatures crested the city walls high above them. It was purplish-pink with feathery ribs, its colour muted in the gloom – except for the blue-green radiance shining from beneath it. *Now*, Melkavesh commanded silently. *Now*. A colourless liquid began to fall from its tentacles. Where it fell upon one of the giants, there was a muffled hiss and great holes began to open up in the metal.

Four more of the creatures drifted to join their companion, then a dozen, and the acid began to fall like rain, indiscriminately searing anything that lay in its path. Im Nerek and her party withdrew hurriedly. Melkavesh endeavoured to keep the Aludrians away from the city walls. There were bubbling, steaming holes eating at the automatons' armour plating, and their vibration changed to a higher, discordant pitch. Then they began to retaliate.

A beam of hot light scythed into the sky with a deafening screech, and one of the creatures tumbled to the ground in flames. Melkavesh was aghast. These were living beings, so easy to kill – and as she watched, another fell, and another, breaking like eggs. The ground was suddenly awash with blue-white fire in which their frail hulks virtually evaporated.

More were coming; wave upon wave of them. It seemed that however many were destroyed, more would still come, an endless tide crashing against impervious rock . . .

Gods, I never intended this, she thought. Her eyes stung

with the heat, endless coppery explosions burst across her sight. *I swore they would never be harmed . . . I did not mean to call them, gods, why did they come?* She flung up her arms to sweep a protective aura around them but it seemed to have no effect against the onslaught of amulin.

But the battle machines were not indestructible either. One, acid-eaten to a skeleton of metal struts, suddenly toppled and crashed to the ground, taking another with it. The Gorethrians controlling them staggered out of the wreckage, screaming as vitriol ravaged their flesh. Fresh horror shook Melkavesh as she stared, unable to tear her eyes away as they collapsed in their dying agonies.

And then Xaedrek did the only thing he could. He diverted his machines to fire not only on the creatures, but on the walls of the city itself.

Another section of wall boiled into rubble, and Melkavesh was thrown clean off her rock and slammed onto the grass thirty feet away. Her protective cocoon of sorcery saved her, and she hauled herself painfully to her feet in time to see the tattered, blackened corpses of Kristillians strewn about amid the rocks. The screams of the burned and wounded shrilled through her head, but through it all she could hear Kharan's quiet words coming as if from another world.

You are more arrogant, and worse, than Xaedrek . . . it will end in the most horrific massacre . . . You frighten me, Melkavesh . . .

Genocide.

She put her head back, thrust with all the force of her will and screamed aloud for the Aludrians to destroy, *destroy*! Acid splashed around her, but sorcery protected her from it as she joined her power to the creatures' and aimed a huge, crackling nimbus at the Emperor's battle machine.

It swayed, but did not fall. She saw the sinister arm pointing at her, and flung herself out of the way as fire slashed from it. She landed in the path of another automaton, but it stepped clean over her – heading for the Kristillian troops.

Haeth Im Nerek saw the machine coming, and she knew there was nothing she could do to avoid it. If they tried to retreat they would never outrun it, and none of their weapons would touch it. Death hovered above them, and all around her there were horses bolting, foot-soldiers throwing down their weapons and running in panic. She was on foot now, already having let her mare gallop to relative safety. She did not try to stop her army's mad flight; if they could save themselves, they must. But she stood her ground, totally calm – except for her burning, blinding hatred of Melkavesh. If her troops were to die, Im Nerek would die with them.

The figure stopped, raised its hand – and in that instant an Aludrian dropped onto it, pumping acid from its tentacles as it wrapped them round the armoured body. The machine began to cave in, dripping inky slime – then there was a crisp detonation, and both it and the creature fell in a sheet of flame.

Haeth Im Nerek ran past the blazing wreckage to get a clearer view of the battle. The Gorethrian army – she had to applaud their courage – were still in their neat ranks with Baramek at their head, simply waiting for the outcome. And whatever she felt for Melkavesh, she could not but admire the woman's spirit.

Melkavesh was in the thick of the carnage, fighting furiously against Xaedrek's colossi with only a frail golden shroud to protect her. The sky was thick with Aludrians, rank upon rank of them, and suddenly Im Nerek knew that Xaedrek could not win, because however many of the creatures he killed, more would still come until all his machines were annihilated.

Xaedrek knew it too, and was determined to inflict as much damage as he could before it happened. But fifteen of his machines were already out of action, and now the Aludrians closed in with lethal efficiency on the rest. Dark metal steamed and turned to foam, the huge shapes staggered drunkenly into ungainly wrecks which continued to dissolve slowly into the ground. There was a marsh of black scum underfoot and the air was thick with noxious vapours. Now only Xaedrek's machine was still on its feet, raddled with holes and walking unsteadily towards the breach in the city wall.

Melkavesh rushed to intercept it, and when Xaedrek saw

222

her waving her arms and yelling furiously at him from the ground, he halted the giant.

She willed the Aludrians to hold back, and yelled, 'Xaedrek, listen to me!'

The panel slid back and she saw his face, no longer serene but almost grey with strain.

'Hold your fire!' she cried. 'I've called the Aludrians off, but I cannot hold them for ever. You must surrender now, Xaedrek. If you don't, they'll wipe out your troops.' She pointed at the Gorethrian lines with a shaking hand. Tears began to flow down her cheeks as she spoke, but she could do nothing to stop herself weeping. 'And they'll fly on to Gorethria if I tell them to, and destroy Shalekahh and everything else.'

Xaedrek said nothing. The figure creaked and sagged.

'For the Lady's sake, Xaedrek, don't make me do it,' she said hoarsely. 'Surrender. You must.'

Still Xaedrek did not speak. He simply looked at her – and with a sudden, hideous shock she wondered if he were conscious or even alive. Then his machine swayed, and with a shriek of metal on metal, its acid-eroded frame gave way and it crashed to the ground.

The battlefield was still. On Melkavesh's silent command, the Aludrians had drawn back and were hanging in unearthly rows beneath the clouds. Many had died, but there were still hundreds, and she had full empathy with them now. They would await her command. Raw with exhaustion, she stumbled forward into the wreckage and began to search for Xaedrek's body.

She was so intent on the task that she did not notice Im Nerek, N'golem, and a handful of others who had not fled approaching her. Nor did she see Baramek and his entourage galloping up the hillside towards them. She found Valamek first, trapped by a metal strut but still breathing; and a few feet away she found Xaedrek, who had been thrown onto a comparatively clean stretch of grass. Only then did she register the hoofbeats and the voices, and she looked up to find the Battle Marshal facing the Gorethrian High Commander barely ten feet from her.

'Your Emperor's dead, and you'd better surrender,' said Im Nerek in a cold, flat voice that held no triumph. 'It must be as obvious to you as to me that if you do not, those – whatever they are – will make short work of your army.'

Baramek let out a slow breath and replied, 'It seems I have no choice. I am not about to sacrifice my men for no good reason, and I do not need an hour to make up my mind.' The bitterness of his voice cut through Melkavesh like winter, and she could not bring herself to look at him. 'But we must discuss terms –'

'It will be unconditional,' Im Nerek said sharply. 'Go back to your men and order them to surrender their weapons. We are not barbarians; you will all be taken prisoner and treated humanely, as long as you co-operate. Do you agree?'

Baramek nodded, and signalled his standard bearers to throw down their banners before Haeth Im Nerek. Then, with contemptuous slowness, he drew his sword and dropped it in front of her so it stuck in the ground, point first. His face did not change, but to Melkavesh his internal anguish was so obvious she could hardly endure it.

'And as for you, Lady Melkavesh,' he said tonelessly, 'I must congratulate you. It was a feat of necromancy that none of us, even the Emperor himself, could have anticipated. I have only one request to make of you, which is that we may bear the body of our Emperor away with us.'

At that, she straightened up and faced him. 'No.'

Baramek's expression darkened. 'I insist. Why do you refuse me?'

'Because he's not dead,' she said quietly. 'And I am taking him prisoner.'

Mind-linked to Melkavesh, a hundred Aludrians detached themselves from their fellows and sailed on towards Charhn.

King Afil Es Thendil had not surrendered. He knew he must, but he could not. He waited, and the whole field of battle waited with him – a nightmare tableau that stretched to the edges of the world.

The Queen was weeping. She sat upright in the saddle like a drawn bow, with the exquisite metal face of Fliya turned impassively towards the Gorethrians. But her shoulders were shaking, and Es Thendil saw the salt water trickling below her visor. She who never wept –

He could not look at her, nor at the people – friends – who waited in devastated silence around him. There was nothing to be said. His eyes clouded over and for a moment he was back in the red mountains of his childhood, away from this – but there was a bitter fog swirling around him, and the landscape became alien, forbidding. Hope had turned to glass dust in his mouth, but no longer could he blame Melkavesh for what had gone wrong. He was alone on the dark and dreadful mountain, just as he had always been, and at the last it was his responsibility. His failure.

'It's no good.' His voice was rough with pain. 'I will not throw my people against those evil machines and watch them all be slain. I will surrender.'

Then the Aludrians came.

Soundless, they slipped down through the clouds like bellied shadows to float above the Gorethrian lines. The two armies stared up, astonished. Es Thendil heard his wife gasp, and he thought, *How many more weapons must they bring against us?*

A few moments later, he began to understand.

The first creature to reach the machines began to drip moisture like fine rain from its chandelier of tentacles. Others joined it. Acidic venom splashed indiscriminately onto the nearest Gorethrians and they broke ranks, screaming with pain. All became chaos; amulin power flamed into the sky, the air shook with brassy detonations. Many of the floating creatures crashed to Earth, their shells cracking and tentacles shrivelling in the heat. But for every one that fell, another came.

The machines were melting now, caving in like the sides of a candle. Their operators sprawled from them, sobbing in agony. General Kadurik had been thrown from his horse, and Es Thendil could no longer see him.

When all the battle giants had fallen, the Aludrians rose up like giant weightless pearls to hang soft as breath below the cloudbase. The flow of venom had ceased, save for the oozing of a few crystal drops. They were an awesome sight; semi-sentient gods of pearl and glass and light. A breathless silence had fallen over the Kristillians, but the Gorethrians did not wait to see what further damage might be inflicted on them. They were retreating.

It took the Kristillians a moment or so to realise. Then a cheer arose, ragged at first, but swelling to an exuberant roar. The King and Queen turned to each other, pulling off their visors, their faces radiant with tears and wonder.

'Mellorn sent them,' Es Thendil cried. 'She did not let us down. She has saved us!'

He half expected the creatures to go after the Imperial troops and slay them all, but they did not. Perhaps Melkavesh was too magnanimous in victory – there was a deep thread at the core of Kristillia's soul that could never forget nor forgive.

Yet no one moved. No soldiers broke ranks to pursue the Gorethrians and turn the retreat into a massacre. In this terrible and splendid moment, it was enough to see the dark lines flowing away from them, to know that the enchantress Mellorn had fulfilled every word of her promise.

11

Reparation

'SIGN IT,' said Melkavesh, holding out the parchment and closing Xaedrek's fingers round a quill.

He glanced coldly at her, then tried to focus on the surrender agreement. He had barely recovered consciousness, and was dazed and in obvious pain. Yet, she noted, he still had the wit not to sign anything without first reading it.

They had carried him to the Prince's keep inside Ehd'rabara, where he now lay wrapped in blankets on a hard leather couch. He was concussed and had suffered bruised ribs and a large acid burn on his left shoulder, but Melkavesh could not bring herself to heal him by sorcery. She had healed as many Kristillians as she had strength for, in the aftermath of the battle; but even if she had still had the energy, some pitiless instinct said, *Let him recover in his own time*.

In the room with her were Rar An Tolis, Haeth Im Nerek, Irem Ol Melemen and a number of other high-ranking Vardravians. All of them hung back from the couch. Even lying injured and helpless, there was something about the Emperor that frightened them, a dark, cold electricity.

'I've read it out to you once,' Melkavesh said impatiently. 'The terms are very simple. The Emperor of Gorethria will surrender completely and unconditionally to Prince Rar An Tolis in Ehd'rabara, and to King Afil Es Thendil in Charhn. He will agree to withdraw troops from Kesfaline and all other occupied countries, relinquishing all claim to them. He will dismantle the Empire and never again make war on other nations. Just sign it, before the ink dries.'

'Tell me one thing first,' he said. 'How did you do it?'

'It's not important.'

'It is to me.' His eyes shone like iced blood under his hooded lids. 'Tell me, and I'll sign the accursed surrender.'

'The truth is, I don't really know,' she replied quietly. 'I called the creatures and they came. I sent some of them on to Charhn, and I saw, as if I were there with them, that they have destroyed your machines there and routed your army.'

Xaedrek's expression did not change. 'So, you've recovered your far-sight?'

'No. It is a link with the creatures alone. But it is a powerful link. They are returning to the sea now, but I can call them again at any time, to destroy every Gorethrian in every part of the Empire, or to annihilate Shalekahh itself. It doesn't matter how many of those machines you've got, the Aludrians will destroy every single one.'

'There were only twenty-five.' She saw him catch his breath with pain as he spoke.

'Good. So you do understand, don't you, what will happen if you don't surrender?'

'Yes. But I am unsure what will happen if I do.'

Haeth Im Nerek, like the others, had never seen Xaedrek in person before, and she had been unprepared for the effect he was having on her. Baramek was one thing, a harsh and daunting adversary, but one she understood and did not fear. But Xaedrek . . . She felt she would sooner thrust her hand between the jaws of a deadly black snake than go near him. Yet Melkavesh, sitting at his side, was leaning over him and touching him with an ease that could only be born of long familiarity; as if – the thought shook her cold – *as if they had once been lovers*.

Melkavesh did not answer Xaedrek's last remark. She only looked at him, and her eyes, although bruised with exhaustion, held the compulsive light of the victor.

Xaedrek signed.

There was an almost audible sense of relief in the room. Haeth Im Nerek, who could never resist defying her own fears, went forward and looked down at the Emperor. 'You ask what will happen now?' she said. 'That is for our sovereign, King Afil Es Thendil, to decide. But I think he will feel, as I do, that as long as Gorethria exists in any form it is a threat – a gangrene for ever gnawing at Vardrav. The only cure is to cut off the offending limb. Burn it. Destroy it. Whatever I've said about Mellorn in the past, credit where it's due. She has given us the means to wipe out Gorethria for good.'

Xaedrek said nothing, only fixed her with a look of such enmity that she had to fight an urge to back away. Then he turned his eyes to meet Melkavesh's, but Im Nerek could read nothing in the glance before he lapsed once more into unconsciousness.

Messengers had preceded Melkavesh from Ehd'rabara, so by the time the Sorceress returned, the inhabitants of the castle knew that Gorethria had surrendered. Kharan was ecstatic, and danced round and round the room with Filmoriel in her arms, while Thaufa En Mianna and her daughter alternately joined in and wept with joy. Only Anixa remained detached, staring out of the window, more closed in on herself than ever.

For some reason, Kharan had expected the weather to improve as soon as the battle was over, as if the two things were connected. Instead, it grew worse. A permanent heavy twilight hung over the castle, pewter clouds soared up as solid as mountains on the horizon and hurled out spears of rubescent lightning. The sea looked like blood. Once the initial relief was over, the storm settled on her heart with the tautness of suppressed panic.

When Melkavesh returned, some five days after the battle, Kharan's happiness was unbounded, to the point of being edged with hysteria. She had been so afraid – still was – and the strain of keeping her anxiety hidden from Filmoriel demanded some release.

The Sorceress was dismounting from Faara in the midst of the crowd milling around in the courtyard as Kharan came running out to her. Seeing her, Melkavesh's preoccupied face lit up in a smile, and they hugged each other for a long time without speaking.

'I don't know what to say to you,' Kharan gasped, half laughing and half crying. 'Do I have to say anything?'

'What about, "There is a meal and a great deal of wine waiting for you"?'

'It will take only minutes.' They laughed together, but Kharan noticed at once that Melkavesh would not meet her eyes, and that the shadow was still in her face. 'Is anything wrong? You must be tired . . .'

'I am tired, yes.' Melkavesh hesitated as if she meant to leave it at that, but then she sighed and added, 'Kharan, I – I have something to tell you. You'd better come inside.'

'What is it? Has someone been killed? Im Nerek?'

'No – no, it's not that bad.'

'You can tell me here, then,' Kharan said firmly.

'All right. Did you see a litter being carried in by the west door?' She pointed across the courtyard.

'No. I was only looking out for you.'

'Ah. Well.' Melkavesh swallowed, and studiedly avoided Kharan's eyes until she began to feel annoyed as well as worried. 'I don't know how to put this. I want you to understand that it was essential –'

'For goodness sake, just tell me!'

'Very well. Xaedrek is here.'

The colour drained out of Kharan's face. 'What?' she gasped.

'I had Xaedrek brought to the castle –' Kharan swayed, and Melkavesh caught her arm and held her up, 'because he is my prisoner. I have to keep him here until I decide what to do with him.'

'But – but I thought he was badly injured at Ehd'rabara, or dead – the messengers said –'

'Kharan, please calm down. I know you must find this upsetting, but it will be all right. He'll be under close guard, and there's no need for you to see him.'

Kharan stared at her, her breathing rapid and her eyes wide with shock. 'How could you, Melkavesh?' she cried hoarsely. 'How could you bring him here? You could have left him at the city – you *sadist* –'

'We'll talk about this later,' Melkavesh said grimly. 'I

didn't realise you'd react this badly, truly I didn't. Let's get you inside before you pass out. You'll feel better when you've got over the shock.'

But Kharan was not seeing the courtyard, nor was she aware of Melkavesh's arm supporting her. All she could see was Xaedrek's face, and all she could think of was her last encounter with him, when he had so quietly and gently informed her that she and Falmeryn were both to be executed.

I can't tell you how much I regret that you have found it necessary to turn away from me to another man . . . Why, Kharan? I thought we had an understanding . . .

She cried out inwardly, but the scene would not go away.

For you, a conventional execution. Beheading. There is a nobility in it which befits what you have been to me . . .

And Falmeryn? she had pleaded. More than three years had gone by, but still the reply came lancing into her mind like a sword of burning-cold white metal, destroying everything that had gone between, destroying everything except her despair.

He will be dead before you.

Melkavesh took Kharan to her chamber and put her in Thaufa En Mianna's care. She sank stiffly into a chair, unspeaking, her eyes focused on some hidden memory that must be causing her terrible pain. She did not react to anything they said, and Melkavesh was distressed at how badly she was taking it. With a heavy heart, she eventually left Kharan and made her way through the long stone corridors to the chamber where Xaedrek was being held.

She had tried to keep Xaedrek's presence as secret as possible, and had selected four Kristillian soldiers for their physical strength and cool nerve to guard him. His pseudo-sorcerous power, which he had only maintained by taking amulin every day, had drained from him, and he was too weak and ill to attempt an escape, yet she could not feel sanguine about him. Being locked in a cage with a wounded moon leopard would have been less nerve-racking. He was as unpredictable and unquestionably more dangerous.

Emperor Xaedrek of Gorethria. She could hardly believe that he was here, at her mercy, the battle over. Yet she felt no joy, no sweetness in the victory. It had been so narrow, more by luck than design, and it had so nearly become the horrific massacre she had dreaded. No thanks to her that there were hundreds dead instead of thousands.

And still the storm grumbled outside, gravid with revelations she could not receive because her far-blindness pressed on her spirit like a lead gauntlet.

She stopped outside Xaedrek's door and exchanged words with the guards, but did not go in. He was resting comfortably, they said, and had given them no trouble. They had lit a log fire in the chamber as she had requested, and he had eaten a small bowl of soup and bread and was now asleep. Melkavesh told them to fetch her if he woke up, and returned broodingly to her office.

She had not spoken to him since she had made him sign the surrender. He had been unconscious or asleep throughout the journey from Ehd'rabara, so she had left him alone – putting off the moment when she had to confront him. The truth was, she was dreading it. Gorethria had been everything to Xaedrek, breath and life and passion; he had lived only to restore her glory, to make her even greater than before. Now Melkavesh had torn up his life's work by its roots and obliterated it – and all she could think of was how he must feel.

She could imagine it, and yet she could not. There was a sick misery in her stomach at the knowledge that Gorethria was her country too. She had loved it with the passion of a true Gorethrian. She was its rightful Empress. Yet she had brought them to this humiliation . . . Yes, she knew her own feelings, and they were not pleasant. But as for Xaedrek, she had never truly understood how his mind worked. She knew he must be devastated, suicidal or mad with grief. But how he would actually react was a different matter.

There had been considerable opposition from Im Nerek and Prince Rar An Tolis to her taking custody of him.

'My lady Mellorn,' the Prince had said gravely, 'we are infinitely, eternally grateful for what you have done for us.

I am not a great user of words. I will not even try to express what we feel . . . but in this matter I don't believe it is right for you to take the . . . the responsibility of imprisoning Xaedrek. He should be taken to Charhn where the King and Queen can decide what to do with him.'

'His Highness is right,' Im Nerek had said. 'Torture and a slow death would hardly be sufficient compensation for the suffering he's caused. But it's up to the King to mete out his punishment – not you.'

'I don't intend to pass judgement on him,' Melkavesh replied, 'but he must be interviewed at length before any punishment is considered – and you must admit, I'm the only person who can cope with him effectively.'

'Really?' said Im Nerek, raising her eyebrows. They had continued to argue, but Melkavesh had remained adamant, and when she had actually lifted the scorpion from the nest, their main emotion seemed to be profound relief.

So she had had her way, and now he was here. The one concession she had made was to let Irem Ol Melemen come to the castle with her.

That evening the castle dwellers held a banquet in her honour. Banks of candles were lit and curtains drawn against the storm, and the Vardravians – as the reality of victory sank in – became uproarious in their celebrations. But Kharan and Anixa did not attend, and Melkavesh retired early, deeply fatigued. The battle had taken its toll of her, and there were darknesses swathed around her that would not let her even begin to enjoy herself.

When she woke, her first thought was of Xaedrek. It was well into morning, and the sky was merely overcast rather than black. She bathed, breakfasted quickly on bread and fruit, and dressed in a long white smock with a green tabard belted over it. There was something deliberately unmilitary and un-Gorethrian in the clothes she had chosen. Then she braced herself and made her way purposefully to Xaedrek's chamber.

Outside Xaedrek's room, she intercepted a guard carrying a breakfast tray for the prisoner.

'I'll take it to him,' she said. 'Unlock the door for me, and don't disturb us – unless I call for you.' The guards nodded. The heavy door swung open to admit her, clunked shut behind her.

She was surprised to find Xaedrek not merely awake but out of bed, wearing a loose-sleeved maroon robe and reclining on a couch near the window.

'I've brought you something to eat.' He did not reply, only glanced disdainfully at the tray. 'Well, I'll leave it here for you.' She placed it on a table near the bed and walked over to him, carefully maintaining a mask of steely politeness.

'This is not Shalekahh, I'm afraid,' she said. She placed a hand on the curved back of the couch and rubbed at the faded brown upholstery.

'That had not escaped my notice,' Xaedrek said coldly. He looked tired and subdued, but otherwise quite well. She was astonished at his resilience – and oddly relieved. 'Where's Valamek?'

'He was taken away with the other prisoners. He'll live. You seem to be recovering very quickly.' She dragged a solid chair across the flags and sat down at his side. 'Are you sure you feel well enough to get up?'

'Yes, thank you, my lady. I am perfectly comfortable in all respects.' His eyes were like cold, red winter suns, distant and impossible to interpret.

'I'm glad to hear it,' she said coolly. 'Is there anything I can bring you to make your stay here less irksome?'

'If they have such things as books in Kristillia. And I would appreciate some paper and something to write with. The only thing I cannot bear is to be idle.'

'I'll see to it.' A tangible silence fell. Melkavesh had come in with no idea what she was going to say to him, and his uncommunicative calmness was throwing her off her stroke. Anger would have been far easier to deal with. The atmosphere between them was so tense that the very air seemed stiff with frost, yet she could not fight the masochistic compulsion to stay in the room – and to provoke some reaction from him.

'I don't understand you,' she said, leaning forward in an

attempt to make him look at her. 'Gorethria has surrendered. The Empire is lost. I had thought to find you broken, possibly out of your mind, or suicidal – and determined to take me with you.'

'You have a colourful imagination.' He folded his arms, his dark, elegant hands cupping his elbows. At least he was speaking to her, and she did not stop to analyse why it mattered. 'If you really thought that, I was a dangerous person to bring inside your household.'

'Oh, I still think you're dangerous. To be so cool after what has happened, you must be. You were always a consummate actor, but to keep your true feelings hidden after this – words fail me.'

Xaedrek gave an unpleasant smile. 'From that I gather you spared my life in order to have the pleasure of gloating over my demise and seeing me broken and wretched.'

'No!' Melkavesh was shocked.

'I could hardly blame you if you had. All I can say is that if our positions had been reversed, I would never have indulged such an impulse.'

'That is not why I spared you!' she exclaimed heatedly. 'I would have hated to see you like that. If you only knew how relieved I am to find you well – unchanged –' She faltered, embarrassed by the feeling that she had said too much.

'I believe you, Melkavesh. So,' he asked softly, 'why did you spare me?'

'You survived the battle. To have killed you afterwards would have been cold-blooded murder.' Then she sat back in the chair and sighed. 'In truth, I don't know. It's possibly the most stupid thing I have ever done. Had you won, I know you would have had no hesitation in dispatching me.'

'Don't be so sure. In your place, I would have spared you too.'

'Oh, yes? With what purpose?'

'Undoubtedly one as foolhardy as yours. You still fascinate me. I believe the world would be a considerably less interesting place without you.'

This hit a raw nerve with Melkavesh. It was as if he had voiced her most nebulous thoughts, and in doing so was exposing her supposedly rational motive of mercy as a false-hood. The truth was that despite everything that had happened, and however much she claimed to hate Xaedrek and all he stood for, her deepest feelings for him had not changed. He knew it, and perhaps he felt the same – but it was him who had the courage to say it. Not her.

'Damn you,' she whispered. 'I should have killed you. Aren't we supposed to be Gorethrian, pitiless? What is happening?'

'You will have to answer that for yourself, my lady. I am your prisoner, and mercy or otherwise is wholly in your hands,' he said evenly.

She glowered at him, cursing her failure to match his coldness and objectivity. How dangerous was he? He had no hyperphysical power left, for the last of the amulin had been burnt out in the battle. He was exhausted, no physical threat to anyone. But he still had his wits about him, and they had always been his most fearsome aspect.

She leaned on the edge of the couch, pushing her hair away from her face. 'I don't know what I'm going to do with you. You're a trickster, a demon who can mimic any human trait he chooses. I don't know what's really inside. The Serpent itself, probably.'

'If you came in here to insult me, a common Vardravian could do it better.' He raised his eyes to meet hers. His voice was very quiet, almost sad, but his gaze was disturbingly intense. 'Stop it, Melkavesh. You know me better than that. I'm Gorethrian, that's all, and you are just the same.'

'No, I'm not.'

'But you are. Have you thought how you look to them?' He waved at the door, and she knew he meant the Kristillians. 'Saving me? It looks to them as though your Gorethrian side has triumphed after all.'

Melkavesh stood up, frozen with so many different, violent emotions that she could not speak.

'Well, hasn't it?' he persisted. She went to lean on the window ledge, staring down at the sheer wall and the iron-grey sea below, sensing the tension in the air kindling to anger. 'There is one thing you owe me, Melkavesh, and that is to be honest. You are the victor. What are you going to do? The King and Queen will want to destroy Shalekahh, obliterate everything that made Gorethria what she was, and they will think it very strange if you have other ideas.'

'Perhaps. The Kristillians think Gorethria deserves utter destruction, and they will do it, if I let them. Should I? If I spare her, will she just rise again and again like some undead thing?'

'Probably. What can I say? I believed in Gorethria with all my heart and soul. I swore I would die before I saw her fall – but she has fallen, and I am still here. What am I to make of that?'

A horrible thought hit Melkavesh, closing round her heart like midnight ice. Xaedrek had once been intensely fond of Kharan – yet the moment she fell short of his standard of perfection, he had ordered her execution without a qualm. Could he now do the same to Gorethria itself? The principle was the same, the conclusion so breathtakingly logical that for a blinding moment she could see him doing just that. Gorethria was no longer perfect, therefore – make an end.

'Gods,' she said through dry lips. 'And you're trying to provoke me to it. Gorethria has lost her Empire, that's all! She must learn to exist in a new way. I am not a wanton destroyer!' She swung round to face him and saw that he was on his feet, walking slowly towards her, his eyes no longer cold but filled with lethal red fury.

'Aren't you? Have you not destroyed Gorethria already, as a child breaks a toy in the mistaken belief that he can make something better out of it? You said you loved Gorethria, yet hated our methods. And I told you, Melkavesh, that you cannot half love something, any more than you can half hate it. You had a choice and you chose the Kristillians. I would have expected you, of all people, to have the conviction to finish what you started. Yet now you have second thoughts? Now, when it is too late? And you think you can leave Gorethria in a state of limbo, only half existing. Do you really not understand what you have done?'

For a few moments she was transfixed by him, and it was as if the fury of all her Gorethrian ancestors were contained in his eyes, searing her like a ruby flame. *Gorethria tolerates no half measures* . . . She had failed, betrayed her birthright, and all around her the faces from the Hall of Portraits were accusing her, despising her, their condemnation like a fierce gale tearing out her soul by its roots. Xaedrek's defeat had not broken his spirit, and he still possessed this insidious power to dissect his enemies' minds and reduce their own ideals to ash.

But Melkavesh was not afraid of him. Part of her hated him, hated the evil things he had done, and she felt an uprush of passionate anger that swept away the trance. She took a step towards him, her eyes as brilliant as his.

'You talk of understanding and honesty. I don't know how you dare say anything to me at all, after what you are guilty of. Putting Gorethria at Ah'garith's mercy, the endless murders in the name of necromancy. And as for what you've done to my friends – the torment you inflicted on Anixa and Irem Ol Thangiol – after that, don't presume to criticise *me*!'

'But you know my reasons,' he said, quietly menacing. 'Everything I have done has been for Gorethria's benefit alone. If it is not to your taste, bear in mind that if you'd stayed with me, much of it would have been unnecessary.'

'Oh, yes! You would have made a slave of me for Gorethria's benefit as well,' she replied with acid fury. 'And you'd do anything for your country, wouldn't you? No matter how vile, how destructive. *Anything.*'

For some reason, her last remark had an intangible effect on Xaedrek. He seemed to withdraw from her, becoming as expressionless as an Imperial statue. 'And would you not also do anything for what you truly believed in?' He paused and added with a knife edge of scorn, 'If only you knew what you believed in. Is it Gorethria? Or Kristillia? Or some twisted vision of your own?'

She swung away from him as if he had hit her. 'I can't talk to you. I was mad to try.'

She found herself striding towards the door, but as she raised her hand to the latch, Xaedrek said, 'Wait a minute.'

She turned, glaring at him – only to be startled by the change in his face. The rage and the coldness had softened to introspection, almost a sadness. She had seen that look before, and it still gave her a jolt. Every time she was convinced he had no soul, not a single redeeming quality, he would suddenly say or do something so human that it turned her judgement upside down. 'Don't go, Melkavesh. This bitterness between us is achieving nothing. I apologise.'

He went back to the couch, and she moved hesitantly to the chair and sat down beside him again. 'You've every right to be bitter,' she said.

'Not really. I started the war and I received a fair and square defeat. With what little dignity I have left I can at least prove that I am a gracious loser. You and I have a lot to talk about.'

'That's why I came. To talk, not to gloat or argue. But I don't know where to start.'

'We could begin by declaring a truce between us. If our points of view are immovable, we may as well accept the fact and put them aside. Do you agree?'

'Yes,' said Melkavesh, bemused. She was sure he was sincere. His eyes glowed like jewels under the long lashes. It was as if he had suddenly abandoned all pretence and was speaking to her with the candour and honesty she remembered from the days when she had first known him. When he had trusted her. 'Listen to me.' She leaned forward and gripped his arm. 'I will not be pressured into making a decision about Gorethria. Perhaps it no longer accords with your vision, but that is no reason to destroy it.'

He closed his hand on hers, and for a few minutes they looked at each other without speaking. Then he said, 'There was a time when you and I walked through the halls of the palace, talking for hours of Gorethria. You spoke of her like a lover, and those words came from your heart. There was no discord between us, and no pretence. Do you remember?'

'Yes,' she said, but no sound came out. She cleared her throat. 'Yes.'

'I know that you could not destroy your country. No more could I. Perhaps the thought crossed my mind, when I first realised it was over . . .' He shook his head. 'No. You see, Melkavesh, what went wrong is not due to Gorethria's failure, but to mine. I am to blame. How can I punish my countrymen for my mistakes, or for their faith in me?'

'You really mean it, don't you?' She eased her grip on his arm, but he did not release her hand.

'You say you were foolish to spare me. Perhaps I am being equally foolish in taking you into my confidence again, but I must. I have a confession to make. Even though it does seem an impossible contortion for a Gorethrian to swallow his pride, I have to tell you that you were right.'

'What about?' she gasped.

'Ah'garith,' he said heavily. 'I have lost control of her. When she first answered my summons, I swore to myself that she would never be allowed to endanger Gorethria, nor to use me as Meheg-Ba once used Meshurek. But her power increased. She tried to possess me. When she failed, she deserted me and fled – taking Irem Ol Thangiol and Amnek with her.'

'Amnek?'

'He betrayed me also. He could not forget Shavarish and he lost his mind, making himself easy prey for Ah'garith.' Xaedrek looked away, and she saw genuine sorrow in his face.

'When did this happen?'

'Some sixty days before the invasion.'

'So you fought the battle without her help?' He nodded. 'But where is she now? What's she doing?'

'What indeed?' Xaedrek met her eyes, and she understood what it must have cost him to make this admission of failure. 'You warned me. I should have listened. Now there is a demon at large, and I have no idea how to find her or how powerful she has become.'

'Xaedrek!' she exclaimed. 'Gods, this is dreadful!'

'I know,' he replied impassively. 'That is why I have told you. Gorethria is in danger not from you or me, but from Ah'garith.'

'Not just Gorethria. Kristillia. Perhaps the whole world.' She sat back, wide-eyed, seeing not Xaedrek but an inward vision of ghastly possibilities. He let her hand slide out of his, lingeringly, as if reluctant to let it go.

'You will agree with me, tempting as it is to go on fighting until we kill each other, we cannot afford that luxury,' he said. 'The Shanin is our mutual enemy.'

'Oh, by the Sphere. Do you understand what you've let loose on the world? When I saw her, it was as if I saw straight through her into a hideous, sick place of pure evil. I told you she must be killed, but you let her go –' She was shuddering, and Xaedrek moved to sit on the edge of the couch and put a hand on her shoulder.

'You said to me that I would do anything for Gorethria, no matter how vile. Well, it is not so. Ah'garith found a new source of power even greater than amulin, but her method of producing it was so disgusting that I forbade her to carry on. That was why she turned against me – and it was indirectly why I lost the war.'

Melkavesh turned her golden-green eyes to stare at him. 'You're telling me the truth. Look, I won't stand in judgement of how badly you handled her. We've got to find her and destroy her. And to do that we have to co-operate and trust each other – for a time at least. Nothing else can be settled while she's at large.'

'I'm glad you agree. Neither of us has a hope against her alone.' There was a brief silence, in which Melkavesh found herself leaning towards Xaedrek, involuntarily drawn to him. His hand, still on her shoulder, moved to caress her neck. Then she recalled herself and stood up abruptly, trying to steady the swift beating of her pulse.

'This is senseless. We've spent three years trying to destroy each other, and now – I'm going. I've things to do, and you had better have something to eat,' she said, hurriedly fetching the tray and thrusting it into his hands.

He looked up at her, his arched eyebrows raised in surprise. 'Not everything we do is sensible, my lady,' he said.

Xaedrek could not sleep that night, but lay staring at the sea-patterns reflecting on the ceiling. The reflection was not of moonlight but of some undefined, unpleasant glow. He thought of everything that had happened, of his encounter with Melkavesh, and of how disconcerting it was to be here and not in Shalekahh. In the morning there would be no servants to do his bidding, no Inner Council nor Senate to see, no sunlight blazing on polished marble – only the guards and the grim walls of the castle. He could adapt to anything – except no longer being an emperor. But Melkavesh had not taken that from him yet. Not yet.

Then he heard the *clunk* of his door being unlocked, and a bar of yellowish lamplight slanted into the room. There was a figure moving in the light. The door closed, and he heard the soft rustle of skirts on the stone flags as the figure approached the bed, invisible in shadow apart from the sea-glow catching on a cheekbone, a glittering eye, and a mass of dark hair.

Xaedrek sat up, startled but curious. There was a sense of danger, but also of something familiar and horribly inevitable. The intruder came up to the bed and stood looking down at him. His eyes were attuned to the darkness, and he saw first the frosty gleam of a long steel knife, then the faint outline of a face that seemed ghostly but was only too alive.

'Kharan,' he said softly. 'I was wondering if you might honour me with a visit.'

'Yes, it's me,' she whispered. 'I'm surprised you recognise me with my head in place. Perhaps you thought I was a ghost, but I am not. If ghosts came back to haunt their murderers, I would not have been able to get in here for the crowd.'

'How did you get in?' He could not imagine the guards letting her in unaccompanied at dead of night. Her presence disturbed him more than he felt it should have done, but he would not let her know it.

'That was easy.' She gave a laugh that did not sound quite sane. 'I always bring the guards a nightcap before I go to bed. Tonight I drugged it with a soporific herb, and they are now sleeping peacefully at their posts. So don't bother to cry out for help.'

'I won't,' Xaedrek said coolly. 'But bear in mind there is no one to help you either.'

He saw her hands fold convulsively around the handle of the knife and her gaze, fixed on his bare, unprotected chest.

Then he realised that she was unbalanced – if only temporarily – and that if he made a move or said the wrong thing she was quite capable of sinking the blade into his heart first and thinking about it afterwards.

'You're the one in danger, not me,' she said. 'For once! How does it feel to be told, "I'm disappointed in you, so I am going to end your life, and no hard feelings"? Well?'

'You're oversimplifying it, Kharan. I could talk to you better without that knife pointing at my ribs.'

'I didn't come in here to talk to you, Xaedrek. I came to kill you. If Melkavesh can't do it, someone's got to.'

'You have a lot to say for someone who does not want to talk,' he said, but she did not move. Her hands shook, so that the blade made tiny stabbing motions in the air.

'You fiend!' she burst out. 'I know why you wanted me put to death! Because I didn't live up to your stupid ideals any longer. I amused you while you thought I was as cynical and cold-hearted as yourself. Then you found out I was only human after all, just a common Vardravian who was as frightened of you as anyone else. For that you despised me. But I'll tell you something. I despise you, too. Now, is my despite worth less than yours? Don't you feel anything at being so hated, anything at all?'

'Thousands of people hate me, Kharan,' he said softly. 'It means nothing – except from you.'

'Why?' she cried. 'Don't say anything – don't pretend I still mean something to you, that you regret sending me to my death and are glad I'm still alive!'

'Not glad, exactly.' Xaedrek looked candidly at her and spoke the thoughts that were in his heart. 'You're not the same person. The Kharan I knew died when she turned away from me. I tried to destroy her shell, but the shell still walks and now it is holding a knife at my chest and there is a stranger looking out of her eyes. You're convinced I have no feelings, yet I find this situation strange – and painful.'

'Bastard!' The eyes that had once looked on him with warmth were glittering with fierce loathing. 'Don't talk to me of pain. You killed Falmeryn. You killed him! Now I am going to do the same to you, and if I could make you feel

243

only one second of the torment you inflicted on us, I should be happy. Just one second!'

She stepped forward, raising the knife. The dull glow caught the gleam of perspiration on her face – and on Xaedrek's dark chest. He *was* afraid; he was human enough to fear death. She hesitated, and then he did exactly what she had known he would, and it had exactly the effect on her that she had dreaded. There was an awful sense that she had been through this before, as he lowered himself back onto his elbows and said quietly, 'Go on then. I won't try to stop you, Kharan.'

She froze, hung her head. 'I can't,' she said wretchedly. 'I've never killed anyone. I can't do it. Not even you.'

She lowered the knife and he saw the curve of her shoulders slump as if under a great weight of shame. She remained there for a moment, then she lifted her chin and looked at him, her eyes glazed but tearless. 'You wanted me dead so badly,' she said. She sat down heavily on the edge of the bed, almost on his leg, which startled him. 'Here's your chance.' She held the knife out to him, hilt first.

He saw that she was not bluffing. She knew him well enough, he realised, to know that if he still saw fit to dispose of her, he would, without a second thought.

He took the weapon from her and balanced it thoughtfully in his hand. She looked older, thinner, marked by what she had undergone since he had last seen her. But she was no less attractive; if anything, the experience and strength she had gained made her seem the more so. It was uncanny to think that all the time he had believed her dead, she had been at Melkavesh's side.

'What about your child?' he asked sharply.

She swallowed, but her face did not change. 'Melkavesh will see she is looked after.'

'I see. And you are so ashamed of being unable to murder me that you do not want to live?'

'In a way. But because I came in here, and I can't kill you, I've brought my fate on myself. The first time you tried to execute me, I was a coward. At least this time you'll see that I'm able to face my death like – like a Gorethrian.'

Xaedrek was silent, testing the point against his thumb. She watched him, and he saw that the mad shine in her eyes had faded. She was composed, trembling no longer.

He reached out and dropped the knife onto the table beside the bed. 'No,' he said. 'I won't kill you, Kharan.'

'Why not?'

'There is no point. At one time it seemed relevant that you died, but now it does not.'

'Oh, yes, I should have remembered. You never did anything that had no point, did you? Never anything that would not benefit Gorethria.' She laughed harshly. 'There was nothing I could do to make you understand how *I* felt. To care. I know I can't change you – I just wanted to make you feel *something*, if only the fear of death.'

'You did that,' Xaedrek conceded.

'Yes.' Her voice was low, intense. 'You have changed. You did feel fear – just for a second. You've learned that you're not infallible.'

'Oh, yes. I've learned that indeed. And to make the best of changing circumstances, which, if you still have your common sense, Kharan, you will do also.'

'I have been trying.' She met his eyes and he saw that all trace of fear was gone from them. 'You are not going to ruin my life a second time. I am not frightened of you any longer. When I first met you I wasn't afraid, I suppose that was just the bravado of youth. For a long time I was terrified, but I'm bewitched no longer.' She stood up, looking down at him with an almost joyous expression. 'After all, what can you do to me? You can't touch me, because I don't feel anything at all for you now. Not even hatred. I'm free!'

'I don't want to harm you, Kharan,' Xaedrek said quietly. 'I'm not that much of a fiend. And I have never thought you a coward. Now go away, take the knife with you, and wake the guards up – before I'm tempted to escape.'

He saw the pearly gleam of her teeth as her lips parted in a half-smile. 'I'm going. I was just thinking, perhaps I've already had a better revenge on you than anyone could have devised. After all, it was thanks to me that you met Melkavesh!'

12

A Messenger from Charhn

WHEN KHARAN left Xaedrek, she could not bring herself to go back to her room and sleep. She had been out of her mind for a time, first with horror at the revelation that he was here, then with the bitterness of her memories, and finally with the mad determination to kill him. Now the confrontation was over she felt wide awake and disturbed. She wished she could still the frantic whirl of her thoughts as easily as blowing out a lamp, but it was impossible.

She craved company, but she could not tell anyone where she had been or why. Nor did she wish to disturb Filmoriel whom she had left in Thaufa En Faliol's care. She longed to be with her daughter, but in her present mood she knew she would only upset the child. She wandered aimlessly in the corridors for a time, and finally she let herself out of a small side door and crossed the darkened courtyard towards the stables.

The sky was overcast, the clouds so thick that they seemed to rest on the castle turrets and extend upwards for miles. It was hours until dawn, yet it was not quite dark. An unpleasant greyish-brown glow seemed to emanate from everywhere and nowhere at once, and the sight of it filled her with a sick depression. She hurriedly opened the heavy wooden door of the stable and sidled in, closing it behind her.

Now she was not alone. A familiar mixture of rank and sweet smells greeted her, and the darkness was friendly with the warm breathing of horses, grunts and sighs and the occasional stamp of a hoof.

She felt her way along the stalls until she found her favourite horse, Sabil. He was on his feet, awake, and seemed pleased to see her. As she let herself in through the half-door he whiffled at her hair, and when she began to weep quietly he only uttered a deep sigh and rested his head contentedly on her shoulder. She put her arms round his neck, comforted yet still wretchedly empty.

She meant what she had said to Xaedrek. Meeting him face to face had driven out the spectre that had hag-ridden her for years. Although the memories would never fade, they were taking on a distance that made them bearable. Even the hatred was gone. She had freed herself – but the meeting had been intensely painful, and at this moment her soul felt as raw as newly flayed flesh.

'Perhaps I should have killed him,' she whispered against Sabil's greasy mane. 'Not for Falmeryn's sake or mine, but because of what he is. Well, it's too late now, Sabil. No . . . It's up to Melkavesh, not me.'

She stayed in the stall for a long time, slowly growing calmer until she felt quite numb. It would be dawn in a couple of hours – if any daylight could penetrate the morbid layer of cloud. Everything feels wrong, she thought. This is not happiness. This is not even living. My daughter sleeps safely upstairs, yet at this moment I feel so black that if I never saw her again, if Xaedrek had killed me, it would not seem to matter . . .

She knew that if she only made the effort to go back to her room, morning would soon come and things would begin to seem more normal. But she could not move. She remained there, paralysed by the black thoughts buzzing in her head, hearing the faint sounds in the courtyard with total indifference.

The large door to the stables scraped open, and a flurry of raindrops blew in, sparkling in a wash of lamplight. It seemed early for the grooms to start work, and as lonely as she felt, she did not want to face anyone. Then she heard voices and the hollow clop of hooves as a horse was led into the aisle between the stalls. She crouched down by Sabil's leg in the darkness, listening, suddenly as tense and alert as a cat.

247

'It's lucky you got here before the rain set in.' Kharan recognised the voice of one of the causeway guards, a good-humoured Kristillian with greying hair. 'Filthy weather to be riding in. Or standing guard. Let's see if we can find an empty stall . . .'

The lamp glow swung from side to side, moving towards her, but stopping a few yards away from her on the opposite side of the aisle. 'Here we are. I'll go and wake the grooms. They should be up by now, lazy louts, but they never are.'

'No, don't,' said a younger, softer voice that sounded bone tired. 'I'd rather stable him myself. If you can just show me where things are.'

'Well, all right.' The Kristillian began pointing out the water-pump, the doors to the tackroom and grain store, while Kharan cautiously stood up and peered over Sabil's withers. The two men were silhouettes against the guard's lamp, and had their backs to her. Something in the new-comer's voice had set her heart thudding, and she did not know why.

'Have you ridden all the way from Charhn alone?' the guard asked affably. 'It must have been a rough journey.'

'I didn't set out alone. There were some soldiers and a priestess with me.' He spoke quietly, and Kharan strained to hear him over the sound of a horse pawing at the flagstones. 'There was an ambush – Gorethrians. I was the only survivor. I've ridden the rest of the way on my own, as fast as the horse could manage.'

'By the moons. Even a priestess,' the guard muttered, shocked. The horse fell quiet, and there was a silence in which Kharan willed the stranger to speak again. After a few seconds the Kristillian added gravely, 'You must have some courage, sir, and it must be an important message you've brought.'

'It's not a message exactly, but it is urgent, and I need to see the Lady Melkavesh at once.'

This time Kharan heard him quite distinctly, and she felt a cold shock as if someone had drawn a knife across her stomach. He sounded so like Falmeryn, so much like him.

She knew it was impossible, but adrenaline surged up through her body and she began to tremble.

'Not a message? What is it, then?'

'It's something – I don't know whether I can explain. Something that is supposed to help Lady Melkavesh to defeat Gorethria.'

Kharan moved softly under Sabil's neck and pressed herself against the half-door, anxious to see him.

'We call her Lady Mellorn, but she doesn't mind either name,' the guard said inconsequentially. Then, 'Wait – what did you say? To defeat Gorethria?'

'Yes.'

'But – well, I suppose if you've been travelling, you wouldn't know, but you're rather too late, sir. The battle's over.'

The stranger gave a deep, barely audible sigh. 'How long ago?'

'Six days.'

'Is that all? I missed it that narrowly? Gods. If only –' He broke off. Kharan's eyes ached with the effort to see him, but he was on the other side of his horse now, and she could make nothing out.

'Don't be despondent.' A lighter note came into the guard's voice. 'Gorethria surrendered. Did you really not know? No, obviously you didn't. They've surrendered!'

'Completely?'

'Yes, sir. It's over!'

The newcomer seemed to be rendered speechless by this. Kharan saw his dark form move around the horse's rump, and she saw the guard clap him on the shoulder, obviously taking great pleasure in being the one to break the good news.

'I don't believe it. Oh, the Lady be praised,' the man said, with a breathless laugh of relief.

It was his laugh. *Oh, let this cruel joke be over*, Kharan thought, biting her cheek until the salt-metal tang of blood burst onto her tongue.

'I still ought to see Lady Melkavesh,' he added, subdued again, as if even the knowledge of Gorethria's defeat did not have the power to raise his spirits.

'Yes, of course. Look, sir, while you finish seeing to the horse, I'll go and wake Irem Ol Melemen. I'd better not disturb the lady herself, she can be rather – prickly, to say the least. But the priest will know what to do. Then I'll come back and take you to him.'

'All right. Thank you.'

'I'll leave the lamp. Some mornings it seems like it's never going to get light.'

Kharan heard the dull clomp of the guard's boots as he strode to the door and went out into the courtyard. The lamp hung from a hook on the side bars, but its ineffectual light revealed only shadows as the man untacked the horse and rubbed it down with a wisp of straw. She ducked by reflex as he came out into the aisle and disappeared to the far end, taking the lamp with him and returning a few minutes later with a bucket of water. As the horse drank he went on rubbing its back, speaking softly to it just as Falmeryn used to when he groomed Xaedrek's horses.

In a trance, Kharan slipped out of Sabil's stall and began to walk slowly, noiselessly towards him. His back was to her, but now she could see the raindrops glistening on his cloak and on his long, red-brown hair.

Something like grief rose in her throat, but she swallowed it. Most Kristillians had reddish hair. This was undoubtedly a Kristillian messenger, she told herself severely – oh, but the resemblance, the coincidence was unbearable. Was her mind playing tricks on her? It was so unfair, after what she had just been through with Xaedrek, to be tormented like this. It was as if she had become the butt of a sadistic jest.

She struggled to master herself, thinking, I am distressed and overtired and when I speak this poor Kristillian messenger is going to jump out of his skin. Why don't I just tiptoe past, leave him in peace?

But she could not. She had to break the spell before she went mad.

She tried to speak, but no sound would emerge from her closed throat. She moved forward compulsively, dreading the moment when he noticed her, but unable to stop herself

250

from opening the half-door and stepping through it as stiffly as a figure made of wax.

He heard the bolt being drawn back, and turned abruptly to stare at her. The light caught the side of his face, and now she saw distinctly that his skin was not the Kristillian mixture of hues but fair, his eyes like shadowed water that in daylight would be a clear, violet-grey –

It was Falmeryn.

But it could not be.

So strong was her conviction that it could not be him, she dared not say his name. Her knees turned to water, and the terrifying feeling swept through her that she was about to make a complete fool of herself. How could she ask him who he was, when she knew?

Then he broke the silence. He looked as stricken as she felt, his eyes wide and lips parted in utter disbelief. 'You look –' he said in a dry, hesitant voice, 'you look just like someone I used to know – a few years ago – in Shalekahh. But it can't be – can it?'

Her ears were singing, the blood rushing whitely through her head. As soon as he spoke, her doubts were gone – but she still could not grasp it. *It really was him.* She hung onto the door, fighting a wave of ecstasy that was as devastating as pain.

'I am Kharan,' she said faintly. 'Don't you remember me – Falmeryn?'

Falmeryn's mind was reeling. Her sudden appearance out of nowhere had alarmed him enough, and now he found himself looking at a woman in Kharan's shape. A stranger, surely – yet the brilliant dark eyes that gathered every mote of light were heart-rendingly familiar, as if it were only a day, not three years, since he had last looked into them. They could belong to no one else. He recognised her but his mind rebelled, insisting that she was dead and could not possibly be standing before him, warm and alive and as stunned as he was.

'Kharan?'

She swayed, stumbled towards him, and he came forward to catch her and raise her up in his arms. There was a

251

suspended moment in which every horrible possibility went through her mind: he had forgotten her, could not believe it was her, no longer loved her – then it was over. 'Dear gods, it really is you,' he whispered. He held her face between his hands and she saw drops of rain shining like tiny diamonds in his hair, and tears soaking his long, dark lashes.

The agonising veil of doubt was torn away. Each knew the other was no ghost, no stranger. Her hands slid round his neck, his encircled her waist, and then they were locked together, weeping, kissing each other over and over again.

It was a long time before they managed to say anything coherent to each other. Kharan felt as if a sun had burst in her chest, and she could hardly breathe for a joy so extreme that it hurt. The previous night's miseries were obliterated, everything forgotten in this dazzling moment.

'Oh, Falmeryn, I was so sure you were dead – I nearly died without you,' she sobbed, disentangling strands of his hair from her mouth. 'Where have you been?'

'But I thought Xaedrek had – had executed you. What happened? Did he reprieve you? I just don't understand why you're here – I can't believe it.'

'*You* can't believe it?' she cried. Suddenly all the bitterness and grief she had been suppressing for months welled up into a torrent. 'Three years – three years I've spent grieving for you, missing you, and all that time you were alive! What were you doing? *Why weren't you with me?*' She struck at his shoulders with her fists, but he held onto her until her rage subsided into deep, shuddering sobs. Her pain tore at him. He tried to tell her what had happened, but his explanation was so disjointed that he gave up and quietened her tears with kisses. There would be time for words later; now they seemed irrelevant, just transient firefly things that could not express what they really wanted to say to each other.

'I'm sorry, Falmeryn,' Kharan said when she was calmer. 'I've got so much to tell you, I don't know where to start. But we can't talk here. Bring the lamp, and come with me.'

'Where to?'

'My room.' Her lips curved in a smile. 'I do live here!'

She had forgotten everything else, but the first thing she

252

remembered was Filmoriel. She gripped Falmeryn's hand and drew him along the aisle to the door, not daring to take her eyes off him in case he vanished again. She could hardly wait to tell him about their daughter – but Filmoriel was with Thaufa En Faliol, and it would be at least three hours before they woke. Somehow she had to keep the news until then, because she knew Falmeryn would want to see the child the moment she told him.

They crossed the courtyard quickly, their arms twined round each other. There was no sign of the guard or Ol Melemen, and Falmeryn did not spare them a thought. In finding Kharan, all else had ceased to matter, and he had even forgotten his need to see Melkavesh.

'Kharan, I can't tell you how much I've missed you,' he said quietly, pausing to kiss her again.

'Then you'd better show me instead,' she said warmly. Her hands were still trembling as she opened the side door, and her breath caught in her throat. 'We have until morning.'

'Longer than that, I hope. Now I've found you, I'm not letting you out of my sight again.'

Melkavesh's office was a large chamber with two tall windows overlooking the Aludrian Sea. The walls were of large blocks of stone fitted seamlessly together, with the curious quality – like the whole castle – of reflecting vividly whatever colours touched it. According to the weather, the room could be golden as sunlight or blue-green as the sea; or, as now, it could take on the brown gloom of a storm. A number of lamps cast overlapping golden circles of light on the ceiling, but every now and then a whip of lightning would turn the whole chamber blood-red or acidic green.

A desk of polished auburn wood stood below the window, and Melkavesh leaned against its front edge, facing Xaedrek. She had had the guards bring him from his own room, and now they waited outside the arched door while she spoke to him alone.

'Another grim morning,' Xaedrek said. 'There is a border-line between natural and unnatural weather, and this seems to have overstepped it.'

253

'You think it has something to do with Ah'garith?'

'I believe so. But you are the true Sorceress. What is your opinion?'

'I agree with you,' Melkavesh said tightly. 'If it is so, it means she is even more powerful than we feared. But I can't find out for sure because I still cannot far-see.' She gave Xaedrek a look of blazing anger and exclaimed, 'And that is your fault! Do you realise that you've crippled me? Every time I try, that accursed Wall is still there. I've done everything in my power to destroy it and it just may be that the damage you have done is permanent. There may be nothing I can do to stop the demon. This is what comes of false Sorcerers meddling with the power!'

She expected an angry riposte to this, but Xaedrek was rarely predictable. He actually looked contrite, and his reply disarmed her. 'If I had known it would come to this, I would not have helped you to create the Wall. In fact I would never have summoned the demon nor created amulin in the first place. When I am wrong about something I do not find it impossible to admit it.'

'Oh. Well.' She sighed, pushed her hair off her forehead and rubbed at her temples. 'I'm sorry, I didn't bring you in here to shout at you. I'm not in the best of moods. The weather's oppressing me, and something strange happened last night.'

'Indeed? What was it?' Xaedrek went to an ebony chair that stood in a corner a few feet to the left of the door. He sat facing her, an elbow on the carved arm and his dark, slender fingers stroking his chin.

'A messenger came from Charhn, insisting he had to see me. The guard left him to stable his horse while he woke Irem Ol Melemen, but when he went back to the stable, the man had vanished. The horse was still there, but no messenger. I've had the castle searched, no sign of him. It's disturbing.'

'I assure you, it's nothing to do with me,' said Xaedrek, a faint smile touching his lips.

'I never thought it was.' She turned away, angered that he still had the power to charm her with the slightest remark.

She determinedly returned her thoughts to Ah'garith, but a brisk knock at the door made her curse. Before she could answer it and tell whoever it was not to interrupt her, the door swung open and two figures came in under the deep stone arch.

One was Kharan, the other a tall young man with a startlingly fair face and glossy chestnut hair. They did not see Xaedrek, who was sitting behind them to their right; they went straight up to Melkavesh, their arms linked and their faces bright with happiness.

'Didn't the guards tell you I wasn't to be disturbed?' Melkavesh said sharply.

'Don't be so miserable!' Kharan exclaimed, too elated to be put off by her attitude. 'Melkavesh, this is Falmeryn!'

The Sorceress opened her mouth to reply, but the retort died and her mouth remained open. Kharan had told her a lot about Falmeryn; the main thing being that he was dead, executed by Xaedrek. It took her a moment to understand the implication, and then she gasped, '*Your* Falmeryn?'

'Yes!'

'But I thought –' She glanced sideways at Xaedrek, but his eyes were fixed in a frozen expression on Falmeryn's back. 'Wait a moment, are you the messenger who arrived last night?'

'Er – yes I am, Lady Melkavesh,' the Forluinishman replied, looking distinctly embarrassed.

'Where on Earth have you been? I've had guards turning Heldavrain upside down trying to find you!'

'Then I apologise.' He met her eyes with a candid gaze that made it impossible for Melkavesh to stay angry with him. 'I was with Kharan.'

'You can't blame us, Mel,' Kharan said, reaching out to touch her arm. 'It's a long story – how we met last night – but you must understand how we felt, finding each other alive.'

'I suppose so.' She gave a rueful smile and added more gently, 'I'm glad for you, Kharan, really I am. And you're very welcome, Falmeryn.' She kissed them both on the forehead. 'Now are you going to tell me what's brought you here from Charhn?'

'From Kesfaline, really.' He held out a soft leather pouch and Melkavesh took it from him, surprised at the weight of it. 'It's stone from each of the moons, Fliya and Jaed. I was told you would understand what it was and be able to make use of it; possibly to defeat Gorethria, although I understand I'm too late for that.'

Melkavesh stole another glance at Xaedrek, and this time Kharan noticed and turned to see what she was looking at. She started violently, having assumed there was no one else in the room, and exclaimed, 'What the hell is he doing in here?'

Falmeryn swung round and stared with utter disbelief at the Emperor. Kharan had told him that Xaedrek was here, but he had assumed that he would be under lock and key in a distant part of the castle. To find him in Melkavesh's office, unguarded, as if he were a respected visitor, shocked him beyond words.

Xaedrek was sitting very still, almost languidly, but his expression had turned glacial. He had known for some time how Kharan had escaped being beheaded, but there had been first-hand witnesses to Falmeryn's death. Amnek and Baramek themselves had seen him savaged by the Gorethrian hound pack, and this apparent resurrection was incredible. Both him and Kharan?

'I did ask you not to come in,' Melkavesh said. 'I was trying to talk to him.'

'What is there to talk about?' Kharan exclaimed, but no one answered her. Falmeryn and Xaedrek were glaring at each other, and Xaedrek, for once in his life, actually had the grace to look disturbed. Then, as if all his accumulated revulsion at Gorethria's evil had focused itself into one lethal arrowhead, Falmeryn lunged across the room to assail the Emperor with his bare hands.

He did not even touch him. Xaedrek stood up with swift feline grace, then something like a fist of light slammed into Falmeryn and thrust him sideways. He collided with the wall and leaned there, gasping. Melkavesh rounded on him with the residual sparks of sorcery still crackling around her arms. 'You may have strong feelings,' she said sternly, 'but I will not have anyone making rash attempts on Xaedrek's life.'

Kharan was pulling at her arm, furious. 'Melkavesh, don't you ever do that again! How dare you! If you ever lay a finger on Falmeryn again, I'll kill you!'

'He's not hurt. I had to stop him.'

Falmeryn recovered and stood upright, rubbing at a bruised shoulder. He was still looking at Xaedrek as if he would attack him again, but Xaedrek was looking back coolly as if it would take an apocalypse to unsettle him. Kharan went to Falmeryn and slid her arm through his, pulling him away gently.

'It's no good, you can't kill him,' she said in a soft, sad tone. 'I've tried. I couldn't do it. Leave him to Melkavesh.'

'What do you mean, *you*'ve tried?' the Sorceress exclaimed, but Kharan did not reply. She looked questioningly at Xaedrek.

'It doesn't matter,' he said. 'I would simply like to know, Falmeryn, how you escaped Gorethrian justice.'

'Justice!' Falmeryn blazed. 'How dare you speak of –'

'For the Sphere's sake, will you all be quiet?' Melkavesh's voice cut the air like steel. She looked at Kharan and Falmeryn, who were now on the far side of her desk, near the windows. 'Listen to me. Xaedrek has surrendered and he is my prisoner, but we have agreed to have a personal truce between us. Before you interrupt me, let me explain the reason. It is not a pleasant one.'

In a grave, abrupt tone she told them about Ah'garith, ignoring their reactions. 'The energy that creates sorcery is part of everything, even the weather. If the power is warped to a very great extent, the weather can be warped also,' she concluded.

Kharan shuddered. 'So these awful storms are a – a symptom of the demon's power?'

'In a way. Or a warning. I don't wish to frighten you, but she's grown very strong. Xaedrek and I must work together to stop her. You know I kept telling you of my difficulties in using sorcery? Well, now I'm certain that it is Ah'garith herself who is blocking my power. She is an anachronism who should have perished with the Serpent, and it is simply her presence on Earth that is diverting the true energy.'

'Well, where is she? How are you going to stop her?'

'I wish I knew.' Melkavesh leaned on the edge of her desk, her hair falling untidily over the shoulders of her green tabard as she stared at the pouch. 'I remember Afil Es Thendil once telling me there was stone from Jaed in Charhn. So they finally found it?'

'The temple itself is built of it.'

Melkavesh smiled. 'Indeed. Well, you'd better tell me everything you can.' As Falmeryn began to explain what Ferdanice and the priests of Charhn had said to him, Melkavesh loosened the top of the pouch and drew out the packages inside, one full of fine, reflective dust, the other containing a thick shard of white crystal. She spread them on the desk top and studied them, trying to probe them with her higher senses.

When Falmeryn had told her everything he could remember, Melkavesh looked up at him, and Kharan noticed how far away and troubled her eyes were. She had often seen that look before, and it never boded well.

'I need time to think about this. I'll talk to you again later, Falmeryn. Meanwhile you can stay in the castle as long as you wish, and welcome, but bear in mind what I said.'

Falmeryn took the hint. He put his arm round Kharan's shoulder and the two of them walked slowly to the door, silent and uneasy. Now Melkavesh was alone with Xaedrek again. He came to her side and looked curiously at the moon stone.

'This was supposed to help you defeat me?' he said. 'You fared well enough without it.'

Melkavesh said nothing. Then she struck the desk with her fist and shouted, 'Damn!'

'What's wrong?'

'Xaedrek, I don't know. I should be resentful that a source of power was denied me before the battle, when I needed it so desperately, but even if Falmeryn had arrived before, I don't think it would have made any difference.'

'What do you mean?'

'The stone means nothing to me,' she said heavily. 'Nothing at all. I can't see into it. Even when I'd lost my far-sight, I could still perceive things closer to me, but now I can't even near-see. It's like everything about Kristillia – I know there's something there, but it's closed to me, lifeless. Oh, curse this blindness!'

She turned her back on him, but he put his hands on her shoulders and she did not pull away. 'So it is of no help against Ah'garith?'

'No. I will keep trying, of course, but I know what the result will be – a dire headache. Gods, Xaedrek, I don't even know where to begin looking for Ah'garith. Is she still in Zhelkahh? Or on the other side of the world?'

'If you had as little sleep as I did last night, you would be wise to rest and think about it when you are less tired.'

'You are very solicitous, suddenly,' she said. 'And what did Kharan mean by saying, "You can't kill him. I've tried"?'

Xaedrek told her. It did nothing to improve her mood.

'I don't know who to be the most concerned for, you or her,' she snapped. 'But I warn you, you had better not touch her, or anyone else. I will not have people in this household trying to murder each other.'

'Melkavesh, listen to me,' Xaedrek said soothingly. 'Evidently Kharan was not meant to die, and I have no intention of harming her.'

'But I don't want to have to keep you locked up because the two of you hate each other.'

'I don't hate her, and I never have. It's true I despised her fear of me for a time, but for the way she has overcome that fear I can respect her. And I will tell you something about Kharan. She only ever hated me as much as she hated herself.'

'Well, it sounds as if the two of you are quite reconciled.'

'Not exactly.' He turned her round to face him, and he was smiling. 'But would it matter so much to you if we were? Surely you are not jealous?'

She cursed the awful black tension that made her tongue so unguarded. 'Don't be ridiculous.'

'She has Falmeryn. It is beyond me how he survived, but I bear him no ill will. They are both quite safe from me. It's true I was fond of Kharan once, but that is long in the past, and I have never met anyone to compare with you . . .'

Then he let her go suddenly, and turned sideways to lean on the desk. Her tension worsened, and now it seemed to have nothing whatever to do with Ah'garith or far-seeing. 'I don't know why I'm saying this to you,' he said. 'I must be insane. You deserved to die for the way you betrayed me, for what you have done to Gorethria. I used to have dreams about you, long before I met you, as if to warn me that you were an angel of destruction. Yet in spite of everything, what I still feel for you is the very antithesis of hatred.'

Melkavesh was lost for words. Surely it was impossible to love someone who was so evil? But her passion for him had never taken any heed of logic. A cynical attempt at seduction she might have resisted, however half-heartedly, but here he was expressing exactly what was in her own heart and it took her breath away. If the terrible things he had done had not obliterated her feelings, nothing could.

She moistened her dry lips and said softly, 'Don't you remember, the time we both far-saw, there was a moment that seemed to be telling us – well, that there are better things for us to do than fight?'

She reached out to touch his arm, and he was already turning towards her, so that she slid straight into his embrace. 'I remember,' he murmured, kissing her half on the cheek, half on the lips. Then his mouth found hers, and her black mood lifted as if the sun had come out.

13

Children of Dark and Light

'ANIXA. ANIXA . . .'

Irem Ol Thangiol groaned and heaved against his bonds, but they held him, greasy against his sweating skin. He was in the midst of a darkness that seemed to rush around him, full of moans and laughs and whispers. Particles bounced off him. There was a sense of water beneath him, a roaring sea that was utterly lightless except for scraps of pewter light winking on the surface.

He turned his head to one side and spat out sour phlegm. There was no water to ease his swollen throat.

He had lost all sense of time and reality. Stretches of oblivion came but offered no relief; as soon as he fell asleep he dreamed, and the dream was just the same as the waking nightmare. He was in hell, truly in hell.

He had no memory of the demon taking him from Zhelkahh, even less awareness of where they were going. He remembered almost nothing at all of his months of torment at Xaedrek's hands, but he hung onto the memory of a woman's face, dark and sombre yet as sweet as a benediction from Fliya.

'Anixa . . .'

Sometimes he was aware of people with him, but they only worsened his dread. There was the thin, unnaturally tall Gorethrian with a face like a vulture's; and then there was the Shanin, who walked in the shape of a benign old woman but whose eyes were overflowing lakes of madness. When she came near him, he would scream until his throat filled with blood – soundlessly, because his voice was gone – but she always knew the moment to stop, the moment to draw him back from the edge of insanity.

There were hallucinations. A dog sniffing at his face. A wave beating relentlessly against a rock, like a flapping sheet. A smooth grey tunnel that seemed made of no earthly substance, like a chute that led down into a ghastly nether-world. And then a vast, dark landscape where naked human beings jostled and cried out in fear . . .

A hissing voice cut into his brain, real yet part of the torment. 'He is no use to us like this. Get him on his feet and make him work.'

'Yes, Ah'garith.' Amnek's hands loomed towards him like black claws, and he felt his bonds being cut. There was a stone cup at his lips, water flooding into his clotted mouth. Later, food was brought, a soft porridge which he managed to choke down, and then he felt his physical strength return-ing. But there was a dull buzzing in his bones, as if he were being animated by an energy as unnatural as amulin and more loathsome.

A peculiar numbness settled on him. He was pulled to his feet and his dazed eyes saw that the dark place and the weeping humans were real. The Shanin was watching him, giggling, and suddenly he understood what was happening and his lips tore apart in a hoarse, curdled yell . . .

. . . And the scream ripped into Kharan's mind and she woke up violently, shivering in a cold glaze of sweat.

She reached for Falmeryn. He was not there.

'Falmeryn?' She sat up in panic, then saw him silhouetted against the discoloured light of the window, standing by the little bed where Filmoriel slept.

'I'm here,' he said, walking back to the bed with the child in his arms. 'She was crying, so I got up to see what was wrong.'

'Oh, did she tell you?'

'No. I picked her up and she's fallen asleep again.' He sat on the edge of the bed with Filmoriel curled up against his chest, her head nestled in his shoulder.

'I usually wake up if she cries, but I couldn't – I was having such an awful nightmare.'

'Are you all right?'

'Yes, I am now.' She knelt on the bedcover and rested her chin on his shoulder. 'Now you're here.'

Falmeryn was quiet for a moment, preoccupied, and Kharan remembered the silent astonishment with which he had gazed at Filmoriel when she first brought her to him a few days ago. Then he said, 'Kharan – this will sound mad to you, but I must tell you. I've seen Filmoriel before. Sometimes in dreams, once or twice in a kind of vision.'

Feathers fluttered in her stomach. 'Not you as well.'

'What do you mean?'

'Melkavesh has said the same thing. Even Xaedrek has dreamed about her: a red-haired child and a little bird. This was even before she was born, and now they look at her and say, "It's her!"'

Anxiety must have given her voice a sharper edge than she intended, because Falmeryn said softly, 'I'm sorry, Kharan, but it's true.'

'Don't you be sorry. It's not your fault. I just find it so frightening. Everyone is welcome to their weird premonitions, but I don't see why they must drag Filmoriel into it. What were these visions?'

'I'll tell you later. Not now, in case she wakes up.' He turned his head and kissed her. 'All the time we were apart I used to dream of finding you alive. I never thought it would come true, still less that I'd find we had a child. Not everything that happens is bad, this is a miracle.'

A light, rapid knock at the door made Kharan's heart leap, and she got up hurriedly to answer it, pulling on an embroidered robe as she did so. Anixa stood in the passage, her arms clasped round herself and her eyes luminous with shock.

'My lady, forgive me.' She still had not lost the habit of calling her 'my lady', although Kharan had often asked her not to. 'I've had a terrible nightmare about Irem Ol Thangiol. He was in an ugly, bleak place, screaming –'

'Oh, you're shaking.' Kharan put an arm round her

shoulders and drew her into the room. 'Anixa, I've just had the same dream. Don't upset yourself. Come and sit with us.'

She helped the slender Kesfalian to the bed and Falmeryn moved up to make room for them. Anixa sat between them with her head bowed, her glossy black hair hiding her face. She hardly ever wept, but Kharan wished that for once she would break out of her sombre self-containment.

'Everything is as I feared it would be,' Anixa said softly. 'Melkavesh and Xaedrek are not enemies after all. And the Earth's secret has been violated. The moon stone is here.'

Kharan looked at Falmeryn over Anixa's head. 'How did you know about that?'

'I know. Just as I knew Melkavesh was the enchantress whom the Kesfalians believed would save us only to deliver us to something worse.' She looked sideways at Kharan, one eye gleaming like an aureate moon. 'Did I not warn you to go to the sages of Kesfaline? Why did you let her come here?'

Kharan stiffened. 'I did try to make her go there, I really did. She just wouldn't listen. You should try arguing with her!'

'You did not try hard enough.'

Kharan felt as if she were falling; she had been through this before, and again it seemed that Anixa was something more than human, a spectre of dark velvet blending into the Earth, sky and moons as if she were part of them and speaking with their voice. *Melkavesh is heading for some great or appalling destiny, and we are not helping her of our own accord but being swept along with her* . . . Outside, clouds the colour of old blood rolled over a grim sea, and everything seemed gravid with horrific, hidden meanings. Kharan suspected that Filmoriel had also shared the nightmare. She longed to shake Anixa out of this mystical mood, but fear had fallen on her like a hand and she could not speak.

Then Falmeryn said, 'I have been with the sages of Kesfaline, Anixa. They said what you have, that Melkavesh would defeat Xaedrek only to bring something worse. But they did

264

not know what it meant, and one of them was not really a sage but a Guardian. He made me bring the stones here. Maybe I've done wrong, I just don't know. But one thing I've learned is that people like you and me and the sages are powerless against the Guardians and Melkavesh. They'll have their own way whatever we do.'

Kharan did her best to shake off the chilling start to the day and concentrate on her work, but it was difficult. She kept away from windows as if she had a phobia of them, but she could not block her ears to the continual sickly belching of thunder over Heldavrain. If she dared to look out, the vista was always the same; voluminous clouds like mountains swirling ponderously overhead, shot through with lightning of bizarre colours. Sometimes spheres of light would roll along the underside of the clouds like clay-red eyeballs.

Filmoriel, normally sweet-natured, would not stop crying, yet it did not seem to be the storm that was upsetting her. Her distress began to drive Kharan to distraction.

'What's wrong, darling?' she asked, carrying her into the kitchens. Rather than leave her in this state with Thaufa En Faliol, she had brought her on her rounds of the castle. 'Is it Falmeryn you want? He's only in the stables. You'll see him soon.'

'No. It's Miril,' Filmoriel said incoherently. 'She's hurting herself.'

'I don't understand you, my love.'

'There!' The child waved angrily at the air. 'Why can't you see her? She can't reach me!'

'Filmoriel,' said Kharan, catching hold of her hand, 'there's nothing there.'

This only made her cry harder. 'She *is*. I've got to make her find me,' she sobbed.

Kharan frowned, wondering if Melkavesh was responsible for putting these ideas into her head. 'Hush. It's all right,' she said soothingly. Filmoriel subsided into hiccuping sobs as Kharan carried her across to the massive hearth, welcoming the fire and the friendly bustle of the kitchen as a relief from the day's gloom.

Thaufa En Mianna came over and greeted her. 'What's wrong with the little one?'

'I don't know. It must be the storm, or something. Anyway, she's quietening down now. How are things here?'

En Mianna, who was supervising the kitchen staff, began to fill her ears with the problems of getting sufficient supplies from Ehd'rabara after the disruption of the battle. Filmoriel struggled against Kharan's grasp, so she set the little girl down and watched her trotting away to receive the effusive attention of the four Kristillian cooks. At least it would distract her for a while, Kharan thought. She tried to sound interested in what En Mianna was saying and to make helpful suggestions, but her mind was elsewhere and hardly a word of it sank in.

When their business was over she took her leave and went to fetch her daughter. She could not see Filmoriel at first, but the kitchen was large and full of tables and hidden corners. Kharan called to her, and the cooks began to look blankly at one another. A flood of panic went through her.

Filmoriel was nowhere to be found.

They all searched frantically, eventually reduced to looking in the most unlikely places. The door to the kitchen had been shut all the time, one of the Kristillians insisted, and she had been working near it so the child could not possibly have gone that way. They looked in every corner of the huge pantries, and then it was Kharan who noticed that the door to the cellar was unlatched.

I've got to make her find me . . .

'Filmoriel, come here! This game has got to stop!' Without pausing to think, she snatched a lamp from the nearest table and rushed into the darkness, shouting her daughter's name.

After the battle, Melkavesh had not expected perfection, but she had expected peace. Instead she had the ominous weather and the knowledge that Ah'garith was at large pressing on the inside of her skull, and now an even more sinister pattern was shaping itself around Heldavrain.

She had been receiving bad news for days. A rider from Alta-Nangra, a moustached man in thick black furs, arrived

266

to tell her that half the people from his village had vanished, and it was not the doing of Gorethria. A Kristillian goatherd had come from the hills above Heldavrain to say that his family were missing. Another messenger reported that a mounted platoon had been sent out from Ehd'rabara, but the horses had returned riderless . . .

People were vanishing, and for once the Imperial troops could not be blamed. Terrified, everyone was turning to the enchantress Mellorn for an answer, never dreaming that she was as helpless as they. She knew it was Ah'garith's doing, of course, but without far-sight she was as good as blind.

Now, on this malevolent morning, she awaited the arrival of a visitor who seemed to presage something even stranger. Baramek was being held with the other prisoners of war near Ehd'rabara, but a few days earlier he had made an urgent plea to see her. It was so unlike him that she had agreed, and ordered her own Kristillian and Mangorian guards to go and bring him to Heldavrain. She had just received word that they were entering the courtyard, and now she sat behind her desk, trying to compose her features into a severe Gorethrian mask.

The door opened. Irem Ol Melemen entered, followed by two Kristillian guards; then came Baramek himself, with the two Mangorians behind him. He strode in under the deep stone lintel, a startlingly severe figure next to the Kristillians. His black cloak was dusty from travelling, his hair plastered down from being encased under the helm that he now held under one arm. His harsh expression burned into her, yet she read something in it that she had never seen before: anxiety.

'High Commander Baramek,' she said, standing up. 'Your request to see me was very unexpected, to say the least. What's the purpose of it?'

'I am not here for reasons of State. It is a personal matter.'

'Indeed?' She frowned, surprised. 'Of what nature?'

'The ill feeling between us, my lady, may well be irreconcilable. Nevertheless, this is a matter of such concern to me that I am prepared to put hostilities aside. I hope that you, as the victor' – there was a vitriolic note in his voice – 'will prove magnanimous enough to do the same.'

'I may be. It depends what it is.'

'You are aware that the Kristillians crossed the Omnuandrix and raided our camps there in order to capture the families of senior officers. My own wife and daughters are imprisoned with me.'

'Yes, but you know it is only a safeguard to ensure the officers' good behaviour. Are you complaining that they are not being humanely treated?'

'No. Not as such.' There was anger in his eyes, and greater pain. 'But my younger daughter, Surukish, has disappeared.'

'From inside the camp? That's impossible.'

'Far be it from me to accuse the Kristillians of abducting her. They showed, or at least feigned, concern, and we searched everywhere for her without success.'

'I hope you are not accusing me,' she said, sharply angry without meaning to be.

He leaned towards her, his eyes like yellow flame. 'I am sure that even you would not stoop so low as to take a child. My only purpose here is to ask if you, with the supramundane powers you have so admirably demonstrated, cannot do something to help me find her.'

She tried to outstare him, but he would not look away. Then he added in a low voice, 'Please, my lady Melkavesh. She is only ten years old. You are my last hope.'

Gods, she thought. *This is the last thing I need.* But at the same time she felt a sudden sympathy for Baramek; whatever his faults, his love for his family was so powerful that he would even undergo the humiliation of pleading with her if it might bring Surukish back. She owed it to him to be honest, at least.

'Listen, Commander,' she began quietly. 'I would help you if I could, truly. I think I know what might have happened to your daughter. You must know that the Shanin Ah'garith is at large somewhere. Others have vanished also, and I fear she has taken them. But I cannot find her, because her very presence on Earth has crippled my powers. There's nothing I can do.'

268

His eyes narrowed, and a frown creased his heavy brow. 'Did you say Ah'garith? The old woman, Ah'garith – a Shanin?'

'Yes, a Shanin, a demon. She deserted Xaedrek at Zhelkahh. You knew, didn't you?'

'He said nothing of this to me. And he spoke of Ah'garith only as a human with a strange power, like yourself . . .'

'I am no demon, but she most certainly is.'

'The same sort as Meheg-Ba?'

'Yes. The same. I knew Xaedrek did not make it common knowledge, but I thought he would have told you by now.'

Baramek was almost trembling with suppressed fury, and she knew why. By summoning Meheg-Ba, Meshurek had destroyed the Empire. Baramek had always hated anything with the slightest taint of the supernatural; he had been prepared to tolerate amulin while he believed Xaedrek's assurance that it was a new and clean power, but to discover after all that Xaedrek was a demon summoner, that the Empire had fallen again because he had repeated Meshurek's mistakes, shocked and repulsed him to the core. Her sympathy for him increased. She had not meant to inflict this dreadful revelation on him.

'You are telling me the truth in this, aren't you, my lady?'

'Yes – I mean – I thought you knew.'

'I did not,' he said acrimoniously. 'I am grateful to you for telling me. And I have another request to make of you. I would like to speak with Emperor Xaedrek.'

'That's impossible.'

'I insist.'

'I'm sorry, it's absolutely out of the question.'

'Then I will not waste your time any further.'

He turned with a swirl of his cloak, but Melkavesh said, 'Baramek, I am sorry about Surukish, and if there's anything I can do to help find her, I will.'

He paused and nodded brusquely. 'Thank you, my lady. You have been honest, at least.' He strode out, surrounded by the guards.

Irem Ol Melemen, who had been standing quietly beside

269

the desk throughout this exchange, looked at Melkavesh and rubbed his chin as he did when he was troubled.

'Is something wrong?' she asked.

'I was only wondering if it is wise of you to have so much personal communication with high-ranking Gorethrians.'

'He wanted my help, Ol Melemen.'

'The Gorethrians would have destroyed us, yet now you wish to help them?' He spoke mildly, but he was a shrewd man and she knew he was trying to question her without antagonising her. She drew a sharp breath. Up until now he had – she thought – trusted her implicitly.

'Surukish is just a child,' she said evasively.

'I was thinking not so much of Baramek, as of Xaedrek himself. For you to spend so much time alone with him may prove that you have a very cool nerve, but it also seems to be an unwarranted risk.'

'I understand your concern, but I am the last person who needs it. I've told you why we've agreed to co-operate. He is not going to murder me – nor put me under his "power", if that's what you fear. I need his help. We can settle other matters when this is over.'

Irem Ol Melemen nodded thoughtfully, as if in agreement. 'I appreciate that. I would just warn you that the King and Queen are on their way here – to thank you – and they may see the matter rather differently.'

Kharan stumbled down the flight of stairs in virtual darkness, gasping as she missed the bottom one and nearly fell. Recovering herself, she held out the lamp in front of her and hurried anxiously between the wine casks and the long racks of cheese and apples.

'Filmoriel!' she cried. The light flashed on grain sacks and stone walls, but there was no gleam of red hair or a creamy robe to relieve her terror. She consciously fought her panic, telling herself that she was overreacting and that all children got themselves lost at times. Her daughter must be here somewhere, probably frightened enough without her mother making it worse.

Two or three others had followed her, but she was oblivious

to them. As the seconds dragged by with no sign of the child, her heart began to beat wildly and she went further into the darkness until she had left the others behind. There were more steps into a deeper cellar. *I must be mad*, she thought as she descended into musty blackness. *The world's supreme coward, and I come down here on my own?*

Feeling her way along a wall, she found the entrance to a small tunnel. She froze, biting her lip. Whether by instinct or precognition, she knew with absolute, horrific certainty that Filmoriel had gone into this tunnel.

As soon as she stepped into it, she knew it was no mere interconnecting passage between storage rooms; it was too black, too narrow. The flame in the lamp began to dance wildly. The cellar had seemed eerily quiet, but here the silence was so intense that the rushing of her own blood became a thunderous roar in her ears.

She paused until the flame steadied. Her mouth was thick, her shoulders ached with tension. The lamp hardly lit a yard in front of her, and the walls threw back only the faintest sheen to guide the way – and she suddenly noticed that the lamp felt almost empty.

This is insane, I must go back, she thought wildly, but the image of Filmoriel down here, lost and terrified, drove her on. She called once or twice, but the silence that answered her seemed to take on a deliberate, sinister indifference.

She almost walked into the door before she saw it: a cracked and ancient barrier of iron-clad wood. Something white flashed in front of her face and her stomach lurched in terror. She recoiled – then sagged with relief, and cursed herself. It was her own hand that had alarmed her, her own hand white against the dark latch.

If there had ever been a lock, it had rusted away long ago, and the door yielded like fungus to her shaking hand. A subtle change in the air, a scent that was more of ice than the mustiness of cellars, told her that she was entering a natural cave. It must have been years since anyone had ventured down here; she doubted that even Melkavesh had explored this deep below Heldavrain.

Gods, I wish I'd waited for the others, she thought. She

had been sweating, and the moisture trickling between her shoulder blades made her shiver. Fear of one sort or another had become part of her everyday life, yet she never seemed to get used to it. To her dismay, the lamp was waning to a faint golden moon that gave her almost no light at all. Reason told her to turn back before she lost her sense of direction – but her desperation to find her child would brook no denial. Step by step she went on, not so much self-possessed as numb with dread, horribly aware of her own breath juddering in and out of her throat.

'Filmoriel!' she called hoarsely. 'If you can hear me, please call out. It's all right, I'm here . . .'

A long, chattering hiss in the darkness cut into her nerves like a whip. She froze, almost sobbing with terror. The darkness itself she could bear, but now an overwhelming sense of malevolence swept through her and it seemed the hiss belonged to some demonic creature, full of mindless, mocking evil. When the hiss came again, she almost screamed.

'Who's there?' she cried, her voice high-pitched and breathless. 'Filmoriel?'

The shuddering breath stopped, became a sob. 'Who's that?' another voice came back like an echo. The voice of a child.

'Oh, thank the moons!' Kharan exclaimed, not hearing the wrongness of the voice, the maturity. 'Where are you?'

'Here. Help me!' Stumbling in the direction of the sound, it took her some time before the glow fell on a small, dark shape, huddled in a corner of the cave as if she had been trying to burrow into the rock.

Kharan fell to her knees, reaching out – until a nauseous shock wave stopped her. It was not Filmoriel. This was a larger figure, wrapped in a black cloak, with dark skin that reflected a purplish sheen in the lamplight. A child, but one of at least ten. A Gorethrian.

'Who on Earth are you?' Kharan cried. The child stirred, and the radiance picked out an insignia on her cloak collar that was distressingly familiar. Baramek's crest. And it seemed she had seen the child before; she was older now, but her almond-shaped topaz eyes were unforgettable.

'I – I am Surukish, daughter of Baramek.' She was shaking uncontrollably and her breath rasped between her teeth, thick with fear and pain.

'How in heaven did you get down here?' Then Kharan's heart melted in pity and she helped Surukish to sit up, hugging her as she trembled and sobbed. 'It's all right. Hush. Did you escape from the prison camp?'

'No, I don't know what happened. I was looking after some younger children, making them play a game. Then everything went grey – I don't remember. There was a thing like a huge dog – carrying me. Where am I?'

'Under Heldavrain Castle. This dog, did it bring you here?'

'It must have done. I don't remember. But there was a sort of red and gold light – and I think the dog was frightened, and dropped me.'

'Where is the dog now?' Kharan stroked the girl's silky hair.

'It's gone. I'm not hurt.' Surukish sniffed and dried her eyes on the edge of her cloak, her natural Gorethrian dignity reasserting itself. 'I wasn't really frightened. Just cold.'

'Well, you're braver than I am, Surukish.'

'That's Lady Surukish to you, An'raagan. Where's my father?'

'I don't know. We'll get you back to him.' An old resentment stirred at the child's Gorethrian arrogance, but her anxiety drowned it. 'Listen to me. Have you seen or heard anything down here that could have been another child? Just a few minutes ago, a little girl of three?'

'No. There was nothing. Only the light.'

Kharan pressed a hand to her face, trying to calm herself and think rationally. The fear was tightening and solidifying under her breastbone with the feeling that however hard she searched for Filmoriel, she would not find her. Perhaps she was not here at all. And now there was the added problem of Surukish; she could not drag her along on a futile and dangerous search. Her only course was to take the child to safety, and get Melkavesh's help.

'Come on,' she said, helping the girl to her feet. 'We'd better hurry back. It's not far.'

They began to cross the cave, but within a few seconds the lamp died. Kharan shook it angrily, then pulled Surukish protectively closer to her side and continued to grope her way in the direction of the ancient door back to the cellar.

Somehow she had known she would never find it. It was all she could do to suppress her frustration and panic as the minutes crawled by and she found nothing beneath her hand except rough, solid rock. The cave seemed huge. Echoes hung in the air as if its fabric were creaking and shifting in the distance. The air sighed around her, cold and gritty as earth, raising prickles all over her skin. And she knew she had turned the wrong way, and was wandering deeper into the cave, not towards safety. Surukish had become very calm and stoical, as if she had transferred all her fear onto Kharan.

Eventually she remarked, 'You're lost, aren't you?'

'It's a bit further than I thought. Don't worry,' Kharan said inanely, hoping the child could not feel her pulse thudding.

'You're lost,' Surukish stated. 'This would never have happened if my father had found me.' She began to extol Baramek's virtues in an arrogant, piping voice, and Kharan's pity slowly faded to irritation.

'You're lucky anyone found you at all, even a common An'raagan. Incidentally, Lady Surukish, my name is Kharan and I used to be called "Lady" as well.' She did not expect Surukish to catch the implication, but she had underestimated the child's intelligence.

'*The* Lady Kharan? I remember you. The one my father –'

'Yes, the one your father so hates,' Kharan snapped, no longer in a mood to be tolerant. 'And did you know why he hates me? Because I was the Emperor Xaedrek's mistress.'

'I know. I'm sure it was nothing personal,' she replied sniffily. 'It's just that the lesser races are so treacherous and inferior. Xaedrek should never have allowed you into his confidence.'

Kharan stiffened, her fear momentarily driven out by anger. She could never forget Baramek, the way his hot ochre eyes had fastened on her with loathing whenever he

274

saw her, his cold and indifferent air of resignation when he had finally found an excuse to arrest her and Falmeryn, as if he was not in the least surprised when she had turned against Xaedrek. He despised her simply because she was a non-Gorethrian, a common An'raagan, less than human. There was so much she could say to his daughter – but the fury bled away. It was not worth it, and she was so tired. She wondered if the intelligent brat was frightened of her now, thinking that she was deliberately trying to lose her as revenge against Baramek. Certainly her voice had sounded a little shrill . . . Kharan sighed, gripped her hand reassuringly, and said, 'It was a long time ago. It doesn't matter now –'

Her words were lost in a rush of air, a blast of light. She tried to cry out, but terror had knocked all the breath out of her. Above and in front of them the air was glittering with a shaft of silver dust particles, as if someone had half opened a door into another world. Then a bird swooped along the beam and hovered there, fluttering wildly in the light. It was hardly bigger than a blackbird, and its colour was the most beautiful Kharan had ever seen, like fire shining through deep red amber. Its wings were outlined by a brilliant white-gold glow.

The Lady help me, I'm going mad, she thought, hanging onto Surukish. Her ears were ringing and she felt on the point of fainting.

'That's the light that frightened the dog away!' the girl exclaimed.

Kharan found her voice. 'Did you see the bird before?'

'No. Just the light.'

'Come on, we've got to follow it. It will show us the way out.'

Breathless, she pulled Surukish along beside her. The bird danced on the air before them and they pursued her with their eyes fixed on the glittering beam that bore her up. And as she gazed at it, Kharan saw a silhouette in the beam, like a child flitting across a doorway to another world. 'Filmoriel!' she cried, stretching out her hand. Her fingers met wood. They had found the ancient door to the tunnel, but the moment she touched it, the bird and the light vanished.

* * *

Melkavesh was alone in her office, deep in thought, when the door flew open and two wide-eyed figures burst into the room. She stood up, astonished by the sight of the tall Gorethrian child at Kharan's side.

'Mel, you've got to help me. Filmoriel's vanished,' Kharan began, but her voice was hoarse and Melkavesh cut across her, not registering what she had said.

'Who is this child?' she said, coming from behind her desk and staring at her.

'I am Surukish, daughter of Baramek.'

'How on Earth –' The Sorceress's face was a mask of incredulity. Kharan started to speak again, but Melkavesh suddenly rushed from the room and could be heard yelling in the corridor, 'Have they taken Commander Baramek out of the castle yet? Then for heaven's sake have him brought back here at once! Tell him Kharan's found his daughter!'

Kharan pushed the sweat-blackened hair off her forehead, trembling with agitation as Melkavesh came back into the room, saying, 'This is extraordinary. I can't tell you how glad I am to see you, Surukish, but however did you come to be here?'

'I'm trying to explain, if you'd listen!' Kharan cried. 'I was looking for Filmoriel.' As she related the story, Melkavesh's expression changed from astonishment to one of brooding grimness.

'Did you both see this bird?'

'Yes. I think it was Miril. You know Filmoriel's had an obsession with Miril since she could speak, I thought she was just making a game out of things she'd heard. Now I'm not sure. I'm frightened, Mel.'

'Ashurek and Silvren told me that the bird sometimes appears in a vision to those in a hopeless situation. I don't know whether she's alive or whether you simply saw such a vision.'

'Does it matter? All I know is that there are horrible things wandering about under the castle, and Filmoriel's down there, and you have got to help me. Now.'

Before Melkavesh could reply, the door swung open and Baramek came in, followed by four guards who looked as if they had been hard pressed to keep pace with him. Melkavesh waved them out into the corridor. Surukish flew to her father and he lifted her up, his arms wrapped tightly round her and his eyes closed with relief and joy.

It was the first time Kharan had seen him show anything like ordinary human emotion. He had always seemed so forbidding, a human monster armoured in black war gear, the very essence of Gorethrian might and evil. Now, witnessing his love for his daughter she felt almost shocked, disorientated by his unexpected vulnerability. She swallowed tears, seeing him through a haze of fear for her own daughter.

Kisses and soft words exchanged, Baramek eventually set the child down and turned to Melkavesh. 'My lady, I do not know how to thank you for this.'

'But didn't the messenger tell you? It was Kharan who rescued her, not I.'

There was an uncomfortable silence. Oh, he knew well enough, Kharan thought. He knew, but he would die before he acknowledged it.

A small voice broke in, 'She was very brave, Father.' Baramek looked at Surukish, and then, at last, he turned to face Kharan. There was no softness in his expression now, not a trace of gratitude or even grudging respect. It was the same contemptuous look he had given her many times before, but now there was something more in it: resentment. Expressionless, she forced herself to hold his malevolent gaze until he turned scornfully away from her. Then, propelling Surukish before him, he strode out of the room and slammed the door. Papers on Melkavesh's desk lifted in the draught.

Both women stared at the door, then at each other. Kharan was shaking, partly with her age-old fear of Baramek, partly with anger. 'You would think – after what I did –' she gasped, '– I did not expect or even want his thanks, but you would think he could at least forget how much he loathes me!'

Melkavesh gazed at her, her eyebrows raised. Then she gave a rueful smile. 'Kharan, don't think I don't sympathise. All I know is that when anyone I hate does me a good turn, it only makes me hate them more.'

'There's a lesson I could have done without learning.' She

277

sagged, leaning on the corner of the desk, and added bitterly, 'Actually, Melkavesh, his reaction wasn't really any surprise to me. In fact I think it was worth going into that dreadful, pitch-black cave, running the risk of meeting something horrible down there, just to spite Baramek and see that aggrieved look on his face!'

'You should not have gone into the cave alone. Why didn't you fetch me?' Melkavesh's tone switched to one of severity. 'It was –'

'Reckless? Stupid?'

'I wasn't going to say that, but as you mention it . . .'

'I've had enough of you calling me that! For heaven's sake, I had to go after Filmoriel – there wasn't time to mess about! But I couldn't find her. Gods, I just don't know what to do.'

Melkavesh put an arm round her shoulders and said gently, 'We'll achieve nothing by panicking. Are you sure there's nowhere else she could have vanished to?'

'No, we searched everywhere. And I told you what Suruk-ish said, that some ghastly thing like a dog had dropped her in the cave. What if it came back and took Filmoriel?' Melkavesh tried to say something comforting, but was prevented by the appalling idea taking shape in her mind. 'Isn't there going to be any end to this? One nightmare after another. I'm going to find Falmeryn before the demon takes him too.'

She pulled away, but Melkavesh caught her arm. 'Kharan, how did you . . .?'

They stared at each other, neither wanting to shape the horror with words. In a strained voice, Kharan said, 'What other explanation is there for what's been happening? Ah'garith is here, isn't she? Near the castle – or under it. She's been here all the time. I didn't know there were caves down there, did you?'

Melkavesh breathed out slowly. She looked out of the window and saw spheres of ball-lightning dropping towards the sea like blood-clots. There was no help the Aludrians could give her now. 'I didn't want to say it, Kharan. As soon as you walked in with Surukish, I began to guess. There *is* no other explanation. Maybe Ah'garith took Surukish as some sort of personal revenge against Baramek. If so, the child had a very lucky escape.' She shook her head. 'Gods! I wouldn't put it past Ah'garith for a second to make her lair right under my nose. I should have guessed weeks ago. How could I not have realised? For that I do not deserve the title of Sorceress, I don't deserve it at all.'

She started towards the door, and Kharan followed her, saying, 'What are you going to do?'

'Whatever I have to do to get Filmoriel back.'

'You're not thinking of going alone?'

'I must. I can't put anyone else at risk.'

'Do you always have to take everything on yourself? You call *me* reckless! How can you possibly face Ah'garith without help?'

Melkavesh paused, then said quickly, 'You're right. Xaedrek knows Ah'garith better than anyone. I'll see what he has to say.'

'All I have to say is that I am coming with you, and you'd better not waste an atom of your breath arguing with me,' Kharan said flatly.

For once, Melkavesh did not.

'She has the audacity to do exactly that,' Xaedrek said, fastening a jacket of quilted black leather. 'To hide in the very last place we expected her to be, and to be quietly mocking our efforts to find her.'

He was the only one among them who seemed unperturbed, but Melkavesh knew him well enough by now to see that his calmness masked a tension as great as hers. After a brief discussion it had been agreed that five of them would go into the caves; as well as herself and Xaedrek, there were Falmeryn, Kharan and Irem Ol Melemen. She had insisted that they all put on battle-dress, and take arms, although what use it would be against the demon, she did not know. It was just an impotent bid to compensate for the inadequacy of her power.

'From what you have said of her, I find it hard to credit that the demon has been hiding under the castle, yet has

279

done us no harm,' the priest said thoughtfully. 'Until now.' He looked incongruous in breeches and bronze-figured breastplate, but the light in his eyes was anything but mild.

'I can understand it,' said Xaedrek. 'She's learned something from me at least – patience. She has probably been busy consolidating her power before beginning her revenge on us.'

'Subtle and very personal revenge,' Melkavesh muttered. There was nothing to be gained by expressing the anger she felt at Xaedrek for unleashing Ah'garith, nor her own terrible guilt at failing to find the demon. The emotions had twisted within her to become a blade of determination, like cold black diamond.

'I wish you'd stop talking about it!' Kharan exclaimed. 'For the moons' sake, can't we just go?'

She and Falmeryn were dressed alike in jackets and breeches of brown leather, with gauntlets and long boots. Both carried short swords. Xaedrek appeared a more breathtakingly sinister figure than usual in the severe black of his war gear, but he was unarmed. Melkavesh lifted a sword and a knife from the rack and held them out to him, hilt-first.

'I am no swordsman,' he said. 'I could cut someone down only if they were good enough to stand still.'

'Just take them,' she said, exasperated. She faced them, dark as earth in her officer's uniform, her hair a flow of phosphorescent gold. 'I will not have any of you arguing with me during this search. You'll all do as I say, or you need not come.'

As she spoke, the door opened and Anixa appeared in the doorway, dressed in breeches and jacket that made her slight figure seem boyish. Her presence seemed to bring an electricity that made the atmosphere, already brittle with tension, vibrate like a shell of black glass.

'My lady, I am coming with you.' There was a flinty resolution in her voice, and Melkavesh knew there was no point in trying to talk her out of it. 'The Shanin took Irem Ol Thangiol with her. I must know what happened to him.'

Her pale eyes were fixed on Xaedrek in a gaze that might have seared him to ash where he stood, but he ignored her.

'Very well,' said Melkavesh. 'As long as you understand how dangerous this may be. And I will have none of you at odds with each other.'

She looked from Anixa to Xaedrek. 'My only concern is yours,' he said evenly. 'To destroy Ah'garith.'

To destroy a demon, Melkavesh thought as she led the party into the darkness of the cellar. Ashurek's and Silvren's faces loomed in the shadows and she heard their voices echoing everything they had ever told her about the Shana. *There is only one way they can be destroyed; by Miril's touch. But Miril is dead. We saw her fall into the Arctic snow, mortal as any Earthly blackbird . . .*

We haven't a hope, she thought. Xaedrek knew it as well as she did. She vividly remembered him telling her that when the Shanin had first come to him, she had stated, *Only Miril's touch could free me from this wretched existence.*

Cold understanding stabbed into her. Kharan's vision of Miril had not been to guide her to safety, but something deeper than that. A warning. *You cannot annihilate the demon without me. You must find me . . .*

How can I find you, Miril, if you are dead? she raged silently. I cannot find anything. I am blind. Falmeryn delivers the secret of the power into my very hands, and still I cannot divine it.

They were through the tunnel now, and venturing across the cave. Each of them carried a lantern, but the blackness seemed to swallow all light before it touched the walls or the roof. The space seemed endless.

'Falmeryn, are you all right?' Kharan said in a small voice.

'Yes,' he replied, though he did not sound it. 'It just reminds me – no, I'm all right, really.'

'Do you know the extent of this cave?' Ol Melemen asked.

'I didn't know it was here. It can't be that big. We are within the plug of rock that supports Heldavrain, so unless there are more caves extending down and under the sea-bed or shore, it has an obvious limit.' She tried to sound matter of fact, but her voice was as thin as wire. It horrified her to know that all the time she had thought the household safe, they might have been in terrible danger. *I have a bad feeling about staying here*, Kharan had said before the battle. Now Melkavesh knew why. Even Kharan had been more aware of it than she, the supposed Sorceress!

The cave widened. The air seemed to speak with staccato echoes. Then the lantern beams began to wink on rough facets of rock, and the party stopped dead in bewilderment. They had come to the end of the cave. There was an unbroken wall ahead of them; no tunnels, no deeper caverns that might lead down to Ah'garith's lair. Not even any real hint of evil.

They moved back and forth around the periphery of the cave for a time, but they could find nothing. There was only one exit, and that was the tunnel back to the cellar. Perhaps this place had simply been used as an extra storeroom in ages past. The longer they remained there, the less sinister it seemed.

'It appears you were wrong, after all,' said the priest.

'If so, how do you explain Surukish being here?' said Kharan. 'And where's Filmoriel?'

'As to Surukish,' said Xaedrek, 'I think Ah'garith has regained her ability to transfer herself – and other people – from one place to another by supernatural means. I described how she vanished with Amnek and Ol Thangiol. The fact that there's no way in from the outside is apparently no obstacle to her or her creatures.'

Such power. How can we ever defeat her? Melkavesh thought.

'All the same, there's nothing here,' said Ol Melemen. 'I suggest we go back.'

'I can't give up just like that! Surukish saw a light, Kharan said, which frightened away the dog creature. Then Kharan saw it herself, and a bird that might have been Miril. It's reason enough to think that Filmoriel came looking for something that was real, not just in her imagination. But I think it was a – a warning.'

'Or a trick played by Ah'garith to lure her away,' Kharan said shakily. 'And the dog dropped Surukish to take Filmoriel instead.'

Falmeryn pulled her to his side. 'Kharan, it can't be that

bad. But she's not here, Lady Melkavesh, and where else is there to look?'

Melkavesh had been casting around the cave with her Way-finding sense, trying to understand the topography. There seemed to be nowhere at all that Ah'garith could hide. Furious with herself, she shook her head in denial of what her senses told her. 'There must be something I've missed.' She raised her hand to the latch of the ancient door. 'We'll go back into the cellars. Perhaps there's another cave or tunnel leading off from them.'

They murmured in uneasy agreement. She opened the door and stepped through –

Only to find that the tunnel had gone.

Instead they found themselves in a shiny grey tube whose walls were as insubstantial as the reflection of glass in glass. An unpleasant furry crackling filled their ears, and there was a hideous sensation like bony fingers poking into their ribs. They fought it, but something had drained them of all power to move, and the tube was sucking them along its length with stomach-turning speed. When they cried out, their voices made no sound.

Too late, Melkavesh recognised the tube as a Way, a passage between dimensions. They had been led into a trap, and again there was the feeling of helplessness, the knowledge that she should have sensed it but had failed them again. Her power dissolved like frost. Then there was the bland, sick lurch of falling, and the tube began to fray out into a cloud of ugly vermilion light.

14

'My name was Ahag-Ga'

THEY STOOD in a landscape that was a warped mockery of Earth. All the colours were wrong. The low rounded hills swelling up out of the vista before them were the blue of veins stretched under skin, and the river that wound between them was a thick substance that undulated like the belly of a snake. It glistened a pale, fleshy pink.

'By the moons, where are we?' Ol Melemen gasped.

'Ah'garith's domain. She must have been trying to lure us here all the time.' Melkavesh's mouth had turned sour and sticky, and she longed for a mouthful of water. 'To have created this in so short a time, not on Earth but in its own dimension – I can't believe it.'

The baleful illumination that bathed the landscape came from above. It was not so much a sky as a skin, red and angry and pitted with sores. Melkavesh was sure she could see figures moving about on it, clinging upside down like insects. Layers of pale red steam peeled away from it and drifted downwards to crawl in sluggish wisps over the hills. It carried a stench heavily redolent of the amulin machines: heated metal and seared flesh, mixed with the brassy thickness of blood. But there were worse taints mingled with it, distillations of human misery and the choking ripeness of decomposition. They gagged against it, sickened.

At first the place had seemed silent; now Melkavesh became aware of a deep undercurrent of sound like the rumbling of a furnace. The vibration sawed at her skull.

'Now what?' said Falmeryn. They were looking fearfully

about them, but there was no sign of Ah'garith – nor Filmoriel.

'Well, we can't just stand here,' said Melkavesh. 'Come on. Let us find Ah'garith before she finds us. This way.'

'Can you sense where she is now?' Kharan asked, but Melkavesh did not reply.

They began to walk down the side of a hillock towards the snake-like river. The ground had a spongy feel and sank with every step. Looking back, Kharan saw a line of footprints, each one with a mass of pale segmented creatures squirming in it, and it seemed to her that the Shanin must have reached directly into her brain to extract that memory of her unpleasant journey through Mangorad . . . she gasped and shuddered. *Filmoriel here, bait in Ah'garith's hands* . . . Screams of white-hot rage coiled in her lungs, and only Falmeryn's presence enabled her to keep herself under control.

She walked hand in hand with him, while behind them, Ol Melemen had Anixa's arm looped protectively through his own. But Melkavesh and Xaedrek were Gorethrians, too dignified to show that they might feel the simple human need of comfort in this alien place. They walked a couple of feet apart, rigidly side by side as if neither would defer leadership to the other.

'I must warn you,' said Xaedrek, 'that the Shanin regained her ability to possess humans. If we meet her, be wary of looking directly in her eyes or listening to her, even you, Melkavesh.'

'And what about you?'

'She tried to possess me once and could not. She has no power over me at all now.'

'Well, it's good to know that one of us, at least, is immune to her,' Melkavesh said with a peculiar edge to her voice.

They were almost at the bank of the river now, and Melkavesh's stomach rebelled at the sight. It had the look of newly flayed muscle fibres. Stripes of shadow and light throbbed along it, peristaltic waves thrusting obscenely towards – what? A lake? Before them, a glow like bloodstained bone glimmered on the horizon, reflecting the colour of the river. Instinct drew her towards it, but with every step her apprehension deepened.

From somewhere ahead of them, a voice spoke suddenly like the slither of metal on leather.

'*Come further in.*'

Melkavesh went cold. Her sword sprang into her hand and a saffron aura radiated involuntarily from her. She could not see what had spoken. 'Ah'garith?'

Then she perceived a shape lumbering towards them on all fours. It was a dog, or rather a hideous travesty of one, huge and hairless with corpse-grey skin covering a network of bulging veins. There was a human look about the domed skull and close-set eyes, and its jaw was large enough to seize and carry a child.

'*Come further in,*' it repeated gutturally. '*Come to my master.*'

Melkavesh looked at Xaedrek, who shrugged. 'I rather thought we were expected,' he said.

They began to follow the dog towards the horizon. Worms chittered malevolently under their feet at every step. The Dark Regions, as Ashurek had described them, had been a domain composed of such evil that most humans would have gone insane within seconds of entering them. The aura of this place was less immediately overwhelming, but it was insidious, introducing its horrors one at a time, with mocking gentleness. Melkavesh glanced round at the others' set faces and regretted allowing anyone but Xaedrek to come.

All the time a slow crescendo of revulsion was building inside her. The buzzing in her skull was affecting her sense of balance, and she had the sour, sick feeling that precedes fainting. She longed to hang on to Xaedrek's arm, but pride would not let her. Rigidly controlled, she forced herself on until they climbed a final mound and came to the source of the light.

The glare flooded up to dazzle them, like long fingers pressed into their eyeballs. It was a sickly pinkish-white, tinged with blood and the discolourations of a bruise, and it pulsed as if to the rhythm of a giant heart. The revulsion it evoked in Melkavesh was instant and devastating.

'No!' she cried hoarsely, stretching out her hands to ward it off. Xaedrek was at her side and now she did hang onto him unashamedly; and only that gave her the strength to master her horror.

Before them, in diabolical mimicry of a lake, lay a vast sheet of muscle fibre. With every throb of light it contracted, causing odd colours to shimmer moistly on the surface. Melkavesh suddenly noticed that the rhythm was in precise time with her own heart, and each beat seemed to be wrenching her closer to the hideous light. The feeling was choking her – that and the stench pasted on the back of her throat, a stench of old armour and chlorine and charred bones.

She hid her face against Xaedrek's shoulder and felt his hand fold round the back of her head to caress her hair.

'I can't stand it,' she gasped. 'What has Ah'garith done?'

Xaedrek did not reply. She looked up and saw Amnek standing on the edge of the lake.

It was a moment of purest nightmare, yet there was no possibility of waking up; it would just go on and on and grow worse with every second. Paralysed, they watched the dog grovelling round Amnek's heels, watched Amnek turn and walk towards them, thin and spider-like.

'Welcome, my Emperor,' he said with a mocking bow. 'Welcome, all of you, to Ah'garith's domain.'

Melkavesh saw the disgust and sorrow come into Xaedrek's eyes. Amnek had never been well disposed towards her, yet she still found it terrible to see him reduced to this, and for Xaedrek it was unbearable.

'I hope you're satisfied with this, Amnek,' he said quietly. 'This cess-pit that goes against everything Gorethria stood for.'

"You failed Gorethria! You rejected the power that might have saved her!'

'This – saved us? What sort of Gorethrian have you become, Amnek? That dog fawns on you just as you fawn on Ah'garith.'

Amnek began to tremble with anger, and there was madness in his luminous eyes – madness and grief. 'No,' he said, pointing a crabbed finger at Xaedrek. 'You were the craven

287

one. I had to help Ah'garith. She made me understand that Earth's future lies with her. All the power we need lies here, but you are too late to share in it, my Emperor.' He turned to stare at Melkavesh. 'And as for you, witch, Ah'garith has promised me my just revenge.'

'What are you talking about?' she said.

'I've no desire for a conversation with you. I've no interest in anything you say. I am here merely to take you to Ah'garith. This way.' He pointed across the lake of flesh.

'Oh, no,' Melkavesh said, horrified. 'No, I am not setting foot on there.' All false power was an anathema to a natural Sorcerer. Amulin had been bad enough; this was infinitely worse, sick and depraved. Even without touching it she felt violated, as if jointless fingers were wriggling into her brain and shredding her inmost beliefs.

Amnek gave a vulturine smile. 'You dislike the prospect? So much the better. I shall sharpen your anticipation, shall I, by explaining – as you were so keen to know – what Ah'garith has created. Is it not obvious, my Emperor?'

'It is the same as the experiment she set up without my permission, the one I made her destroy,' he said grimly. 'She described it as a lens which draws power from the Earth. But this is on a far greater scale.'

'A lens which draws only evil and filters out all the good,' Melkavesh whispered.

'Evil is a matter of viewpoint,' said Amnek. 'To me, nothing is more evil than a Gorethrian who betrays his or her country.'

'A description which could equally apply to you,' Xaedrek said. Amnek's face twisted with malevolent fury.

'Your words mean nothing,' he hissed. 'Just follow me, all of you, and let me show you a sample of what the Lens can do.'

Reluctant, yet too dazed to disobey, they let Amnek lead them along the edge of the shore. The canine monstrosity followed, muttering and snapping at their heels, until they came in sight of a pale mound lying on the Lens, a few yards away but close enough to be seen quite clearly.

Melkavesh hugged her stomach and fought not to scream.

She had seen it before, in a far-vision, and had not known what it was. But now she knew.

It was a living being – or rather, three beings warped and deformed by the Lens into a three-lobed monstrosity. They had once been human, but now they retained almost nothing of a human shape save for rudimentary faces squashed down between bloated shoulders. They were as pale as corpses yet they were horribly alive, their sides rising and falling like bellows with each wheezing breath. A throbbing glare sweated from their pores. She understood that they were the focus of the Lens's power, dehumanised vessels for a boundless, vile energy. Yet there was an embryonic quality about them, as if their metamorphosis were not complete.

Melkavesh heard her companions' sharp breaths of horror, Kharan's faint sobs, but she could not look at them. Even Xaedrek seemed shaken, not impervious to horror after all.

'It's just the same,' he said. 'Ah'garith offered me all the power I wanted through this necromancy. I was right to reject it. I thought I could look at anything scientifically – but not this. It's an abomination.'

None of them could take their eyes from the wretched faces, nor forget that these had once been men. The closed eyes, the white foreheads creased in permanent frowns, the puffy lips parted around globules of saliva – all gave the impression of beings in such overwhelming pain that they could no longer move nor cry out against it, only wait paralysed for death to release them.

'Of course, this is only the first stage,' said Amnek. 'We have hundreds at various stages of development, and the ultimate one is most interesting . . .'

Kharan uttered a stifled cry. The thing *was* moving, trying to heave its pallid bulk towards them. They backed away, drawing swords – only to see that its attitude was not one of aggression but supplication. The three mouths opened simultaneously and three thickly distorted voices said as one, *'Help me.'*

'I've got to stop this.' Melkavesh raised her arms and flung out a whorl of yellow light, but it had no effect on the beings. It simply sank into them like water into a sponge. She reeled

289

away and only Xaedrek's quick reaction prevented her from falling to the ground. As she pulled herself upright, gasping with horror, she saw that there were pale lumps dotted all over the Lens, as far as the eye could see. *All those people who vanished – fodder for Ah'garith –*

'Don't be so foolish,' Amnek said acidly. 'I'm losing patience with you. You had better cross the Lens, if you want to see the child again.'

At that, Kharan flew at Amnek, but Melkavesh grabbed her and held her back. 'And I said no. Let Ah'garith come to us.'

'My master bids you cross the Lens,' said a guttural voice. With its lips drawn back from its teeth, the dog began to circle them, muttering words that were unintelligible yet full of sinister implication; and it was not its physical grotesqueness that was terrifying so much as its aura of witless, malignant brutality. It was trying to harass them onto the Lens. As they tried to evade it, it suddenly rushed at Irem Ol Melemen and sank its teeth into his thigh. He screamed, and cried out again and again, 'It burns – gods, by Jaed, it burns!'

Falmeryn was the first to react. His sword flashed down onto the brute's neck. A long split appeared and a pewter-coloured ooze bubbled out, but the dog hardly flinched. It twisted on itself, veins and muscles bulging under the death-bleached skin, and leapt for Falmeryn's throat.

In the same moment, Melkavesh's own sword, lambent with power, crunched into its skull and felled it. It lay in a pool of gore, still twitching and muttering to itself, but it did not rise again. She shuddered with a mixture of revulsion and pity.

'Ol Melemen, are you all right?' she asked. He was leaning heavily on Anixa, his breath emerging in staccato grunts.

'No – yes – agh, yes, I can still walk.'

'This undignified resistance ill befits you,' said Amnek, looking with distaste at the dog. 'The Lens will only harm you if you linger on it. Walk across swiftly and you will be quite safe.'

Melkavesh shook her head convulsively. *Why, why was Amnek raising a hand into the air? He looked like a prophet, a skeletal, mad prophet, a death-figure* . . . 'I'd rather die.'

Amnek grinned. His long fingers curled like a dancer's, expressive. 'Behold, then, the culmination of the Lens's creative energy.'

It appeared over the hillock behind them as if it had been waiting there all the time; a pyramid of flesh, three times the size of a man, bloated with vile power. It had the look of a fleshy white slug. Its swollen base was supported on six legs, six arms protruded radially all around the tapering thorax, twitching and grabbing at the air. There was no neck, and the head was a three-lobed thing squashed onto the body, with six eyes arranged around it; human eyes, whose madness and pain corroded her soul like acid. It dipped up and down with the sinister menace of a hunting spider – and then it came towards her.

She tried to back away, to sidestep it, raining spears of sorcery at it. But her energy only dissipated into its skin, feeding its power. Out of the corner of her eye she saw Falmeryn rushing towards it, his sword raised, and she yelled, 'Stay back, all of you! It'll kill you! Stay back!' Though it seemed to move ponderously it was faster than her and neither sword nor theurgy touched it as it forced her backwards, off the lip of ground and onto the surface of the Lens.

I can't, I can't touch it, she thought wildly. Her whole being curled up in horror as she slammed into the taut, fleshy surface and the impact bounced her back to her feet.

The shock wave of evil that went through her almost tore her sanity away. All the feeling went out of her limbs and for a few seconds she seemed suspended in hell as the Lens's pulse, synchronised with her own, began to pump fire into her blood. There was a sense of heinous power, an intense discomfort beyond the worst pain or nausea. The wrongness of it cut into her mind like wire, weaving a cage that pulled tighter with every leaden beat . . .

And then it was part of her. She *was* the fire and the pain, she was Ah'garith; her blood had become an ichor that uncurled along her arteries like silk ribbons. Yes, like silk was the power, evil and sensuous, and she was laughing as the monster lumbered towards her, laughing as it attacked

291

her with silvery ovoids of light. They were evenly matched now. A sheath of electricity sparkled along her sword, extending in a spike beyond the tip. She swung it to deflect the creature's power with ease, then closed in to slash at its flesh, grinning as it bellowed with pain. Three mouths, one voice. It rotated as it advanced on her and she turned with it, circling round and round until they were working their way across the Lens in a bizarre dance, swathed in coils of evil light. The monster could not win; but neither could she.

I must get out of here, said a voice in a distant part of what had once been her self. *I must get out . . . make a Way back . . .* The hideous power was inside her now as her true sorcery had once been, giving her the ability to see beyond her surroundings into other dimensions. That was when she realised that Ah'garith's domain was greater than she had thought. It was not a single entity but multi-layered, mirrors in mirrors, dimensions fitting inside others like an onion. She was whirling faster and faster, reality shattering and falling around her like snowflakes, her own being disintegrating under the force of a negative energy that could only defile and destroy.

And suddenly the power was gone, snuffed out like a candle. She was on her hands and knees on a goose-pimpled surface that emitted not energy but misery. It was blue, like cyanosed skin. As her head cleared, the first thing she made out was a human being a few yards away to her right. He was emaciated, his hair streaked with grey, his face sunken with untold suffering – and yet she recognised him. It was Irem Ol Thangiol.

A silvery light was playing on the upper rim of her vision. She looked up to see Ah'garith standing on the mound above her, smiling with obscene benevolence.

'Well, and how did you like my flesh warrior?' she said. Melkavesh sat back on her heels and saw the monstrosity crouching behind the demon. It seemed wounded and was wheezing with pain. She groaned. Now the Lens's power had left her she felt filthy, disease-raddled. 'A melding of three men. It has perfect radial symmetry, you see,' the demon went on. 'It has no back, therefore it can anticipate and attack in all directions at once. Each hand can hold a weapon – just in case its enemies have not already died of fear! It is impervious to death. Imagine an army of such beings.' She looked past Melkavesh and raised her voice. 'This is what you could have had fighting for you, my Emperor. This would have won Gorethria's stupid war – no overgrown molluscs could have defeated my creations. But it was not to your delicate taste and so you have lost everything!'

Melkavesh looked round as Ah'garith spoke, and saw the others stepping from the Lens onto the base of the mound, with Amnek following them like a shepherd. They had all been forced to the far side of the Lens. Because she was a natural vessel for power she had been the worst affected, but she could see from the numb horror in their eyes that they had not crossed it unscathed. Anixa exclaimed at the sight of Irem Ol Thangiol, and she and Ol Melemen hurried to his side to kneel by him and bear him up in their arms.

'Anixa? Am I dreaming?' said Ol Thangiol in a faint, cracked voice.

'No. I really am here.'

'Ol Thangiol, don't you know me?' the priest said. 'It's me – Ol Melemen.'

'Melemen?' Hazy recognition came into his eyes and he gasped, 'Oh, my brother. I had never thought to see you again.'

'Hush. We're here now. Melkavesh has come with us to rescue you.'

'It has been terrible for me without you, Anixa. I have thought of nothing but you. Please stay with me.'

Bending her dark head over him, she said softly, 'I will never leave you again.'

They wept. The sound of their weeping cut into Melkavesh's soul as even the Lens's evil could not, bringing her back to herself – and to an insufferable sense of guilt and degradation. She had brought them into this, and if they did not escape soon it would be too late for all of them.

'Melkavesh?' Xaedrek said quietly.

'I'm all right,' she said, climbing to her feet. She did not want to look at the demon, but she made herself. Ah'garith still had the body of an old woman, but the ghost of her true demon form shimmered round her more strongly than ever.

'Oh, I'm *so* glad you're not hurt, witch,' came her sneering reply. 'You realise it was only a game. I hope it has made you understand that you can only defeat my monsters by becoming like them. Serve me and I will give you power; resist me and be destroyed. Isn't it so, Amnek?'

'Yes, Ah'garith. But you promised her to me.' Amnek stepped forward and looked from her to Xaedrek. 'You called me evil, but it was you who lost us everything – and as for you, you witch –' Amnek extended a finger at Melkavesh. He did not look fearsome, she thought; he looked old and horribly frail. 'You are two of a kind. You pretended friendship to Shavarish and then you cut her down, like the traitor you are.'

'It wasn't like that!' Melkavesh cried, but as she spoke, Amnek lunged towards her. Before she could react, Xaedrek stepped between them and she saw the flash of his knife as he stabbed up into Amnek's stomach. The Councillor sagged forwards with a grunt. Xaedrek stepped clear and the fleshy ground quivered as the body slumped onto it, spilling a dark stream of blood.

Xaedrek stood gazing down at the body, absently wiping the blade on his sleeve. He seemed unmoved, but Melkavesh, touching his arm, could feel him shaking through the leather of his jacket.

'It had to be done,' he said as if to himself. 'He was a good Gorethrian – the finest. Better he is dead than that he exists like this.' He looked up, his eyes burning. 'A mindless tool of yours, Ah'garith.'

There was a moment of stillness, broken only by the heartbeat of the Lens and the noisy breathing of the flesh warrior. Then the Shanin's laugh hissed through their ears. 'He was worth a thousand of you, *Sire*. No matter. I can reanimate him later. He'll never be the same, of course.'

'By the gods and all my ancestors, Ah'garith, I swear I'll destroy you!'

'You can't,' she said, giggling. '*She* knows. But she's too pathetic even to try. Look at her. Sorceress! Silvren, curse the bitch, was worth ten of you!'

Melkavesh felt something pulsing behind her eyes, evil power stirring in her veins. Perhaps she was mad, but she could listen to no more of this. She loathed the demon with a pure burning hatred that drove out fear, thought, everything except the need to avenge the suffering this being had caused Silvren. She had dropped her sword somewhere, but she reached out to take Xaedrek's instead. Kharan was saying something about Filmoriel, *Filmoriel*, very faintly as if something had knocked all the breath out of her, but Melkavesh ignored her. With the sword held two-handed, she rushed up the mound and struck Ah'garith's head from her shoulders.

The flesh cleaved, the head fell, but the body remained standing. Melkavesh staggered backwards, aghast. She put up a hand to shield her eyes as a fountain of noxious light came spewing out of the neck stump, twisting, curling, feeding on the flesh from which it came until the old woman's body was gone and a new one had taken its place.

They stumbled back in panic; all except Xaedrek, who simply stood and watched. Even the flesh warrior scuttled away as if it retained enough humanity to be terrified of the Shanin. When the light became bearable they hardly noticed that it had gone, for they were looking on the realisation of a nightmare.

Ah'garith had returned fully to her true form. It was no longer ghost-like but solid, as perfect as a statue, beautiful and poisonous as mercury. The eyes were silver glass, the mouth a blood-red gash. It was sexless, so Ah'garith could no longer be called 'she'; and it was all they could do to resist the desire to fall down in worship and terror.

Melkavesh turned away, facing Kharan and Falmeryn, trying to obscure their view of the Shanin. She was shaking, sweat running down her body. 'I can get us out of here,' she said quickly. 'I can't destroy the demon but I can create a Way and get us out.' Kharan was gaping at her as if she could not grasp what she meant. Melkavesh felt like shaking her.

'Don't look at the demon or it'll possess you! I'll get the others and –'

Kharan was shaking her head now, pointing mutely at the Shanin, finally uttering one strangled word. '*Melkavesh!*'

The Sorceress turned. The glare had died down and she saw that Ah'garith was holding a small red-haired child. She was struggling, whimpering. The demon gave her a spiteful pinch, at which Kharan, distraught, sprang forward and screamed, 'Give her to me, you vile fiend – devil – what do you want?'

It took both Falmeryn and Xaedrek to hold her back. They looked at each other over her head as she struggled, while the Shanin smiled down on them and filled the air with its sibilant mirth.

'I don't want anything of you, dear lady. I just want you to suffer – you and her.'

Kharan fought the restraining arms, almost deranged. Falmeryn met Melkavesh's eyes and said helplessly, 'We can't go without Filmoriel.' There were tears on his face. 'Go if you like. You'll have to leave us here.'

I can't accept this, I can't, Melkavesh thought desperately. But she was transfixed by the Shanin's soulless stare and hypnotic voice, which seemed to go on and on like the rustle of a spider on paper.

'I owe you my thanks, Xaedrek. If not for you, I would never have discovered a way to tap the power. We have had our differences, I know, but at the end of all you have only helped me find my freedom. How do you like my creation?' Ah'garith swept a hand in an arc from the Lens to the pestilential sky. 'So much more colourful than the Dark Regions, is it not? And this time the Guardians are not going to interfere. My domain exists separately from Earth, but I stole a part of Earth to create it. As yet it is small, just an egg – but like an egg it will hatch into something greater. Little by little I shall swallow the world until only my domain is left, and the crust will be one huge Lens, filtering the power to my desire, shaping all life to my purpose.

'My name was Ahag-Ga, in the old days of the Serpent. I shall find a new name, suitable to my new status. I was bitter when I first met you, Emperor, but no longer. I am glad M'gulfn and my siblings died, for it has enabled me to ascend to absolute power. And I would have you all serve me for a while before you die . . . a while being as near eternity as makes no difference.' She leered gleefully at their stricken faces. 'I did warn you of my plans, my Emperor. You told me to be quiet and get on with my work! What say you now?'

Melkavesh had felt despair before, but never such absolute, black hopelessness. She could not believe it had come to this. The enormity of what she had allowed to happen could hardly be grasped, yet it was bearing inexorably down on her, crushing the last spark of her spirit. *Disaster*. She had thought herself the only being on Earth with true power, the demon a mere irritation. Now that arrogance had cost everything. When the birth of sorcery was over, it would produce not a healthy child but a monstrous, amorphous tumour. That was what the Lens was – a cancer rooted deep in the Earth. It had been her task to tear it out, but from the beginning she had misread the signs, and this was the outcome.

She had brought mankind to its death – or worse, to the eternity of suffering that Ah'garith had planned.

'Well may you look so stricken, *Sorceress*! What better revenge could I have had on your filthy mother and father than to crush your dreams and turn the world inside out like a pig's stomach?' The demon bounced the child up and down in its hands. Kharan cried out. 'You want the brat, don't you? Is there anything you wouldn't do to save her wretched skin? Well, she's nothing to me. Rubbish.'

With that, Ah'garith suddenly flung Filmoriel away to their left. The tiny body landed with a sickening thump, and there was a wrenching moment of silence as Kharan ran to her and bent to lift the little body. Then she gave a low, hoarse scream and sprang away.

'What's wrong, what is it?' Falmeryn cried, torn between hanging onto her and seeing to Filmoriel.

'It's not – they've killed her – she's –' Her eyes were wild, her voice raw with horror. With foreboding crawling under her skin, Melkavesh bent to examine the child. She brushed the hair aside – and found underneath a skeletal thing the colour of raw meat, hardly human, decomposing yet still twitching with life.

For Kharan's sake, she had to control herself. 'Kharan! Kharan, listen to me,' she cried, gripping the An'raagan's shoulders. 'It's not Filmoriel. Do you understand me? It's not her. It's a trick.' Then she turned to the Shanin, yelling, 'What have you done with her? What the hell have you done?'

The demon's amusement was sickening, hideously incongruous. 'She isn't here. She is hidden safely in one of my inner dimensions. Oh yes, Melkavesh, this region is far more complex than it looks. I could tease you for hours, days, trying to guess where she is and what I might have planned for her!'

'For pity's sake, Melkavesh, what are we going to do?' said Falmeryn.

'I don't know.'

'Why didn't you bring the moon stone? Perhaps this was what it was for, to –'

'I have brought it!' Her anger was at herself, but she turned it on him. 'There's no power in it, Falmeryn, nothing! Perhaps Ferdanice misled you – perhaps you misinterpreted what he said, I don't know, but the moon stone is useless!'

Kharan turned to her, pressing one hand to her face as if trying to calm herself, the other clutching at Melkavesh's sleeve. 'Listen.' Her voice was tremulous, but under control. 'Didn't I tell you, I thought I saw a beam of light like a half-open door, and a shadow moving across it, a shadow like a child?'

'Yes, of course you did.'

'Well, doesn't it tell you anything? Can't you try to find her – somehow?'

Melkavesh looked up at the Shanin. It seemed that nothing she did could make things worse. 'I can try,' she said softly.

'Oh, too amusing,' said Ah'garith. 'Be my guest. I shall possess you at once, of course.'

'I've got nothing to lose,' she said grimly. The fury was rising in her again.

298

Xaedrek gripped her arm and said, 'Don't, Melkavesh. I've had a taste of it. It'll destroy you.'

But she seized his hand in a stronger grip, pulling him with her. 'But you survived. That's why you're going to help me.'

With that she made a running leap at the Shanin. The power she summoned was the vile power of the Lens, but she steeled herself against its repellent sensuality. It was all she had. The demon was taken by surprise, but did not fall under the assault; instead it stretched out its arms to take her and Xaedrek in its embrace.

Its touch burned their flesh through their clothes, but they were tangled up with it now and could not break away. *The Sphere help me, give me strength*, Melkavesh thought as she forced herself to look into the glaring eyes, forced herself to let go and enter the demon's brain. And Ah'garith did not simply let her in. It sucked her in and held her inside with touch as delicate as that of a scorpion's sting in its prey.

What she saw there almost tipped her into insanity. The virulent glee, sadism, hatred of life, and all its other base emotions scoured her soul, though they were no surprise to her. They lay like glittering slime over the demon's psyche. But she had to thrust through the slime into what lay below – and it was what she found there that destroyed her reason.

She was in a bald, sick landscape more terrible than the Wall. Its aura twisted into her heart like a worm, and all other horrors paled beside it. It was the secret vista of the demon's mind and it was not even despair, it was *nothing*, and somehow she knew that she would travel through that terrible place for ever, while her body went through the motions of gibbering and pleading and worshipping, anything to send the nothingness away . . .

Then Xaedrek was with her. Their minds were entwined like hands. He kept her sane.

It was his detachment that saved her. It enclosed her like a shell, a cool silver eye from which she could see the truth. *Look. Look carefully,* he said. *What are you so afraid of? Ah'garith's power is a sterile thing that can never touch the essence of your self.*

Was it true? The Shanin had the power to dissect peoples'

299

souls if it chose . . . but Melkavesh's fear was gone. She was simply an observer. Calm, detached, she sought what was hidden in the landscape, connected herself to the demon's own vision, and saw – layers of mirrors again – all the other dimensions that made up Ah'garith's domain. They were all infinitely inventive in their horrors, but ultimately they were all the same. She looked through them, one at a time, never realising that she was far-seeing, until she found Filmoriel.

The true Filmoriel was sitting on a rock by an acid-green sea, huddled in her thin robe, staring at the sky. The sky was colourless yet reflective, like a sheet of glass, and behind it fluttered the bird Miril.

She can't reach me. I've got to make her find me, the child seemed to say.

It was all so clear then. Miril's task on Earth was unfinished while there was still a demon alive, but for some reason she could not find her way back into the circles of the world. Filmoriel was the only link. But still Miril could not break through.

That was when the Shanin attacked. It flung all its power, all its scalding, annihilating venom at Melkavesh, trying to break her detachment; it trickled insidious torments into her mind, magnifying all her worst fears and guilts. *You are nothing, Sorceress. You are a worm, a parasite, a disease . . .* Execration poured over and through her like a torrent of white flame. Yet Xaedrek steadied her, and when the fire died, she came through it whole.

And you, Ah'garith, you are a fool, she replied, laughing. *When you took the child, did you not know that she was linked to Miril? You've sealed your own fate!*

Of course I knew! The Shanin's wrath shook her and her laughter died. *You think I didn't? Why do you imagine I've imprisoned her in that other dimension? I tried to kill her, but the brat evaded me!*

Evaded you? Or you could not kill her? It was still a mistake, Ah'garith, to bring her here.

I did not bring her. She came seeking me. So I've imprisoned her and there she will stay for all eternity – she and the accursed bird.

300

Melkavesh drew back from the demon's thoughts, shaken. God-like she looked at the bleak shore where Filmoriel sat in patient misery; but unlike a god, it seemed she could do nothing. *Here I am again – adrift and helpless. No Sorceress at all. Missing everything, misreading all the signs . . .*

Oh, not this time, no. It was not anger that stirred in her but something that came from Xaedrek – and from herself, from the inmost core of her soul – a diamond-hard thread that would always endure, always turn loss to victory. When she began to draw power, it seemed to be coming from everywhere – from the Lens, from herself, even from other worlds and from Silvren herself – and whatever evil there was in the power, she herself acted as the Sphere, the filter that purified it. The Shanin was trying to stop her, but it was Xaedrek who held it back. It seemed they were all with her, all their different essences feeding her strength; Kharan's warmth and resilience, the steadfast soul of Kesfaline through Anixa, Ol Melemen's faith in the moons and even the dark suffering of Ol Thangiol. And most of all Falmeryn, closest in spirit to H'tebhmella and to Miril, the very antithesis of the demon. And all of it she forged into a single golden needle which she held within herself for a split second before pulsing it out at Filmoriel's sky.

The glass shattered.

There were layers and layers of it, bursting all across the vastness of the universe. The barriers between Ah'garith's dimensions were gone. A rent opened up in the atmosphere and Filmoriel rolled from it to lie at Kharan's feet, dirty and weeping.

Kharan snatched her up. Simultaneously Melkavesh and Xaedrek wrenched themselves out of the demon's mind and staggered backwards down the mound, their detachment driven out by a hideous, disorientating noise. There was a moment of confusion and terror, in which Melkavesh put her hands over her ears and looked round frantically for Miril. There was no sign of her. There was only the ghastly Lens-light, the mounds and the pitted, scarlet sky.

And the noise, she realised with amazement, was that of Ah'garith screaming. Its mouth was a crimson square, its forehead creased and the eyes glazed, and its metallic scream went on and on until Melkavesh feared they would all go mad.

Irem Ol Melemen came limping towards her. His face was lined with strain, his hair sweat-darkened. 'What's wrong with the demon?' he cried.

'Can't you see?' said Falmeryn. 'Look!' He pointed into the air, though Melkavesh could see nothing.

Ah'garith no longer looked awe-inspiring, but like some fossilised thing caught in an attitude of overwhelming disbelief. It shrieked, 'If that bird comes near me, this whole domain will cease to exist and you will all die! Make her keep away!'

'Miril is here!' Melkavesh exclaimed.

'I know, I can see her quite clearly,' said Falmeryn, but she cut across him urgently.

'Ol Melemen, can Ol Thangiol walk? No matter, carry him if necessary – but bring him and Anixa here *now*. I can get us out of here, but you must all stay close to me!'

Even as she spoke, she was beginning to draw power again – any power, good or evil, she did not care – and swiftly shaping it into a Way. The effort and the accumulation of stress almost made her pass out. Gradually a tunnel of transparent blueness began to whirl around her, but Anixa, Ol Melemen and his brother were still outside it.

As she worked, Miril became visible to them all in a cloud of silver-gold light.

She was just as Kharan remembered from her vision in the caves; just as Melkavesh, Xaedrek and Falmeryn had seen her in dreams. Her colour was that of Filmoriel's hair, rich and deep as fire seen through amber, or crimson light splashing on rubies. She hovered in the light with wings outstretched, and in her presence the whole of Ah'garith's kingdom seemed to shrivel. Miril was the only living thing there.

The demon was retreating from her now, moving down the side of the mound towards the Lens with a horribly plastic slowness. And the bird was descending towards it, her beauty as dazzling as the Shanin's evil had once been.

She was singing. Her song drowned its screams. Their exchange was deafening, wordless, yet the sense of it echoed in Melkavesh's mind. *You died with the Serpent, you cannot touch me, I have only just found life!*

No, Ahag-Ga, Miril replied. *I stayed alive for you, I have returned for you. You are the Serpent's own and your time is over. Look at me and accept your demise.*

No . . .

The Shanin stepped onto the surface of the Lens and began to run. The bird kept pace easily, but Melkavesh thought, *Run, Ah'garith, run! Give me a few seconds more!*

Xaedrek was at her side, Kharan and Falmeryn behind her with Filmoriel. The Way was almost ready, but she could not extend it or move it, and the other three were still outside. She was burning hot, ice cold. Miril was beyond communication; only Filmoriel could have told her to wait, wait until it was time, but it was too late for that.

They were crawling towards her like snails, Anixa and Irem Ol Thangiol. The priest was almost within range, but he was turning anxiously to tell them to hurry. Too slow. If she waited any longer none of them would escape.

Her teeth were clenched, her eyes streaming, as she made the decision. The tunnel was whirling faster and faster around them, still transparent but catching flashes of light on its surface, crackling with zigzags of colour. Out on the Lens, all the wretched deformed beings were groaning, writhing, trying to rise up as the silver figure ran between them. The Lens's glow outlined the demon with a sickly, pulsing halo. The scene was awash with light, but the palpitation of the membrane was becoming frantic, dying under the bird's brilliance.

Then Miril swooped. She did not attack the Shanin; she merely brushed its back with her wings, unleashing a shower of ruby light. Ah'garith's unhuman cry throbbed in their heads as if the whole domain was screaming and convulsing. Then the Shanin's body flashed into acidic white fire. There was a moist cracking of bone, and they saw it curl up like the dried husk of a fly and fall to ashes.

It was over in a moment. The Lens and the sky began to

heave, pale figures fell screaming into fire. But the glassy smoothness of the cylinder was spinning round them and the scene was fading as Melkavesh drew them along the Way back to Earth.

Passing from one dimension to another was never pleasant; but this was the worst Melkavesh had ever experienced. The weight of centuries seemed to be crushing her. The domain was collapsing, natural space and time reasserting themselves; and there was nowhere for the fabric of it to go, except to rip loose and come spewing through the tunnel with them.

Gods, all those poor people I could not save. Anixa, Irem Ol Thangiol, oh, forgive me. Miril, Miril . . .

There was a rumbling sound, a sense of pressure like an unimaginable force ploughing through solid rock – and suddenly, the brilliance of daylight. They were flying, falling, flung out like dolls in an uprush of soil and stones.

If she flung out a sorcerous blanket to cushion them, it was purely instinctive. Melkavesh could not remember. The next thing she knew, she was lying uncomfortably on a pile of earth, her head full of murky colours. Every bone was aching, and the borrowing of Ah'garith's power had left her feeling degraded, dirty, and totally drained. Dizzy, she found her feet as gracelessly as a new-born colt.

There was relief, and there was pain.

She was on a hillside half a mile above Heldavrain. All around her was devastation. The Way itself had not caused the physical wound to the Earth; that had been made by the ripping out of the Shanin's domain. Amid the rubble, she saw scraps of the Lens glinting dully like flesh – or perhaps it really was human flesh. She turned away, sobbing.

'Melkavesh?' It was Xaedrek's voice. His hand was on her elbow, supporting her in an impersonal kind of way. She looked round at him; and for some reason the fact that he was dishevelled and exhausted yet still as collected as ever made her want to laugh. Now she could see Kharan and Falmeryn further down the hill, picking themselves up from the wreckage, hugging each other, doing their best to console a wailing Filmoriel. They seemed more shocked than injured. Melkavesh and Xaedrek went down to meet them.

'Where's Anixa?' said Kharan. Melkavesh met her eyes, but could not speak. The silence was understood. They stood in mutual grief, not weeping – not yet – but looking up at the sky. It was as if the shock wave of power had rammed a hole in the clouds, and was now tearing them into wisps of vapour. Patches of harebell blue were appearing, veils of sun falling through to gild the distant red mountains. The Aludrian Sea looked like a plain of gold-tipped beryl, with Heldavrain gleaming like an emerald on its edge.

'Lady Mellorn, quickly,' came a breathless voice twenty yards away. It was the priest. He was limping towards her, trying to brush soil from his clothes. When he saw her turn, he beckoned, and they all scrambled across the rocks to look down into a small crater. Two bodies lay there.

Melkavesh stared at them. Somehow she had brought Anixa and Ol Thangiol through, but they lay so still, entwined like children amid the earth and dust.

'If there's a spark of life left, I'll heal them,' she said, and climbed down to kneel beside them. The others followed, but she waved them to stay back. They watched anxiously as she bent over them, and the healing light began to flow gently from her hands to shimmer around them.

Irem Ol Melemen, unable to bear the silence, said, 'Are they still alive?'

Melkavesh did not reply. But Kharan saw the light die, saw her face change, and she turned to lean against Falmeryn, whispering, 'No more. I can't bear any more.'

15

Ashes of Ice

THERE WAS a vision.

Melkavesh saw a line of horses, as shiny as brown satin, their gold-shot manes rippling from arched necks. The riders were all in velvet and leather, a tapestry of leaf-green and gold, blue and bronze and silver. In their midst rode a man and a woman in the bright armour of the moons, and they were winding their way across the sun-washed fells towards Heldavrain.

She opened her eyes wide. The vision had come without warning, even as she bent over Anixa's inert form. A sudden flower of light bloomed within her; the heart-sickness and defilement that ravaged her were obliterated by a crystal surge of joy that brought one clear thought. *It's over. Ah'garith's dead. It's over.*

Only for the joy to be smashed by a fist of searing, impossible, familiar pain. The shock froze her where she knelt. She knew her face had twisted in horrified denial, but she could not compose herself, could not think, and when Anixa began to stir and groan, it meant nothing to her at all : . .

But Ah'garith is dead! How can this be?

'My lady.' Irem Ol Melemen shook her arm very gently. 'My lady, what's wrong? Look, Anixa is alive. You've healed her. They're both alive!'

The Sorceress turned her head slowly, blinking as if totally bewildered. Kharan, her hands full with Filmoriel, watched her worriedly. Tears were half blinding her at the sight of the Kesfalian's eyes fluttering open, the incomparable thrill of realising that she was not dead after all; but why did Melkavesh still look so desolate?

Falmeryn went to Anixa and helped her to sit up, holding her as she coughed the dust and soil away. Still dazed, her first thought was of Irem Ol Thangiol. She turned to lay her head on his chest, then stretched out a hand to the priest, croaking, 'His heart is beating! Oh, thank Fliya! Help me, help me take him –'

'It's all right, little sister,' said Ol Melemen gently. 'I'll carry him down to the castle, and Falmeryn shall carry you. Lady Mellorn?'

Perhaps Xaedrek would have helped her, had the others not been there. But as it was he stood apart, watching them without emotion. Even what they had just endured could not annihilate the past and forge any links between him and the others, and he wanted such comradeship least of all. It was left to Irem Ol Melemen to lift his brother's frail form over his shoulder, and help Melkavesh to her feet with the other hand.

'My lady, they are alive,' he repeated. 'Let me help you. You look ill.'

'Whatever's the matter?' Kharan asked anxiously.

It took Melkavesh some time to answer as they began to make their way very slowly down the hillside. If Xaedrek had made a bid for freedom, there was not much they could have done to stop him; but strangely, he did not. Below them, folk from Heldavrain were pouring across the bridge to see what had caused the explosion and the sudden clearing of the storm.

'Eventually she said, 'The King and Queen are on their way here.'

'Yes, my lady, I told you so myself,' said the priest.

'What I mean is that I have just seen them. I can far-see again.'

'But that's wonderful!' he said. 'Isn't it?'

She extracted her arm from his grasp. Her eyes were bleak, but she was calm, and once she could walk unaided she

307

would not accept help. Sometimes this Gorethrian dignity drove Kharan mad. 'Yes, it's wonderful,' Melkavesh said spiritlessly. 'How can I say this? It's hard, because I don't understand it myself. I feel like a bone with all the blood-marrow sucked out of it.

'I can't restore the dead. Anixa and Ol Thangiol are alive because they were – lucky, I suppose. I haven't healed them. You saw my power die when I tried.'

'Yes,' said Kharan. 'Yes, but what do you mean?'

She took a breath. Her voice sounded raw and empty. 'I told you that Ah'garith was blocking the power of true sorcery, and I thought that when she died, everything would be all right. The Wall's gone, it's true. But when I attempted the healing, my power failed. I'm back where I was before – not a wholly crippled Sorceress, just a half crippled one.'

Kharan wished desperately that she could say something that would help; but there was a gulf between them and Melkavesh was on the other side, bereft of those who could truly understand and help her.

Ol Melemen began, 'My lady, are you saying –'

'I'm saying that I was wrong!' she cut in bitterly. 'It wasn't Ah'garith blocking the power at all, it was something else, and I'm still no closer to discovering what it is!' With that she turned her back on them and strode away down the hill, alone.

There was a serenity over Heldavrain, but darker threads ran through it. Outwardly, life was returning to normal – or as normal as it could be with Melkavesh and Xaedrek there – but whispered anticipation, suspicion and fear netted the air, drawing tighter hour by hour.

Melkavesh had saved them from the demon Ah'garith, but she had not warned them of the danger, nor of the vile fate that would have awaited them had the Shanin triumphed. The horror of it was barely comprehensible, but it caused a powerful undercurrent that brought profound relief to some in the castle, nightmares to others.

As soon as she regained her own strength, Melkavesh exhausted herself again by healing the mental and physical harm her companions had received in Ah'garith's domain. Kharan, Falmeryn and Ol Melemen were comparatively easy; she left them in a palliative haze, subdued but able to recover and forget. Anixa, closed to her, refused to be touched; Xaedrek insisted that he had incurred nothing worse than a few bruises and needed no help. But Irem Ol Thangiol was so far gone in the anguish he had suffered at Ah'garith's hands that it was several weary hours before she hauled him out of the darkness and left him sleeping peacefully with Anixa at his side.

She had poured out her restoring energies until she was wrung dry, and she knew that what she was really pouring out was her own guilt and frustration. But when she had finished, they were still there.

She went to Kharan and Falmeryn's room to see Filmoriel. The child had said very little about her experience, except to ask once or twice where Miril was, and they all hoped she was too young to have been badly affected by it. Melkavesh was relieved to find her abandoned to the baby-like tranquillity of sleep.

'I don't think you needed my sorcery to heal you,' she whispered, touching a finger to the child's forehead. 'Miril was with you and she protected you. But my power sustained you when you were too tiny to live unaided, and one day your own power will blossom in you and I will be here to guide you, my own Sorceress. One day I'll be able to tell you that you are the first Sorceress born on Earth since my mother, and since the Serpent died. The first true Sorceress, the Earth's future . . . and perhaps by then I'll know the answers.'

Her voice was too soft for Kharan and Falmeryn to hear. With a brief, weary smile at them she went out into the deserted corridor. The walls were a cold, pearly grey in the dawn. She felt calm yet torn apart, empty. There was no one to heal her, no one to show her the answers; but there was something that came close to the release she craved, and she was too tired, too human to fight the need.

It was a simple matter to cloak herself sorcerously against being seen, to take Xaedrek past the guards and cloud their memories so they would not know he was gone; a simple matter to bring him to her own room and close the door behind them, something they had done many times since they had agreed to set aside their differences.

She knew it was wrong; it was breaking her Oath to use her sorcery for deception; it was betraying the Kristillians' faith in her. She envied Xaedrek's lack of conscience, for her own gave her no peace; but even through the torment she could not stop herself, and it seemed the only relief she could find from it was in Xaedrek's arms. And all the time she convinced herself that she could be two things at once.

Although Melkavesh had repeatedly warned them of the danger from the Aludrians if they went down to the sea's edge, not everyone listened to her. Anixa and Ol Thangiol did not spare a thought for the danger as they climbed down the rocks and onto the sands. They were simply anxious to escape the castle for a time and find solitude.

They spoke little as they walked arm in arm along the beach, but understanding passed between them without words, and Anixa's eyes were sad. She imagined how Ol Thangiol must once have looked: a broad, strong Kristillian warrior, the wind tangling his bronze-red hair and beard as he rode into combat, joyfully defending Kristillia against Gorethria. He still held himself upright, but he could only walk very slowly on his skinny legs, and his face had the gouged-out look of an old man's. His every movement seemed edged with difficulty and pain. Melkavesh had done her best, but there was only so much even she could do.

Anixa said, 'We are so far adrift from happiness that we've forgotten how it feels.'

'I am happy, my love. I'm with you.'

Anixa squeezed his arm. 'We need not go back to the castle. We could simply walk and walk, leave it behind and never again be reminded of what has happened. I used to believe I was destined for some personal vengeance against Xaedrek; perhaps all Vardravians have had the same delusion. But now I can accept what Falmeryn said, that there's

310

nothing people like you or I can do. Let us go away, and forget, and learn how to be happy.'

They walked on, and Heldavrain dwindled along the curving ribbon of the beach. The sky took on the glassy paleness of twilight.

Then Ol Thangiol said, 'I can't forget, Anixa.'

'Why not?' There was fear in her voice, fear she had been trying to deny.

He paused, and began to climb up towards a flat rock a few feet above them. She followed him and sat pressed against him amid the tussocks of grass.

'Melkavesh has healed you. She said you would feel better in time, with rest . . .'

'Yes, she did all she could. I am sane. Perhaps it's because I'm sane that I cannot forget.' He looked away from her, and seemed to be twisting something in his hands, a piece of grass, perhaps. When he turned back to her there were tears running down his face. 'I am burned out, my love, destroyed. I have seen too much evil. I fall asleep and the demon's eyes haunt me . . . Melkavesh did her best, but my soul is too sick and the despair is inside me now, part of me. For your sake I have tried, but I can't see past it.'

'What are you trying to tell me? That you are giving up? If Melkavesh –'

'No one can take this greyness from me, not even the enchantress herself. It will never fade, and I'm so tired. I just want to fall asleep with you beside me – and not wake up.'

'We survived the demon and Xaedrek, and now you're letting them win after all? I won't let you!'

'It's too late,' he said. 'Do you know what this is?' He opened his right hand and she saw a tiny tube of colourless liquid, and a ring with a minute needle on its outer surface.

'That's the ring and the phial of daelammion poison that Xaedrek gave me,' she said, her throat burning. 'Where did you get them?'

'You told me she took them from you. I went to her office while she was not there and found them in a desk drawer. So I stole them. One drop on a pin is enough, isn't it?' Then he turned his left hand over and she saw the dark bead on his palm where he had stuck the ring's spike into his flesh. *Oh, why didn't Melkavesh destroy the poison? But if she had, if she had, he would only have found another way . . .*

'No. You cannot leave me alone. I lost my husband and my son, and I had no one until I found you. You can't leave me!'

'I'm so sorry, Anixa. I didn't mean to hurt you, but it's the only thing I can do. Give me this at least, that you'll stay with me until I die. Then I will die happy, if I cannot live so, and if there's anything beyond I will wait there for you.'

'Oh, may Fliya guard you, Jaed and Fliya both,' she whispered.

Anixa being what she was, acceptance rose in her almost as quickly as grief. She did not weep. She held Irem Ol Thangiol as the poison crept through him and he began to choke. The pain did not last long.

He was calm at the end, all despair washed from him by Anixa's dark, sweet presence. Her face became the night sky; her eyes two gold-frosted moons across which a bird flew in silhouette and swooped down to perch on his chest. For a moment he met her gaze, and then a beam of light lifted him out of sorrow and into an infinite sky.

Anixa held him for long after he was dead. When she moved, it was to pluck the fatal ring from his hand and hold it poised over the soft crook of her elbow. But after a few minutes she flung it away from her with a cry. The sea and beach were deserted, there was no one to witness her grief; but their very impassiveness seemed to breathe something into her soul, and with that her decision was made, her pain gone.

She prised the little glass tube from Ol Thangiol's hand. Then she began to make her way back to the castle, soft as a black candle flame in the dusk.

Melkavesh woke from a dream of warmth, of tangled limbs and disarrayed sheets, to find that she was not dreaming. Sunlight poured through the windows, turning everything to the colour of honey; even their skin looked like dark honey against the creamy bedcovers. Xaedrek was awake, regarding her with a smile that was more in his eyes than on his lips. As she blinked in the light, still half asleep, he kissed her and lifted a hand to trace the curve of her face.

How forbidding, how unapproachable Xaedrek could seem to those who did not know him – and there were very few who could truly say they knew him. If there had been no more to him than that coldness, however attractive Melkavesh had found him, she might have resisted. Yet beyond that, beyond even the charm which came just as naturally to him, she had long ago discovered that he was anything but cold. He had a way of making people believe whatever they wanted, but there was nothing feigned in his passion for her. In Shalekahh the fondness between them had been light-hearted, almost detached; she had expected and wanted nothing more this time. But the affection – she hardly dared call it love – he had shown her in the past few days had deepened far beyond that, and was so unprecedented that it took her breath away.

'I trust you are feeling better now?' he asked softly.

'Much,' she sighed, stretching. 'Far better than I deserve.'

'I did miss you, Melkavesh, in those three years we wasted.'

'I'm sure you did,' she replied with gentle sarcasm. 'In between trying to assassinate me.'

'I'm glad I failed. The mistake I made was not in trusting you in the first place, but in letting you go.'

'*Letting* me –?' She raised herself from the pillow and leaned on his chest. 'I seem to recall dire threats of what would happen to me if I did not co-operate, following which I had to flee for my life!'

'I would never have done anything to harm you.' His hands were warm on her shoulder blades. 'But I was less than diplomatic, I'll admit.' She laughed, and he went on, 'In the event you were proved right – about Ah'garith.'

'Only about her?' she murmured.

'I never wanted to believe that what you call "false" sorcery is impossible, but I've come to accept it. Hyperphysics is something for natural Sorcerers only. I believe this is what they call learning the hard way.' His tone was lightly

313

self-mocking. 'Anger never achieves anything. If we had talked, instead of fighting, none of this need have happened . . . Still, it is over now, and we need not make the same mistakes in the future. I am not a defeatist . . .'

He smiled at her in a way that sapped what little will-power she had left, drew her down into a golden chasm. Groaning, she said softly, 'If only the world would fade away and leave us in peace, I'd be more than happy.'

Xaedrek kissed her again. 'But it won't.'

'I know. And I wish I knew where this conversation is leading.'

'You know we can't put this off any longer. We agreed to a truce until Ah'garith was dead. Well, now she is. So, my love, what next?'

What next? she thought. She leaned back on the pillow, closed her eyes, feeling the red-gold warmth through her eyelids and the smoothness of Xaedrek's body beside her.

'You must have an answer, Melkavesh. Have you not thought beyond this moment?'

'I have, and I haven't. What is there to think? The King and Queen are on their way here. They will expect me to deliver you into their hands. And I don't want to, gods, I don't want to, but how can it be avoided?'

'Not long ago you would have been happy to see me dead.'

'Never happy. But that was before . . . Now, if you must know, I can't bear the idea.' She left the bed and began to move around the room, putting on a robe and combing her hair. Xaedrek sat against the carved bedhead, watching her.

'Well, there is an answer,' he said.

'Which is what?'

'To decide what you believe in?'

'I know what I believe in. The nations of Vardrav being free. That is what I have fought for.'

'But it isn't that simple.'

She had known this moment must come, and had dreaded it, but again Xaedrek was not behaving as she had expected. His tone, far from being full of insidious threats, was grave and gentle and wholly free from artifice. He went on, 'This is what I should have said to you, Melkavesh, instead of dealing so harshly with you and letting you think me an unmitigated villain.' She had sat down in a chair in front of her mirror, and in the reflection she saw him push back the covers and cross the room to her. He took the comb out of her hand and began to draw it through her hair as he spoke. 'Without the Empire, do you think there will be peace? While Gorethria survives, the Vardravians will remain allies against her, it's true. If you leave Gorethria intact, she will still be a strong country. All the troops recalled from the Empire will be there to defend their motherland and she will fight like a cornered leopard for her survival. War could drag on for decades. Without a strong Emperor, Gorethria cannot be kept in check. How do you propose to control her – unless you go back and rule her yourself?'

She met his eyes in the glass and said nothing.

'But you could not do that. You have to devote your energies to founding your School of fledgling Sorcerers. Your alternative is to command the Aludrians to lay waste to Gorethria. That is what the Vardravians will want.'

'I told you, I cannot do it!' she said hotly. 'I doubt if even the King could countenance such genocide. In the heat of revenge, maybe – but not after days of thought. I believe that Gorethria and the other nations can exist peacefully together.'

Xaedrek's eyebrows lifted slightly. 'Try telling the Cevandarish that. They are as warlike as Gorethria, given the chance. Without us to subdue them, they will turn their attention elsewhere – Kristillia, for example, or a weaker nation. The Gorethrian Empire may be harsh but it is not barbarous; a Cevandarish Empire would be a thousand times worse. And there are others; Bagreeah may break her boundaries, Mangorad turn on Ungrem. There are endless possibilities for war. You take my point.'

'You're telling me that in dismantling the Empire, there can only be something worse?'

'I'm telling you exactly that,' he said quietly. 'No Emperor and no Empire will mean anarchy, all of Vardrav tearing itself apart. I know, Melkavesh, that this is not what you set out to do, but you have achieved it all the same.'

315

'By the gods,' she said flatly, and stood up to face him. 'If that wasn't the most beautifully eloquent plea for me to let you return to Gorethria and let everything go on as it was before! You would try anything, wouldn't you?'

'Yes, I would – for what I believe in. And that is the key. I am being honest with you, I am telling you what I know is right and for the best.'

'Ah, and now we are back to the very thing on which we could never agree. I knew this moment would come, and there is still no way to resolve it.'

'Yes, there is. Because in your heart you know I'm right. *You know it*. You can't let Gorethria go.'

Her head dropped forward against his shoulder, and she groaned, 'She won't let *me* go!'

'I know,' he said, very softly. 'That is always the way it is. Gorethria loves her children – even the ones who have strayed, Daughter of Ashurek.'

His words seemed to tear something loose in her soul, like a ship suddenly wrenched from its anchor. 'I don't know what you're assuming, Xaedrek, but I cannot turn against the Vardravians. The Empire is over. We will never agree about this.'

'We might.' She looked questioningly at him. 'If you could bring yourself to compromise with me, Melkavesh, I can with you, because there is only one way to heal this situation.'

'You – compromise?' she gasped.

'Yes. For Gorethria's sake. And because I do not want to lose you again. Will you hear me out?'

He really means this, she thought. Her tone guarded, she said, 'Very well. What do you suggest?'

'Do not give me to the Kristillians. Let me return to Shalekahh as Emperor,' he replied. 'I may not be greatly popular there at present – but I am still their ruler, and I am the only one who can steer them from disaster.'

'And if I were to allow this, what would you do in return?' she asked with a touch of scorn.

'I would not try to reinstate the Empire. I would keep Gorethria whole, but separate, as you wanted. And I would ask you to rule with me.'

316

She tried to keep her astonishment from her face, and almost succeeded. 'You would share the throne with me?'

'Of course. I don't know why you are so surprised. I asked you once before to marry me, and I am asking you again, but this time, no threats, only a heartfelt request. My fate is in your hands, as they say.'

'And what would I tell the Kristillians?'

'Tell them whatever you think fit. You are a Sorceress; they have no hold over you. When did you ever fear anyone's disapproval?'

'Disapproval is putting it mildly,' she gasped, sitting down suddenly on the arm of the chair.

'It's to everyone's benefit, even theirs. While I keep stability in Shalekahh, you would have the freedom to establish your School of Sorcery wherever you wish.'

Melkavesh thought on this, and what had seemed a chaotic mess resolved itself into a pattern of clear, sparkling symmetry. Xaedrek was right. Her own most nebulous ideas were coalescing into a perfect round diamond that sent rays of hope and excitement dancing through her. She waited until she was sure she had mastered the feeling, and said very carefully, 'You are a manipulator, Xaedrek. I can imagine how you must have lain awake after the battle, planning to manoeuvre me into this. I can't be defeated, I can't be intimidated, so all you have left is to get me on your side by the most unfair means possible – taking advantage of – well, of my feelings for you.' He was leaning on the back of the chair, looking at her with a tranquil, open expression that did not change. 'Gods, you are a devious bastard!' she burst out. 'No wonder you were such a good Emperor.'

' 'I am unsure if that is meant to be a compliment, but I will take it as one. All I can say, Melkavesh, is that if your feelings for me are as strong as they appear to be, and you can *still* give me to the King, then you are a better, more ruthless Gorethrian than I am. I presume your answer is no.'

'I didn't say that.' There was a perverse pleasure, for once, in having the advantage over him. 'In another way, you are

317

the most straightforward person I know. Whatever you do, however warped, is always with Gorethria's best interests at heart.' She rose and walked slowly away from him, so he could not see her face. 'I agree with you. Gorethria needs a strong ruler. I am the link between Kristillia and Gorethria, the only one with the power to control both sides. You may be in the Kristillians' hands, but they are in mine, and whatever I decide, they will have to acquiesce. Xaedrek, you are right. If we work together, there *can* be peace in Vardrav.' She went back to him and placed her hands on his arms. Her eyes were shining. 'Very well. Let us be Emperor and Empress. I could rule Gorethria in my own right, but I don't want to, so what better solution could there be?'

Xaedrek's eyes softened, and she thought she saw surprise there, mingled with triumph. 'In spite of your harsh judgement of me?'

'I want you to understand that I am entering this with my eyes wide open. I am doing it because it's for the best, not because you've blinded me with passion. You have yet to prove that I can trust you.'

'You are not being altogether fair, my love. I could have escaped the night Kharan came to me, I could have run after we emerged from Ah'garith's domain, but I did not. I stayed for your sake. The first time I asked you to be my Empress was for political reasons. This time there is far more to it than that, and you know it.'

'Yes,' she murmured. 'Yes, I know.'

'I always thought myself destined for a solitary existence. You told me once that you felt the same, but we were both wrong. Did we not both dream of each other, long before we met? What was it for, if not for this?' His arms were round her, enfolding her, and she closed her eyes and gave herself over to the bliss of no longer being alone. 'There is no one else to love us, Melkavesh. But we can love each other.'

Melkavesh was on the mainland, in one of the orchards, when Irem Ol Melemen found her. She had gone there on her own, needing time to reflect on the decision she had

318

made that morning. There was peace here, sunlight slanting through the leaves, a carpet of flowers underfoot, a sweet sea breeze carrying the haunting cries of gulls. Then she sensed someone nearby and turned to see the tall, robed figure of the priest approaching.

His face was twisted with grief, and he made no attempt to brush his tears away. 'My lady, my brother, Ol Thangiol, is dead.'

Something sank away inside her. 'What? But I healed him!' she cried. 'What happened?'

'Anixa came to me – she said he had killed himself. I went with her to bring back his body from the beach. He poisoned himself with some daelammion he stole from your chambers. He had – seen too much evil, she said, and could not bear to live with it. I thought – I thought you might have known already.'

By far-seeing, he meant. Suddenly a cold, sad wind seemed to be blowing on her. She might have seen, if she had not had so much else on her mind, but she knew that in the long run she could not have stopped him, that it would have been cruel to try. With the grief there was a terrible sense of failure.

'I didn't know. Ol Melemen, I'm so sorry,' she said. 'I can't believe it. How is Anixa?'

'Very calm, but strange – too quiet. Will you come back with me and speak to her?'

'Of course, but you go on ahead, Ol Melemen. Give me a few minutes, and I'll be there.'

He nodded, wiped his eyes with a shaking hand, and walked away. Behind him, out of sight, Melkavesh sank involuntarily to her knees as if an invisible hand had forced her down.

Irem Ol Thangiol's death had taken her like a cramping blow to the stomach, a far greater shock than she would have anticipated. There was a vortex spinning inside her, and it seemed to go beyond shock and into something physical, a sucking blackness that was swallowing her mind and body together, wrenching and stretching her as it did so. She could not feel the grass under her knees; she could not see anything except the blackness, and there was a sickening sensation of weightlessness, or an unstable surface like the sea beneath her.

It was her dream of the moons again, but this time far more vivid and terrifying than it had ever been before. And it had not crept into her slumber but jumped her, fully conscious, like an assassin, riding on her wave of sorrow. There were the stars, the unbearably heavy, menacing globes of rock sliding above her, the sea tipping beneath – but this time there was something horribly slow and precise about the vision, as if it were spelling out its meaning and would spell it out again and again, for eternity if necessary, until she understood. Each star was an adamant point of pain. The moons drove at her with an intolerable, muscular force until she could feel her bones aching and cracking, her ears ringing as if her head would burst. *Let it stop, oh, let it stop*, she chanted over and over to herself in the void; and when it had gone on for a hundred years, and she finally felt the choking rush of water in her mouth as the sea claimed her, even that had a ghastly deliberateness to it. The water rippled and cleared, and as through a block of glass, she saw Filmoriel. This time the child was not on a ship; she was in a room of polished red wood, the study in Silvren and Ashurek's house, and she was playing with the exquisite model of Earth that Silvren had crafted for Melkavesh long ago. She looked up at Melkavesh, pointing at the moons in a meaningless yet significant way that cut into Melkavesh like a spear of white light.

And she understood.

She yelled and struggled in the vision, desperate to return to reality before the understanding eluded her again, but she was embedded in the glass, helpless. And Filmoriel transformed into the slim golden figure of Silvren and came towards her through the glass as if it were no denser than air to her.

'Mellorn, my daughter, I told you how hard, how lonely and dangerous this would be. But I did not foresee what would have to be done. I beg of you not to go through with it; let things alone.'

'It's not in my nature to do that, Mother,' she heard herself reply, calmly, in spite of her distress. 'The change must take place, or the Earth will never progress.'

'But you don't understand what you are doing!'

'I love you, Mother, but you must not fear for me . . .' And Ashurek was there, his eyes freezing her, flaying her, his voice grim and dreadful yet so beloved.

'There is something pitiless in you, Mellorn. A core of iron that no gentle feelings can ever touch. It's not strength; it's a kind of blindness. I don't know how to explain it, and the coldness will never warm, unless you see Miril's eyes. But Miril is dead.'

They were among the last words he had ever said to her. Tears ran down her cheeks and froze there; a crystallising coldness drenched her, and the glass prison crazed and shattered outwards in a silent explosion, millions of diamond shards spiralling outwards into nothingness. She watched them, so cold now that she had become a statue caressed by the frigid wind, so brittle that if she tried to move she too would shatter and blow away like glass powder. Ashes of ice, she thought, and a laugh was painfully stillborn in her chest.

She was standing on a perfectly flat plain of snow, and on the snow she saw a dark grey figure and a light grey figure, stiff and stylised as if their reality were an abstract thing. But the woman between them, while not human, seemed the embodiment of life, all that was graceful and lovely. A sapphire light enveloped her, and her hair was like the silken grain of oak. *She is the Lady of H'tebhmella*, Melkavesh thought, *and I have seen this before.*

The Lady was going from one figure to the other, imploring them each in turn, *Why have you done this, why?* But neither would answer; and when one did not reply she returned to the other to ask the same question again and again, as if expressing the world's grief. It was a ritual step, achieving nothing but doomed to continue through eternity.

Stop, you must stop, you don't understand, Melkavesh tried to say, but the cold had frozen her mouth as solid as marble. It came to her that she really had become a statue.

Already the essential understanding was sliding away from her, a pebble trickling across a sheet of ice, growing smaller and smaller like a snowball in reverse. She must seize it before it was lost for ever. To forget again, now that she had finally understood, would be unbearable.

Don't try to move. Try to be very still, she thought, and with that her consciousness folded in on itself and she was no longer on the plain but moving up towards leaf-dappled sunlight. And she was screaming in silent panic, because the mote of comprehension was evading her like a reflection sliding off the edge of a mirror.

She came back to herself very suddenly, disorientated and feeling that several years had passed by. She was lying at an awkward angle on the grass, uncomfortable and shivering. And Kharan was bending over her, her face an inexpressibly welcome sight.

'Melkavesh?' she said anxiously.

The Sorceress groaned, straightened her limbs and sat up very carefully. 'I'm all right – I think.'

'Thank goodness! Whatever happened to you?'

'A vision, Kharan. I've never had anything like it before – well, I have, but never so intense, to the point of knocking me out. It was frightening.' She shook her head. 'Still, it's gone now.'

'Mel, did you know about Irem Ol Thangiol?'

'Yes. Oh, gods.' Kharan put her arms round Melkavesh's neck and for a minute or so they shed tears together. Then Melkavesh said, 'Help me up. I think I've done something to my shoulder. I must talk to Anixa.'

Kharan supported her, and as Melkavesh rose her jarred shoulder sent a fountain of pain up into her head. She winced, but the discomfort was as nothing to the sudden, icy clarity of her thoughts. The pain had jolted her, and to her astonishment the elusive idea flashed back into her mind and remained there, a transparent pearl, recaptured. Melkavesh gasped and clutched Kharan's arm, hardly daring to believe it.

'What's wrong?'

'Something in the vision I couldn't remember, it's come

back to me. And I think . . .' She probed the idea, tentatively at first in case it vanished again, then with growing exhilaration. 'Yes, there is sense in it, I feared it was a delusion. You know – when you dream you have learned some profound secret, and then wake up and realise it was something ridiculous? But this is real. It's the answer I've been searching for.' She was trembling, dazed with too many emotions, but the dominant one was hope – edged with terror. 'Everything will be all right now, Kharan. I know why I have been given the stone of Jaed and Fliya.'

There was a village in flames. There were people crying out and running, and through the smoke and flying ash there came soldiers clad in black cloaks and winged helmets. Anixa dropped the cloth she was carrying and ran until she could see the flames tearing at her own house, the bodies of a man and a young boy thrown down by the door like sacks of grain. And then there were hands gripping her, dragging her to join the other Kesfalians who would be taken to Shalekahh as slaves . . .

I served them well, too well, Anixa thought. From nothing she had become court dressmaker, won the Gorethrians' trust, even had her own house. She had survived, but at what cost? Melkavesh had entered her life like a sunburst, awakening the rebellious urges she had denied for so long, filling her both with hope and dread. But there had also been Kharan.

And there had been Irem Ol Thangiol. She had never known the man he must once have been. She had only known the husk, wrecked by Xaedrek's experiments and Ah'garith's malevolence, and all she could remember now was the burned-out blankness of his eyes, which even Melkavesh could not cure. She thought, *What did I say to him? That my vengeance against Xaedrek could never be realised, that we should go away and forget? I was wrong, so wrong.*

She saw Melkavesh entering a room in a swirl of silk and lamplight, saying, 'Xaedrek is utterly charming!' She saw the Emperor's red eyes, felt his arm round her as he forced her to endure the awful visions that the ichor had brought. All

323

of us, all of us his victims – all except Melkavesh, who for all her fine words was his equal not because she opposed him but because she was just the same as him.

There is nothing that people like us can do, Falmeryn had said. For a time Anixa had believed him, but now she knew her first instinct had been right after all. The time for standing by helplessly was over.

Xaedrek and Melkavesh were linked. Melkavesh should have stopped Xaedrek, or he should have stopped her, but instead they were acting as one, carving the world to their own dark design. So the answer was blazingly simple. Anixa must stop them both.

It was a Gorethrian who had first distilled daelammion, a poison so virulent that a single drop on a pin would kill . . . Oh, she should have done it long ago, the day she had been fitting Xaedrek with a new robe, just before her meeting with Ol Thangiol had changed everything. She had had the chance then, but not the will – nor the courage.

Courage, however, was not needed now. She needed nothing, felt nothing. She simply was, like an eye at the centre of the universe, unseen but seeing everything. And although she was just a speck beneath the sky, it also seemed that she had become boundless, the soul of Kesfaline itself. And like Kesfaline there was a power inside her: not sorcery but a passive strength, Fliya's gift, smooth and still and unyielding as obsidian shining under the moons.

16

Moonrise

IT WAS several days before the King and Queen arrived with their entourage, but Melkavesh's far-vision had not misled her. They came to Heldavrain in a rippling line of colour, and suddenly the bridge and courtyard were blazing with life, noise and celebration.

Melkavesh had fulfilled her promise. Gorethria had fallen. That was all Afil Es Thendil knew, and he did not notice her slight reserve as he pulled off his helm and strode forward to embrace her.

'Oh, Mellorn. I am completely lost for words. So many times I dreamed of this, when Xaedrek would have surrendered and we would be rejoicing, but the reality of it is – oh, what's the use? Words can't express it.' And he kissed her on both cheeks, leaving her face damp with his tears of joy. There was nothing diffident about him now; he was confident, unquenchably high-spirited. Even the Queen looked happy, and there was a closeness between them that had been absent before.

His smile faded only once, and that was when he saw Kharan with Falmeryn. He greeted her warmly, listened in grave silence as she explained how Falmeryn had come to Heldavrain, and at last kissed her formally as if saying farewell. 'I am happy for you, my dear, truly happy,' he said, and she knew he meant it.

When he had passed by, Queen Afil An Mora favoured her with only the briefest glance, and said coolly, 'Now you are a ghost in truth. As far as I am concerned, you do not exist.'

'What on Earth did she mean by that?' said Falmeryn in astonishment.

'Nothing. Nothing at all.' Kharan slid her hand through his arm. 'I'll tell you one day. Look, Haeth Im Nerek is here. Come and meet her.'

The Battle Marshal had come from Ehd'rabara to rejoin the King. She greeted Kharan with obvious pleasure, and after some light-hearted conversation, she said, 'Well, how is my beloved Lady Mellorn?'

Kharan grimaced. 'In a much better temper since Ah'garith died.'

'Not since Xaedrek's been here?'

'What do you mean?'

'Well, she and Xaedrek were lovers once, weren't they?'

Kharan stared at her, feeling suddenly cold. 'However did you know that?'

'It was written all over them when he was signing the surrender. I notice these things.'

'Look, Im Nerek, it was a long time ago – you can't be suggesting – no, there's nothing but hostility between them now. Xaedrek is kept under guard. It just isn't possible.' She looked round anxiously to make sure no one could overhear them. Melkavesh was deep in conversation with Prince Rar An Tolis, and the King was exchanging a formal greeting with N'golem and U'garet, praising the Mangorians' bravery. There was only Falmeryn, listening in startled silence.

'Come on, Kharan,' Im Nerek said quietly. 'You're not naïve, and why are you defending her? Melkavesh can do anything she wants. Would you put it past her?'

To admit that Haeth Im Nerek might be right seemed a betrayal of Melkavesh. It had only been a suspicion, one she had tried to deny to herself, but to hear it from someone else shook her. 'No. I mean, no, she wouldn't –'

'Melkavesh can't do anything wrong for the King, but even he would take a dim view of this – what do they call it? Fraternisation? Or reverting to type?'

'Im Nerek, you'd better not repeat a word of this to anyone else, King or otherwise.' Kharan was angry now. 'The thought is horrifying, I agree, but you've got no proof.'

326

'I wouldn't dream of saying it to anyone but you,' said Im Nerek, putting a friendly hand on her shoulder. 'I'm just warning you. If it's true, she'll be found out. And she'll have to bear the consequences.'

A feast was held in the visitors' honour, and the mood in the castle became uproarious. Many of the other Vardravian war leaders had come from Charhn and Ehd'rabara, and it soon became apparent that the King intended to hold a post-war council at Heldavrain. It was what Melkavesh had dreaded. The evening became a blur of wine and candlelight and noise; she made a faultless show of joining in the celebrations, but inside she was burning.

In the face of all the love and gratitude they were heaping on her, the secret she held to herself became intolerable. She felt she had no right to their friendship, even less to turn round and grind their loyalty into the dirt. Yet that was exactly what she must do. They had to be told. The knowledge was like a wall of ice round her and she went through the evening with an acute sense of being an observer, not a participant.

'. . . And on top of all his other crimes, Xaedrek let a demon roam loose and almost destroy us all,' Es Thendil was saying. 'By the moons, he's got more to answer for than a thousand slow deaths could expiate!'

'Your Majesty, I did not think you were a vengeful man,' she said, carefully keeping her expression neutral.

'I am not, usually. But you must admit Xaedrek's case is different.'

'I did tell you how much help he gave in killing the demon,' she said, then tried to change the subject. 'Anixa is looking happier, thank goodness. The Queen seems to have taken her under her wing. I was surprised, but of course the Queen herself is half-Kesfalian. Some friendships are instinctive.'

The King, however, was not to be diverted. 'Anixa is a brave woman who has suffered terribly at Xaedrek's hands. There are many to whom I shall present bravery awards. Of course, you do appreciate that the Council is likely to last several days. We have a great deal to talk about, not least of which is the fate of the Gorethrian tyrant. I want him brought before the Council as soon as possible.'

'I don't think that's a good idea,' she said abruptly.

'Why ever not?' He refilled her glass from a flagon of wine, but she did not touch it.

'Isn't it obvious? With everyone harbouring such vehement feelings against him, it could only result in an unpleasant and undignified scene.'

Es Thendil put a hand on her arm and looked gravely at her. 'Mellorn, I appreciate the way you've kept him here and coped with him so skilfully, but the time has come when I must relieve you of the burden. I've no wish to see him in private, or there really might be murder done. He must be brought before us all.'

The King could be strong-willed when he chose, and she could find no argument to change his mind. 'Very well,' she sighed. 'But it must be on the condition that everyone keeps their emotions in check.'

'Good. It's a difficult matter, deciding what to do about Gorethria now, but I think we have no choice. I do not trust them to abide by the surrender, especially as the man who signed it will presently be dead.' He scratched at his beard, his expression troubled. 'We are a civilised people, and it sickens me to think that we must do this to a conquered race. But the Gorethrians have forfeited their right to be treated as human. I have to safeguard my people's future. Gorethria must be destroyed before it rises again. Completely destroyed.'

His eyes had a faraway look and he did not seem to require an answer. Perhaps he took her silence for agreement, but she could not speak for the ball of ice that had formed in her stomach. She drank the wine, and several glasses more.

Under its influence it became easy to believe that there was a way to break the news and reconcile everyone to it without undue enmity. But even as the feast came to an end, that illusion was torn away. She had said her final good-nights and was making for the door, when she overheard one of Im

328

Nerek's generals and a Cevandarish warrior discussing in sickening detail just what they would do to Xaedrek if he fell into their hands – and if she had needed a reminder of the depth of feeling against him, that one impaled her like a steel spike.

Two days later, the scene in the banqueting hall was very different. The long table had been moved towards the wall and rows of benches arranged on each side, facing a central space. Behind the table sat the King and Queen, Melkavesh, Irem Ol Melemen, Haeth Im Nerek and Prince Rar An Tolis. Kristillian and other Vardravian officers occupied the benches to their left, and on the right were Heldavrain's senior staff, with Kharan, Falmeryn, N'golem and U'garet on the front row. Light filtering through the high windows smudged the hall with gold and rust and grey.

The Council had already been in progress for some hours, and so far had been an interminable reiteration of the war. For Haeth Im Nerek and many others there was a slight air of unreality in discussing a victory that had been won not by strategy but by the summoning of supramundane creatures from beneath the Aludrian Sea. Yet it was real enough; they had seen it with their own eyes, and more importantly, they knew it was their most effective means of destroying Gorethria completely.

Melkavesh felt that they had exhausted the subjects of the Aludrians and Ah'garith, and was wondering, now they had reassembled after a meal, what more she could find to say about them. The alternative, which she wanted to avoid, was to discuss Xaedrek.

As she was brooding on this, the King stood up and said, 'My friends, as you are all aware, our enemy Xaedrek of Gorethria is being held captive in this castle. I now command that he be brought before us that he may answer to his crimes. Lady Mellorn?'

It was unexpected, and she looked up with a jolt of annoyance. 'Your Majesty,' she whispered, 'you might have informed me in private of the precise time you wanted him here.'

'I have only just decided,' he said, 'that now is the right time. I'm sorry, Mellorn, but would you –?'

The hall had filled with a murmuring of excitement; a sight of Xaedrek was what they had all been hoping for, and the imminent prospect brought a palpable tension to the air. Melkavesh stood up and said in her severest tone, 'Very well, the prisoner shall be brought before us, but only on one very strict condition. No one is to speak to him, abuse him or assault him, and if anyone tries, they will be ejected at once. Is that clear?'

They grumbled their agreement. Reluctantly, Melkavesh sent the guards to fetch him from his room. It was only a minute or so before the doors opened again, at which the massed anticipation leapt in the air like static.

It was not Xaedrek. It was Anixa, dressed in an embroidered black robe with gathered sleeves.

Walking to the front of the table, she bowed to the King and Queen and said quietly, 'Please forgive my lateness, Your Majesties.'

'Not at all,' Es Thendil said kindly. 'Sit down, and Fliya bless you, my loyal sister.' Kharan moved up to make room for her.

It was another ten minutes before the guards returned, and by then everyone was muttering and fidgeting restlessly. A brisk pounding on the door silenced them. Then it swung open, and six Kristillian soldiers marched in with the tall, slender Gorethrian between them.

As they led him to stand before the King – at a respectable distance – the only sound was the faint hiss of many indrawn breaths. Then the quietness hung thick as dust in the air. Those who could not quite see him were craning their necks to discover whether the legendary Emperor Xaedrek really was a man or a devil.

He did not disappoint them. He stood quietly dignified between the guards, not looking at anyone – not even deigning to acknowledge the King and Queen – but his aura of graceful menace had not been diminished by his defeat. If anything, it shone more darkly brilliant in this stronghold of his enemies, and the atmosphere slowly became saturated

330

with unease and fear. They hated him, but he fascinated them like an exquisite snake.

Then someone stood up, and almost before the curse began to unfold from his lips, Melkavesh was on her feet and yelling him into silence.

'I warned you! Anyone else who chooses to disregard my conditions will be ejected head first through that door – and I do not guarantee to open it first.'

'Please – please,' Es Thendil added placatingly, 'do not make this situation more difficult than it is. Please remain quiet, all of you.' His throat sounded dry. To Melkavesh's dismay, he proceeded to break the condition himself as if out of a perverse desire to hear the Emperor speak. 'Xaedrek of Gorethria, your crimes against Vardrav are legion, but you have been brought to justice at last. Have you anything to say for youself?'

Oh, no, Melkavesh groaned inwardly. She saw Xaedrek fix his freezing red gaze on the King, and she saw how nobly Es Thendil tried to hold the look. Xaedrek said, 'I trust your victory has not been soured by the knowledge that it was not your own strength or superiority that saved you, but factors over which you had no control.'

Es Thendil tensed with anger. 'Not at all,' he said thinly. 'Victory is victory. I thought that was your own philosophy.'

'It is,' Xaedrek replied, 'and I congratulate you. But there is always a price to be paid for such things, as I'm sure you realise.'

'What are you implying?'

'Your Majesty, please don't get into an argument with him,' Melkavesh whispered.

Xaedrek gave a slight, sardonic smile. 'Gorethria has stumbled before and risen again. Beyond that, I have nothing to say to you.'

'Well, I have this to say to you,' the King said. 'You are to be delivered into our custody and dealt with as my countrymen see fit. Whatever the manner of your punishment, Xaedrek of Gorethria, you can be sure that it will not even begin to expiate your crimes!'

'Not yet,' Melkavesh said sharply, standing up. She had

braced herself for this moment, but the wave of hostility that Xaedrek's presence induced still shook her.

'What is "not yet" supposed to mean?' the Queen enquired.

'I explained to you all earlier about the Shanin Ah'garith. Xaedrek was instrumental in helping us to destroy her. This excuses nothing he has done, I know, but there is a further purpose in which I need his help.'

'Help?' cried Im Nerek, standing up. 'The only help he could give anyone is to kill himself!' Voices were raised in agreement, and Melkavesh brought her hands down on the table in anger.

'Hear me out!' she said so fiercely that they subsided. 'I am a Sorceress. On the world Ikonus, where I was trained, sorcery was an easy, flowing power that pervaded everything, but here it is not so. I've been trying to discover the reason, and when my far-sight returned after the demon's death, I finally understood what is wrong.'

Kharan looked at Falmeryn, clasped his hand.

'The power is an energy that circles round the Earth. But it is out of alignment with Earth. When the power first came into being at the Serpent's death, the process was incomplete, imperfect. That is why I've had so much difficulty, and why there has been only one Sorceress born that I know of. Now I have to finish what was started.'

'And what,' said Es Thendil, 'what will that mean?'

'It will mean a new age for the Earth. Sorcerers will exist freely, oh, not in their thousands, perhaps a handful in every country, but the hidden strength in Kristillia's soul leads me to believe that this land may be doubly blessed with them.'

'Blessed, or cursed,' Im Nerek put in. The King frowned her to silence.

'It is our own prophecy that the enchantress will bring the powers of the moons into their own,' he said dubiously. Irem Ol Melemen nodded. 'But how do you intend to – er – to bring the power into alignment?'

'I have had endless premonitions about it. I could never understand them, until I had a far-vision some days ago that suddenly showed me what it meant. Except to say that it involves the stone of Jaed and Fliya, it is not something I can explain. Not yet.'

That was not strictly true, but she had no intention of telling them anything until it was over.

'But is there anything dangerous in it?'

'There may be danger to myself, but to no one else, I swear. How can I put this? It is not *my* decision to do this, it's something that must happen for the Earth's good, and I am the instrument chosen to do it.'

Haeth Im Nerek stood up again. 'Forgive me, Sire, but I don't like the sound of this at all. She is asking us to trust her *and Xaedrek* in something she can explain nothing about, but which involves interfering with – well, with cosmic powers about which we know nothing – and she expects us to stand meekly by while she carries on?'

There were a few calls of agreement. N'golem suddenly rose from the bench, his slate-blue face savage with anger. 'How dare you question the word of the enchantress?'

'Someone ought to, or are we all sheep?'

'N'golem, Battle Marshal, please sit down,' said Es Thendil, agonised. 'When has our faith in Mellorn been misplaced? She brought us to victory. She destroyed a monstrous demon. We do her a great disservice in questioning her integrity. You should be ashamed!'

Overwhelming concurrence. Melkavesh gave Haeth Im Nerek a burning look, and said, 'Do you think I would do such a thing as this if it were not essential? Do you want the Earth to stay the same, to stagnate, like some creature only half-way to giving birth? I am the midwife, if you like, and my duty is to help the Earth.'

The chamber was hushed; unspoken questions hung in the air. They were out of their depth. Such was her conviction and authority, the power of her presence, that they could not disbelieve her. 'As soon as I sense that the time is right, it will be done. And I need Xaedrek to help me.'

The King cleared his throat and swallowed. 'Why? Surely, my lady, a priest of Jaed and Fliya would be far more appropriate. Why not Irem Ol Melemen?'

'Because Xaedrek shared my premonitions since long

before I knew him, and he is the only person I know who has. There must be a reason. He is connected with this.'

The King floundered, unable to form an argument, but at the mention of Xaedrek the chamber was again filled with grumblings of dissent. They were blind where Xaedrek was concerned, and she could hardly blame them; it just made things so difficult.

Es Thendil raised his hands for silence. 'I am sure the enchantress knows best in this. But how soon will it take place? We must insist on Xaedrek being handed to us immediately afterwards.'

'Immediately!' a few angry voices shouted.

'Afterwards,' Melkavesh said, 'we will discuss the arrangements.'

'Arrangements?' said Haeth In Nerek incredulously. 'Your Majesty, why do you allow this? Let's take him now, and leave!'

Over the shouts of agreement, Melkavesh said, 'I understand your feelings, Battle Marshal, but I must insist that no one obstructs me in this.'

The room seemed to be gathering, darkening around Melkavesh, while the light ran through her hair like sunlit water. Something in her eyes – the charismatic power of her personality – silenced them, but she felt their suspicion swelling through the silence.

Then someone said, 'Be honest with them, my lady.' A small dark figure rose from Kharan's side and walked towards the King and Queen. 'She has no intention of giving Xaedrek to you. No intention of destroying Gorethria. Ask her what she intends! Ask her if she does not mean to let Xaedrek go back to Shalekahh – and to go with him.'

'Anixa!' Melkavesh was furious, but the damage was done. The Queen's eyes were blazing, the King suddenly dumbfounded.

'Is this true?' Im Nerek shouted.

'These insults to the enchantress shall be avenged –' N'golem began, but his voice was lost among others.

Melkavesh ignored them. Suddenly the shouts died away and everyone stared at Anixa, who was walking calmly and purposefully towards Xaedrek. Her right hand fumbled for something in her left sleeve. In a sudden flash of intuition, Melkavesh knew exactly what she meant to do.

Xaedrek, held by the guards, could not defend himself, and they would not protect him; more likely, they would happily hold him still for her. Even as she thought it, Melkavesh flung out a crackling streak of power to halt her, fling her aside.

Showers of sparks fell around Anixa, but she did not even flinch. There was a power in her, not sorcery but something deeper, passive yet unassailable. The bolt that should have stunned her dissipated in a whisper of gilded sparks and she walked on as if nothing had happened, drawing from her sleeve a long, shining pin.

Melkavesh was out of her chair, over the table and across the floor almost as fast as her sorcery bolt. She seized Anixa just as she reached Xaedrek, just as her hand was raised and the pin hovering an inch from his chest.

'Get him out of the way!' Melkavesh screamed at the guards, but to her enhanced senses they seemed to obey her in agonising slow motion. She had Anixa's shoulders, but somehow could not seem to catch hold of her wrists. There was an incredible strength in the woman. It was all she could do to drag her backwards, pull her round – then they were grappling frantically, and the pin was dancing before Melkavesh's own face.

She never saw how it happened. Suddenly she had Anixa's wrist; the dark fingers came open painfully and the pin clattered onto the flags. But Anixa's mouth was open in mute agony and she was rigid in Melkavesh's grasp. Whether by accident or design, in the struggle the Kesfalian had somehow pierced herself with the pin.

At once Melkavesh left the physical world and plunged into Anixa's body, desperately trying to halt the poison. But all she met was an image that impressed itself on her mind for ever: a dark tunnel, and Anixa's soul fleeing, fleeing along it as if she could not escape fast enough. Then there was only the tunnel, and silence, and Anixa was gone.

Melkavesh returned to the physical world, shivering, to

find herself on her knees and the Kesfalian half in her arms, half on the floor.

'Kharan, could you help me, please?' she said. It was like someone else speaking, incongruously calm. She became aware of a crowd gathering around her, the King and Queen, Kharan and Falmeryn and all the others, pressing in on her, their concern stifling her. She gave the small body into their hands and stood up with the room tipping vertiginously around her in a dense, ringing silence.

A moment later, they knew. She could not bear their eyes on her; Kharan's white, accusing gaze.

'I had to stop her,' she said hoarsely. 'I did not mean her to die.'

'My lady, is there nothing you can do?' Ol Melemen cried.

'I tried. I can only heal the living, not the dead. Guard!' She turned and beckoned to a stocky Kristillian. As she did so she caught Xaedrek's emotionless gaze and quickly looked away. 'Take Anixa to her room. I'll come as soon as we've finished here.'

'What for?' Kharan said bitterly. 'She's dead, she needs nothing from you!'

The atmosphere in the chamber had turned as grim as a demon storm. As Anixa's small frame was taken away, all the Kesfalians in the hall rose and filed out after her. Their voiceless protest affected everyone. As the rest returned to their places, Melkavesh had to dredge every last atom of Gorethrian pride to regain her composure. She wanted to order that Xaedrek be taken back to his room, but she could not seem to find her voice.

'We understand that it was an accident – a very unfortunate event,' the King said at last. A derogatory grunt was heard from Haeth Im Nerek. 'Poor, poor woman. My lady, she must have been unbalanced to make such an accusation against you.'

How the hell did she know? Melkavesh thought. *A guess, a logical conclusion?* She hated to lie, but in their present mood there was no way she could make them understand that what she planned to do was for everyone's benefit – not just Gorethria's.

336

Her voice measured, she replied, 'Anixa was deeply unhappy. In such a state of grief, any delusion can seem real.'

'But was it a delusion?' Haeth Im Nerek asked harshly.

Melkavesh's head snapped up to glare at her. 'How can you doubt me, after all I've done to help you?'

'Quite easily.' Im Nerek caught the King's gaze. 'She and Xaedrek are lovers. Ask her if it is not so, and see if she can look you in the eye as she answers!'

'Battle Marshal!' Es Thendil cried, shocked. 'It hardly befits you to say such a thing. I suggest you withdraw it at once.'

'Very well, I withdraw it,' said Im Nerek. She gave a sardonic inclination of her head.

And then the Queen said, 'But can the Lady Mellorn deny it?'

Embarrassed on all sides, the King scowled her into silence, but his eyes on Melkavesh were troubled, questioning. She knew he was only defending her because the truth would have been unbearable. Betrayal. They could take it no other way.

'The King is right,' she said with a cool dignity that surprised herself. 'I will not be pressured into defending myself as if I were on trial. I have told you what must be done and I have explained why Xaedrek is the only one who can help me.' She sensed Xaedrek's approval, and did not want it.

Her words did not quiet them this time; the babble of voices in the chamber grew louder, and she stood up, her fingers gripping the edge of the table. A new voice cut through the noise, 'Help – to do what?'

'I've just explained,' she said thinly.

'What you mean to do, yes – but not the consequences.' The speaker was the only Kesfalian who had not left, a short, plump man in a brown robe. As he stood up from the rearmost bench, Falmeryn stared at him in amazement.

'That's Cristan!' he said to Kharan. 'I didn't know he was here!'

'Silence, everyone, please,' said Irem Ol Melemen. 'If you have something to say, state your identity.'

'I am Cristan of Kesfaline. I arrived this morning, and I've travelled here from – from Imhaya, because I'm greatly concerned at what the Kristillians are allowing to happen.'

The King turned his sharp gaze upon the man. 'Explain yourself.'

'I was a witness to the Stone of Fliya being taken. I don't know the purpose of it, but the deceptions and mysteries surrounding it prompted me to come and find the enchantress for myself. Kristillia and Kesfaline have each had their prophecies that such an enchantress would one day save us, presumably from Gorethria. In Kesfaline it is also said that she will then destroy us.'

'How?' the King demanded. 'My country and yours have never quarrelled before, and I do not mean to start now – but I cannot agree with you. We believe she will bring the powers of Jaed and Fliya into their own, and we should be doing everything to help her!'

'No, no, you're wrong. Friends we are, and as a friend I am trying to warn you. The nature of the disaster is not specified, but –'

'For the Sphere's sake, I am not going to destroy anything!' Melkavesh broke in. 'My only purpose is to free the power of sorcery.'

'How can you say that she is acting destructively?' said Es Thendil. 'She might have denied us this, jealously kept the power to herself, but instead she is willing to share it. She's fulfilling the prophecy.'

Thank you, Melkavesh thought. The level of noise fell, and for a moment it seemed the King had swayed them.

'At what cost?' Cristan persisted. 'What will these Sorcerers do?'

'They will help you; I will train them as I was trained, in the strictest –'

'Oh, you were trained to switch sides on a whim, were you?' Haeth Im Nerek again. 'So Kristillia will swarm with enchanters just like you, will it? And what about Gorethria?'

An instant hush, like an axe falling.

The King said, 'Now, Battle Marshal, you know there can be no more danger from Gorethria. Gorethria is to be destroyed.'

'And Melkavesh is going to do it, is she? Ask her. Go on, Your Majesty, *ask her*!'

'My Lady Mellorn, forgive me, but I must ask you to set everyone's minds at rest,' the King said heavily. 'You alone hold the power to put an end to Gorethria's evil once and for all, and I think these doubts would swiftly be answered by your assurance that you mean to do so as soon as possible.'

Again the silence that drove into her breastbone like a spike of granite. Should she lie now, tell them the truth later? Or say one thing and do another?

They could not read her face, but she hesitated too long, and she could feel the hostility gathering, poising itself like an arrow on the bow. She looked at Xaedrek, and saw his lips form the words, *Tell them*. Yes, the least she owed them was honesty; she must make them understand – or take the consequences if she could not.

'You have put your faith in me, and I have given all I could in return. Gorethria has fallen. You are free and nothing, I swear, shall take that from you. To turn on a defeated country and wipe them out would be genocide –'

Her words were drowned in uproar. She had gambled and lost; even the King had turned on her now and was shouting his rage with the others. Everyone was on their feet, even Heldavrain's staff – everyone except Kharan, Falmeryn and the Mangorians. Swords were being drawn, and in a flash flood of anguish she discovered how it felt to be universally reviled.

Someone scurried past the table towards the door: Cristan, alarmed at the chaos and hurrying to join his countrymen. Then everyone seemed to be converging on her at once, Kristillians and Cevandarish and Alta-Nangrans, their blades shining like teeth. The Mangorians surged forward to defend her. And Melkavesh, with no choice left, drew energy into herself and held it there like a breath.

Then she released it.

The power birthed itself from her forehead like an egg, ballooning outwards in a sphere which flung her attackers aside. Chairs were upturned, those alongside her hurled back against the wall. There were screams. People stumbled over each other, some rushed for the door. It was more in fear than pain, for she had not aimed the power to harm anyone; but light particles danced madly over the skin of the sphere, throwing out miniature lightning darts that lashed anyone they touched.

Outside the sphere there was panic; but within it, cocooned by golden radiance, Melkavesh stood untouched. She drew the shield back in on itself until it was just large enough to protect her – and Xaedrek, whose guards had retreated. Then she cried, 'Enough! Be silent and listen to me!'

This time they obeyed, turning faces to her that were pale with fear and acrimony. She could not control the emotion pushing up in her throat. 'It's the last thing I wanted, to have to use force against you, who were my friends – and I hope will be again. But I have to make you understand.'

'You've made yourself clear enough, my lady,' said Es Thendil, leaning heavily on the edge of the table as he dusted himself off. 'We see that you are protecting Xaedrek. We may assume that Anixa's accusations were no delusion after all. We understand that our point of view counts for nothing, when with your power you can do whatever you please.'

Haeth Im Nerek added, 'Why don't you dye your hair its true Gorethrian colour? Black, black to its roots!'

Melkavesh hardened her heart. She had to, or she would have broken. But as she began to reply, there was a strange light in the hall, something beating against the high arched window in the opposite wall. She held her breath. *Something was answering her power* –

The glass in the window bellied out and burst, showering the hall with glass, and through the aperture came a shaft of pure violet light. It fell on Melkavesh and her own power flamed violet in response. She had become oblivious to everything except the beam, and releasing the breath she lifted her head and stretched out her hands to receive its meaning.

It took her several moments to realise that it was moonlight.

Then she understood.

340

'The moons are full tonight.' She spoke quietly, but her voice rang through the hushed chamber. 'The change I've tried to explain to you must take place now. You may come and witness it if you will; I don't want to obstruct or harm anyone. But I cannot allow anyone to try to stop me.'

She walked round the table and looked at Xaedrek. With the same cool dignity he had maintained throughout he went to her side, allowing himself to meet the King's gaze as he passed. It was a look of cynical amusement that scored Es Thendil's heart like acid. *Even in defeat, I have won*, it said. Still wrapped in amethyst light, he and Melkavesh went out through the double doors together.

It was several moments before anyone moved. Then, exchanging many speaking looks but few words, the rest of the assembly began to file out of the hall and follow them.

By night the Aludrian Sea became other-worldly, a plane of spangled ink under the moons. Melkavesh and Xaedrek, barefoot and clad only in dark breeches and shirts, pushed a flat skiff out onto the water and climbed into it as it began to glide across the wrinkled surface. Jaed and Fliya were poised overhead like matched pearls webbed with palest silver.

Melkavesh thought, *Will they still look as beautiful after . . .?*

There was a crowd on the beach behind them. She felt almost sorry for them, in a way, only able to watch in impotent anger. But if they were afraid, so was she. Her hands were damp, and now the moment had come she dreaded finding that she did not have the strength needed.

Sorcery propelled the vessel, and the beach was soon out of sight. A slight swell rocked them, moonlight shattered and re-formed on the water. In the dreams there had been nothing more substantial than a raft between herself and the sea, and somehow it seemed important. In any case, Heldavrain had no larger boat to offer. The vivid light that had called her had diffused, but its after-glow still clung to her and guiding the skiff took almost no effort at all.

Xaedrek said, 'I appreciate that you did not want to tell the Kristillians too much, but aren't you going to tell me what we are doing?'

'Don't you know? But you've had the dreams as well!'

'Yes, Melkavesh. But you admitted that you only understood them yourself a short time ago.'

'Of course. I couldn't expect you to –'

'I can make an educated guess. But tell me, anyway.'

'The energy circling the world is not physical as such, but it is affected by physical bodies.'

'Such as the moons.'

'Yes. And it can only be pulled into its correct alignment if the moons themselves are moved, their orbit changed.'

Xaedrek took this in, and said eventually, 'Well. I can certainly appreciate why you did not want the Kristillians to know that. How do you plan to achieve it?'

'We,' she corrected. 'One moon each. I'll show you when it's time.'

'Why on the sea, though, instead of land?'

'Because this is the way it was in the dream. Perhaps the Aludrians have something to do with it. Or it may be that great pressures will be unleashed that the sea can absorb, which on land would have crushed us. Xaedrek . . . you didn't have to come.'

He gave her a hard look. 'I am asking questions because I want to know, not because I am apprehensive.'

'Perhaps you should be. I don't really know what will happen.'

The castle was still visible, but dwindling now. She felt the build-up of energies, like a machine sliding into life simply because she was there, the essential pivot round which all else would revolve. Xaedrek said, 'There's something else I must know. If this has the result you hope, might the transformation give me true sorcerous power as well?'

'I don't know,' she said, surprised. 'It's very unlikely. Sorcerers are born, not made. So much on this Earth is strange that I can't be sure, but don't hope for it.'

'I was merely curious. To have such power would be useful, but I can cope quite well without it.'

342

'I've noticed.' She gave a fleeting grin, and his gaze on her softened.

'Melkavesh, don't let yourself be perturbed by the Kristillians. You cannot waste time always trying to please people. Be calm in the knowledge that what you're doing is right.'

'I'm glad someone thinks so.'

'It is. How far are we going?'

'Further yet. Where the water's deep enough, and the moons are at their apex.'

'Then we'd better find a way to pass the time.'

They kissed, but after a few moments she pulled away and said softly, 'This would be very pleasant, but we'd best conserve our energy. You know, even when we were at odds with each other, I would sometimes have this strange feeling that the world had faded away, that none of this had happened and we weren't good or evil; we simply *were*. Wishful thinking, I suppose, but this is the nearest I have come to that feeling in reality. I wish it could last.'

'So do I. But we can't turn away from the world,' he replied. 'We are nothing without it. And when this is over, the prospect of returning to Shalekahh is very welcome.'

'If I can trust you.'

'As much as I can trust you not to let Es Thendil have me after all.'

'What if I did?' She was half teasing, half serious.

'I would expect no mercy, and I would certainly ask for none. They'd have no satisfaction of me. However –' He placed a gentle hand on her shoulder, 'I don't mind admitting that I would much rather live.'

She smiled, touched her lips to his. 'I'm glad you're here with me.'

They talked about their shared dreams, and it seemed like a dream, the two of them adrift in the calm silence of the night. It was an hour or more before Melkavesh knew the moons had reached their highest point, and then she slowed and stilled the skiff. It spun a little before coming to rest on the obsidian surface.

Then she took a pouch from her belt, removed two packages from it, and placed the stones of Jaed and Fliya side by side on the planks at the bottom of the boat. Dull at first, the solid fragment seemed to absorb light until it became luminous, while the dust of Fliya began to shine like powdered silver.

'I know their purpose now,' she said. 'There is no power in them as such, they are a focus, a link between myself and the moons along which I can direct my power.'

She knelt on the planks and Xaedrek knelt alongside her, taking care not to rock the skiff. She noticed that his hands were perfectly steady, while hers were trembling. 'What do you want me to do?' he asked.

She moistened her lips. 'Take the stone of Jaed. I am going to channel part of my power through you, so that you can move Jaed while I concentrate on Fliya. We will be connected, so I can let you know exactly what to do. We must lie flat on our backs, so that the pressures don't over-balance us.'

Side by side they lay down in the skiff, Xaedrek with the rock-shard held to his chest, Melkavesh with the dust carefully rewrapped in its vellum but shining through it. They joined hands. As she began to feel the swell of electricity through her body, two threads of light coalesced in the air, leaping from the moon stones and soaring up into space to touch the very moons themselves. Jaed to Jaed and Fliya to Fliya. She felt a thrill of excitement. The link was visible now, the thread with which she would manipulate the change.

The radiance that flowed through her was stronger than anything she had felt before, even on Ikonus. It was almost involuntary, insistent as a birth pang, and the force of it lifted her out of her physical body and into the astral. It was exhilarating, not golden or violet now but silver-white. Struggling for control, she split the power into two streams and diverted one to flow through Xaedrek; and as she did so he was there with her, disembodied yet warm and close as life.

In the same moment she felt the throb of cool fire from beneath the waves, and knew that the Aludrians were joining their power to hers. They gave everything, asked for nothing. From above she saw her own body and Xaedrek's shrouded in the lunar glow, saw the delicate aquamarine flood into it and seep upwards through the light threads until the faces of Jaed and Fliya took on the tint. And on those silver-blue cords she and Xaedrek were being borne upwards.

They were rising at great speed. The moons were growing to fill the entire sky, their angles changing dizzily until they became as huge as planets, Jaed hanging above them and Fliya below.

Blackness. They were beyond the moons, on the dark side where no sunlight reached. Two souls flying through space, no longer in conflict, just as in her prescient dreams . . . Stars crystallised on the darkness. She thought they had left the Earth behind, but now they were curving towards it again, and for the first time she saw it from a distance, not dark against the sun but blue-green and white, just like the model that Silvren had made for her as a child.

And like the model, the lines of energy circling around it were visible. She knew she was seeing them with supernatural vision, the whirling rings as fine as spider silk, glittering with colours she could not even name. But instead of forming a perfect circle round the Earth, they orbited in a distorted ellipse, scattering energy uselessly into space.

This is what I was seeking all along, this is what I was blind to, she thought. The sight was sublime, overwhelming, and she wanted to weep with awe.

I see it too, Xaedrek said without words. A cold observer no longer, he was as rapt with wonder as a scientist making an incredible discovery. *I knew – I always knew – but I could never put a shape to it . . . What now?*

Now, she said, *we are not only borne on the power. We are* the power. There was a sense of falling, and two great globes rose before them, swallowing all light. Melkavesh struggled to keep the Earth in sight before they eclipsed it. *Take Jaed. Act with me. I will tell you how far . . .*

They sped nearer the moons, two arrowheads of light connected to a single shaft. She understood now that they were to move the moons by pushing them. All her training, skill and instinct were in flight as she pressed towards Fliya, all the knowledge she needed pervading her. She knew how to force the body onto a new path and how to fine-tune the adjustment so that the energy shifted into perfect synchronisation.

She did not dare to think of the consequences if either of them lost control, if one of the moons fell to Earth.

Xaedrek's thoughts blended with hers, myriad impressions and possibilities. Where Ah'garith had failed, this experience succeeded in tearing his detachment from him, and he could think only of the Earth's beauty, the devastating, sublime power that whirled through him and all around him. They were poised in the immensity of space like stars. *Compared to this, even Gorethria seems insignificant*, he thought. *And after this, what can have any meaning?*

Oh, Xaedrek, she answered him. *This gives everything meaning, everything!*

They did not touch the moons; they were poised a long way from them, feeling a resistance like the smooth, round repulsion between two magnets. The harder they pushed, the stronger the repulsion became. There was an inertia to be overcome, and Melkavesh desperately drew more power, feeling it gather through her physical form and flow upwards along the thread. She saw the energy-lines contract and shimmer in response. When she knew she had enough power to counteract Fliya's vast mass, she unleashed herself like a steel ball, while Xaedrek sped towards Jaed.

It was then that the pressure began. No harmless jewels now, the moons seemed, with hideous preciseness, exactly what they were; unimaginably heavy globes of rock, weighing billions of tons. *No power in them? Wrong. I was wrong*, Melkavesh thought. The dream had only been a shadow of this. Something was flowing from them, not theurgy but their own slow heartbeat, wave after wave of dense luminosity. She and Xaedrek were caught in it. Awe crossed the threshold into dread and kept going into terror, but she could not cry out, could only keep driving and driving against the pressure as if the moon were struggling to be born from her own body.

Xaedrek remembered the first time he had dreamed of this. The poignant sense of weirdness and profundity that dwarfed all else, the yearning both to escape and capture the feeling, were with him again, but this time they received fulfilment. It was here – an end to the desperate seeking that had brought Ah'garith to him . . .

And suddenly the pressure was released. Jaed and Fliya gave way. There was a horrible sense of slippage, then the two dark spheres were drifting towards the Earth with crescents of sunlight silvering their rims. *Stay with them, guide them*, Melkavesh cried silently. Once the moons were moving, the hardest part was to stop them. She kept her gaze fixed on the world and saw the rings changing shape, the distortion flattening as if pushed by an invisible hand as the moons sought their new orbit. Everything that had ever mattered was swallowed by the slow cosmic dance, time itself measured by it. Melkavesh felt less significant than a flea in the face of such immensity. *And yet*, she thought, *only we could have done this. No one else, not even the Guardians themselves. Only us* . . . And the thought came not with pride but with utter humility.

Only us, my love, Xaedrek agreed softly. *Joined in a destiny even greater than Gorethria.*

The rings spiralling round the Earth appeared to be springing back into shape, as if the distortion had been a forced thing. A perfect shining web enclosed the planet, slightly flattened over the poles. It was as it should be . . . but Jaed and Fliya were still moving, gathering momentum and falling, the web beginning to fray –

Xaedrek! I've misjudged it, used too much power – we must – but she was already swooping down between the moons, and he was with her, part of her –

Strange, came a fleeting thought through the urgency, that in reality Jaed and Fliya were thousands of miles apart, yet now they seemed almost to touch, as if far-sight cut out all that did not matter . . .

– And then they were between the moons and Earth, two tiny crystal arrows trying to halt the irresistible forces of gravity. An intolerable pressure was crushing them; the two immense bodies were poised above them bearing them down, down towards the sea. The weight was not only the great mass of rock but the weight of billions of years, and an

347

impossibly heavy flow of power was pulsing from them, terrifying, annihilating. They could not breathe, could not cry out. It was only the effort to do so that made Melkavesh realise she was back in her physical body.

Xaedrek –

The weight was on her chest, unbearable. She felt the skiff being forced under the surface, and she could not move to save herself. Water slopped in over the sides. Then its coldness came in a rush, filling her mouth and nose and ears. She began to flail against it, felt Xaedrek's hands catch at hers, and only then realised that her contact with him was lost.

Her power was gone. She could not save herself with sorcery this time. She was being thrust deeper and deeper, and the shock of cold and darkness and crushing weight left no space for thought or even fear; only a fleeting image of two silver threads breaking, a stone sinking, and the dust of Fliya swirling round her like a cloud in the water.

On the beach they waited in grim silence, not even knowing what to look for. They waited a long time; some began to grumble, to move back towards the castle in twos and threes. But eventually, those who stayed saw the faint platinum strands spring from somewhere out on the sea and touch the faces of the moons.

They moved closer together, clasping hands, shivering although it was not cold. It happened so slowly that they did not see at first, and could not believe their eyes when they did.

Kharan said, 'The moons – they're growing larger!'

'Nonsense. You're staring at them too hard,' someone replied.

'No, she's not,' said Irem Ol Melemen. 'They are moving. Look.'

Fliya seemed to be curving sideways in the sky, an unnatural motion far swifter than her normal orbit. And Jaed seemed to stay where it was, slowly but inexorably increasing in size.

'Not moving,' said An Mora quietly. 'Falling.'

Fear enfolded them like a soft cold breath, but no one moved. 'Why?' cried the King. 'Why is Melkavesh doing this to us?'

'The Kesfalians were right.' Ol Melemen said, peculiarly calm because the true nature of the doom was beyond him. 'Yet I'm sure she did not mean to destroy us in this way.'

Kharan swung round, almost hit him, suddenly frantic with the need to run back to the castle – as if there were anything she could do to save Filmoriel. But Falmeryn hung onto her. There were gasps all round her, and as she focused on the sky again she saw why.

Jaed was huge now, but its size was stable. It was no longer falling. Weird bands of colour were flickering across its surface. Fliya was sailing near the horizon as if she had dropped across the sky and been cushioned there by clouds.

'Gods. Jaed and Fliya help us,' the King said in a choked voice. 'The moons are – are – For them to have fallen to Earth would have been quite impossible . . .' His words faded. An eerie light was weaving across the heavens. It was not daylight, for this glow came from the whole sky at once, and it was striated with bands of blue and violet, green and silver and copper. They rippled and shimmered with supernatural beauty, and they could not be mistaken for the aurora; they were too ordered, and they shone against a sky that seemed to be made of beaten gold. For a few moments the night flared brighter than day.

Then the vision faded. Night lapped around them, and they blinked against sudden blindness. All seemed normal – and yet everything seemed different.

'I'm worried,' Kharan said. 'Shouldn't we go and look for Melkavesh?'

No one replied. No one knew what to say or do. More torches were brought from the castle, but they waited a long time and almost gave up hope before Falmeryn spotted a dark shape in the water.

'She's coming back. She's all right,' he said. Uneasy murmurs broke out and they moved nearer the waterline. In torchlight and moonlight they saw two figures swimming towards them – or one swimming laboriously, pulling the other through the water. They reached the shallows and the swimmer rose out of the water, swaying, weighed down by sodden clothes.

It was Melkavesh. She was coughing, and trying to shout to them between coughs, 'Help me. There's nothing I can do – someone else must try –'

She seemed out of her mind with panic. She was struggling now to pull the unconscious form out of the water, stumbling in the wet sand as if she had almost no strength left. They surrounded her and Falmeryn helped her to haul Xaedrek to a drier place. She bent over him, shaking.

'Help him, please,' she said hoarsely. 'We both nearly drowned. I lost contact with him, I can't reach him. Please –'

'It's all right, my lady,' said Irem Ol Melemen. 'I will do what I can.' As he knelt down to listen to Xaedrek's heart, Kharan shook Melkavesh's arm and pulled her to her feet.

'What happened?' she cried.

Melkavesh pushed the wet hair off her forehead with a violently trembling hand. Her eyes were unfocused, irrational. 'The boat was pushed down into the water. I didn't know we'd righted the moons; all my strength went out of me, I was sure I was going to drown. Then I started to rise again, but when I broke the surface the skiff had sunk. It took me an age to find Xaedrek, and when I did he was floating, face down.' She coughed and shivered. 'My sorcery started to come back then so I tried to heal him, but I couldn't – couldn't reach him. I don't know why. I tried so hard, but then all I could do was swim ashore. He will be all right, won't he?'

They were all staring at her. Irem Ol Melemen stood up slowly and looked down at Xaedrek's dark, motionless form, unable to meet her eyes. He took a breath and released it. 'He's dead, my lady.'

Her eyes widened. 'Don't be so ridiculous! He can't be!'

'But he is.' Falmeryn and the King and Queen were bending over him now. 'He is, truly. Why do you doubt me?'

'It's impossible. *I* survived – how can he have died?'

'He must have drowned. He was undoubtedly dead when

350

you found him, which would explain why you were unable to heal him.'

Melkavesh wrenched her arm out of Kharan's grasp. A dangerous power flickered on her hands and she took a step towards the King – but then she swayed, and it vanished. 'Get away from him,' she said in a raw, husky voice. 'Go on, get away from him, all of you!'

Stunned, they obeyed. Melkavesh dropped to her knees by Xaedrek's side, pressed her fingers under his jaw, listened for the faintest heartbeat. Her sorcerous senses had already told her that there was no spark of life left, but in desperation she had to make a last, futile search for something she knew she would not find. Oblivious now to the crowd staring and staring at her, she kissed the cold eyelids, ran her fingers over the face that even in death kept its sculpted beauty. Her tears mingled with the droplets of sea water on his cheeks.

Open your eyes, look at me. I am a Sorceress, you are Xaedrek of Gorethria. Have we not survived what would have killed ordinary mortals a hundred times over? We succeeded, we brought the moons to their new orbit, unlocked the power. You can't be dead, we've got too much to do. What about Shalekahh? Oh, by all the gods and demons, Xaedrek, you cannot choose this time to leave me. You of all people, my love, you cannot simply have drowned . . .

Acceptance came at last, very slowly, but unbelievably painful and saw-edged. The pain dragged her down like the weight of the moons until she was lying across Xaedrek's body, heavy as death herself. Then came the sobs of grief, wrenching themselves from the roots of her lungs and scouring a throat already thick and sore. And the sobs, horrible for the onlookers to hear, went on and on.

No one could feel sorrow for his death, even less for the woman who had betrayed them and now swept away all lingering disbelief that she could have loved such a man. Yet her grief was too human not to tear at them. The King was the first of many who walked away, outwardly in disgust, inwardly so that he did not start to weep with her.

351

17

The Circles of the World

Twins no longer, the moons looked as strange as new planets rising in the night sky. Kharan and Falmeryn stood alone on a hilltop, watching them glide on their slow path around the Earth. Fliya was only slightly larger, like a swollen harvest moon, but Jaed seemed eight times its original size, no longer a faraway disc but a very round, solid sphere hanging impossibly close above the hills.

And they were no longer white. Inexplicably, Fliya had taken on a hue of pale gold, veined with amber, while the larger moon was a soft plum-blue with every detail of its surface etched in shadow. They were beautiful, weird, and wrong.

'I don't think I'll ever get used to it,' Kharan said. 'Every day for the rest of our lives the moons will look like that – never again as they used to be. I can't believe Melkavesh has done this.'

'I wonder if she understands what she has done. I don't think anyone does . . . except the Guardians.' Falmeryn spoke quietly, uneasily. Below them, the Aludrian Sea raged like the open ocean. Purple lightning crackled on the horizon and there was a feeling of strain in the air as if the sky were composed of plates grating against each other. 'If this is the disaster the Kesfalians feared, it doesn't seem that disastrous . . . but it's so far beyond me I don't know what to think. What really shocked me was Melkavesh's reaction when she realised Xaedrek was dead. I couldn't believe any of the accusations – until I saw her grief. Didn't it shock you as well?'

'No. Not at all.' She half smiled without humour. 'I knew from the first time she met him, that she was in love with him. Even when she was fighting him. Oh, at the time I believed everything she told me, but in my heart I always knew she would find a way back to him. No. It was no surprise.'

'But how could she? To betray everyone –'

'Falmeryn.' She laid a hand on his arm, looked up at him with gentle eyes. 'I feel sorry for her. How can we choose who we fall in love with? And I know how it feels to lose someone you love. She has no chance of finding him again.'

He nodded, lowering his eyes. 'And maybe we both find it too easy to forgive, instead of fighting back. I wonder what she'll do now?'

'I don't know.' Kharan shivered, suddenly chilled by the night. She pictured oceans torn into violent turmoil by the moons' new paths, ships capsizing, coastal villages engulged by tidal waves. 'Falmeryn, I've had enough. I don't belong with Melkavesh any more. I want – to go home, I was going to say, but I don't have one. I don't belong anywhere.'

'Yes, you do.' Falmeryn pulled her against him, wrapped her in his cloak. 'There's somewhere we both belong, and it's time we went back. I promised we would.'

'I hope you don't mind me coming to see you. There's no one else I can talk to, really.'

'I am grateful that you came to tell me the news yourself,' said Baramek. Melkavesh glanced out of the window and saw the grey walls of the prison camp outside, and the Gorethrian men and women moving restlessly beneath them. Most of the prisoners of war were accommodated in tents, but Baramek and the senior officers were in cells which, if not luxurious, were at least clean and supplied with fresh water. There was nothing the Gorethrians hated more than squalor.

'I didn't want you to hear it from some gloating Kristillian,' she said.

'I would not have believed it.'

'But from me you believe it?'

353

He nodded. Even without his war gear and helm he was still a menacing figure, in no way diminished by imprisonment, but the look in his eyes was one of stunned grief. It reawoke her own sorrow and she had to turn away from him until she could control her expression.

Yet there was no need. She felt his hand on her shoulder, and she could almost have imagined it was Ashurek with her. 'My lady, I loved him too,' he said. 'I did not always agree with his methods. But he was my Emperor.'

She said haltingly, 'I've had an officer released so the news can be taken back to Shalekahh – and to any Gorethrians he meets along the way. I've no wish to conceal the fact.' Then her shoulders rose and fell with a deep sigh. 'Baramek, now he's gone, we must talk. I need your help, and I want to help you in return.'

'Indeed?' There was an odd indifference in his tone. 'I am in your debt, my lady, over Surukish, but I think there is no further help we need from you.'

'Because of what I've done,' she muttered, then swung angrily to look at him. 'Damn it, Baramek, I couldn't stand by and see Vardrav crushed by you! But now I can't let the Kristillians do the same to Gorethria. I want all the Gorethrian prisoners of war released and sent home, but I can only effect it if I am absolutely certain that you won't attack Kristillia again.'

He understood. His eyes clawed into her. 'You are asking a lot, Lady Melkavesh.'

'I know. I am asking you to make an Oath of Loyalty to me.'

'An Oath of Loyalty is made only to the Emperor.'

'I know that, too.'

Astonishment looked incongruous on Baramek's heavy features. 'You mean to take the throne?'

'I don't know about "take",' she said. 'Didn't Xaedrek ever tell you who I am?'

'The daughter of a Gorethrian soldier and a Tearnian woman . . .'

Melkavesh burst out laughing, and controlled herself before the laughs turned to sobs. 'Well, that's true enough.

Oh, typical of Xaedrek! Of course he would not have wanted anyone to know. That Gorethrian soldier, my father, was Ashurek.'

'Prince Ashurek – Meshurek's brother?'

'That's right. Heir to the throne of Gorethria, as I am now the rightful heir.'

She let this news sink in. Part of her did not care how he reacted, but part of her was desperate for approval. He took a breath, folded his arms, and said sharply, 'I should demand proof, but somehow I do not need to. After all you've done, do you think you can simply walk into Shalekahh and declare yourself Empress? They will never accept you.'

'Oh, yes, they will! They'll have no choice!' She saw no contempt in Baramek's face, nor any doubt that she had the strength and other qualities to achieve her ambition.

'Would you force yourself on us?' he said.

She swallowed and softened her voice. 'Gorethria must have a strong ruler. I am the only one who can do it, and keep peace in Vardrav. Baramek, let me confide in you; I can't bear this feeling of belonging nowhere. Ashurek said that this was all I ever wanted, to take the throne. I've denied it all along, but he was right – my blood is stronger than I am. When I first saw the palace, my only thought was, "That is my family home – my birthright." The first time Xaedrek took me in the Hall of Portraits I knew it from a hundred dreams. The eyes in the paintings were alive, my ancestors' eyes following me, compelling me to serve Gorethria as they had done. It was like a storm bursting in my head and it's still there. I can't refuse them any longer. Do you understand? I have to go back to Shalekahh, it's where I belong.'

Baramek seemed unmoved by this confession. 'And of course you need the backing of a loyal army.'

'Please, Baramek. We always got on well, you and I. You are the most straightforward man I know. I could force you by sorcerous means but I won't. The alternative is for me to leave you here to be massacred by the Kristillians. What use would it be for Gorethria to lose half her army, when by a simple Oath you could all be set free?'

'Will the Kristillians agree to it?'

355

'They will have no choice, either.'

He paced slowly round the cell. She gave him time to think and waited patiently until he halted by the window and turned to look at her. 'I also have a confession to make, my lady. I have an inbuilt hatred of the supernatural. I tolerated Xaedrek's methods while I believed they were more scientific than anything, but the discovery that there was a demon behind it all the time was more than I could stomach. I – I could not have gone on serving him after that.'

'I thought not,' she said quietly.

'I am a traditionalist. Furthermore, though it is unfashionable to admit this, I respected Ashurek. He was a good man and the finest of soldiers, until demonic evil destroyed him. I served under him when I first entered the army.'

'You did?'

'He would have made a fine Emperor. I see the same qualities in you, Lady Melkavesh. I'm less than happy about the power you have, as I am about your part in the war,' he said heavily, 'but no situation is ever perfect. I believe there is nothing corrupt about your power. I know you hold the power of life or death over Gorethria . . . but I believe you love her as much as I do. And there was Surukish . . .'

'Do you mean that you will give me your Oath?' she asked guardedly.

'I must speak to my officers, of course, but they will not gainsay me,' he said. Then, quite matter of factly and without any trace of subservience, he fell to one knee and bowed to her, pressing his lips to her hand. She was taken aback. The moment seemed to last for ever in her mind, golden-dark, while she could not put a name to the emotions that twisted through her. She could not weep or make any sound at all.

'From henceforth I will serve you as my Empress,' said Baramek. 'But I warn you, even with the army's support, you face a hard struggle in Shalekahh.'

When Melkavesh returned to Heldavrain, she found the gates and portcullis locked against her. The locks and chains yielded like butter to her power, but it put her in a furious mood. How pathetic of them to try to keep her out of her own domain. She stormed past the guards and other folk in the courtyard, lashed by the looks of fear and suspicion they gave her, they who had once been her friends. Speaking to no one, she went straight to her office and slammed the door, cursing.

'Wherever did you learn such language?' said a voice, making her jump. Kharan was sitting behind her desk, a shadow in the violet-blue dusk filling the room. 'I've been waiting for you for ages. What's wrong?'

'They tried to lock me out. Idiots.'

'I didn't know.' Kharan sounded nervous, not herself.

'It doesn't matter.' Melkavesh threw her cloak across the desk and pulled off her gloves. 'But the sooner the King goes back to Charhn, the better. I'm glad you're here, Kharan. At least there is one person in this place who hasn't turned against me.'

'Er – yes,' Kharan muttered. Melkavesh could hardly see her face, only the anxious white gleam of her eyes.

'Would you like some wine?' She filled two goblets and balanced them in one hand as she dragged a chair from the corner and sat down at Kharan's side. 'Gods, I'm exhausted.'

'I've obviously picked a bad time . . .'

'What are you talking about? I said I was pleased to see you. I'm not angry with *you*, Kharan.'

'Oh – good. I – well, er, where have you been today?'

'You've been sitting here waiting to ask me where I've been?' Melkavesh said, frowning. 'If there's something wrong, I wish you'd just say it. You've never been afraid to speak your mind to me before.'

Kharan sat forward, staring into her wine. 'It's rather difficult. I've got something to tell you, and I don't know how you'll react. Falmeryn wanted to come with me, but I thought it was better if I told on my own.'

'Told me what? You will make me angry if you don't explain.'

'We're leaving, Mel,' she said softly. 'Filmoriel, Falmeryn and I. We're going back to Forluin.'

Melkavesh did not answer at once. She took a mouthful

357

of wine and reached forward slowly to put the goblet down on the desk. 'Oh, no. Not you as well.'

'Falmeryn's always wanted to go back, and there's nothing to stop us now. It's peaceful there. Filmoriel can be brought up in peace, instead of with all this –'

'Gods, I might have known this would come. Everyone else has turned against me – my fault, I know, but do you think that makes it any less painful? And now you – you turn round and tell me you're leaving? You can't, Kharan. I need you!'

'No, you don't. You'll miss me for a time, perhaps, but that will pass. I'll miss you as well. But you certainly don't need me.' Melkavesh's shoulders were taut, her eyes cold. Kharan put a hand on her arm. 'Please don't be upset about it. I haven't turned against you, I've given up trying to judge right from wrong. But I just can't see any end to all this madness. Enough is enough, and I've got to protect my child.'

'No, Kharan.'

'I'm sorry, Mel. I didn't know you'd take it so badly. I thought you'd understand.'

'I'm not taking it badly.' She looked round, and Kharan flinched at the cold metal shine of her eyes. 'I do understand. You can go whenever you please – but you are not taking Filmoriel.'

Kharan's goblet slid through her fingers and smashed on the floor. 'What did you say?'

'I said, you are not taking Filmoriel. Go if you like, she stays here.'

Kharan was on her feet, her face wild. 'How the hell can you –'

'Listen to me. I know it sounds hard but I cannot let her go. She is a latent Sorceress.'

'So you keep saying!'

'I have to keep her with me to teach her! When the power begins to manifest itself, she could be a terrible danger to herself and others if she is not taught how to control and use it. It's for her sake, not mine.'

'I don't care. I'm not leaving without her.'

'Then stay.'

'As your prisoners! That's what it would be! You've got no right to do this. She's my daughter.'

'Who, if not for me, would not even be alive.'

'I know – I know – but that does not mean you own her! How do you know she's a Sorceress? I've only got your word for it!'

Melkavesh stood up. In the gloom she seemed angular, threatening, with no softness about her at all. 'If she was not a Sorceress, she would not have lived. I could not stop you from miscarrying – I was only trying to heal you – but it was as if a spark leapt from her mind to mine, telling me what she was and crying for help. That's why I nearly killed myself to keep her alive, and that's why I can't let her go now.'

'I don't believe it,' Kharan whispered. Her face was white, her eyes glittering. 'You heartless bastard. You're telling me that you only saved her because she was a latent Sorceress – that if she had been an ordinary child, you would have let her die?'

'I'm saying –'

'I don't want to hear any more of this. Ye gods! I trusted you after she was born – I loved you, I thought you were my friend. We sat and hugged each other and cried tears of joy over her. Now I feel as if I want to cry and I can't. I've watched you doing all these terrible things and all the time I've thought you can't be bad, you can't be like Xaedrek, because you saved Filmoriel. But I was wrong. You were using her!'

'That's not true! Kharan, can't you understand, she's the Earth's very future –'

'She's just a baby! From the very second she was born, all everyone's done is try to use her and it's going to go on and on unless I take her away so she can have a proper childhood and know what it is to be loved, not used. Why don't you just go back to Shalekahh where you belong? Leave us alone!'

She ran to the door, but Melkavesh followed her and seized her arm. The loathing in Kharan's eyes stunned her, and roused her to bitter anger. 'Where are you going?'

359

'Away from you. To think I felt sorry for you when Xaedrek died! We're taking Filmoriel to Forluin and you had better not try to stop us.'

'And you had better not try to take her,' said Melkavesh. 'I have my far-sight again, and I can watch every move you make. If you or Falmeryn try to take her out of the castle I will know at once, and be assured – I will stop you. Now get out of here, Kharan. Just get out.'

Kharan fled, but the image hung dimly behind Melkavesh's eyes of her running along corridors, finding Falmeryn, pouring out the wretched story in his arms. Sickened, Melkavesh tried to detach herself and think of them only as shadow puppets. She felt – she felt almost nothing, she discovered. She left her room and climbed flights of stairs until she came out onto the battlements, and there she felt the warm night breeze blowing straight through her as if there were nothing left to stop it.

They would not try to leave at once, she was sure. She leaned on the edge of the battlements and stared at Jaed, hanging low over the sea. They would wait until they thought she was off her guard – if they dared to try at all. She could not lose Filmoriel now.

The sea was calmer this evening. The Earth seemed to be settling into its new state and the electric tension had faded from the sky. Yet there was still something strange; there seemed to be a third ghost-moon glowing azure against the darkness and increasing in size as it spun slowly towards her . . .

She watched it in alarm. Instinctively she had extended her higher senses to perceive its nature, and her vision of Kharan and Falmeryn was blotted out by a powerful image of two figures in another dimension, two figures so vast that they overshadowed the Earth itself. They were struggling against each other, and the echo of their voices made Melkavesh stagger backwards, futilely blocking her ears.

'You must let me through to Earth,' said a ringing, female voice. 'The Guardians have broken all laws in preventing me. Stand aside, Ferdanice, and let me pass.'

'Oh, I will let you through now, my Lady.' The second

speaker sounded amused. 'The change has been effected. You are too late to prevent it, so there's no more reason for me to detain you.'

The image vanished, but the sphere was still drifting purposefully towards Melkavesh. It was like a cloud of frosty blue stars, no more than ten feet across. As it crossed the battlements it began to spin on the spot like weightless gossamer, and from it stepped a woman of ethereal beauty.

Melkavesh had never seen her before, but she knew at once that this was the Lady of H'tebhmella herself, the sphere an Entrance Point to the Blue Plane. The sapphire glow that shone from the Lady's pale robe and hands was like no light ever seen on Earth, and the other-worldliness of it made Melkavesh catch her breath. Nothing she had heard of H'tebhmella could ever have prepared her for the electrifying reality of the Lady's presence, the sweetness and strength that flowed from her like a song.

'Mellorn,' the Lady said. How she knew her real name – or knew her at all – seemed unimportant. 'Mellorn, daughter of Silvren, I have been seeking a way to reach you for countless days. Would that I could say we were well met.'

'My Lady.' Melkavesh was not accustomed to bowing to anyone, yet before the H'tebhmellian she could not help herself. 'I am honoured – but what do you want of me?'

'Oh, Mellorn, Mellorn. Do you not know? I sought you to give you a warning, but the Guardians blocked every Entrance Point I made.'

'Why would they do that?'

'Their power is greater than ours – and certain of them were willing to misuse it for their own ends. Now I am too late. I come not to warn you but to tell you what you have done.'

Melkavesh suddenly felt as if the blue light were freezing her. 'What do you mean?' she asked guardedly. It was not easy to confront the Lady as an equal; her face was like an angel's, her rain-grey eyes filled with a stern sadness that could devastate a mortal. Not easy, but Melkavesh steeled herself to it.

'You shifted the moons in their orbits,' the Lady said.

361

'Yes. Surely you know the reason?'

'Your concern was only for the power of sorcery. The Guardians' concern, as always, was that certain energies should be brought into balance. But none of you considered the other disruptions that your action might cause. You did not know. The Grey Ones knew, but they did not care.'

'My Lady, I was not unaware that there might be side effects, but whatever they are, the advantages outweigh them.' Melkavesh tried to sound self-assured, but her mouth had gone dry.

'I do not think you understand the delicate relationship between the moons, the Earth and the three Planes, Hrunnesh, Hrannekh Ol and H'tebhmella.'

'Does anyone?'

'Not fully. Not even I. The Planes are in other dimensions, but the balance between them and Earth is essential and fragile, and without it – I cannot say what will befall any of us.'

'Do you mean that by moving the moons I have destroyed that balance?'

'Yes, Mellorn. It is not gone yet, but over the coming days it will slowly erode until the links between Earth and the Planes are severed for ever.'

'Does it matter?' Melkavesh asked through the sour aching of her throat.

'Yes. It matters. Perhaps Earth will not suffer from loss of contact with the White and Black Planes; or she may suffer in subtle ways that I cannot foresee. But think of the Blue Plane H'tebhmella, where tranquillity and beauty and healing energies are distilled. Our influence over the Earth has been greater than you can imagine. It was greatest in Forluin, clearly visible in the beauty and peace of that land. But without us, not only Forluin will suffer. The whole world will grow darker and crueller, and the power of sorcery itself will be used more for evil than for good.'

'No,' said Melkavesh. 'No, I can't accept this! The Guardians obviously don't agree with you, or why did they take such pains to stop you from warning me and to bring me the moon stone?'

'Because nothing matters to them except the balance. The power has been aligned, the world is free to evolve into one permeated by sorcery. They do not care if the Earth loses H'tebhmella's healing influence. They might welcome it. There has often been conflict between us.'

'I should have known . . .' Melkavesh said, half to herself. 'Why wasn't this revealed to me by my own far-sight?'

'The Planes are outside sorcery. It is a young power, but the Planes are as old as the Earth itself. You will find many things in this Earth that are outside your power. Never imagine that you know everything.'

'I don't. But even if I had known, I would still have done the same. My Lady, it had to happen, whatever the consequences! The moons were calling me from the beginning. Everything that has happened has been inevitable.'

At that, the Lady seemed to diminish. Her wide-spaced, shining eyes were filling Melkavesh with an indefinable but ghastly anxiety. 'Perhaps,' she said. 'I have done all I could. Earth loses us, but she may find contact with other Planes or dimensions of which even the Grey Ones know nothing. Whether this will be good or bad, I do not know.' She stepped forward and pressed her fingers to Melkavesh's forehead. The touch was so sweet that she wanted to cry out in happiness and pain, beg the Lady to tell her how the link with H'tebhmella could be saved. But she could not.

The Lady lowered her hand and said, 'I grieve for you, Mellorn. How could you set yourself upon this path, after all that Ashurek and Silvren suffered? The Guardians have chosen well in you, for I think there is no gentleness or pity in you at all.'

'I'm sorry you think that,' she said tightly. 'I have a job to do in which such feelings are only a hindrance.'

'You are wrong, but it's beyond my power to make you see it. I shall leave you now, Mellorn, and I shall not see you again. I hope you understand, within a few days, no H'tebhmellian will ever again be able to set foot on Earth, nor anyone be able to find an Entrance Point to H'tebhmella. Pity Forluin, at least. You have driven us from the circles of the world.'

The Lady drew back into the cloud of stars, faded to a silhouette, and vanished. The Entrance Point floated on and dwindled into the darkness. All the time a voice was screaming inside Melkavesh's head, *Don't go, please don't leave us, oh, show me a way to put this right* – but she felt like a creature of steel, one of Xaedrek's machines, with no way to express her despair.

She turned towards the little tower enclosing the top of the stairs, and there she saw Falmeryn, leaning against the doorway, staring at her with a kind of bewildered horror.

She made to push past him, but he caught her arm. 'What did the Lady mean, "pity Forluin"? Melkavesh, what in heaven's name have you done?'

'You heard.' She felt a cruel, Gorethrian smile curving her lips. 'You may as well give up all ideas of returning home. It sounds as if there's nothing to go back to. Will you let go of my arm?'

He did so. She brushed him aside, but his voice followed her down the stairwell. 'This is what the Kesfalians were afraid of, isn't it? This is the disaster you've caused, nothing cataclysmic, just an insidious corruption of everything that was good. Who needs demons, Melkavesh, when we've got you?'

The Lady had told Melkavesh less than she might have done. In Forluin, they knew the worst.

The vitreous shimmer of the sky – caused by the reverberation of the Lady's conflict with Ferdanice – persisted for so long that it no longer seemed remarkable. Only when the conflict ended and the sky returned to normal, did the Forluinish notice the change. It should have been welcome, but the poignant softness of the air only seemed to presage something more ominous.

It was close on seven years since Falmeryn had gone missing. Arlena rarely spoke of him now, and when she did it was with tender sadness rather than anguish. Falin was grateful for that, and for the happiness they still found in Forluin and in each other. Life went on, and life was normal.

Until an evening when without warning the moons rose

not as shining pearls, but like soft-hued, unrecognisable planets. The Forluinish gazed on them in wonderment, too astonished even to think of being afraid. Foreboding came stealthily, in the hours that followed.

It was the next afternoon when Estarinel came to Falin's and Arlena's cottage and said, 'There is an H'tebhmellian here. It's Filitha. Do you remember her?'

'Of course,' Falin said. 'We couldn't forget, could we?'

It was Filitha who had first come to Forluin to comfort them after the Serpent's attack. The H'tebhmellians did not come to Earth without dire cause.

'Where is she?' Arlena said anxiously. 'Why is she here?'

'She's waiting in Sinmiel's Grove. She can't stay long, and I must gather as many folk as I can to hear what she has to say. I don't know what it is yet.' He put an arm round his sister's waist. 'But it is nothing bad, Arlena, I'm sure. Don't worry.'

The grove in the late sunlight seemed jewelled, all rich melting shades of green and gold and red. Deer moved softly through the trees. Some twenty Forluinish men and women had gathered there, and in the centre – glowing with a cool blue light that was not of Earth – stood Filitha. Even among the Forluinish she was exquisitely beautiful. Her hair was dark, her eyes sapphire flames.

'All through the time of the Serpent, H'tebhmella watched over Forluin,' she said. 'We watch over you still. You have witnessed a change that is as momentous as the coming of the Serpent, in its way. The Lady did her utmost to prevent it, but she could not prevail against the will of the Guardians.'

'The Guardians again!' Estarinel exclaimed in disgust. 'You hardly need to say any more, Filitha. The shifting of the moons is something to do with their sacred "balance", isn't it?'

'It is so,' she replied, and explained what Melkavesh had done. 'The Blue Plane's strength is a passive one, alien to the power of sorcery. Perhaps the two cannot co-exist. This is the hardest thing I have ever had to say; in a few days' time, the links between Earth and the three Planes will be severed.'

They took this in with quiet horror. Estarinel was the first to voice their thoughts. 'You mean that the whole world will lose H'tebhmella's influence?'

'Yes.' Her eyes mirrored their pain. 'And without it, life can only become more grim.'

'And Forluin will become no different from the rest of the world?' The question hung in a chasm that seemed to reverberate with their thoughts. Forluin's safety was so fragile; without the Blue Plane's protection they would be vulnerable to invasion; or worse, the change might be within themselves, a slow erosion of the love that held them together, until they destroyed themselves.

Falin said, 'It sounds as if we are going to lose everything we gained when the Serpent was defeated. Was it all for nothing?'

'No,' she said gently. 'Such sacrifice is never for nothing. I have more to tell you, and I do not know what your reaction will be. Because Forluin is different, because she is linked so closely to the Blue Plane, she cannot easily be severed from us. When H'tebhmella is cut off from Earth, Forluin will be torn away with us. She will not become part of our Plane. Rather, she will hang in a different dimension, still under our influence, still part of the Earth – but separate from both.'

At this, there were exclamations of guarded relief, but Filitha's eyes were still grave. 'It is not necessarily more desirable. No choice can be given you. In effect, we will be taking Forluin against her will. I can best explain it by saying that things may seem no different, but you will be an island in an infinite ocean. If you leave, you could sail for ever and never reach any other part of Earth, and no ship sailing here will ever find you. Forluin will remain peaceful; no harm will come to you. But divorced from Earth, who can say what less visible damage may result? I am sorry, truly sorry.'

They were solaced, alarmed, bewildered; everyone began questioning her at once, but Arlena turned and made her way shakily out of the grove. Her face was colourless.

'Arlena?' Falin said, following her. 'Beloved, there's no cause for despair.'

'Isn't there? What about Falmeryn?' The old anguish was back in her eyes, and it tormented him. 'I've tried to stop hoping he's alive, but I can't. Now – even if he is – this means he'll never, ever come home to us. How do you think he'll feel, when he can't find Forluin? And he won't even know why.' Tears matted her eyelashes. Falin gathered her to him, but he could find no words of comfort, even to say, *He is gone, we must accept it,* would be a cruelty. They had never overcome the pain, only suppressed it, and even under H'tebhmella's sweet shadow he did not know how they could face a lifetime of not knowing.

The King and Queen were leaving the castle at last, along with most of their Vardravian allies. There was a sullen acceptance that Melkavesh would not be ousted from Heldavrain before she was ready, and that there was no point in trying.

Now only the Mangorians were left. They were the first supporters she had found, and now the only ones who had not deserted her. Their devotion to her was almost religious, and she sensed that even her becoming Empress would make no difference. Still, she thought bitterly, they could worship the Serpent, so why not me?

'We wanted to be free of Gorethria in order to practise our religion,' N'golem told her. 'Now we are free, but you have subverted our religion by proving that the Serpent is dead. My people must have something in its place. We must have sorcery, and we must have you.'

The thought of a Mangorian Sorcerer made her shudder, but she replied quietly, 'I'm grateful for your loyalty, N'golem. It will be good to have you with me.'

The Mangorian raised his slanted eyebrows in surprise. 'Oh, no, my lady, we cannot stay. My people are unhappy in this dry land. I must take them back to the jungle, where we can spread word of you, and I also have certain unfinished business with my father. We shall stay only until the Kristillians have left Heldavrain.'

That blow, however, was as nothing compared to her last meeting with Es Thendil. She had kept nothing from him; she had related what the Lady of H'tebhmella had said, even her meeting with Baramek. She noticed his hands shaking as she spoke to him, alone in her office, but his uncertain air had gone and there was a resolute set to his shoulders.

'You mean to release Baramek and all the prisoners?' His manner was almost painfully formal.

'Your Majesty, the whole point of my getting him to make the Oath of Loyalty was so that I can ensure they pose no more danger to Kristillia,' she said.

'You are playing a dangerous game, my lady. I would stop you if I could. But I will not plead with you.'

'Oh, Es Thendil, I wish I could make you understand! To have wiped our Gorethria would have been as great a crime as theirs against Vardrav. The only way to control them, to keep peace, is for me to go back and rule them.'

'If they'll have you.'

'I'm doing the best I can for everyone. I haven't turned against Kristillia. I am still your friend, Es Thendil, and I wish you were still mine.'

He clenched and unclenched his hands on the desk, and a tremor shook him. 'What have we done to you, Melkavesh, that you have betrayed us like this? I trusted you! We did not ask you to help us – you came to us, offering miracles and begging us to believe in them. You won the war for us – so why, why afterwards did you turn into the arms of our enemy? Xaedrek, of all people! How could you?'

She felt the blood draining out of her face, pooling like lead in her stomach. This meeting was torment. She could not bear the grief in his eyes, his agony at being betrayed, and would have done anything to heal it. She was a Sorceress, she could do anything – except restore his trust.

She said quietly, 'I may have acted wrongly. But before you condemn me, ask yourself how much thought you gave to An Mora when you met Kharan.'

He seemed to flinch. 'It's no excuse.'

'No. No excuse.'

'It doesn't matter to me, Melkavesh, whether you blame it on love or perversity, the outcome is the same. You are

Gorethrian at heart, and all Gorethrian Emperors are the same. There can never be friendship or trust between us, and I will believe in peace when I see it.'

'There will be peace. If you don't believe me, be patient and let me prove myself.'

'Oh, I pray that it will be so. But it is not only Gorethria. What you have done to our moons is beyond me, beyond even our priests to understand.' He stood up, giving her a cold look that she had never seen in his eyes before. 'You can do whatever you like now, because you are the only Sorceress. But you've said yourself there will be others. When there are, you had best beware.'

'They will not know how to use the power until I teach them,' she said sharply.

'And how will you make a School of Sorcery, Empress of Gorethria, while you are occupied in Shalekahh? Even you can't be in two places at once. I wonder if you really know what you have started.' His sorrow and his quiet dignity distressed her beyond words. She could say nothing that would touch him, bring him back. 'Goodbye, my lady. I doubt that we shall meet again.'

'I'm sorry it's come to this.' Her voice was almost a whisper, a thread of ice. 'I'm doing what I believe to be right. I wish it could be otherwise. I'm sorry, Es Thendil.' But he had gone, and did not hear her.

And now the courtyard and bridge were thronging with soldiers and horses, and all the people who had formed her household were leaving with them. Melkavesh watched them through a window. She had not meant to watch, but having glanced once she found herself leaning on the deep stone sill as if magnetised there. A few Mangorians stood sullenly around the edges of the courtyard. The Vardravians ignored them. She saw Irem Ol Melemen walking under the portcullis with Cristan, the King kissing Afil An Mora on the cheek as he helped her to mount her horse. Melkavesh felt the bitter disappointment in her heart solidifying into contempt, Gorethrian contempt, because it was her only defence.

'I cannot afford to care,' she said to herself. 'Ashurek told me that I was pitiless at heart, and I suppose he was right.

369

But what is the point in being otherwise, when it can only destroy you?'

The royal party were moving off now. She saw Thaufa En Mianna and her daughter En Faliol coming out of a side door, wrapped in travelling clothes, and somehow that was infinitely worse than seeing Es Thendil leave. I can bear no more of this, she thought – and as she thought it, there was a strange, dark fluttering in the back of her mind, like something calling to her. She straightened up in surprise.

Far-sight now came easily to her, and was an almost unconscious attunement to anything that might affect her. Falmeryn, Kharan and Filmoriel were still inside the castle; this signal was nothing to do with them. It was something dark, like a night wind washing along a beach. She closed her eyes, discovered its source, but not the reason for it. She blinked, bewildered. Then she turned and ran into her room and was pulling on gloves and boots, desperately grateful for a reason to forget the Kristillians and to miss the rest of their wretched departure.

Minutes later she was outside Heldavrain, conjuring the golden Spectre of a horse which would bear her along the beach to the estuary. She was wrapped in two cloaks; one of green velvet, and one of invisibility. No one had seen her pass.

The call drew her for many miles, across the river mouth itself, where the horse skimmed like ball lightning across the water. Beyond, she followed the beach under the shadow of overhanging cliffs until she saw a small Gorethrian vessel at anchor, all ebony and scarlet elegance, dipping on the water like a black swan. It was evening. A few miles north were the mountains separating Omnuandria from Cevandaris.

She let the horse fade, let herself become visible, and deliberately crunched her boots in the pebbles as she walked towards the cliffs. She felt casual, immune to harm. When three Gorethrian warriors stepped out from the lee of the cliff with swords drawn, she felt no surprise at all.

'Who goes there?' shouted one.

She continued to walk towards them, smiling. 'Do you not

370

recognise me? Please, sheathe your blades. There is someone here who wants to see me.'

Out of the shadow stepped a fourth figure, and that was no surprise, either. She was shrunken with age, her dark head crowned with a milky wisp of hair, and she was wrapped in a grey cloak. Her bearing was all arrogance, but her face was aghast.

'My greetings, Lady Lirurmish.' Melkavesh gave the formal nod of an equal. 'Are you in mourning?'

'You should know for whom!' Lirurmish snapped. She waved a hand at the ship. 'We were coming to your castle. I – I cannot imagine how you knew, or how you managed to find us, Lady Melkavesh, but I confess myself amazed.'

Her tone was stiff, indignant. Melkavesh had never liked her. She replied pleasantly, 'I am glad to have saved you a journey. But you surely cannot have come from Shalekahh. There hasn't been time for the news of Xaedrek's death to reach them yet.'

'They'll know soon enough. I was in Cevandaris before the battle and Omnuandria after, near enough for the news to reach me.'

'Then why did you want to see me, Lady Lirurmish?' Melkavesh softened her tone. There were bound to be questions over Xaedrek's death; perhaps this was the beginning of it, and there was no point in antagonising a powerful Inner Councillor.

'You mean you don't know?'

'No, my lady. I received a strong impression that you were here, and that it was me you sought. As to your reasons, I can only guess.'

'Indeed. Your miraculous talent did not extend to reading the inside of a scroll?'

Now it was Melkavesh's turn to be puzzled. 'No, Lady Lirurmish. Please explain.'

The Councillor withdrew a hand from the folds of her cloak, and in it she held a roll of parchment, like a luminous bone in the dusk. She unrolled it but held onto it, so Melkavesh was forced to read it over her shoulder.

'It's Xaedrek's will,' said Lirurmish. 'Just before the battle he made a will, leaving one copy in Shalekahh and one with me for safe-keeping. He has named you his heir.'

Silence. Twilight drawing the world into a circle of cliffs round her. Time measured by heartbeats and a soft, indrawn breath that went on for ever.

'. . . in the event of my death that the Imperial Throne and Crown should revert to its rightful heir, Princess Melka-vesh of the House of Ordek in Shalekahh, daughter of Ashurek, son of the Emperor Ordek XIV, on condition that she forswears all other loyalties except that which she owes to Gorethria . . .'

Melkavesh swallowed hard. 'He wrote this *before* the battle?' she said incredulously. 'Before –' She almost said, *Before we were reconciled.*

'Yes, Your Highness. Valamek and I witnessed it. We were as amazed as you are, but it was not for us to question Xaedrek's intentions.'

'I can't understand it. We were mortal enemies.'

'Then give yourself time to think on it, Your Highness, as I have,' Lirurmish said, not altogether pleasantly. 'Perhaps he knew you better than you know yourself. He obviously thought there was no one better fitted to rule after him, and as you appear to be the legal heir anyway, it will at least save the years of wrangling that preceded his reign. Or perhaps he simply did not expect to die.'

'This means that I will be accepted in Shalekahh? That I won't have to contest my claim to the throne?'

'As long as you can meet the conditions of loyalty.'

'Yes,' Melkavesh said softly. 'Oh, yes, the Kristillians and I have already broken with each other. That condition I can meet.'

'I am glad to hear it. I cannot say that things will be easy for you. But the law is the law. When the news reaches Shalekahh, they will be waiting for you.'

With a rather more grudging respect than Baramek had shown her, Lirurmish and the three soldiers knelt and bowed to her. Melkavesh had to help the Councillor to her feet afterwards.

'I am grateful to you for telling me,' she said, then realised it was not the right thing to say. Emperors were not required to be grateful to their minions. She had a lot to learn.

'Your Highness, may I suggest you come back with us now? Surely there's no need for you to return to the castle?'

Filmoriel. Even as she thought it, other shadows began to move in her mind, and alarm shivered through her. She had been too concerned with Lirurmish.

'No, I must go back to Heldavrain. Lirurmish, is that your ship?'

'Not as such, Your Highness. We were going to sail to the castle in it, but the Kristillians make it impossible for us to return to Gorethria along the Omnuandrix.'

'Well, if you're going to Shalekahh overland, you won't object if I take the ship.'

'All Gorethrian vessels are yours to command,' said Lirurmish acerbically. 'But there is no crew.'

'I don't need one. Lady Lirurmish, I will bid you farewell now, but I'll see you again in Shalekahh. Tell them to prepare for an Imperial funeral – and a coronation.'

By the time she splashed through the waves to the ship, found a rope and climbed on deck, her alarm had turned to cold rage. Falmeryn and Kharan had left Heldavrain some time during the afternoon – with the child, of course – and were travelling directly east towards An'raaga under the protection of the Kristillians. Had they known her attention was elsewhere, or had they just taken a risk? She suspected the latter. With a lash of power that burned through the anchor rope, she ran up to the prow and willed the ship out into the waves. The energy seemed to be flooding in through her heart, like red-gold blood, seeping down through the planks to fire the vessel with unnatural power. Moments later, the sails still furled, *Karvish's Hawk* was arrowing towards Heldavrain.

Half-way across, her sense of urgency abated and she let the ship slow down. She needed to sleep. It did not matter how far they got, she would still catch them up, because she could swift-travel and they could not. The morning would be time enough to pursue them. Until then, let them bask in the illusion that escape was possible.

373

She lay down on the planks, but sleep would not come. Fliya was shining into her eyes, and the stars seemed to be pricking her like diamond needles. There was a bird following the ship. Every time she came near sleep, the sudden whirr of its wings would jerk her back to wakefulness.

It was just like the dream she used to have – the ocean, the ship and the bird – only the ocean was not pearl-green and the ship was blacker than the night, and the bird was not –

'Miril?' She sat up violently, her heart pounding.

'I am here,' came the answer, the answer she had both longed for and dreaded. 'I was here all the time, Mellorn, waiting, waiting for you to see me.'

The voice, not human but melodic as a thrush's, came from somewhere above her. She looked up, saw the bird silhouetted on the rail. Then Miril spread her wings and fluttered down onto Melkavesh's knee. She had no colour in the moonlight, which burnished her feathers to a gold so pale it was almost silver.

'Miril – I don't – why have you come to me?'

'You had need of me.'

'I don't need anyone, Miril, and I particularly don't need a lecture from you. Leave me, please.'

'I cannot leave you, Mellorn. You brought me back to the Earth.'

'I?' She tried to push some moisture past the dry ache in her throat. 'But I thought Filmoriel –'

'I came back through Filmoriel. But I came back for you, Mellorn, Ashurek's daughter.'

'Ashurek could hardly speak of you without weeping. You made him hate Gorethria, Miril. You made him hate himself. Is that what you want to do to me?'

The bird put her head on one side. Melkavesh was trying to avoid looking into her eyes, her depthless black eyes in which truth hung suspended like sunlight in dew, but she could not help herself. She looked, and felt that a vein deep inside her had ruptured and was spilling her soul like black blood onto the deck.

'I want nothing of you, nothing,' the bird sang. 'Take from me what you need. Whatever Ashurek told you of me, he

374

did not teach you my true name. He could not, for you can only discover it for yourself. I am not hatred, Mellorn. You know this. Look at me, look at me.'

'I'm looking,' she groaned. *I'm looking and I'm bleeding.* 'Don't do this to me, Miril. I can't afford pity, I need to be strong.'

'You think that lack of compassion is strength?'

'I don't know. It's all I've got.'

A core of iron in you, Mellorn . . .

'Oh, Mellorn, will you ever know me?'

She fell back onto the deck, striking her head. The bird was on her chest now, her eyes, as beautiful as night, dark mirrors that spared her nothing. Her eyes were the sky. Melkavesh had lost, Miril had won.

. . . And in her eyes, guilt. The blood and pain and utter wrong of Gorethria's atrocities . . . and a child crying in hunger because its parents had died in battle, and that battle had not made the conqueror glorious, but less than the rat scuffling in the straw at the child's feet . . .

It was what Ashurek had seen and it had turned his love for Gorethria into loathing. She let the dark core of her self bleed out into the ocean, and in its place she drank in the truth.

Gorethria is beyond redemption. Father, Father . . .

And it was nothing she did not already know.

'Miril,' she said. She sat up with a huge breath as if she had just broken the surface of the sea. 'Miril.'

I want to cry and I can't.

'Yes, I am here.' The bird was on her knee again, fluffed up and blinking like a fledgling. She was softness, love, hope, a shining creature that seemed too fragile to survive the harshness of Earth. 'For as long as you need me, I am here . . .'

'It's no good. I do know you, Miril, and it makes no difference. I know what I am and what I should be. I still have to follow the same path. You're only making it harder.' Melkavesh hugged herself as she spoke, as if trying to keep the words in. But they spilled out of her like dust, and a terrible bleakness was wrenching her heart into pieces.

'And this I know as well,' the bird cheeped softly. 'Alas, Mellorn, I was mistaken. You need nothing from me, and yet, and yet you have taken everything.'

'No! No, Miril, don't go –'

She drooped one wing as if it were broken, fluttered and fell to the deck. But when Melkavesh bent frantically to pick her up, there was nothing there.

She tried far-sight, she tried everything; dawn bleached out the stars, and she had not slept at all. Miril was beyond the reach of sorcery – or Miril had ceased to exist, and Melkavesh had destroyed her.

Near Heldavrain, she grounded the ship on the sand and continued her pursuit on the spectral horse. She rode with grim speed, not really hurrying, but inexorably gaining on Kharan. Sometimes it seemed she was observing the scene from a great distance; a group of people as tiny as flies toiling desperately to escape; and herself like a dreadful airborne creature gliding after them, each heavy wingbeat propelling her nearer to them until their whole sky turned black.

She caught up with them on a fellside crowned with trees, but she did not let herself be seen at once. Instead she circled ahead of them, let the horse fade, and waited on foot. Presently they came into the trees and, as she had guessed they would, dismounted to rest their horses and eat.

There were ten Kristillian soldiers with Kharan and Falmeryn, the King's own men. An army would not have protected them. Filmoriel was curled up in Falmeryn's arms, sleepy, not really understanding why they had had to leave the castle which was the only home she could remember. Melkavesh waited until they had finished eating and were least on their guard, and then she stepped from the trees and let them see her.

Their faces, oh, their faces. Filmoriel woke up and started to cry. The soldiers formed a protective circle round them and made to draw their swords, but Kharan stepped between them and said, 'It's all right. Let me talk to her.'

'Kharan, don't,' Falmeryn exclaimed.

376

'She won't harm me. Stay with Filmoriel.'

She came forward to meet Melkavesh, her face very white against her rust-red cloak.

'Hello, Kharan,' Melkavesh said quietly. 'You knew I'd find you.'

'Oh, yes, we knew.' Her mouth was a bloodless line and she was trembling with exhaustion and fear. They were all afraid – terrified, Melkavesh realised with a shock. She had never meant to inspire such dread, such hatred. When she had confronted Kharan before, it had only antagonised her, but now it was as if Miril had removed a layer of skin and left her defenceless. Fear rolled off them like a hot wind and stung her newly flayed soul to agony.

'Then why did you try to escape?'

'Escape,' Kharan said with a short laugh. 'First there was Xaedrek, and now there's you. I still foolishly believed you'd spoken in the heat of the moment, and couldn't really be that inhuman.'

'I meant what I said. Filmoriel will find life hard without a teacher and guide.'

'I know we can't stop you taking her. If you do, you take us all prisoner. I'll never forgive you, Melkavesh. If you care – if our friendship ever meant anything to you at all – I hope you can live with that.'

Dignity again. They were all so collected, these people she was destroying, while Melkavesh felt the pieces of herself fraying out on the wind of their despair.

'No, Kharan, I can't.'

'Well, how unfortunate, because you'll have to – unless you mean to follow Xaedrek's tradition and kill us.'

Melkavesh looked at Filmoriel. The child gazed back with eyes just like Falmeryn's – just like the Lady of H'tebhmella's, through an amethyst lens. It seemed there was a being behind those eyes who knew more by instinct than Melkavesh did by training. It's so hard to let you go, my love, my Sorceress.

'Oh, Kharan,' Melkavesh said. 'Kharan, I can't take her from you. Go to Forluin, if it's what you want. I won't try to stop you.'

377

Kharan's face transformed: a flash of pure joy, then a look of guarded hope. 'Do you mean it?'

'Yes. More than that, I'll help you. It will take you for ever across land. I've a ship near Heldavrain. You can take it, sail across the Aludrian Sea and along the Nanuandrix to the open ocean. I have enough power now to propel the ship by sorcery from a distance. I can send you very swiftly to Forluin.'

'Do you believe her?' Falmeryn said. 'How do we know this isn't just a trick to get us back to Heldavrain?'

'I suppose I deserved that. But I give you my word, on my very Oath of Sorcery, that I'm not deceiving you.'

'She doesn't need to trick us, Falmeryn,' Kharan added. 'What happened, Mel? Was I not so wrong about you after all?'

The hatred had gone from her eyes, but Melkavesh knew she would never again see warmth there. She said, 'I don't know. I don't know anything now.'

'Are you all right? You look strange.'

'Yes – yes, I'm all right. Well, shall we go?' But Melkavesh still hesitated, unable to break away from Kharan's eyes. And suddenly, involuntarily, they were hugging each other, a harsh embrace that contained as much pain as love, and Melkavesh was whispering, 'Forgive me, Kharan. I couldn't see what I was doing to you, or to myself. Forgive me.'

She was alone in the castle now, and outside her window the Aludrian Sea moved softly, violet turning to gold, as if nothing had ever happened.

There is not an atom of sentiment in my body, Melkavesh thought. How can I grieve for someone like Xaedrek? A man who loved his friends one moment, destroyed them the next. Who thought his country's right to rule others justified any act of cruelty. And yet. And yet.

Yet her hands were pressed to her face, sliding on a salty glaze of tears, and no power outside or inside her could stem the rough sobs. The waves swallowing her now were waves of grief, and there was no vision of Filmoriel and Miril to shine through them. She wished the moons had fallen after all.

It was so hard to accept that he had simply drowned. Had he seen something at the last moment, Miril's eyes revealing the truth of his nature to him, so that he had drowned himself in despair?

She had let him delude her, of course. He had not really changed; he would have twisted and broken all his fine promises. She knew, oh, she knew.

Or perhaps his feeling that after the moons even Gorethria seemed insignificant was so deep-rooted that it had truly left him no reason to live. She would never know. He would never come back to tell her, nor to say again, *No one else can love us. But we can love each other*.

When the spasm was over, she automatically went to wash her face and pull a comb through her hair. She felt like a hollow figure made of lead. Then she went back to the window, where she had propped a little mirror on the sill.

It showed not her reflection, but a distant scene of the ship *Karvish's Hawk* flying across the wave crests, trailing creamy veins of foam behind her. Sorcery shimmered like pollen dust on her masts. It was hard work to send her power over such distance, but since the moons had taken their new orbit, it was not impossible. She no longer suffered the bone-wrenching pain. Sorcery was natural to her again, a spirited horse that she could turn to any obstacle – yet what had she achieved?

She was absolutely alone.

'We are all alone, Mellorn,' a voice said, causing her nearly to jump out of the lead shell that was her skin. There was a bird on the sill, hardly bigger than a blackbird, a deep reddish amber in colour.

'Miril! Oh, gods, I thought you were dead!'

'Me, dead? Am I not the Hope of the World? Every night I perish, and with every sunrise I am reborn, for as long as there is someone to think of me. Why do you weep, Mellorn?'

'Because of Xaedrek. And because of you.'

'And not for Filmoriel?'

'Her, too. Everything.'

379

Miril was silent, her head cocked on one side. Then she said, 'Where are you going, Mellorn?'

'Back to Gorethria. I am going to be their Empress. You cannot change that.'

'Nor would I wish to. But, Mellorn, what path will your life take from there?'

Melkavesh's eyes were focused on the ship, yet not focused. 'When I became a Sorceress, I took an Oath which was intended to constrain us to using our power only for good. The Oath restricted us so severely that there was almost nothing we could do, except to heal the sick, or farm or teach. But the Oath was everything. I have broken it a thousand times since I came to Earth. On Ikonus now they would make me an outcast, not fit to be called a Sorceress. Can I begin again, remake my Oath, and with it a new one? I swear to you, Miril, that I will do everything in my power to rule Gorethria fairly – and to control them, so that the rest of Vardrav can live without fear. I know it will not be easy. Xaedrek and my father would say impossible.' A deep sigh heaved out of her and she said bleakly, 'Oh, Miril, I do not want this!'

'But it is the path you have chosen.'

'I know, and I would choose it again. I was always destined to become an Empress, and I wanted it, thinking it was something glorious. But you made me understand the truth – that it is a responsibility, a terrible burden. I'm afraid – not for myself, but for the people I may fail. When my ancestors called me, they were calling me to fulfil my responsibility, which is to put right all that Xaedrek and Meshurek and Ashurek did wrong.'

'You are strong enough. Do not think yourself weak because you can weep,' Miril sang gently.

'I don't. I believe in myself. But if things had been different, I would rather have stayed here and made Heldavrain my School of Sorcery.'

'How will the new Sorcerers fare without your help? You are responsible to them, also.'

Melkavesh reached out and stroked Miril's breast with one finger. 'You mean I must do both? I am human, not a god.'

380

'Will you do less than you can?'

'No. Never. Believe me, Miril, if I find time to start the School I will. And I hope that when Filmoriel is old enough to decide for herself, she will come back to me from Forluin.'

There was a strange, sad look in Miril's eye that Melkavesh suddenly began to find very disconcerting. Eventually the bird sang, 'Alas, Mellorn, they may never reach Forluin.'

'What do you mean?'

'Did not the Lady of H'tebhmella tell you? When the Blue Plane is lost to the earth, Forluin will be lost also.'

'No, she did not. You mean, destroyed?'

'No, no harm will befall her. But in another dimension, no ship from Earth will ever reach her.'

Melkavesh closed her eyes and reached out into far-sight, far beyond *Karvish's Hawk*, to the white and green shores of Forluin itself. The island was still there, but there was a fracturing of the atmosphere, as if the sky were splitting into plates and the light of another plane streaming through the cracks. A ring of mist undulated slowly round the coast, while the waves rose like towers and collapsed in walls of foam. A day or two and Forluin would be gone behind a veil of mist and light. *Karvish's Hawk* would never reach her destination.

'Gods, Miril, they don't know. Falmeryn doesn't know. Can't you do anything?'

'There is nothing I can do, Mellorn. If you will send the ship faster, take care, she may be swallowed by the waves.'

Melkavesh stared at the mirror, biting into the tip of her thumb until she felt the flesh break. It was the perfect reason to turn the ship about and bring them back to her. *I could never have got you to Forluin, it would have been too dangerous to try. Forluin is gone, Falmeryn, gone, and you will never walk on her shores again . . .*

They would never believe her. What proof could she give them? They would see it as betrayal of the most terrible kind, as if she had let them run in the illusion of freedom for a time before slowly reeling in the chain.

'No, I can't do it,' she whispered.

'You cannot send them to Forluin?' Miril hopped onto her

hand. Melkavesh felt the warmth and weight of her small body, and it felt like a benediction.

'I cannot bring them back here,' she said tightly. 'I'm going to make sure they reach home. Safely.'

'Even though Filmoriel may be lost to you?'

'Even though,' she replied, leaning towards the mirror. 'It's all I can do for them. But I need your help, Miril.'

'I will go to them and guide them. Don't fear, Mellorn. Grief passes, but strength will remain.'

Melkavesh began to summon energy, felt it swirl like streams of multi-coloured fire from the sky and sea, filling the void inside her and turning her flesh from lead to amber and crystal. Then she unleashed it, saw *Karvish's Hawk* hurtle forward like a spear – and in the same moment Miril flew at the mirror and vanished.

The sea was wild, the waves leaping up to smack into the ship as she skimmed above the them. The speed was terrifying; Kharan sat huddled on the deck, white-faced and soaked with spray. She had Filmoriel well wrapped in a cloak on her lap. Perhaps it would have been safer inside the cabin, but it did not feel so; the ship, not designed for such speed, was shuddering as if it might break up.

Falmeryn came down from the forecastle deck, hanging onto the rail. Kharan's heart was in her mouth until he reached her safely.

'Can you see anything?' she asked anxiously.

'No. There's too much spray.'

A wave the size of a hill hurtled towards them, and they held onto each other until *Karvish's Hawk* had made a sickening leap over it. 'What's Melkavesh trying to do to us?' Kharan cried.

Falmeryn said nothing, because to speak his thoughts would have terrified her. He had a dreadful intuition about the journey. It seemed to him that it would go on for ever, because Forluin was not there any more. At least they were together. He put his arms round Kharan, encircling her and Filmoriel.

When he looked up again, he saw Miril perched on the

382

mast. She flew down to sit on Filmoriel's shoulder, and this time she did not seem dazzling or supernatural but a simple, living creature. But there was no mistaking the deep red plumage, the liquid beauty of her eyes. Filmoriel lost her look of weariness, and smiled.

Then Miril sang to them; and the song said, 'Do not fear. I am with you now. Whatever befalls, I will guide you through it.'

And from a cliff on the western coast of Forluin, Arlena watched the sea.

Filitha had said that when Forluin was finally separated from the world, the transition might be visible. Many had travelled to the coast to witness it, to look on the ocean which soon would lead nowhere. As a people they rarely travelled abroad, but that had been by choice; this imposed isolation was unspeakably disturbing.

'We could have gone to any part of the coast,' Estarinel said to Falin. 'Do you think it was wise to come here?'

'It was Arlena's choice,' Falin replied sorrowfully. 'It's a way to say farewell, I suppose. Perhaps it will help.' Estarinel gripped his shoulder briefly, and they went to join Arlena and Lilithea on the cliff edge.

They had come to the small natural harbour from which *The Silver Staff* had sailed with Falmeryn aboard – and to which it had returned without him. Several of the crew from that voyage had come with them, including Edrien and Luatha; all had been Falmeryn's friends, all took on themselves the guilt and sadness of his loss. Estarinel's mother Filmorwen was there too, and his children – Falmeryn's beloved cousins – Farinel, Arviel and Filmorwyn.

It was dark when they arrived and all night they stayed awake and listened to the roaring of the sea. The separation was not completed yet, but already the threads holding Forluin to Earth were under great strain, and it was as if a sheet of crystal had come down across the heavens.

'What light will shine on us when we are no longer part of the world?' Lilithea whispered. No one could answer her.

When morning came, the sun rose as always in a perfect blue sky. In the strange hours that followed, it remained the only constant, as if it were a star whose rays fell on more than one dimension. They were grateful for that; all else was chaos. The waves thrashed in clouds of diamond foam; the sky seemed to be shattering and flaking away like a china glaze. Even the ground rose and fell under them, making them cling to each other in dizziness and wonder if they were not to be destroyed after all.

Then, when the sun reached its apex, there came a sense of dislocation that told them it was over. The sea foam ceased to thrash but rose upwards to form a curtain of shimmering vapour. Within it, the sea became abruptly calm. The land felt steady once more.

They began to loosen their hold on each other, to look about them and to breathe again. The sunlight seemed gentler now, but otherwise nothing seemed different – until Falin cried, 'Look at the sky!'

It was blue still, but it was as if an opaque film had been stripped away from it. The clarity and delicacy of its colour were breathtaking, and all across it they could see shapes like transparent images etched on crystal: the rock formations and shimmering lakes of the Blue Plane.

'It's H'tebhmella,' Estarinel said softly. 'We can see H'tebhmella.'

'Almost close enough to touch,' Falin said, hugging Arlena in joy. But her eyes were as blank as the wall of mist that was raining down on the ocean, severing Forluin from the world and from her last hope of seeing Falmeryn again.

Then her expression changed. The impossible happened. A ship came sailing out of the mist, a dark slender vessel with sunlight gilding her spars. She was listing as if she had only just made it through the worst of a storm. There were figures on deck – two, or was it three? – and above them there circled a solitary bird.

'By the Lady,' someone murmured, but Arlena was already away and running for the cliff paths that led down to the harbour.

She did not pause to consider that the chances of it being

Falmeryn were virtually non-existent. To her there was only one explanation for the ship's arrival, and it was as if the very strength of her belief made it come true.

Exhausted, soaked to the skin, Kharan and Falmeryn looked up at Forluin's shores and wept with joy.

They had been thrown by a tidal wave into a writhing mist; Melkavesh's contact had been lost, and they feared the ship would capsize. Instead there was a sudden, eerie calm. They slid out of the mist to find white cliffs, edged with green rising up before them, unutterably welcome.

Only now did they begin to realise how close they had come to losing Forluin for ever. But Melkavesh had kept her word, done her utmost; and Miril had been like a lodestone, to guide them safely home. Her task over, she wheeled away and dwindled into the sky, singing.

Behind them, the vapour cleared to reveal a calm pearl-green ocean stretching as far as the eye could see. And gliding across that unearthly tide came *Karvish's Hawk*, the last ship that would come from Earth. As she slid into the little harbour, there were already people on the wooden quay, others streaming down the cliff paths to greet them, hands held out to take the ropes and tie her up, to help with the gang plank.

'All these people,' Kharan exclaimed. 'It's as if they knew we were coming.'

Then a voice on the quay cried, 'Falmeryn!'

He held onto Kharan's shoulders, unable to believe what he was seeing. 'They're my family,' he said breathlessly.

'All of them?'

'No – no, but I know them all.' Then the gang plank was down and they were on the quay; and his parents were waiting there with Estarinel and Lilithea and all his loved ones, and they were laughing and crying as they embraced him. Kharan found herself and Filmoriel drawn into their welcoming arms as if they were not strangers but beloved friends. And there was so much to say that for a long, long time, no one said anything at all.

*   *   *

385

'Falmeryn promised me a long time ago that we'd come to Forluin one day,' Kharan told Arlena and Falin. 'So many things conspired to stop us that I can hardly believe we're here. Oh, but Forluin is everything he said, and more.' She turned to clasp his hand, her eyes shining.

They had all come inland to the shelter of a wood to rest and talk as evening fell. It never grew quite dark, and H'tebhmella cast a dim blue radiance that was sweeter than moonlight filtering through the leaves. The moons and stars could still be seen like faint reflections of themselves, lace and glass.

'I never, ever gave up hope that you'd come back,' said Arlena.

'Mother, I knew I'd come home,' Falmeryn replied, smiling. 'When I was ill once I dreamed you were at my side and Filmoriel was with you. This was before I knew Filmoriel existed. In the dream you said she was always under your feet!'

Arlena laughed. 'And I hope she will be,' she said, reaching out to stroke the child's hand. She stirred on Kharan's lap, but did not wake.

'I've dreamed of the future, too, sometimes,' said Estarinel. 'Such dreams aren't always evil.'

'And they aren't always dreams,' Falmeryn murmured. His face became thoughtful, and Kharan slid her hand through his arm and said, 'What are you thinking about?'

'Filmoriel. Did you ever tell her about the time I was trapped in the caves?'

'Of course not, why?'

'Because this morning, while we were still on the ship, she told me she'd dreamed that she and Miril found me in a tiny cave. She was frightened I would die if I didn't move, so she made me dive through a pool of water and follow her to safety. When she knew I was all right she woke up, but she was upset that I hadn't recognised her . . . Do you understand? What happened for me several months ago only happened for her last night.'

Kharan and Falmeryn looked at each other in a moment of shared foreboding that seemed to intrude on the glade

386

like a breeze blowing from a darker plane of existence. It could not help but exclude the others. A nightbird began to sing in the shadows, and the liquid poignancy of the notes made Arlena draw closer to Falin, Estarinel gather Lilithea to him. They all had their shared darknesses and joys, and they all knew Miril's song.

Then Falmeryn smiled. 'It's all right, Kharan. We're home. The Earth can't touch us here, nor ever take Filmoriel away from us.'

Kharan believed him.

A BLACKBIRD IN SILVER

FREDA WARRINGTON

They were three.

From Forluin, green, half-fabled land of beauty and peace, had journeyed Estarinel, grave and strong in his thoughtfulness.

From the terrible Empire of Gorethria, hated and feared among all the victim peoples of the planet, rode Ashurek, once High Commander of the Armies, scourge of the subject races.

And the third was known only as Medrian. Coldly wrapped in her cloak of mystery, her eyes deep-shadowed with suffering long endured, she spoke nothing as to her reasons.

Theirs was the Quest. Together they were to seek out and slay the great Serpent that had come down from the far frozen limits of their world to lay waste and utterly destroy.

HODDER AND STOUGHTON PAPERBACKS

MORE SCIENCE FICTION AND FANTASY AVAILABLE FROM HODDER AND STOUGHTON PAPERBACKS

FREDA WARRINGTON

☐	41903 7	A Blackbird in Amber	£2.95
☐	40161 8	A Blackbird in Darkness	£3.50
☐	05849 2	A Blackbird in Silver	£2.95

Ed. JOHN CLUTE, DAVID PRINGLE AND SIMON OUNSLEY

☐	42853 2	Interzone: The Second Anthology	£2.95

JEAN M. AUEL

☐	26883 2	The Clan of the Cave Bear	£3.50
☐	39311 4	The Mammoth Hunters	£3.50
☐	32964 5	The Valley of Horses	£3.50

DIANA L. PAXSON

☐	43054 5	White Mare, Red Stallion	£2.95

MICHAEL WEAVER

☐	42206 2	Mercedes Nights	£2.50

All these books are available at your local bookshop or newsagent, or can be ordered direct from the publisher. Just tick the titles you want and fill in the form below.

Prices and availability subject to change without notice.

Hodder and Stoughton Paperbacks, P.O. Box 11, Falmouth, Cornwall.

Please send cheque or postal order, and allow the following for postage and packing:

U.K. – 55p for one book, plus 22p for the second book, and 14p for each additional book ordered up to a £1.75 maximum.

B.F.P.O. and EIRE – 55p for the first book, plus 22p for the second book, and 14p per copy for the next 7 books, 8p per book thereafter.

OTHER OVERSEAS CUSTOMERS – £1.00 for the first book, plus 25p per copy for each additional book.

Name ....

Address ....

....